Midnight

COLLECTION

January 2015

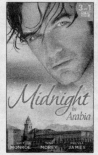

February 2015

March 2015

April 2015

May 2015

June 2015

D1513431

Midnight in *Arabia*

LUCY MONROE
TRISH MOREY
MELISSA JAMES

MILLS & BOON

Published in Great Britain 2015
by Mills & Boon, an imprint of Harlequin (UK) Limited,
Eton House, 18-24 Paradise Road, Richmond, Surrey, TW9 1SR

MIDNIGHT IN ARABIA © 2015 Harlequin Books S.A.

Heart of a Desert Warrior © 2012 Lucy Monroe
The Sheikh's Last Gamble © 2012 Trish Morey
The Sheikh's Jewel © 2012 Lisa Chaplin

ISBN: 978-0-263-25354-2

024-0215

Harlequin (UK) Limited's policy is to use papers that are natural, renewable and recyclable products and made from wood grown in sustainable forests. The logging and manufacturing processes conform to the legalenvironmental regulations of the country of origin.

Printed and bound in Spain
by CPI, Barcelona

Heart of a Desert Warrior

LUCY MONROE

Lucy Monroe started reading at the age of four. After going through the children's books at home, her mother caught her reading adult novels pilfered from the higher shelves on the bookcase... Alas, it was nine years before she got her hands on a Mills & Boon® romance her older sister had brought home. She loves to create the strong alpha males and independent women who people Mills & Boon® books. When she's not immersed in a romance novel (whether reading or writing it), she enjoys travel with her family, having tea with the neighbours, gardening and visits from her numerous nieces and nephews. Lucy loves to hear from her readers: e-mail LucyMonroe@ LucyMonroe.com, or visit www.LucyMonroe.com.

For Helen Bianchin… It is said that good writing inspires good writers. Your writing has inspired me both in my life and in writing for years.

I thank you from the bottom of my heart for the many hours of pleasurable reading, the wonderful bits of advice and kind words when I was the new kid on the block. Your stories continue to inspire, your books are my dear friends and your characters beloved to my heart. Thank you.

CHAPTER ONE

"You look like you're ready to face a firing squad."

Her field assistant's words stopped Iris at the top of the grand palace staircase.

Suppressing a grimace at what she could not doubt was his all too accurate assessment, she turned to face the college intern and forced a smile. "*You* look hungry."

"Seriously, this is just dinner right?"

"Of course." Just dinner.

Where they were supposed to meet their liaison while in Kadar; Asad, Sheikh Hakim's second cousin, or something, and sheikh himself to a local Bedouin tribe, the Sha'b Al'najid. Asad was a fairly common Arabic name, meaning lion. An appropriate name for a man destined to be sheikh. Right? There was no reason to think that the man was *her* Asad.

No reason other than this awful sinking feeling that had not gone away since Sheikh Hakim had mentioned the liaison's name earlier. Ever since agreeing to this Middle Eastern assignment, she'd had a feeling of foreboding that she'd done her best to ignore.

But it was getting harder with every passing moment.

"I'm not feeling reassured here," Russell said as

he stepped onto the stairs, his tone only half joking. "Dinner isn't a euphemism for *kidnap and sell to white slavers,* is it?"

The ridiculous assertion shocked a laugh out of Iris. "You're an idiot."

Still, her legs refused to move.

"But a charming one. You've got to admit it. And who wouldn't want to kidnap this?" he asked with a wink, having stopped to wait for her.

With his shaggy mop of red hair and pale skin, he could have been her baby brother. If only. Her childhood would have been a lot less lonely with a sibling. Her parents hadn't been cruel, only supremely uninterested. Their lives were complete with each other. They worked together, they played together, they traveled together and none of it included her.

She'd never understood why they'd had a child at all and had long since decided her advent into the world had been one of those "accidents" of faulty birth control. Though nothing had ever been said.

She couldn't imagine what they would have done with a child like Russell; he didn't fade into the background with grace.

No, no matter how many surface resemblances they shared, he would have been an even bigger cuckoo in their family nest than she'd been.

Nevertheless, Iris and Russell really did look like they could have come from the same gene pool. Oh, he had freckles and she didn't, and his eyes were green rather than her blue. However, they both had curly red hair—like her mother—slightly squared chins—like her father—and skin as pale as the white sands of New Mexico. At five foot ten, Russell was average height for a man, just like she was for a woman at five-five.

They both tended to dress like the science geeks they were, though tonight she'd donned a vibrant blue sheath dress and a black pashmina. Instead of her usual ponytail, she'd pulled her hair back in a loose knot and even gone so far as to put on mascara and lipstick, though she almost never wore makeup. She was dining with a sheikh and his family after all.

Two sheikhs, her worried brain reminded her.

Russell was in his own version of dress formal, khaki slacks and a button-down oxford instead of his usual T-shirt and cargo pants.

Still, neither of them were all-that-and-a-bag-of-chips.

She groaned at his humorous conceit. "Anyone with half a brain would know better than to go through the trouble of kidnapping you."

He laughed, not taking offense and not entirely masking a concerned expression she didn't want to see.

No matter what, she would be fine. She *would.* She was no longer a naive university sophomore, but a professional geologist with an eminent private survey firm.

"So, why the long face?" Russell asked, taking another step down as if coaxing her to do the same. "I know you tried to get out of doing this assignment."

She had, but then she'd realized how foolish she was being. She couldn't go through her career refusing lucrative assignments in the Middle East just because she'd once loved a man who came from this part of the world. Besides, her boss had made it clear that this time, she didn't have a choice.

"I'm fine. Just a little jet-lagged." Forcing her feet to move, she started down the stairs.

Russell fell into step beside her when she reached him. He put his arm out for her and she took it.

She wasn't dwelling on the possibility that Sheikh Asad was *her* Asad. Not at all.

After all, what were the chances it was the same man who had done such a good job decimating her heart six years ago that she hadn't gone on another date until after she graduated? That it was the one man that she had hoped to live the whole rest of her life without ever seeing again?

Small. Almost nonexistent.

Right? *Right.*

So, her Asad had been part of a Bedouin tribe and, as she'd found out at the end, slated to be sheikh one day.

It didn't have to be the same man. *She was praying it wasn't the same man.*

If it was *her* Asad—or rather *the* Asad: he'd never really been hers and she had to stop thinking of him that way—she didn't know what she would do. Working toward the coveted position of senior geologist with Coal, Carrington & Boughton Surveyors, Inc., she couldn't refuse this assignment based on personal reasons. Not when she had been back in the office and definitely not now that she was already in the country.

She wasn't about to commit career suicide. Asad had taken enough from her. Her faith in love. Her belief in the rosy, bright future she'd ached for and dreamed of. He didn't get her career, too.

"What did the diamond say to the copper vein?" Russell's youthful voice pulled her out of her less than happy thoughts as they made their slow way down the stairs.

She rolled her eyes. "That joke is as old as the bedrock in Hudson Bay. The answer is—nothing, minerals don't *talc*."

It was a hoary old joke, but when he laughed, she found herself joining him.

"I'm glad to see you still have a sense of humor." The deep voice coming from the hall below didn't sound happy at all.

In fact, it sounded almost annoyed. But Iris didn't have the wherewithal to worry about that little inconsistency. Not when the rich tones that still had the power to send her heart on a drumroll and to spark little pops of awareness along her every nerve ending belonged to a man she had truly believed she would never see again.

She stopped her descent and stared. Asad looked back at her, his dark chocolate gaze so intense, she felt the breath leave her lungs in a gasp.

He'd changed. Oh, he was still gorgeous. His hair still a dark brown, almost black and with no hint of gray, but instead of cropped close to his head like it had been back in school he wore it shoulder length. The different style should have made him seem more casual, more approachable. It didn't.

Despite his European designer suit and their civilized surroundings, he looked like a desert warrior. Capable. Confident. *Dangerous.*

His brown eyes stayed fixed firmly on her. Serious and probing. The humor that used to lurk there nowhere in evidence.

He had close-cropped facial hair that only added to his appeal, as if he needed any help in that department. He'd filled out since university days, too, his body more muscled, his presence every bit that of a man of definite power. At six feet three inches, he had always been a presence hard to ignore, but now? He was a true Middle Eastern sheikh.

Wishing, not for the first time, that she *could* ignore

this man, she forced herself to incline her head in greeting. "Sheikh Asad."

"This is our liaison?" Russell croaked, reminding her that he was still there.

It didn't help. The young intern was no competition for her attention to Asad and the feelings roiling up from the depths where she'd buried them when he left her.

Putting his arm out to Iris, Asad showed no sign of noticing Russell at all. "I will escort you to the others."

Her frozen limbs unstuck and Iris managed to descend the remaining stairs. Giving in to her urge to ignore at least his suggestion, she stepped around his extended arm and headed to where she'd met earlier with Sheikh Hakim, his wife and their adorable children. If she was lucky, the dining room would be in the same part of the palace.

"Do you know where you are going?" Russell asked from behind her, sounding confused.

Asad made a sound that almost sounded like amusement. "I do not believe Iris has ever let a lack of certainty stop her from going forward."

She spun around and faced him, long-banked fury unexpectedly spiking and with it not a little pain. "Even the best scientist can misinterpret the evidence." Taking a deep breath, she regained the slip in her composure and asked with frigid politeness, "Perhaps you would like to the lead the way?"

Once again, he offered his arm. Again she pushed the bounds of polite behavior and ignored it, simply waiting in silence for him to get on with showing them where they were going.

"Just as stubborn as you ever were."

And she wanted to smack him, which shocked her

to her core. She was not a violent person. Ever. Even in the past, when he'd hurt her almost beyond bearing, she'd never had a violent thought toward him. Just pain.

"That's our Iris, as immovable as a monolith."

Asad didn't ignore Russell this time. He gave the younger man a look meant to quell.

Seemingly oblivious, the college intern grinned and put his hand out to shake. "Russell Green, intrepid geological assistant, one day to be a full-fledged senior geologist with my own lab."

Asad shook the younger man's hand and inclined his head slightly. "Sheikh Asad bin Hanif Al'najid. I will be your team's guide and protector while you are in Kadar."

"Personally?" Iris asked, unable to keep her disquiet out of her voice. "Surely not. You are a sheikh."

"It is a favor to my cousin. I would not consider relegating the duty to someone else."

"But that's unnecessary." She wasn't going to survive the next few weeks if she had to spend them in his company.

It had been six years since the last time she'd seen this man, but the pain and sense of betrayal he'd caused felt as fresh as if it had happened only the day before. Time was supposed to heal all wounds, but hers were still bleeding hurt into her heart.

She still dreamed about him, though she called the images she woke to in the dark nightmares rather than dreams.

She'd loved and trusted him with everything inside her, believing she finally had a shot at a family and a break from the loneliness of her upbringing. He'd betrayed both her emotions and her hopes completely and irrevocably.

"It is not up for discussion."

Iris shook her head. "I…no…"

"Iris, are you okay?" Russell asked.

But she had to be okay. This was her job. Her career, the only thing she had left in her life that mattered, or that she could trust.

The only thing Asad's betrayal had left her with. "I'm fine. We need to join Sheikh Hakim."

Something glimmered in Asad's dark chocolate gaze, something that looked like concern. She wasn't buying it, not even if someone else gave her the money to do it.

He hadn't been concerned about her six years ago when they had been lovers; it was too far a stretch to think he was worried about her now, when they were little more than strangers with a briefly shared past.

Asad did not offer his arm again, but turned and began walking in the direction she'd been going to begin with.

So she had guessed right in this instance.

Go her. Sometimes her intuitive thoughts were on target, at least when it didn't come to people.

"So Asad tells us you went to the same university." Catherine smiled without malice, genuine interest shining in her gentian-blue eyes.

Nevertheless, the memories her words evoked were not happy ones for Iris. Iris forced something that resembled a smile and a nod. "Yes."

"It's funny you should have met."

At the time Iris had believed it destiny. She'd been studying Arabic as her second language, a common practice for those in her field, but it had felt like more. Studying the language of his birth had felt like a common bond between them, as if they were meant to be together.

She had believed him to be an incredible blessing after nineteen years of feeling like she never really belonged to, or with, anyone. She'd thought she'd belonged to Asad; she'd been convinced he belonged to her.

She'd been spectacularly wrong. He didn't want her, not for a lifetime, or even beyond their few months together. And he was not hers, not in any sense.

"It was one of those things...." Asad had come on to her in the Student Union. He'd flirted, charmed and when he asked her out, she hadn't even considered saying no.

"The Student Union building knew no class distinctions," Asad added when it was clear Iris wasn't going to say anything else.

"Not in age or social standing," Russell agreed. "I met a billionaire's daughter in the Student Union at my university."

And Iris had met a sheikh. Not that she'd known it. Back then, he'd just been plain Asad Hanif to her. Another foreign student availing himself of an American university education.

"She was sweet," Russell continued, "but she doesn't know the difference between sedimentary and igneous rock."

"So, not a friendship destined to prosper," Sheikh Hakim observed, his tone tinged with undeniable humor.

"*Our* friendship prospered." Asad gave her a look as if expecting Iris to agree, even after the way their *friendship* had ended. "Though I knew little of geology and Iris had no more interest in business management."

"The friendship didn't last, which would indicate our differences were a lot more important than they seemed at first." She'd managed to say it without a trace of bitterness or accusation.

Iris had never really considered herself much of an actress, but she was channeling Kate Winslet with her performance tonight. She'd managed to get through predinner drinks and the first course of their meal without giving away the turmoil roiling inside her to her hosts, the Sheikh of Kadar and his wife, *just Catherine please.*

Asad laid his fork across his empty salad plate. "Youth often lacks wisdom."

"You were five years older than me." And worlds wiser and more experienced.

He shrugged, that movement of his shoulders she knew so well. It was his response to anything for which there was no good, or easy to articulate, answer.

"Anyway, I hope my words haven't made it seem I'm looking to renew any old friendships." Chills of horror rolled down her spine at the thought. "I'm not. I'm here to work." It was her turn to shrug, though it was more a jerk of one shoulder.

She'd never done casual well when it came to Asad, but it didn't matter. She *was* in Kadar to work and then she would be out of his life once again, just as fully and completely as before. As she was sure he would prefer.

And she was never returning to Kadar. Not ever. No matter how lucrative a promotion depended on it.

"It would be a shame to travel so far from your home and spend no time experiencing the local culture." Asad's gaze bored into hers with predatory intent.

She remembered that look and her heart tightened at receiving it here, in this place, after everything that had passed between them and in his life particularly since their breakup.

"I'm sure living amidst your tribe will give both Iris and Russell the perfect opportunity to experience much of our culture," Catherine said with a smile aimed first at Asad and then Iris. "I love staying with the Bedouin. It's such a different way of life. Though why it always seems there's more trouble for our children to get into in the city of tents than at home, I don't know."

She winked at her husband and Sheikh Hakim gave her such a look of love and adoration, it was both wonderful and painful to see. Here was a couple who loved each other every bit as much as Iris's parents, but who adored their offspring with equal, if different, intensity.

Then the full import of Catherine's words hit Iris. "We're staying with Sheikh Asad's tribe?" she asked in shock. "But I thought *this* would be our home base."

The beautiful Middle Eastern palace that still managed to feel like a home for all its glamour and size.

"Our current encampment is far closer to the mountainous region you will be surveying," Asad said, an inexplicable tone of satisfaction lacing his words.

CHAPTER TWO

"STAYING WITH the Sha'b Al'najid will save you a lot of time in travel," Sheikh Hakim added.

"But…"

"You'll love it, trust me," Catherine said. "While Asad has taken the tribe in a different direction than Hakim's grandfather did, their way of life has much in common with that found millennia ago. It will be an amazing experience, believe me."

Iris would be in purgatory, but at least the encampment would only be their home base, she tried to tell herself. "I'm sure I will enjoy it very much," she lied through her teeth. "What time we spend there, at any rate."

Catherine looked inquiringly. "I'm not sure I understand."

"When we're in the field doing the type of survey Kadar has requested of CC&B, a team spends most of its time in a portable camp," Iris explained. "It really wouldn't make much of a difference if we maintained a home base here, or in the Bedouin encampment."

"You are not staying alone in a camp with nothing but this pup for company." Asad's voice, laced with possessive bossiness, brooked no argument.

And shocked Iris to the core. She didn't understand

why it mattered to him. And that possessiveness was completely at odds with a man already taken himself. She must have imagined it.

The first to admit that reading people was not her strong suit, she nevertheless felt a shiver of apprehension skate along her spine.

"It's not as if we share a cot, just a tent," Russell said, no doubt trying to assuage any conservative sensibilities.

And doing a really bad job of it, Iris thought.

Asad's features set in a mask she was sure had more in common with his warrior ancestors than modern man. He gave Russell a look that made her self-defined intrepid field assistant shrink into his chair.

"Not acceptable." Just two words, but spoken with absolute authority in a tone she'd heard only once from Asad.

When he was telling her they had no future in words that could not be denied.

Russell squeaked. Catherine's look tinged with concern. Iris's heart ached with memory while she fought to maintain a facade of indifference.

Sheikh Hakim frowned. "My cousin is correct. It would be neither safe, nor appropriate for you to camp in such a manner."

Iris could see her escape route disappearing in front of her eyes while the chilly sense of dread inside her grew. She couldn't give up without a fight, though. "I assure you, I've been on several field assignments, in the States and abroad, and never had a problem with it."

Just not in the Middle East.

"Nevertheless, I am responsible for the safety of those within my borders," Sheikh Hakim said with a shake of his head. "Asad is right, a two-person camp in the mountains is an unacceptable option."

Asad simply looked at her with an immovable expression she would never forget. He'd used it also when he said goodbye. "As I told you earlier, I will see to your safety."

"My safety isn't your responsibility."

"On the contrary. I have decreed that it is." Sheikh Hakim's friendly manner dissipated in the face of his arrogant assurance.

Right. And Sheikh Hakim was a very important client. His country was paying CC&B a great deal of money for this survey. She was compelled to accept the way he wanted the field work handled. Either she backed out of the assignment, or accepted the constraints surrounding it, including Asad as her liaison.

She'd accepted that backing out of the assignment wasn't an option before she ever left the States.

"Not having a moving camp could make the initial sample gathering and measurements take significantly longer," she said by way of her final sally.

"Swift is not always better," Sheikh Hakim said implacably. "Your safety must come first."

"Would you be more comfortable with a male team lead?" she asked, seeing a possible way out. If the sheikh asked for it, her career wouldn't be affected adversely. It was understood that some parts of the world did not deal as well with female geologists. "My superiors could arrange for my immediate replacement if that would make you more comfortable."

"Not at all. I am confident your work will be more than acceptable," Sheikh Hakim said smoothly.

Russell was staring at her like she'd offered to dance naked on the tabletop. Okay, so normally, she'd bristle and fight tooth and claw to avoid being replaced simply on the basis of gender, but these were special circumstances.

"It surprises me you would make the offer." Asad sounded just as disbelieving of her words. "I remember a woman who would not stand for the idea that men made better geologists than their female counterparts."

"I didn't say he would be a *better* geologist."

"Naturally not. You graduated at the top of your class, did you not?"

"I'm surprised you know that." But then it might well have been included in the information CC&B had supplied about her to Sheikh Hakim.

Asad shrugged again. "I kept up with you."

No, really, he hadn't. She'd never heard from him again after he left, though a mutual friend had told Iris when Asad had married a year after returning to his home. She'd spent the weekend crying off and on, for once Iris's studies unable to assuage the ache of loneliness and grief.

Then she'd buckled down, determined not to let anyone or anything stand in the way of the one dream she had left. She'd even continued her studies in Arabic, though until this assignment, she'd had no chance to use them in more than a few written translations and phone calls.

"I'm surprised your wife isn't with you," she said to change the topic and to remind herself forcibly why this man could not be allowed past her defenses.

No matter what the circumstances she would be forced to live in over the coming weeks.

And really? Where *was* the man's wife? What woman would prefer to stay at a Bedouin encampment when she could be visiting the local palace? And how did his wife feel about Asad promising protection and guidance to his former girlfriend?

But then, that at least, was an idiotic question. No way did the princess know anything about Iris.

Iris certainly hadn't known anything about Princess Badra when she'd been dating and sleeping with Asad.

Asad had known, though. He'd known he had no intention of spending his future with Iris. He'd known he planned to marry the virginal princess, not the American geology student who spent every night in his bed for ten months.

He'd seduced her anyway, treating Iris like his girlfriend when she was nothing but his mistress.

An old-fashioned word for an ugly, outdated position she would never have willingly taken. Or so she told herself.

The most painful truth of all, the one that had woken her in nighttime sweats more than once, was that even had she known he would never be hers, Iris was not sure she would have been able to walk away from what he offered her naive, love-struck, nineteen-year-old self.

"My wife died two years ago." Asad's voice pushed into Iris's raw thoughts.

She met his eyes in genuine shock and polite words tumbled out of her mouth in stark reaction. "I'm sorry."

Asad didn't reply, but looked back at her with an expression both predatory and implacable.

The room and people around them faded from her awareness for a frozen moment as she met his gaze, her body frozen in shock, her mind blank with reaction and her heart stuttering in horror.

A married Asad was bad enough, but a widower? The thought sent terror shaking through her not-so-mended heart.

* * *

The helicopter blades whirled overhead, making discussion within the bird impossible except over the shared radio pieces. Asad had his fill of public discourse the night before when all he'd wanted to do was drag Iris out of the dining room and take her somewhere they could be alone.

He could not pretend what he wanted to do was talk, either, though it was not entirely off the agenda.

It had taken considerable self-control to stop himself from going to visit her in her room, but he needed to follow his plan. A plan that had a better chance of success once she was living in his encampment, not minutes from the royal airfield at the palace.

The level of animosity in Iris's expression and voice when she wasn't doing her best to suppress it, surprised him. It had been six years since he'd returned home. Surely she was not still angry at the admittedly abrupt end to their association.

Had he to do it over again, he would have handled it differently. But when they'd been together, he hadn't realized she'd been thinking in terms of the future, either. He'd assumed from her actions and circumstances that she knew nothing they did together could be permanent. He hadn't counted on her Western viewpoint on feminine sexuality, or her ignorance of his status.

In his arrogance, he'd believed everyone knew he was a future sheikh. It was no secret after all. But Iris did not gossip, and she was a geology student who, he learned later, knew next to nothing about the students in her own discipline, much less the others that attended the large university with her.

When she'd told him she loved him, he'd taken it as his due. The usual response of a female in a sexual relationship with a man, but he hadn't believed she meant it.

He still wasn't sure he bought the idea of everlasting love, though his cousin's marriage to Catherine was something special. Even Asad could see that.

Nothing like his own marriage, which had been nothing more than a series of lies and subterfuge.

Still, he could have been kinder when he had to end their months-long affair. He realized that now.

He would never admit to anyone but himself that his harsh and immediate withdrawal had been the result of feelings he wasn't used to dealing with. He'd become more attached to Iris than he'd expected to. And much to his chagrin, had realized at the end of their time together, that she, more than anyone or anything else, had the possibility of undermining his carefully laid plans.

So, he had walked away. And stayed away.

And had forced his mind to shut down every time he thought of her until his ill-fated wedding night, when inevitable comparisons and conclusions had to be drawn. Conclusions that had destroyed what was left of his own naive beliefs about women and sex.

Iris hadn't been a virgin, but she'd been honest, loyal and surprisingly innocent. He'd believed Badra untouched, but that had been a lie of monumental proportions, as was so much about her. The woman who had considered herself too good for a Bedouin sheikh had traded on deceit and Asad had not even had a glimmer until their wedding night.

Even so, his anger at Badra had muted over time to be replaced with indifference. So that when she had died all he had felt was relief to be free of her, only marginally tinged by sadness for their daughter, who saw less of her mother than the Parisian clothiers Badra favored.

Once married, he'd been unable to keep thoughts of

Iris completely banked. Though that surprised him, he chalked it up to the fact that they had been even better friends than they were lovers. He'd kept up with her academic and work career, but had stayed away from her personally. He was not Badra. Asad did not cheat.

He did not understand this passionate fury barely contained in Iris, not after so much time. He slid a glance at her only to find her looking out the window of the helicopter, her eyes too unfocused to be seeing anything of real interest in the desert below.

Her body and attention turned from him, but he would change that. It had been six years. Two years since his wife's death. Enough time for all that he had planned. He would wait no longer.

The low mountains loomed much closer than at the palace when the helicopter made its descent for landing.

"Hey, where are the camels?" Russell asked as he climbed out of the helicopter right after the pilot.

Asad did not answer. He had not liked the way the field assistant referred to Iris proprietarily, and with such familiarity, the night before. Though he doubted very much that the two shared a relationship outside of work, Asad felt possessive of the friendship that had not been allowed to flourish by his marriage.

He offered his hand to help Iris alight. After a moment of inaction while she stared at his hand as if it were a snake set to strike, she very clearly gritted her teeth and then reached out to take it.

He smiled into her lovely sky-blue eyes, carefully blanked of emotion. "Welcome to the Bedouin of the twenty-first century."

Iris looked around them at the landing pad and the SUV parked on its edge. "I understand camels are not quite the mode of transport they once were." She met his gaze again and choked out a laugh which he enjoyed hearing very much. "But a Hummer?"

He shrugged. "What can I say? Our tribe is more affluent than most."

"Why is that?"

"My great-grandfather purchased land rights in three adjoining countries along our usual travel route so our tribe would always have a place to camp. At the time, political unrest dictated the move, but we rarely avail ourselves of that land for encampment anywhere but in Kadar."

"But the land in the other countries, it's making money for you?"

"It is." The once-beautiful landscape was marred by oil rigging that pounded away with a noise that others might learn to sleep through.

He never would. "Oil."

"Lucky you."

"Some might say so."

"I think pretty much everyone would say so."

He didn't reply, but turned to give instructions to the tribesmen waiting for them to move the geologists' luggage and equipment to the Hummer. Asad made sure Russell ended up in the other SUV for the drive.

The Sha'b Al'najid encampment was nothing like Iris expected. Erected in the shadows of the small mountain range in the southernmost part of Kadar, it truly looked like the "city of tents" Catherine had referred to.

"You must have high-producing wells."

"They are sufficient as a base for our needs."

"A base?"

"My grandfather invested intelligently if modestly on behalf of our people. I have continued that tradition, though perhaps not as modestly." Satisfaction glowed in Asad's dark gaze. "We continue to do what we are best at as a people, as well."

"What's that?" she asked, her curiosity stronger than her desire to avoid conversation with him.

"The Bedouin are known for their hospitality. Our tribe offers the opportunity to live the Bedouin life for tourists from the cities of Kadar and abroad. The Sha'b Al'najid still run trading caravans across the desert and for a sufficient fee, one may join in this venture, also."

"Like a Dude Ranch?" she asked in disbelief.

"I have never been to a Dude Ranch, but I believe the intent is similar. Others of my brethren tribes do this, as well. It provides our people the opportunity to continue with millennia of cultural and living tradi-tions while others are afforded the opportunity to ex-perience this unique way of life."

"You sound like a travel brochure."

"I have written more than one of them."

A grin sneaked up on her, despite her feelings to-ward him. "It can't be too traditional with Hummers instead of camels."

"We still have many camels, I assure you."

"Do you still move camp?"

"Twice a year, rather than seasonally, but yes."

"Do you stay in Kadar?"

"We do. This too is different, but preferable to other tribes who have settled permanently on lands granted by the government."

"I see." Though she wasn't really sure she did and was afraid he could hear it in the uncertainty of her tone.

"Within our encampment you will find modernizations mixed with traditions that are thousands of years old." And he was clearly proud of that fact.

"Are those electric cords?" she asked in shock as she noticed the thick black rubber-coated cords snaking through the sand.

"They are. We have a bank of solar panels strategically placed five hundred yards in that direction." He pointed away from the mountains to a spot that was no doubt ideal for sun exposure.

Incredible. "So, I can use my laptop?"

"It is better for you to charge your battery between uses. Our power is limited and certain measures must be taken, but there is even a television in the communal tent."

"I didn't know there was such a thing in a Bedouin encampment. I thought most of the socializing happened in individual homes." Or outside in the courtyard-like areas between the tents.

At least according to the research she'd done on Bedouin living back when she'd thought she'd had a reason to do so.

"The communal tent was created for the tourists to gather in groups, but my people have found they enjoy its use, as well."

"And its television."

"Some British and American programs are very popular." His shrug said some things must change, but others would remain the same. "I confess to a craving for *Law & Order* when I returned home six years ago."

They'd used to watch it together. He'd called the crime drama his weekly mindless entertainment. She never quite got that, but she'd suffered through the program's dark plots and emotional angst for the sake of spending that time with him.

"Do you still watch it?" he asked.

"No."

"It was never your favorite."

"No." Though she hadn't stopped watching until the series was canceled.

"Yet you watched it, for me."

This trip down memory lane was getting distinctly uncomfortable.

"I'll admit this is not what I expected." She waved her hand, indicating the encampment around her.

"You had expectations?"

"Naturally. It's a poor geologist who doesn't do her homework on the area she'll be surveying."

"But you had no idea you would be coming to a Bedouin encampment."

"You never know." It was not quite a lie, but not the admission he was looking for, either.

"This is true. Six years ago, neither of us would have suspected you would be here."

Actually, she had…right up until he'd broken up with her. She had no more interest in rehashing that particular bit of history than anything else about the months they'd been together. "You said some things are still traditional?"

"Many things."

She saw what he meant when they entered a huge tent toward the center of the encampment. A curtain bisected the area horizontally from the entrance. In the center, was a single overlapping panel embroidered with two giant peacocks, their feathers fanned out in a display of the beautiful jeweled tones the birds were known for.

The curtain created the public reception area the Bedouin homes were known for, but it was much larger she was sure than the average tent boasted. With no evidence of the famed television, Iris had to assume this wasn't the communal tent he'd mentioned earlier.

Rich Persian rugs covered the ground of the main area, but instead of chairs, there were luxurious pillows in silks, velvets and damasks with lots of gold, purple, teal and a dark sapphire blue. Low tables dotted the expansive area and while the outer walls were the typical woven black goat hair, inside the walls were covered in richly colored silks.

"Russell and I are staying here?" she asked with a sense of foreboding.

This was no normal Bedouin tent. Situated where it was in the compound and considering the luxury of the interior, she had no doubts who this particular dwelling belonged to. Sheikh Asad bin Hanif Al'najid.

"You are, yes. Russell will stay in the tent with your equipment."

"What is this tent, a harem, or something?" she asked in faint hope.

"This is my home."

CHAPTER THREE

"I'M NOT staying in your tent."

"It has been arranged. Your accommodations are behind that partition." He pointed at a blue silk hanging. "My late wife insisted on a nontraditional division of the women's area of the tent. So, you will have your own room rather than sharing the entire space with the other single women of my family."

"Other single women?" she asked faintly.

"My daughter and a distant cousin."

"I can't stay here with you."

"I assure you, you can."

"I'll share the tent with Russell."

Oh, Asad did not like that suggestion. Not at all. His expression went very dark very quickly. "You will not."

"But it makes the most sense." And might actually save her sanity, not to mention her heart.

"It is not acceptable."

"You and your cousin, Sheikh Hakim, have an affinity for that word," she grumbled, feeling like the Persian rug beneath her feet was actually quicksand.

"You will stay here." There was no give in Asad's voice or his posture.

"How is it better for me to stay here with you than to share a tent with Russell?"

"As I said, my daughter and cousin share this tent, as well, but so do my grandparents."

Her whirling brain latched onto the plural *grandparents* and she asked, "Your grandfather is still alive?"

"Of course."

"But you're sheikh."

"What did you think, I had to kill my predecessor to take over for him? It was much more prosaic. He retired and enjoys the increased freedom of his days like any other man who has well earned such."

"He retired?"

"Yes."

"That's just…"

According to what Iris had read, the concept of the next generation taking over the majority of sheikh responsibilities when the current holder of the office became very old was not completely unheard of. But to refer to it as *retirement?* It was just so, so…*modern.*

"The way of things." The words were spoken by an elderly woman carrying a tray with tea things on it as she entered through an opening in the blue silk partition.

Dressed in traditional Bedouin garb, the older woman's hair peeked from under a heavily embroidered and beaded sheer scarf that did not completely hide the long white tresses. Her face, though showing the wear of sun and years, was still beautiful, though paler than Asad and more Gallic in bone structure.

"Grandmother, may I present Miss Iris Carpenter." Asad bowed his head toward his grandmother while indicating Iris with his right hand. "Iris, my grandmother, the Lady bin Hanif."

"You will address me as Genevieve."

"Thank you. That is French, isn't it?" Iris asked, pretty sure the woman's accent was Gallic, as well.

"It is. Though my family has made its home in Switzerland for nearly two centuries. My husband found me when we were both attending university in Paris and convinced me to leave all I knew to share his life here among his Bedouin tribe." She smiled as she set the tea tray on one of the low tables. "I have never regretted it. The Sha'b Al'najid soon became my people."

"And Grandmother became the favorite lady to them in generations."

Iris smiled. "It's a pleasure to meet you, Genevieve."

"Come, sit." The older woman indicated the cushions on the floor with a flick of her elegant wrist. "It is always a pleasure to meet an old friend of my grandson."

About to deny the classification, Iris thought better of it. She suspected that the Lady bin Hanif was the type of woman who would demand an explanation.

"We knew each other only for a few short months at university," she said to downplay the relationship as much as possible.

Genevieve poured tea into fine china cups painted with Arabic design. "And yet those short months were particularly impacting for my grandson, I believe."

Iris turned to glare in shock at Asad. He'd told his grandparents about their affair? Heat crawled into her cheeks while her stomach rolled in humiliation.

Asad's eyes widened at her glare and then narrowed in what seemed like comprehension. He shook his head just slightly, as if saying he had not told them the intimate details of the friendship.

"Oh my, yes. Our boy, he spoke of hardly anyone

from his university days. But Iris, the budding geologist? We heard much of her academic and career exploits." Genevieve serenely sipped her tea. "His late wife did not enjoy Asad's university reminiscences, I think. She had attended only a year of finishing school in Europe you see."

Completely flabbergasted by the idea that Asad had kept track of her like he claimed, Iris could think of no other response than to nod and sip her own tea. Hot, very strong and almost equally sweet, it had a smoky flavor something like Earl Grey and yet not. There was almost a flavor of sage in the blend, as well.

"This is delicious. I can see why the Bedouin tea is so famous."

"Yes. There is a knack to making it. You must brew it over a wood fire, not on the hob."

Iris's gaze flicked to the silk divider. There was a wood fire burning behind that, *inside* the goat hair dwelling?

"Not to worry, the cooking fire is under the open awning behind our tent," Asad said, showing more disconcerting proof that he could still read her all too well.

When they had been together, he had known her better than anyone else, though she'd kept her secret shame to herself and never admitted to him the extent of her parents' indifference.

Genevieve smiled and reached out to pat Iris's arm. "Do not worry. You will soon grow accustomed to our ways."

"My favorite mentor always said that one of the marks of a good field geologist is the ability to acclimate to different surroundings so nothing can get in the way of accuracy in one's fieldwork."

"A wise man," Asad said, "was Professor Lester."

"How did you know I was talking about..." Iris let her voice trail off as Genevieve laughed softly.

"Oh, my grandson, he remembers everything, does he not?"

"Yes." Asad's eidetic memory was one of the reasons they'd had as much time together as they did.

When he had almost perfect recall of everything he heard, read and saw, the need to study for tests or reread information for papers was severely mitigated. He'd even helped Iris study for her own exams.

Genevieve's eyes glowed with pride as she looked at her grandson. "It makes him a very good sheikh and political advisor to my great-nephew, Hakim, ruler over all Kadar."

"You're one of Sheikh Hakim's official advisors?" Iris asked Asad, storing the information on their actual family relationship for future reference.

He merely nodded before taking a drink of tea.

But Genevieve was more forthcoming. "Of course, they are family. However, Asad has proven himself wise in the ways of our people and the modern world we must live in, as well. Hakim listens with a bent ear to our Asad. It was his idea, after all, to get your company to do the mineral survey and to request you be the on-site geologist."

Asad's jaw tautened, as if he was trying not to frown, but the look he gave his grandmother was tinged with something that looked very much like exasperation.

"You're the reason I wasn't given the option of refusing this assignment?" Iris demanded, catching on quickly even if her memory wasn't precisely eidetic.

Asad shrugged.

She opened her mouth to tell him that wasn't a good

enough answer. Not this time, but his grandmother forestalled Iris. "But why should you wish to?"

And Iris remembered where she was and why she was here, despite the helpless fury burning in her chest. "I have yet to do any survey work in the Middle East. Another geologist would have been a better choice."

"Nonsense. If Asad believes you will do the best job, then I am quite confident you will. Surely it is time you expanded your vita to include work in the Middle East."

Iris could not deny it. She would never be promoted to senior geologist while she lacked field experience in the Middle East, which was one of the points her boss had made when insisting Iris take this assignment.

That didn't make her feel any better about the revelation that Asad was responsible for getting Iris to Kadar. He was a man who always had an agenda. If she had only realized that when they'd been dating, she would not have been so sideswiped by the knowledge he was already practically engaged to the Princess Badra.

What was his plan now?

Iris had the awful feeling it had something to do with her. And since the only thing he'd wanted from her was her body, she didn't think she was too far outside the realm of probability to believe he had his sights set on renewing their affair.

For a short time anyway.

Why not? She'd fallen into his bed with barely a push back in the day. Practically a virgin, she'd still allowed him to make love...*or have sex rather*...with her on their first date. She'd been overwhelmed by her reaction to him and thought he felt the same. She knew better now, but wasn't entirely sure it would make any difference in the outcome.

"Where is your father?" she asked in a desperate attempt to change the subject and get her mind on a different pathway. Why hadn't *he* taken over the sheikh role?

And then she considered the possibility that the older man was deceased and wished she could bite the words back. Particularly after her similar faux pas the night before when asking about Asad's wife. It was too late, however, to do anything but hope she would not be given the same answer.

Thankfully, Asad did not look like he was remembering a traumatic loss. "He does not live with the tribe. He oversees our European interests from his home in Geneva."

"Your father lives in Switzerland?" Considering they clearly had family there, that was not entirely surprising. Still, it seemed odd that Asad would be sheikh to the nomadic Sha'b Al'najid while his father lived in one of the most sophisticated cities of Europe.

"As do his mother, sister and two brothers." Genevieve's tone did not sound altogether pleased by that fact.

Iris gave Asad a look in which she felt incapable of hiding her abject shock. "You have siblings?"

He had never mentioned it, but then he'd left a lot out of their discourse six years ago. So, the fact that none of them lived among the Bedouin tribe was even more surprising to her than their existence.

"It is so."

"But…"

Genevieve refilled the teacups without asking if Iris or Asad wanted more. Something about the set of her features told Iris this conversation was no easier on her than the earlier topic had been on Iris.

Asad leaned back on the cushion, looking like a

pasha and said, "You wonder why they do not live with the Sha'b Al'najid."

"If your parents live in Geneva, I suppose it's natural that your sister and brothers would, as well."

"They are all of an age to make their own decisions about how and where they live."

She didn't know what to say to that. She could understand that the Bedouin way of life might not work for everyone, but for all of them to turn their backs on thousands of years of tradition seemed wrong somehow.

"In order to gain permission to leave the tribe, my father had to allow my grandfather to raise me here as his own son to take over leadership of the tribe." Asad said it so casually, it took a moment for the import of his words to sink in. "It is why I am called bin Hanif instead of bin Marghub. Not that my father uses his tribal name. He goes by Jean Hanif."

In Western culture such a name similarity would show the family connection, but in Kadar, Asad not carrying his father's name was as good as disowning him. Though it sounded like the decision had been made for him.

"That's barbaric." Iris slapped her hand over her mouth, unable to believe she'd said that out loud, no matter how much she thought it.

She looked askance at the tea; was there something in there that she didn't know about?

Genevieve smiled reassuringly, clearly having taken no offense. "Jean found much about the Bedouin way of life to be barbaric. He never wished to return from our visits to Geneva to my family. He insisted on attending an American university and ended up married to a European like his father."

If they no longer lived among the tribe, Iris thought

that Western origin could be the only thing Asad's mother had in common with Genevieve.

"Celeste and Jean came here to live after their marriage, but neither were happy. Eventually, Jean told us that he had no desire to follow his father as sheikh to the Sha'b Al'najid. My husband could have named a cousin or nephew as his successor. It is how he became sheikh himself, but he saw the fire of the Bedouin burning brightly in our grandson and offered the alternative of us raising him here instead."

"How old were you when your parents left?" Iris asked.

"I was four."

And they had seen the Bedouin spirit burning bright in him? At such a young age? Iris supposed it was possible, but it was still barbaric. "How old were your siblings?"

"My sister was two. Mother was pregnant with my younger brother, as well."

"She did not want to give birth in the encampment." Genevieve shrugged, the movement exhibiting her Gallic ancestry. "All of her children were born in a Genevan hospital after Asad."

Despite their past, Iris could not help the rush of pity and understanding she felt for Asad in that moment. She knew exactly how it felt not to be necessary to one's parents.

Asad shook his head at her. "I know how you are thinking. Stop it. My parents did not abandon me. We continued to see one another often and I always had my grandparents. I had the Sha'b Al'najid. Doing things in such a fashion was necessary. My father did not want the less luxurious life of the Bedouin and my grandfather knew one day I would make an excellent sheikh."

No arrogance there. Not at all. She almost smiled. "It looks luxurious enough to me."

"We have satellite access to the internet for four hours in the afternoon only. We do not have modern kitchens, appliances or bathrooms."

She knew what he meant and shrugged. "I'm sure your facilities are better than what I have on most of my camping field assignments."

"No doubt." He smiled as though her words had pleased him, then the smile melted away as if it had never been. "What we have now is beyond what my father experienced in the encampment. Though when he and the others visit, they still find it abysmally rustic."

"All of them?"

"All but my youngest brother. He was born four years after they moved to Geneva." Asad's lips twisted wryly. "An unplanned blessing added to my parent's family. He has said he plans to make his home here once he finishes university."

"And your parents are okay with that?"

"Naturally. My father relies on the tribe's business investments for his income. He knows better than to reject our way of life completely." So, regardless of how unaffected Asad would like to appear regarding his father's rejection of his way of life, there was something there.

"He gave up his oldest son to the tribe," Genevieve chided. "Any parent would feel that was a sufficient sacrifice."

Iris begged to differ, but she wasn't about to say so out loud. Her parents would have happily given her up if it meant getting what they wanted. In fact, they had often made the trade-off of time with her for travel on their own. She'd never told Asad that she'd been sent to boarding school at age six, but then the fact had always shamed her.

She'd thought there was something wrong with her that her parents had preferred to have her live with them only on school vacations. And even then, they weren't always "at home" when she was.

"Perhaps," Asad replied to his grandmother, not looking particularly convinced. "I do not know how difficult the decision was for them. I know only that they made it, choosing life outside of the encampment rather than living here to raise me."

Genevieve clicked her tongue twice, as if gently chiding her grandson without saying anything overt.

"You never told me this." And Iris wasn't sure that hadn't been for the best.

She'd been head over heels in love with Asad, but how much worse it would have been for her if she'd believed they had this pain in common and allowed herself to identify with him on such a deep level?

"There was much we did not talk about."

"True. I didn't even know you were going to be sheikh one day." And he knew nothing of her childhood or her parents' supreme indifference. She'd never told him the story of how she'd lost her virginity. Asad was oh so right; there was *a lot* they'd never spoken of. "Looking back, I realize I should have guessed based on your bearing alone."

"I did not mean to hide that from you."

She believed him. He had been so certain she knew the score, she did not believe he'd meant to hide anything from her. For the first time in six years, she admitted to herself that they'd both been spectacularly wrong in reading the situation between them. Not just her.

That didn't do a thing to alleviate her current anger

with him for manipulating her into coming to Kadar, however.

Genevieve rose gracefully to her feet. "I will refresh the tea."

Iris went to stand, intent on helping, but the older woman placed a staying hand on her shoulder. "No. Another time, I will teach you to make tea the proper way. Now you must stay here and renew your acquaintance with my grandson. He has so looked forward to seeing you again."

Nonplussed, Iris could do nothing but nod with as much graciousness as she could muster. She didn't think it would do her company's relationship with Kadar a good turn if Iris admitted she would rather renew the acquaintance of the rattlesnake she'd met on her last field survey than Asad's.

Asad waited until his grandmother had gone to say, "I never lied to you. I thought you knew I was meant to be a sheikh."

"I heard you the first time." She glared at him, her current anger sufficient to fuel the nasty look, their past notwithstanding.

"And?"

What? Was he expecting her to congratulate him or something?

"Do you believe me?" he asked with a tinge of frustration in his usually urbane tones.

"Yes."

"Then why the look when grandmother left us to talk?"

Really? He could not be that dense. "I guess an eidetic memory does not equate to people smarts."

His eyes narrowed in affront at her sarcasm. "You have changed."

"Yes." She was no naive idiot anymore. "But seriously? How could you think knowing you would be a sheikh one day would have made a difference to me back then? I wouldn't have been any more prepared to be dumped like I was."

"I did not dump you."

What happened to that famed honesty of his? "Excuse me, *you did*."

"I had obligations, a plan for my life I could not abandon."

"You didn't want to abandon it. You didn't leave me out of duty—you left because you *never* wanted me for a lifetime. I was just stupid enough to believe you did. That's all." And equally painful, she'd lost her best friend.

"I am sorry."

He had said *that* six years ago too, with pity in his eyes. But not regret. If there was regret there now, she wouldn't let herself see it.

"It's in the past."

"Yet I still see pain in your eyes when you talk about it."

She couldn't deny it, but she sure wasn't going to admit to it, either. She'd had all the pity she could stand from this man when she'd been that foolishly naive nineteen-year-old. Besides, she had something much more recent to deal with.

"I can't believe you engineered me coming to Kadar." She made zero effort to hide how much knowledge of his manipulation infuriated her.

He looked shocked by her anger. "I was doing you a good turn, making up for my abrupt departure from your life, if you will."

"You have absolutely got to be kidding me. You

think being forced to work in close proximity to you is in some way a good thing?"

"I am no monster. You used to enjoy my company very much, and I do not just mean in the bedroom."

"We were friends. We aren't anymore!" She swallowed her next words and fought for control of her vocal cords. The last thing she wanted was for Genevieve to return to Iris shouting at the man she was beginning to realize was more dense than metamorphic rock.

"We could be again."

"Why?" Why would he want to be?

"I missed you. You missed me."

And to him, it was that simple. Never mind the fact she'd been so totally in love with him that she'd felt like her heart had been ripped from her chest when he left. "You could have just called."

"You needed the Middle East experience to move forward with your career."

"Just how close tabs have you been keeping?" she demanded.

"Close enough."

"So, you thought you'd do me a favor?" Why did she think it hadn't all been altruism on his part? Oh, yes, because she no longer trusted him and never would again. "Didn't it occur to you that not coming to the Middle East had been my decision?"

"No."

She dropped her head in her hands and groaned, her fury losing its heat. The man just had no clue, none whatsoever.

And there was no point in continuing this discussion. He was never going to get it, but he wasn't going to drop the subject unless she did.

So she observed, "You said you share this tent with your family."

"I do."

"Where is everyone else?" Were the tent walls so thick, they would mask the sounds of a child?

It was surprisingly quiet, no sounds from outside filtering through, nor from any other part of the tent.

"My grandfather spends this time each day with the other old men, drinking coffee and telling stories. No doubt he would have stayed to meet your arrival, but my grandmother knows how to get her way and she wanted to meet you first," Asad revealed in a fond tone.

"Where is your daughter? In school?" Iris guessed.

He shook his head. "She will be playing with other small children under the watchful eye of my cousin."

Since, presumably, if his grandparents had more children than Asad's father, the barbaric bargain would not have been made, he didn't mean *cousin* literally, but referred to a female relative. "She's not old enough for school?"

"We do not run a school precisely, though the concept is similar. We train our children in every aspect of life, not merely to read, write and cipher, though we do not neglect their book learning. Some will want to attend university one day." He reached out as if to touch Iris and let his hand fall, an unreadable expression in his dark eyes. "But you are right, my daughter is too young for any formalized training."

"Does your grandmother have someone to help her with…" She let her voice trail off, not knowing the child's name.

"Nawar. My daughter's name is Nawar and she is four. My grandmother and cousin help me with Nawar, but she is *my daughter*."

"That is a commendable attitude to take," she grudgingly admitted. "But I would have thought that since you're the sheikh, you'd be too busy for full-time parenting."

"Is it so unusual for a father to have a career? I do not think so. I spend as much time with Nawar as possible."

Once again, Iris believed him, but wished she didn't. It would be a lot easier on her if she could simply see him as a complete and utter bastard. Instead, he made himself all too human. If they did not have the shared past they did, she would not only respect him, but she might even like him, as well.

Something she simply could not afford to let herself do.

CHAPTER FOUR

"I would be more comfortable staying in another tent." Iris knew this was her only chance to argue her viewpoint and she should not have wasted time discussing their past.

"Would you really?"

"Yes."

"You wish to stay with strangers?" he asked in a tone that said he knew she would not.

"That's not what I meant."

"But that is the only other option."

"Well then, maybe it would be best." As much as she hated the idea, it was better than living in his home.

"No."

Typical Asad-like response. He didn't bother to justify, or excuse; he simply denied.

"You've gotten even bossier since university," she accused him.

Though back then, his bossiness had not bothered her. He'd convinced her to try things she never would have otherwise, like the ballroom dancing class they'd taken together a month after they'd met, or attending parties she wouldn't have been invited to on her own and learning to dance to modern music amidst a group of her peers.

She'd suppressed so many of the good memories from their time together and now they were slipping their leash in her mind.

He did not look particularly bothered by her indictment. "Perhaps."

"There is no perhaps about it."

"And you are surprised? I am a sheikh, Iris. Bossiness is in the job description." He sounded far too amused for her liking.

"Asad, you've got to be reasonable."

"I assure you, I am eminently reasonable."

"You're stubborn as a goat."

"Are goats so stubborn then?"

"You know they are."

"I would know this how?" he asked in an odd tone.

She rolled her eyes. "Because everybody does."

He nodded, tension seeming to leave his shoulders, though she had no clue what had caused it. "You will stay here."

"You're a CD with a skip in it on this."

"First a goat, now broken sound equipment. What will you liken me to next?"

"You're changing the subject."

"There is nothing further to discuss in it."

She opened her mouth to tell him just how much more there was to discuss when a flurry at the door covering caught Iris's attention. A second later a small girl with long black hair came rushing into the tent and threw herself at Asad's legs. "Papa!"

He leaned down and picked her up, giving her a warm hug and kiss on her cheek. "My little jewel, have you had a good morning?"

Other than the coloring, Iris did not see the family

resemblance. The little girl must take after her mother. The observation made Iris's heart twinge.

"I missed you, Papa, so much. I even cried."

"Did you?"

She nodded solemnly. "Grandmother said I needed to be strong, but I did not want to be strong. Why didn't you take me with you, Papa?"

Asad winced as if regretting his decision to leave his daughter behind. "I should have."

"Yes. I like playing at the palace with my cousins."

"I know you do."

"Next time, I must go."

"I will consider it."

"Papa!"

"Stop, you are being very rude. There is someone here for you to meet and you have spent all this time haranguing me."

Watching the two together caused that same delight tinged with pain she felt around Catherine and Sheikh Hakim. It was so clear that Asad loved his daughter and that pleased Iris because it meant she had not been entirely wrong about this man six years ago. She'd thought he would make a wonderful father and she'd been right, but knowing he'd had his child with another woman sent salt into old wounds.

"Oh, I am sorry." The little girl looked around and locked gazes with Iris, her dark eyes widening. "Who are you?"

"Nawar," Genevieve chided, coming back into the room with a laden tray the cousin jumped forward to relieve her of.

It was clear from the extra cups and amount of food that Genevieve had expected the child's return with her minder, a woman about fifteen years Asad's senior with soft brown eyes.

The little girl looked properly chastised, her expression going contrite. "I did not mean to offend." She put out her little hand from her position in her father's arms. "I am Nawar bin Asad Al'najid."

She sounded just like a miniature grown-up and Iris was charmed. She took the little girl's hand and shook gently. "My name is Iris Carpenter. It is a pleasure to meet you, Miss Bin'asad."

"Thank you. Why do you call me Miss Bin'asad?"

"Iris is being polite," Asad answered before Iris could.

"Oh. But I want her to call me Nawar. It is my name."

Iris had spent very little time around small children, but she thought Nawar must be exceptional. "I will be honored to call you Nawar and you may call me Iris."

"Really?" the girl asked. She looked to her grandmother. "It is all right?"

"If she gives you permission to do so, yes," the older woman said with firm certainty.

"Iris is a pretty name," Nawar offered.

"Thank you. It is my mother's favorite flower." She'd decided her mother chose the name so she would not forget it as easily as she and Iris's father forgot their only child. "Nawar is lovely, as well. Do you know what it means?"

"It means flower. Papa named me."

Iris did not know why Asad had named his daughter rather than his wife doing so; perhaps it was a Bedouin tradition, though that sounded rather odd considering the other cultural norms she had read about among his nomadic people.

It was those norms that made it possible for Iris to

stay in Asad's familial tent, but would have made it impossible if he did not live with his grandparents. She could wish he'd broken more cultural norms and moved into his own dwelling, so she didn't have to.

"Your papa is very good at naming little girls, I think."

"I do, too." Nawar smiled shyly. "What is haranguing? Do you know?"

Asad huffed something that could have been a laugh.

Iris stifled her own humor and answered, "It's like nagging."

Nawar turned her head to glare at her father. "I don't nag, Papa."

"Sometimes, little jewel, you do."

The little girl sniffed and it was all Iris could do not to burst out laughing. An urge Iris surprisingly felt several times over the next hour, while sharing more tea and refreshments with Asad's family. His grandfather joined them not long after Nawar had arrived, evincing the same pleasure in Iris's presence as Genevieve had done.

Iris expected Russell to arrive any minute, but the minutes ticked by and he didn't. When she asked, Iris was told he had been given a tour of the encampment by one of Asad's tourist liaisons.

She couldn't quite suppress her disappointment at the news. "Oh, I would have liked to have joined him."

"I am glad to hear you say so. I planned to give you a tour later," Asad said with satisfaction.

Iris just stopped herself from gaping and said, "I wouldn't want to take up more of your valuable time as sheikh."

The man was relentless. He wanted to renew their friendship and he would make that happen. One way or another. Maybe he did regret the way things had happened between them and this was his attempt at making up for it, but still…she hadn't imagined that predatory look in his eyes, either.

He probably saw nothing wrong with adding sex to their friendship. He'd done it once before, after all.

"Nonsense, you are a guest in our home. Asad would not dream of neglecting you while you are here," his grandfather said with finality.

Iris thought she knew where the younger sheikh had gotten his arrogance, and it wasn't from a stranger. But the older man's point about the Bedouin tradition of hospitality could not be ignored, either. From what she had read, it was not a matter of pride, but one of honor.

And honor could not be dismissed.

"May I go, Papa?" Nawar asked.

Iris smiled at the little girl in encouragement, but Asad shook his head. "You will be napping, I am afraid."

"I'm not tired." Nawar negated the words almost instantly by rubbing her eye with her small fist. "I want to go."

Her father pulled Nawar into his lap and kissed her temple. "You need your rest, but be assured Iris will still be here when you wake and for many days after. Won't you, Iris?"

Iris could do nothing but agree. Asad and his cousin had maneuvered her neatly into a situation she saw no way out of without severe damage to her career.

Genevieve showed Iris to her room while Asad put Nawar down for a nap.

"It's beautiful. Thank you." Both private and luxurious, the apartment was larger than she'd expected.

The bed was ground level and a single, though. Covered in rich silks a deep teal color she'd always loved, it looked very comfortable nonetheless. Graced with fluffy pillows Iris was certain just from looking at them were of the finest down, the bed tempted her to simply sink down and take her own afternoon nap.

Genevieve nodded and smiled. "Asad had someone come in and change the decor to better fit in with the rest of our home after Badra's death. During their brief marriage, moving this room alone was almost as big of a job as moving the entire encampment."

"I'm…this used to be the princess's room?" Iris asked faintly, relieved that while still luxurious, it wasn't anywhere near as ostentatious as Genevieve implied it had once been.

Though the fact the princess had called it her own would explain the amount of space dedicated to it in a Bedouin tent, regardless of the fact the sheikh's dwelling was probably one of the largest in the encampment.

"Oh, yes." Genevieve indicated the fabric wall the bed butted up against. "Asad's room is just on the other side."

"But isn't that…I mean, aren't the male and female quarters separated?"

"In a traditional tent, yes, but I must admit to making some changes in our home when I married Hanif and Badra made even more. While the receiving room is traditional, the way we divide what used to be considered the women's space is quite different."

"I see." Though honestly, Iris felt very much in the dark.

"Hakim and I have the room at the end, beyond the interior kitchen. Fadwa and Nawar share the room between it and us. And you are correct, in the Bedouin culture, usually a single woman would stay in that room with them, but Asad has decreed you would be more comfortable in Badra's old lodgings."

The older woman waited as if expecting Iris to say something, so she said, "Um…I'm sure he's right."

Neither woman commented on the fact that the sheikh and his wife had not shared sleeping quarters. But Iris couldn't help speculating on the why of it. Had the virtuous Badra found the wedding bed too onerous?

Unimaginable. How could any woman not fall under the sensual spell Asad created in the bedroom? When they were together, she'd craved his touch with an intensity that had shamed her after the breakup. At the time though, she'd been enthralled by the beauty and passion of their lovemaking.

It was simply unfathomable to her that another woman would be indifferent to Asad's sexual prowess.

Needing to redirect her thoughts, Iris reached out to touch the brass pitcher beside a matching basin on top of the single chest of drawers. "This is lovely."

Decorated with an intricate design surrounding a proud peacock, it was polished to a bright sheen.

"The water in the pitcher is clean. You may drink it, or use it to wash," Genevieve said. "Someone will come to dispose of the water in the basin for you. It will be used to water my garden in the back, so it is important you only use the soap provided."

Iris picked up the bar of handmade soap and sniffed. The fragrance of jasmine mixed with sage. "I'll be happy to. This is wonderful."

"I am glad you think so." Something in her tone said that perhaps the perfect princess, Badra, had not. "We make it here in the encampment."

Iris noted that her case was beside the chest, but she

hadn't seen anyone come in while they were visiting over tea. "Is there another entrance to the tent?"

Genevieve nodded with a warm smile. "Through the kitchen. I will show you the rest of our humble home, if you would like?"

"Oh, yes, please."

The tent dwelling was anything but humble, the private compartments all endowed with the same level of luxury as Iris's room, if not a plethora of furniture that might make their twice-a-year resettlement difficult. Or at least, Iris assumed Nawar and Fadwa's was, but she had been unable to see for herself as the child was settling into her nap.

One thing she did note was that the single women's quarters that housed Asad's daughter and distant cousin were actually smaller than the apartment Badra had commandeered for her own use and that Iris would now use.

When she said as much to Genevieve, the other woman shrugged. "Perhaps when Asad marries again, his wife will reapportion the sleeping quarters again. So long as she does not attempt to change my and Hanif's room, I will be content."

"Is he thinking of remarrying then?" The thought of Asad taking another wife sent a shard of pain that absolutely should not be possible straight through Iris's heart.

"But naturally. Though he has not set his sights on any woman in particular." Genevieve led the way through the inner kitchen and outside. "Enough time has passed since Badra's death though, I think."

"How did she die?"

"In a plane crash with her lover," Asad said with brutal starkness from behind Iris.

His arrival taking her by surprise, she jumped and spun to see him standing with an old familiar arrogance, but an only recently familiar harsh cast to his features.

Genevieve tutted at her grandson. "Really, Asad, you needn't announce it in such a manner."

"You think I should dress it up? Pretend she was simply vacationing with friends as the papers reported?"

"For the sake of your daughter, yes, I do."

Asad inclined his head. In agreement? Perhaps, but the man wasn't giving anything away with his expression.

"What do you think of my home?" he asked, dismissing the topic of his unfaithful wife in a way that shocked Iris.

The Asad she had known at university would never have been so pragmatic about such a betrayal.

Forcing her own mind to make the ruthless mental adjustment of topics, she said rather faintly, "It's fantastic."

"You like your room?" he asked, the stern lines of his face relaxing somewhat.

She tried to keep the hesitation she was feeling from her tone. "Yes."

"But?"

"I didn't say anything."

"Didn't you?" Asad's tone was borderline cutting.

"It's just that, well…it's kind of big for just me, isn't it? I mean, it's gorgeous, but I could set my lab up in the room and still have plenty of room to spare." She felt guilty about that fact, though she wasn't sure why.

Not to mention, it was right next to Asad's room. That in itself was enough to cause immeasurable anxiety and probably sleeplessness on her part.

One of his now rare but gorgeous smiles transformed Asad's features. "That will not be necessary. You and your coworker have already been assigned quarters for your tests."

"Thank you." What else could she say?

"I will do all that I can to make your stay here a pleasant one." The words were right, but the look that accompanied them sent an atavistic shiver down Iris's spine.

She turned to take in the charming courtyard created by the surrounding tents. Jasmine and herbs in pots decorated with bright mosaics made the space seem anything but desert austere. Despite the heat, other women cooked over open campfires, their curious gazes sliding between their sheikh's guest and the watch they kept over children playing in the communal area.

"I had read that the tents are grouped by family ties. Is that true here among the Sha'b Al'najid?" Iris asked.

"It is," Asad answered while his grandmother conferred with the woman cooking what Iris assumed was to be *their* dinner. "The dwellings around us are those of the family closest to my grandfather's predecessor. Had my grandparents had more children, it would be their tents that occupied these spots around the sheikh's home."

It must have been a great disappointment to the elder couple to have only had one child, but Iris kept her lips clamped over the much too personal thought.

"Come." Asad took Iris's hand and placed it on his arm. "I will show you the rest of our city of tents."

"Do you have the time, really?" she asked, trying to tug her hand away to no avail.

His other hand held it implacably in place and his

dark gaze told her he wasn't about to let go. "I have made time. The law of hospitality is very important among the Bedouin. Not to show you proper consideration as a guest in my home would be unacceptable."

"There's that word again."

A tiny lift at the corner of Asad's lips could have been a smile of amusement, but he was such a serious man now. She could not be sure.

"The way of life among my people is thousands of years old. Some things are considered absolute."

"Like hospitality," she guessed.

"Yes."

"But your home is not as traditional as it appears."

"No."

"You are not afraid of change."

"I am not, though I do not seek it for its own sake."

"You want to keep the Bedouin way of life viable coming into the next generations."

"You understand me well." His hand tightened on hers. "You always did."

"No." If she'd really understood him six years ago, she never would have deceived herself into believing what they had was permanent.

"Perhaps you understood me better than I did myself."

"Oh, no. We are not going there." She tried to yank her hand away again.

But he held on. "Be at peace, *aziz*. We will shelve the discussion of our past friendship for now."

If only he was simply talking about friendship. She'd become friends with Russell since he started his internship, but Iris was under no illusions. When he returned to university, if they never spoke again, she would not be devastated.

Not like after she'd lost Asad.

When she'd believed they were far more than friends who had sex. "No. Don't. You don't mean that word. Don't ever use it with me again. I don't care if you see it as a casual endearment, I do not...I didn't back then and it hurt more than you'll ever understand to learn it meant less than nothing to you."

"What?" He'd stopped with her, his tone filled with genuine incomprehension. "What has you so agitated?"

He really didn't know and that said it all, didn't it?

"*Aziz.* You will not call me that. Do you understand me? If you do it again, I will leave...I promise you." She knew she didn't sound superbly rational, or even altogether coherent, but she wasn't backing down on this.

Shock and disbelief crossed his face before the sheikh mask fell again. "You would compromise your career over a single word?"

"Yes." And she meant it. She'd tolerate a lot, but not that.

Not ever again. That single word embodied every aspect of pain that had shredded her heart six years ago. It meant *beloved,* but he didn't mean it that way. He'd never once told her he loved her, but every time he called her *aziz,* she'd believed that was his way of doing so.

She'd been so incredibly wrong, but darn it—the word had only one translation that she knew of. Only Asad used the word as flippantly empty as a rapper calling his female flavor of the week "baby."

Iris and Asad stood in the middle of a walkway between tents, others walking by them, but no one stopped to converse with their sheikh. It was as if they could sense the monumental emotional explosion pressing against the surface of normality she'd been striving for since seeing him at the bottom of the stairs the night before.

"You do not wish me to call you *aziz,* but surely—"

"No. Promise me, or I'm going to pack my things up right now."

"Your company would not be pleased."

"They'll probably fire me."

"And yet, you would leave Kadar anyway." The confusion in his tone hurt as much as his casual use of the word a moment before.

"Yes." She didn't care if he understood; she only wanted his compliance. "Are we in agreement?"

After several seconds of charged silence he said, "I will not use the endearment unless you give me leave to do so."

"It will never happen." That was one thing she was sure of.

"We shall see."

"Asad—"

"No. We have had enough emotional turmoil this day. I will show you my desert home and you will fall in love with the Sha'b Al'najid just as so many have before you."

And then leaving them would break her heart, but that seemed par for the course with this man for her.

She could do nothing but nod. "All right."

He showed her the communal tent he was so proud of. Even in the middle of the day, it was busy with people, some watching a tennis match on the large projector screen while others occupied themselves more traditionally with a game as old as their lifestyle played with pebbles or seeds.

"So, this is where the tourists congregate?" she

asked, doing her best to ignore the effect his nearness had on her body.

After six years and a broken heart, no less. It wasn't fair. Not one little bit. But he was right; they'd had enough emotional upheaval today and she wasn't going to invite more by letting herself get lost in her reaction to him.

"Usually, but we have no guests at present."

"Why not?"

"The most recent group left and the next does not arrive for a few days."

"You timed it, didn't you?" She didn't know why or even how he could have maneuvered her arrival to fit his liking, but she knew he had.

He didn't even bother to shrug, just gave her a look that she had no hope of reading and wasn't sure she'd want to if she could.

CHAPTER FIVE

By the time they had seen a good deal of the encampment, Iris's head was spinning with images and thoughts.

She'd met women who spent their days weaving amazing rugs and fabrics, others who beaded jewelry, and some even making the soap Genevieve preferred. A much smellier occupation than the fragrant bar Iris had sniffed earlier might have implied.

She saw much she expected to, traditional Bedouins doing traditional things and she really loved it. Few experiences could live up to imagination, but life here among the Sha'b Al'najid? It absolutely did.

"But where are the herds?" she asked, as they approached a tent that stood off by itself.

It was near his home and where they had started and she knew they were close to the end of the tour. Inexplicably, she was not ready for her time with him to be over. She tried to convince herself that was because she wanted to know more about the Bedouin, but she'd never been very good at lying to herself.

Sheikh Asad bin Hanif Al'najid was every bit as fascinating to her as he had been when he was simply Asad Hanif. If she were honest with herself, he was even more so. She needed to get to work quickly and get her mind occupied elsewhere.

"Herds?" he asked, his tone curiously flat after the animation with which he'd described his home over the past two hours.

"The goats and things. I'd always read that Bedouins kept flocks." Only the encampment had been surprisingly bereft of animals, except, surprisingly, some peacocks and peahens wandering between the tents, which she assumed they kept as a curiosity for the tourists.

From what she could tell, the birds had free rein of the encampment and were quite friendly. However, they'd been the only evidence of animals she'd seen. Unless others were kept in the courtyards, but there hadn't been any in the one behind his tent.

"And you thought all Bedouins were goatherds?" he asked with a stark tension she did not understand.

"Don't be ridiculous—no more than I think everyone living in the Midwest is a farmer, but isn't herding part of the traditional Bedouin way of life?" Not only would it not make sense for the Sha'b Al'najid to get their meat and fleece elsewhere, considering how independent a people she'd already witnessed they were, but wouldn't the tourists expect it?

"We do keep herds, rather a lot of them in fact, but they are grazed in the foothills. If they were not, the stench might be too much for our guests."

"That makes sense." Though somehow, she wasn't sure how she felt about them pushing a traditional part of their lifestyle into the outskirts.

He lifted a sardonic brow. "I'm glad you think so."

"I didn't mean to offend you." Wasn't even sure how she had done so.

Asad shook his head. "You did not. It was an old argument I had with Badra. That is all."

Surprised again by his candid comment about his

deceased wife, Iris nevertheless asked, "Did she think it wrong to cater so carefully to the tourist's preferences?"

Asad's laughter sounded more like glass breaking. "Not at all. Quite the opposite, in fact. She could not stand the smell and would have preferred we got rid of the herds altogether."

He'd already alluded to the fact his wife had not been faithful—an eventuality Iris simply could not comprehend. What woman would want another man when she had Asad in her bed? But this latest revelation pointed to only one conclusion: the perfect princess had been a perfect idiot.

Because the woman would have to be absolutely brainless not to realize how foolish it would be to give up the herds of a Bedouin tribe.

"Marrying the virginal princess did not turn out to be all it was cracked up to be, I guess."

"If that odd English idiom means it was not what I expected it to be, you are correct. Does that please you?" he asked darkly.

"You probably won't believe me, but no. Losing what I thought I had with you hurt more than I believed anything ever could, but I never wished you ill." Her own honesty surprised her a little, but with only a couple of glaring exceptions, she'd always found it far too easy to reveal her deepest thoughts and emotions to Asad.

Perhaps because in the past, he'd proven himself a worthy and safe confidant. It was hard to change that viewpoint despite the pain he'd put her through, maybe because he'd walked away and she hadn't had a chance to shore up her defenses against him in person.

Whenever she'd revealed a fear or disappointment in the past, he did his best to alleviate it. She'd told him she was worried about passing a difficult class and though it was not in his discipline, he'd helped her study and even write one of her papers. She'd admitted to feeling awkward in the way her body moved and he'd talked her into ballroom dancing lessons.

Asad stopped before they entered the strangely isolated tent and looked down at her. "You are a very different sort of woman, little flower."

He'd used to call her that, too, a play on her name that was just silly enough to be endearing. Somehow, his using it again didn't hurt with nearly the pain the betraying *aziz* had done.

"I don't think so. When you love someone, you want them to be happy. Even when it's not with you." That truth had sustained her through some of the darkest nights of her soul.

He jolted as if she'd hit him with a cattle prod. "You love me?"

"I *loved* you," she emphasized.

"And that prevented you from hating me?" he asked in a curious tone. "Even though you considered my leaving a betrayal."

"It was a betrayal of my love. But no, I don't hate you."

She never had, even in her darkest moments of pain. A love as deep as the one she felt for him simply had not allowed for that emotion, no matter how devastated she'd been.

He went as if to touch her face, but then let his hand drop after a quick glance around. They were not alone, though no one was close enough to hear the subject of their conversation. It would not do for him to be seen taking such liberties with a single woman, even one from the West.

The tribe might be part of the small percentage of

Bedouins that had not converted to Islam in the seventh century, but that did not mean that such behavior would be any more culturally acceptable in this place.

"Your love for me was true," he said as if just realizing that.

"And you really *didn't* love me. Life is peppered with little inconsistencies like that," she said with a wry twist to her lips.

She was really proud of the insouciance of her tone and stance. Maybe seeing him again had been for the best. Perhaps once this assignment was over, Iris would be able to move forward with her life…and maybe even fall in love with someone who would return her feelings.

Though trusting someone else with her heart was not something she was sure she ever wanted to do again.

"So, what is this place?" she asked, indicating the isolated tent.

"Let me show you," he said as he led her inside.

She gasped out in shock as they passed under the heavy tent flap that operated as the door.

The interior of this particular structure was nothing like the others. An undeniably modern office, either side of the main area, was taken up by two desks facing each other, all manned by people clearly at work. In the center, there was even a secretary/receptionist speaking into a headset while typing at a laptop on her desk.

No one sat on cushions on the floor, like in other Bedouin tents. In fact, there were no cushions. They all used leather office chairs and the receptionist had a small grouping of armchairs covered in Turkish damask in front of her desk. The potted plants to either side of her desk looked real and native to the desert, and the desks were made from dark wood with a definite Middle Eastern vibe, but other than that, this room could pass for any office in corporate America or Europe.

The receptionist looked up at their entrance, nodded at Asad in acknowledgment and gave a small smile to Iris, but then went back to her phone conversation. He didn't seem bothered by the lack of formal greeting.

"What is this? Command central?" Iris asked.

That surprised a laugh out of Asad that sounded quite genuine and she had to stifle her own grin in response.

"I suppose you could call it that. Come." He led her through the busy room to a curtain similar to that in any other Bedouin tent, except this one had an arched opening cut out in the center that led to a hall.

On the right side, they could see through the opening to a room with a bevy of monitors on one wall. Two men and a woman watched, taking notes and calling out observations to each other, or speaking into headsets as they did so.

"This is where we monitor our caravans, the encampment and other business interests."

The room to the left proved to be Asad's office. She had no doubts as to who it belonged to as soon as they entered. For one thing, it had the equivalent of a door, heavy fabric that fell into place cutting off the sound of the others working within the tent office.

For another, the space was decorated with dark wood and rich colors similar to those in his home. And it simply *felt* like it belonged to Asad.

"I thought Bedouin sheikhs conducted business over the campfire," she remarked, still a little flabbergasted by this modern hive of corporate activity in the midst of a Bedouin camp.

"We are not so primitive, though I still settle most disputes among our people over a traditional cup of tea."

"That's good to know. I wouldn't want to think you'd abandoned your old ways completely."

"I have not abandoned them at all. I've simply made them work in a modern age as you guessed earlier."

"You're a very wise man." She didn't mind giving the compliment. It was well deserved.

But that was all he was getting from her. No matter how heated his dark gaze had gotten since their arrival in the private room. She didn't miss the fact that there was a low divan that could easily be used for sleeping when he did not return home at night.

"You're just as much of a workaholic here as you were at university, aren't you?" She'd bet even more so.

Asad shrugged. "I have the welfare of many people on my shoulders. It does not make for long nights of sleep."

"If I remember right, you weren't fond of sleeping as a student, either."

"But for entirely different reasons." The look he gave her could have melted iron.

But she wasn't going to let it melt her heart. "Get that look off your face. I'm here to do a geological survey for Sheik Hakim, nothing more. And we were enjoying this tour. Don't ruin it."

"I assure you, that is not my intention." He moved closer and being smarter than she had been six years ago, she backed up.

Only, when her thighs hit his desk, she knew she was trapped. She put her hands up. "Stop. What happened to having enough emotional drama for one day?"

"I have no intention of indulging in drama. I have something else entirely in mind."

She shook her head, doing her best to look firm while her body yearned for his touch with a reawakened and near-terrifying passion. "We aren't doing this."

"Are you certain?" he asked, his muscular legs coming to a stop only a breath of air away from hers.

"I am. I mean it, Asad. I'm not here for a dalliance. I'm here to work."

"A dalliance." He reached up and caressed the outer shell of her ear exposed by her hair pulled back in a ponytail. "An interesting and strangely old-fashioned word for a modern-day geologist."

"Maybe I'm a little old-fashioned."

"The woman who allowed me entrance to her body on our first date? One who had others before me? I think not."

She shoved at him, hard, his words a better deterrent to her giving in than anything she could have come up with. "You don't know anything about me."

He actually stumbled back a step; maybe in surprise at the strength of her attack. He might be playing, but she wasn't. She slid away from him quickly, stopping only when she was near the door and could make an instant escape if necessary.

The arrogant assurance in his stance and demeanor did not change at all. "I think I know some things about you very well."

"You knew me six years ago. Things change. People change." Please God, let her have changed enough.

"If that were so, you would not be afraid of what you would reveal with my nearness."

Oh, he had more nerve than a snake oil salesman and was just as trustworthy to her heart. She had to remember that. "Maybe I simply don't enjoy being sexually harassed on the job."

"You do not work for me."

"I work for your cousin."

"But not for me. You and I both know your job with Hakim in no way relies on what happens between us."

"Or doesn't happen?" she taunted.

But he nodded decisively. "Or doesn't happen. You want me, Iris. I can see it in the flutter of your pulse here," he pointed to his own neck. "And the way you lose your breath when I am near."

She slapped her hand over her neck, as if she could hide the evidence, but knew he was right. "I am not controlled by the urges of my body."

"So, you admit you desire me? I will take that as a start."

"You're a fantastic lover, Asad, but you're lousy odds for a relationship and I'm not interested in a brief sexual encounter."

His nostrils flared, like they used to when he was particularly turned on. "When we make love, it will be anything but brief."

"And anything but love." Regardless of the corresponding heat pooling in her womb. "It's not going to happen."

"You are lying to yourself."

"You go right on believing that and while you are at it, leave me alone." She fled from the office and then the tent, heading back into the encampment toward the one Asad had pointed out earlier that housed both Russell and their equipment.

Asad had refused to stop and let her explore then, saying there would be plenty of time for her to spend in that particular dwelling. She intended to make that true.

She didn't care if her hasty exit and walk through the city of tents was considered dignified. She didn't have to be a general to know when all-out retreat was called for.

She was only surprised when Asad did not pursue her, but then perhaps he was more aware of his own dignity than she was of hers.

Russell evinced no surprise at Iris's arrival and commenced a steady stream of chatter regarding his own observations of the encampment while they set up their equipment and portable lab. All he required from Iris was a noise of agreement every now and again.

While most of the analysis of the samples and measurements they took would happen back in the real lab, some things were best handled in the field. And she was lucky enough to work for a firm that could afford the latest in portable geological lab equipment.

She reminded herself of that pertinent fact as her fight-or-flight instincts prompted her toward booking the next plane seat back to the States.

"So, what's the deal between you and the sheikh?" Russell asked when he'd exhausted the topic of the city of tents.

"Sheikh Hakim?" she asked, trying for ignorance.

"Get a grip, Iris. It doesn't take a scientist to interpret the facts. You and Sheikh Asad have some kind of history."

"We went to the same university."

"Right. My freshman year, a CEO of one of the newer dot.coms attended my school. We even met, but that doesn't mean we're friends."

"Asad and I *were* friends." At one time, she'd considered him her very best friend.

And then he'd betrayed her love and her belief in their closeness.

"A whole lot more than that, I'm guessing, or the guy wouldn't have such an effect on you."

"It doesn't matter. The past is exactly that and we're here to—"

"Work. Yeah, yeah, I know." Russell fiddled with a microscope. "You can't blame me for my curiosity. Everyone at CC&B thinks you're more interested in rocks than people, especially men."

He gave her a probing look.

She tried to ignore the pang in her heart that his words gave her. It was true that she hadn't gone out of her way to make friends, and well…rocks couldn't hurt you. But that didn't mean she wasn't interested in people at all.

"I date."

"Really?" he asked with clear disbelief.

Bringing up the one dinner she'd shared with a fellow rock hound in the past year probably wasn't going to count, particularly since all they'd talked about was, well…rocks. "It doesn't matter."

"It does when you're acting like a *woman,* not a scientist."

"That's ridiculous. I'm always a scientist first."

"Sure, until we got here. You offered to let Sheikh Hakim bring in a *male* geologist if it would make him more comfortable." Russell's tone gave that fact the inexplicability it deserved. "This Sheikh Asad had you on the run and he'd only spoken a few words to you."

"I'm not on the run."

"Could have fooled me."

"You're being annoying."

"I'm good at that. You don't usually mind." Russell

stopped looking at his microscope and gave his attention solely to her. "I'm being a nosy friend. So, spill."

It went against the deep sense of privacy she'd always lived with, but then that privacy had left her lonely. Perhaps it was time to make more friends, true friends…not just work acquaintances.

She'd clicked with Russell on both a working and friendship level when he'd first begun his summer internship with CC&B three months ago. She'd been pleased when the college student had been assigned the role of her assistant on this survey.

"Asad and I were together for a few months in my sophomore year," she admitted.

"*Together* together?"

"Yes."

"Wow."

"You didn't suspect?"

"Hell, no. You're not exactly the kind of woman who ends up in a sheikh's bed." The other redhead had the grace to blush at that observation. "I don't mean you're a troll or anything."

"He wasn't a sheikh then."

"I bet he was the same in every other way, though."

"No. He used to smile a lot more."

"Oh-ho."

"Now what?"

"Nothing."

"Stop being cryptic. What is *oh-ho?*"

"You're sad he's not as happy as he used to be. I can tell."

"Don't be an idiot. I didn't say he wasn't happy." But that's what she'd meant and hadn't realized it until Russell brought it up.

"But he's not, is he?"

"His wife died two years ago." And the pampered princess Badra had been nothing like what he'd expected her to be. "He's probably still mourning her."

"Not the way he looks at you, he's not."

She didn't ask what way that was because she already knew and wasn't up to false protestations.

Russell told her anyway. "Like he wants to devour you. If a woman looked at me like that, I'd have a heck of a time staying out of her bed."

"Right." That at least, deserved some proper skepticism. From what she'd seen over the summer, Russell didn't have any more of a social life than she did. "You're as wrapped up in your work as I am."

"But I'd take time away from my precious rocks for something that intense."

"That's why you go clubbing every Saturday night, because you're looking."

"I never go clubbing…oh, you were making a point. I still say if I walked into it like you have here, I'd go for it."

"You wouldn't. You're every bit as gun-shy as I am. You're just being an idiot," she said fondly.

Russell should know just how damaging such a course of action would be to her. He'd had his own broken heart, as he'd confided to her over a bottle of potent wine on their first assignment in the field together.

"You've said that before. Good thing I've got such a high IQ, my confidence in my own intelligence is bulletproof."

She snorted. "IQ measures your ability to learn, not your common sense."

"You saying I lack common sense?"

"If the fossilized fragment fits…"

"Aren't you the clever one?"

"How far from here to our first sampling site?" she asked.

"According to my satellite GPS, about an hour in a Jeep, provided we can travel pretty directly."

She nodded.

"We should ask Sheikh Asad. After all, he is our guide while we're in country."

"He's a sheikh. I'm sure he's got someone else we can go to."

"And you call me an idiot."

"What does that mean?"

"The sheikh's not leaving our guiding up to anyone else and you know it. He wants to handle you...um, I mean this little geological expedition personally."

CHAPTER SIX

IRIS rolled her eyes, but didn't reply to Russell's obvious innuendo.

At any rate, she couldn't exactly deny it. Her field assistant was right. Not only had Asad insisted on being their go-to guy, she was pretty sure he'd want to accompany them on their first foray out of the encampment. She could only hope he would limit himself to the one time.

Her instincts told her to hope all she wanted, but the man was going to become her shadow, big-time busy sheikh or not.

Asad proved her first supposition right later that evening when they were all sharing dinner in his tent.

For the sake of her own sanity, she tried to talk him out of it. "That's not necessary. I've been doing this for almost four years, Asad. I know what I'm doing and Russell can read his pocket transit with the best of them."

"Nawar is looking forward to an excursion. Would you deny her?"

The little girl in question was looking up at Iris with pleading brown eyes.

Oh, not fair. Iris shook her head. "Of course not."

"But can this wait until the day after tomorrow?

Grandmother has planned a welcome feast for your arrival."

"What? Why?"

"You are our guest," Genevieve said, as if that explained everything. "It would be bad manners not to do so."

"But surely Russell and I can start our work tomorrow and return in time for dinner?" she asked, feeling desperate.

She had to get away from Asad's home and remind herself why she was in Kadar.

"It will be much more than a simple meal," Asad said.

Genevieve smiled in a way that was catching. "I thought perhaps you would enjoy witnessing the preparations and this aspect of our way of life."

It would be churlish to refuse, but how Iris wished she could do so. "I would love to. Thank you for the offer."

"I could go on my own and start the measurements," Russell offered.

Surprisingly, it was Asad who shook his head before Iris had a chance to veto the idea. "While traditionally, men do little to prepare the food, we will have our own things to attend to for the feast. You must not miss the opportunity to experience this part of our world."

"Thank you, Sheikh Asad." Russell smiled, his youthful eyes glowing with excitement at the thought. The traitor.

Asad inclined his head.

"Grandmother has said we will have *mansaf.* It's my favorite, but we don't have it very often," Nawar piped up.

"Is it?" Iris asked with a smile for the tiny girl so

unlike her father in looks, but so similar in every other way. "If I remember correctly, that used to be your father's favorite, too."

She'd even tried to make it for him once, looking up a recipe online for the traditional stewed lamb and yogurt sauce served over rice. An indifferent cook, Iris had been disappointed but not surprised when the dish had turned out only so-so, even to her palate. Asad had thanked her for the effort, but informed her that traditional Bedouin food had to be prepared in the traditional way—over a campfire—to carry the full flavor.

It was a criticism and excuse for the dinner's mediocrity all-in-one and she hadn't been exactly sure how to take it. Any hurt feelings she might have had were dispelled by the passionate lovemaking that followed dinner, however. He'd made it clear that no matter the outcome, her efforts had been very much appreciated.

She didn't repeat the mistake of attempting to cook food from his homeland for him again.

"It still is," Nawar said with a giggle. "Grandmother says we are just alike."

"I'm sure your grandmother is right." Iris ruffled Nawar's hair.

"Tomorrow I will show you the baths in the caves," Genevieve said. "I'm sure my grandson showed proper decorum and skipped that part of his tour with you."

Iris didn't know about proper decorum, but the older woman was right. "Asad didn't mention any baths."

She had to admit to a feeling of relief at the thought that the next few weeks would not be spent without a proper soak.

"There are natural hot springs in the caves to the south of the encampment," Asad said now.

"The women use the upper caves and the men the

lower ones. I suppose they think they can handle the hotter water better," Genevieve said with a loving smile for her husband of several decades. "Hanif discovered them when he was a boy and gifted the caves to the tribe upon our wedding."

It was a romantic story and Iris found herself smiling, as well.

"It just goes to show that for the thousands of years our people have wandered these lands, they remain a mystery to us," Hanif said. He turned to Russell. "Mr. Green, you will join me for coffee in the morning with the other men, yes?"

"Russell, please," her field assistant said with a grin. "And I would be honored. I've been eager to try the real thing ever since I learned we were coming to Kadar."

"Ah, so you understand that what comes out of an automatic drip maker is nothing like it?" Asad asked sardonically with a look at Iris that said he wasn't talking only of coffee.

"I'm willing to be convinced of it," Russell said unsurprisingly. The man was a caffeine addict with a particular fondness for coffee.

If Asad had researched Russell, he couldn't have made a better ploy to get him otherwise occupied in the mornings.

Somehow, regardless of her best efforts, Asad managed to accompany Iris on her trek to her room when it came time to find her bed later that evening.

Which said something about his efforts versus hers, she supposed. Or, perhaps it was the level of determination she should be looking at. The possibility that Asad's might be stronger than hers in this regard was disturbing on more than one level.

She liked the idea that she might not be wholly dedicated to minimizing their contact no better than the thought that he was far more determined to spend time with her than he should be.

"So, what do you think of my city of tents?" he asked just as she reached her doorway and thought to slip inside without incident.

Her hand on the edge of the curtain that covered the entrance to her apartment, Iris stopped. "It's amazing."

"You do not find the remoteness too disconcerting?" he asked with a certain level of disbelief.

A wry smile curved her lips and she met his dark brown gaze squarely. "Asad, last month I spent two weeks in the middle of the East Texas desert doing an updated geological assessment for an oil company. The truth is, your nomadic home is more sophisticated and busy than ninety percent of my assignments."

"Do you enjoy being away from home for such long periods?"

Prepared to give the answer she always offered when asked that question, she was surprised when honesty spilled forth instead. "At least when I'm on assignment, there's a reason for me spending so much time alone."

"Your work."

"Yes."

"It's very important to you."

"It's all I have." She looked around them, noticing his grandparents had already made it into their chamber down the long corridor that ran the width of the tent.

Nawar and Fadwa had gone to bed hours earlier. But still, the sense of family permeated the impressive dwelling.

"We're not all like you, with relations who miss us when we're gone," she added in an even tone.

"Your parents are still living."

"The last time I saw them was Christmas two years ago. We took a winter cruise together." She'd bought it for them as a gift with hopes of building something more of their relationship now that she was an adult.

It hadn't worked. They'd been no more interested in getting to know the grown-up Iris than they had the child. And as much as it hurt to admit, looking at them through adult eyes, she realized her parents were not people she would particularly care to know well, either.

She'd finally given up hope of having anything resembling a real family and hadn't bothered them with so much as an email since. Though now she realized that she'd begun to give up that particular dream when Asad had left.

She simply hadn't been aware of it until her parents' continued indifference pounded the final nail into the coffin that had been her hope.

"Two years ago? But that is criminal. Why would you neglect your parents so shamefully?"

His absolute inability to understand charmed her when she thought probably she should have been offended. But to discover the worldly sheikh so naive in even one area was rather captivating.

"When was the last time you saw your parents?" she asked curiously.

"Last month." He cocked his head to the side, studying her like a specimen under glass. "I travel to Geneva three times a year."

So the decision to allow his grandparents to raise Asad, and groom him to take over as sheikh, had not destroyed their relationship completely. He might resent it somewhat, but he still cared for his parents and she was certain they cared for him, as well.

"Your family is happy to see you when you do, I imagine."

"But naturally."

She nodded. Lucky him. Even after the barbaric bargain, he had parents and siblings who loved him and wanted to see him. And probably a lot more often than the three times a year he went to see them. "For your family, yes. We aren't all so lucky, Asad."

His expression turned thoughtful. "In the ten months of our liaison, you never mentioned a visit from or to your parents. I assumed it was because you saw no reason to introduce me to your family."

It was a reasonable hypothesis, considering the fact Asad himself had not been thinking in terms of a future together. He'd no doubt assumed that while he'd returned home on winter and spring break to see his family, she'd been doing the same. Instead, she'd spent those weeks by herself on campus missing him more than she ever had her parents.

He'd never made any move toward introducing her to anyone in *his* family and because of her past, she hadn't found that odd. Only later had she realized that a man did not introduce his relatives to a casual lover. Particularly not a man slated to one day become sheikh.

Silly her. Iris had thought he was waiting for the right time when the truth was, there was never going to be any such thing for them.

"Once again, I guess we were both guilty of making assumptions." She shook her head, tired and in no mood to prevaricate. "I don't have a family, Asad. I had an egg and sperm donor who were kind enough to financially support me until I graduated from university."

He jerked back as if she'd slapped him. "That is a

very cynical thing to say about the people responsible for giving you life."

"I don't expect you to understand. Your parents allowed your grandparents to raise you in the ways of the Bedouin and while I'm sure you felt abandoned by them, no matter how much you might deny it, the truth is, they never gave you up. Not really. My parents kept legal rights to me, but for all intents and purposes, I was their unwanted ward, not their daughter."

"And you called my grandparents' deal with my parents barbaric," he said in a tone laced with a heavy dose of shocked disapproval.

She just shook her head. He was right. She was in no position to judge and certainly Asad had far more of a family than she did. Though she noticed he didn't deny feeling abandoned by his parents.

He frowned, looking like he wanted to say something more.

She put her hand up in a silent bid for him to leave it. "Like I said, I don't expect you to get it. Why should you? I never did, and they were supposed to be my family. I'm tired and I want to go to bed. All right?"

Though why she was asking him, instead of just going into her room, she didn't really know.

"I don't suppose I could persuade you to share mine," he said in the same teasing tone he used to employ to lighten things when they got too serious when they'd been together.

She'd avoided telling him the truth about her parents because it shamed her to admit she was unloved, but she remembered now the other reason that she'd kept the truth buried. Asad had been so very good at keeping her smiling and happy, she'd been loath to bring the pain of her left-behind childhood into the present.

And, back then, there had still been that tendril of hope that one day her parents were going to realize Iris was someone they could enjoy having in their lives.

She gave him a smile now, not nearly as forced as it should have been. "You're an idiot."

She'd said the same words, or something like them, to Russell earlier, and knew it was because, even after everything, part of her still considered Asad to be a friend.

Perhaps, for a woman like her—who trusted with such difficulty—once trust was given, it could never be withdrawn entirely. The ramifications of that possibility were not good for her heart, not at all.

Unaware of her inner turmoil, Asad gave her a lazy smile she hadn't seen in a very long time. "No, an idiot would let the opportunity slip by."

For a terrible uncertain moment, Iris was tempted to take him up on the offer. She'd never felt like she belonged anywhere like she did in his bed. It had all been a fantasy, but it had *felt* real. In his arms, she'd felt like she had a family.

And it had almost killed her to lose him.

She wasn't setting herself up for that again. She couldn't.

She didn't bother to reply, but simply slipped into her room. Tying the cords that would keep the curtain snugly over her doorway while she slept, she ignored the tears tracking down her cheeks.

The next day, as much as she tried to hold herself aloof, Iris found herself falling under the spell of the four-year-old daughter as easily as she had the father six years before. Nawar had spent the entire day, except her nap, acting as Iris's shadow.

It had been a busy day, filled with preparations for the feast and chatter with Asad's female relatives.

Iris had enjoyed herself so much that she'd felt guilty for not working, despite the fact a phone call from Sheikh Hakim had made it clear that he did not expect Iris to begin her geological assessment until after she'd been officially welcomed into the city of tents.

Now that the food and party preparations were over, Genevieve had told Iris it was time for their personal preparations. Iris had intended to wear the single dress she'd brought with her for what she'd believed was to be a remote field assignment, but Genevieve would not hear of it.

She and Nawar had made a big production out of choosing a galabia from Genevieve's wardrobe for Iris to wear to the feast. And the small girl had now appointed herself as Iris's instructor in the ways of bathing in the communal baths of the Sha'b Al'najid.

They were now soaking in the largest of the pools fed by an underground hot springs in the women's section of the caves, after a cursory wash with fragrant soap and water left to cool in large bowls near the pools.

"You must rest. No splashing or swimming," the small girl said with a very serious mien. "After a long time, we wash again with the sand from the bottom of the pool."

Iris wondered what a long time meant to a small child and smiled. "I bet that makes your skin very soft."

Nawar gave her a solemn nod. "Grandmother says so."

"And our hair?" She'd found it odd that they didn't shampoo before coming into the communal pool of mineral waters.

"We're supposed to wash it first," Nawar admitted with a frown.

Oho, the little one didn't like washing her hair. "Don't you want your hair soft like your skin and shiny like silk?"

"The soap gets in my eyes." Nawar gave a childish pout. "It stings."

"I think I can help you wash your hair without getting soap in your eyes."

"Fadwa tries, but she says I move too much," Nawar replied doubtfully.

"You seem very good at staying still now."

"Thank you." Nawar gave Iris a guilty look. "I don't like to wash my hair."

"So, perhaps you move more when Fadwa is trying to get it clean than you should, hmmm?"

"Maybe."

Iris nodded. "Well, you will simply have to do better for me, because if I get soap in your eyes it will make me very sad."

"I don't want you to be sad."

"Thank you."

Iris successfully washed the child's long dark hair without getting soap or water in her eyes after their soak and then sand scrubbing. Nawar was ecstatic and begged Iris to promise to wash her hair from now on.

"As long as I am here, I will. All right?" More than that, Iris could not promise.

They dressed for the party in the bathing caves after drying and brushing their hair. Genevieve had insisted on lending Iris a sheer silk scarf to be worn over her head and around her shoulders in the traditional manner. It matched exactly the heavily embroidered peacock-blue galabia she'd given Iris to wear earlier.

Walking back to the sheikh's tent, Iris felt like an Arabian princess.

"I have not seen that galabia in a long time," Asad's grandfather said when Iris and Nawar entered the dwelling. "It was always one of my favorites."

"Oh…I shouldn't have worn it, but Genevieve insisted," Iris said, feeling awkward.

"Nonsense." The old sheikh gave her a rakish smile and Iris could see what had attracted Genevieve all those years ago. "Naturally my wife chose it for you to wear. It is the perfect color to bring out the cream of your skin and that red shine in your hair so uncommon among our people. The other guests will be in awe of the beauty of the women of my house."

Iris blushed at the praise.

"I agree, Grandfather. The peacock galabia is lovely on Iris." The words were complimentary, but Asad gave his grandmother what couldn't be mistaken for anything but an admonishing look.

The older woman returned his gaze, her own serene. "Nawar chose it."

Asad's brow rose. "It is the traditional dress of the women of my house."

It had seemed rather a coincidence that the brightly colored trim around the skirt of Nawar's little party dress was styled after peacock feathers. And Genevieve's peach silk galabia had peacocks amidst the intricate gold needlework covering the garment. Even Fadwa's dress had tiny peacock feathers embroidered along the hem.

Iris's borrowed galabia was not only the shade of blue in a peacock feather, but had the birds embroidered on either side of the collar with sequins stitched into the tail feathers. More stitching ran around the collar, down the center of the garment and around the hem.

It was one of the most beautiful things Iris had ever worn.

Nevertheless, she should probably go change. "I'm not a member of your house. I shouldn't be wearing this."

"You are our guest." Which seemed to be Asad's answer to everything. "It is fine."

"But—"

"It is your favorite color." He reached out and tweaked his daughter's hair. "Nawar is partial to that shade of blue, as well. It is no wonder she chose this dress."

"I like purple best, though," Nawar said with a smile for her father.

"I know you do, little jewel." He met Iris's gaze then, his own somewhat rueful but unmovable. "It would be an insult to my grandmother to refuse to wear the galabia she offered you."

Knowing she wasn't about to win that particular argument, Iris gave in gracefully and smiled at Genevieve. "Peacocks are my favorite bird. It isn't just the color. Thank you for letting me wear this beautiful garment."

"No thanks are necessary. You must keep it if you like it," Genevieve said firmly. "I would have given it to Badra long ago, but she preferred Western dress."

"Oh, no. I couldn't take it." Particularly not a dress that was to have been passed down from Genevieve to the woman who had wed her grandson.

"But you must. You will offend my wife if you do not," the old sheikh said with that all-too-familiar arrogance.

Like grandfather, like grandson. Iris found herself amused instead of annoyed by the overt manipulations. Particularly when she saw the look Asad gave the old sheikh.

For whatever reason, it appeared he felt like he was being maneuvered just as neatly as she was. That couldn't help but make it easier for her to accept his grandmother's generosity.

Iris found herself grinning and winked at the old man. "We can't have that, can we? I would be honored to accept such a lovely gift," she said to Genevieve.

"Your old college friend is impertinent, Asad. Did you see her wink at this old man?" Hanif asked.

"I saw," Asad said with one of his infrequent smiles. "Grandmother will have to keep her eyes open at tonight's feast."

"Oh, you." Genevieve slapped her grandson's arm lightly. "Don't encourage him. He'll be flirting with the tourists again."

"The tourists love me. A desert sheikh of the old ways." Hanif pointed at himself importantly.

"I'm sure they do," Iris said with a smile, letting her gaze slide to Asad.

She imagined the tourists loved him as well, especially the women. Did he flirt with them like his grandfather? If Asad did, it wouldn't be innocent fun like with the old man—of that Iris was certain.

Realizing she really didn't want to think about Asad flirting with and conducting liaisons with the tourists, or anyone else for that matter, Iris forced all thoughts of the like from her mind.

CHAPTER SEVEN

THE feast was far more than a simple dinner, just as Asad had said it would be.

Platter after platter of food came in from the outdoor kitchens—far more than the ones Iris had helped Genevieve and the cook prepare the other night. The other women in the courtyard had all been cooking as well, but Iris hadn't known it had been for the feast.

They ate in the public receiving area of Asad's tent, the large room filled with his family and guests who Iris learned were all related to him, if distantly.

Russell, who had been seated at a different table from the immediate family, didn't seem in the least offended, but appeared to be enjoying himself every bit as much as Iris was.

After everyone had eaten, the men played their instruments and sang traditional songs, some stories of love and romance, other songs Nawar told Iris were for the camels.

"It helps them to be strong and carry heavy burdens," the small girl explained very seriously.

Iris nodded her understanding, though she found the idea fanciful.

Even Asad joined in the singing, his deep masculine voice making the song of love lost he'd chosen to share unexpectedly poignant. Then he sang a song in a dialect Iris did not understand, but the cadence of the song and tone of his voice made her thighs quiver with unwanted longing.

Her discomfort only increased when several of the guests gave her assessing glances. She tried looking everywhere but at Asad. Only his voice inexorably drew her gaze back to him.

He met her eyes, singing the last stanza in a low, melodic tone that brought moisture to her eyes, which she did her best to blink away.

"You enjoyed my humble efforts?" he asked Iris as he allowed Nawar to climb into his lap and rest against his chest.

The small girl had been allowed to stay up past her bedtime and looked ready to fall asleep right where she was.

Iris caught herself staring at the charming domestic picture they made as she answered, "Just as I'm sure everyone does who hears you. You're a man of many talents."

Iris's desire to be part of that scene was so strong, her chest ached with it. Though she knew there was no hope of that ever happening. She wasn't Asad's future.

No doubt there was another perfect princess in store for him, hopefully one with a stronger character than the deceased Badra.

"I am glad to hear you say so."

"I'm sure you hear it often enough."

"Perhaps."

She huffed out a small laugh at his arrogance. "You don't lack confidence, that's for sure."

"And do you think there is a reason why I should?"

"No, Asad, you are everything a desert sheikh should be."

"My daddy is the bestest sheikh ever," Nawar said, her tiredness showing in the childish pattern of speech so rarely exhibited by the young girl.

"Even better than Sheikh Hakim?" Iris teased. "After all, he is king over all of Kadar."

"Daddy is sheikh to the Sha'b Al'najid," Nawar said around a yawn. "That's bestest."

"I suppose it is, sweetheart."

The little girl's eyelids drooped.

"So, why is the peacock the symbol for your house when your tribe is called the people of the lion?" Iris asked Asad.

Even he had been named for the large predatory animal.

"The peacock is a symbol for the *women* of my house."

"But it's on the panel that leads to the..." And then Iris understood. "It covers the doorway that leads to what is traditionally considered the women's chamber."

"Yes."

"So, how did a bird become the symbol for the women of your house?"

"Many generations ago, one of the first sheikhs of our line, gave a peacock and peahen pair to his bride as a wedding gift. They were very exotic birds, something none of the Bedouin of their tribe had ever seen though as nomadic people they saw more wonders than the settled dwellers of our part of the world."

"Where did he get the birds?"

"I do not know, but his wife was so taken with them that she embroidered their likeness on all of her clothing."

Nawar made a soft little snoring sound and Iris couldn't help smiling. "And it became tradition to do so in the following generations."

"It did, though not all adhere to this tradition any longer."

"Why do you?"

"I did not, for a while, but my grandmother finds the birds beautiful, even the less-flamboyant peahen."

"Badra was not as impressed with the tradition," Iris guessed.

Asad's featured turned stern. "She was a princess of a neighboring country, but she preferred Western ways to anything the desert had to offer."

"Even you."

"Even me." Asad's clenched his jaw and Iris felt badly for reminding him that his marriage had not turned out anything like he'd anticipated when he'd dumped her to marry the virginal princess.

"I'm sorry. I shouldn't have said that."

"It is the truth."

"I'm still sorry."

"Come with me to put her to bed," he invited, indicating his sleeping daughter.

Iris nodded before her brain could even finish processing the request. She shouldn't. She knew she shouldn't. Keeping her distance from him was the only hope she had of keeping her heart intact this time around.

But keeping her distance from his daughter simply wasn't an option. After the years of rejection at her parents' hands, Iris did not have it in her to disappoint the child.

Besides, she liked Nawar.

Iris helped Asad undress Nawar and put a nightgown

on the sleeping child like she'd done it a hundred times before. It should feel awkward, but it didn't. Maybe the old saying was true, some things were just like riding a bicycle. You never really forgot how to do them, no matter how young you were when you learned.

While Iris had no experience with children as an adult, in boarding school she had often taken care of the younger ones.

She tucked the little girl into her bed, soothing her back to sleep with a soft lullaby when Nawar started to wake after her father laid her down.

"You're good with her," Asad said as they left the room moments later.

"Thank you. I've had some experience."

"I wasn't aware you had small children in your life." He talked like he knew a lot more about her life than he possibly could.

"I don't."

"But you've had experience?" he prompted.

"I learned how to tuck little girls in when I was a child myself."

"Explain," he pushed.

"My parents sent me to boarding school when I was six. I was terrified at night without our housekeeper there to tuck me in and tell me a story."

"I know this is a common practice, sending away one's children, but not one I could ever approve of for my own."

She didn't imagine a man who considered family as important as Asad did would. That knowledge cemented her certainty that his parents' defection to Geneva had hurt him badly, though he might never acknowledge it.

"It's actually not as frequent a practice in America as

it is in England, particularly not for children as young as I was, but there are some schools who will board their students from the age of six."

"And your parents saw fit to send you to one of these?"

"Yes."

"But how does that explain your experience with small children?"

"When I had been there a year, another six-year-old girl came to board, as well. Though I was second youngest of all the boarders, I was seven then and used to the life. The rest of the children in our grades were day schoolers."

"Day schoolers?"

"They came for the day, not to live."

"I see." He stopped her before they returned to the feast. "But you were a night schooler? No that would not be right."

She smiled at his attempt to get the word right. "I was a resident, or a boarder."

"Oh, yes, of course. And this little girl…"

"They put her in my room because we were so close in age. I could hear her crying in her bed that first night. She missed her parents terribly."

"So, you comforted her?"

"I had a little flashlight. I used it to read her a book. Then I sang to her until she fell asleep." Iris had returned to her own bed after that, more comforted than she had been at bedtime since going to the school.

"It became a routine."

"Yes. She was only there for a semester. Her parents had been in an accident and couldn't care for her, but as soon as they could, they came and got her."

Iris had been without a roommate until the next

year, when they'd put the two newest and youngest residents in a room with her again, since she'd been so good with her other roommate. "The girls' dormitory mother made sure that the youngest residents were always put in my room."

"Even when you were older? That must have put a cramp in your style."

Iris laughed. "Not so you would notice. I was a very shy girl, but I knew how to comfort the little ones and help them transition to boarding school life."

"They were lucky to have you."

"It was mutual. I would have been very lonely otherwise."

"Didn't you have friends?"

"Of course."

"But not close ones," he guessed far too perceptively.

"I made the mistake of growing close to a couple of girls in the beginning, but then they left." And she'd learned not to let people get too close.

They always left. But then Asad had come along and she'd opened her heart again...only, he'd left too.

"And now?"

"Now?"

"Do you have friends now?" he asked in a strangely tense voice.

"Russell."

"*Russell?* Your assistant?"

"You say his name like it's a dirty word. He's a really great guy." Iris liked the geological assistant who told corny jokes only another geologist would get.

"Are you attracted to this really great guy?" Asad asked with dangerous quiet. "He is a great deal younger than you."

A junior at his university, Russell was about as much

younger than Iris as she had been than Asad when they were together. "He's twenty. Anyway, what difference does it make to you?"

"Answer me. Are you two in a relationship?" he said, the last word laced with disgust.

She rolled her eyes. "If I didn't know better, I'd think you were jealous."

"Who says I am not?"

She laughed, the sound cynical. "Oh, come on, Asad. Like you are going to be jealous of a geeky science boy."

"Are you attracted to geeky?"

She could have been, she realized. Not Russell, necessarily. He was very much like a younger brother, but maybe to someone else like that. If there hadn't been Asad to spoil her for others. "You asked me if I had friends, Asad. That's what he is. My friend."

And a pretty new one at that.

"Good."

"I'm glad you think so."

"But you *don't* have a lot of friends back home."

"No."

"Yet you are a very good friend to have."

She made a sound of disbelief. If he'd really believed that, he wouldn't have given her up so easily. Would he?

"You were my friend once. It was only later that I realized what I lost when that friendship had to end."

"There was no *had to,* Asad. You were done with me and you dumped me. Stop trying to rewrite history."

"I am doing no such thing. Do you really think we could have remained friends when I married Badra?"

He had a point. And Iris probably shouldn't care that he'd missed her friendship, and yet coming to believe it dulled some of the old pain of losing him.

"I would like to be friends again," he said when she made no reply.

She didn't believe him. "You want me back in your bed. That's not friendship."

"For us it can be."

"Really? And when I return to the States, what then?"

"I do not intend to eject you from my life again," he said in a tone that made the words a vow.

It disconcerted her, and frightened her, as well. Because those words were not merely a promise…they were a threat, too. "I don't think I'm any more prepared to be your friend after leaving here than I was before."

What she meant, but didn't say, and hoped he clued into, was that for Iris it had been more than casual sex and friendship. And unfortunately, probably always would be.

"Give it a try. Let us see where it goes."

It wouldn't go to the altar; at least this time she knew that. Knowledge of the truth had to make some kind of difference in the outcome, didn't it?

"You want me in your bed."

"I do." At least he admitted it.

"And you want to be my friend." For now, anyway.

"Yes."

"What will that make us?" she asked uncertainly.

"Whatever we want it to."

This time she heard what he said, not what she wanted to hear. He wasn't making any promises.

She wanted to be his world like he'd been hers, but that was never going to happen. What did she say to this offer, though? She'd missed Asad so much because she'd let him into a place in her heart she'd kept protected from her very earliest childhood.

Now he was offering more than a tumble in the sack.

He was offering a renewal of their friendship that supposedly would last into the future.

She wasn't sure she wanted that to happen, but she was equally unsure if she wanted to hold herself back from him while she was in Kadar. Iris had spent six years avoiding intimacy, taking no other lovers and dreaming of Asad more nights than she cared to count.

Could having what he called a liaison with him help her to let go of him forever? Just being away from him hadn't done the trick. Psychobabble said people needed closure to move on. If she ever wanted to break the lonely boundaries of her life, Iris had to move forward. She had to take a chance again.

So, maybe that was exactly what she needed…closure on a relationship that was never meant to be in the first place.

One truth she could not escape: Iris had missed this man every day since he had walked away.

Losing him the first time had nearly destroyed her, but maybe being with him again, knowing it was temporary, would help to heal her now. Maybe letting him in again was the only way to break the boundaries she'd set around her lonely life.

She'd like to believe she could refuse him, but recognized that putting it to the test might see her disappointed. Regardless, she realized she didn't really want to.

Understanding better what had been going through his head six years ago—and realizing how betrayed he'd been by Badra—changed Iris's view of their shared past. At the very least, it made her realize Asad was not invulnerable to hurt.

Why that should matter, she was not sure, but it did.

And she wanted him, more than she would have

believed possible after everything that had happened. But there it was.

She had a choice, one that only she could make. If she got back into Asad's bed, it would be with her eyes open to both the reality of the past and what the future would hold.

Could she live with that? She thought maybe she really could. She was almost positive she *couldn't* live with the other...the not having him and the richness he brought to her life for whatever time available to them.

When the silence stretched between them as her thoughts whirled inside her head, Asad slipped his hand beneath the scarf covering her head and cupped her nape. "It is not in me to lose you again."

Asad saw the flash of disbelief in Iris's blue gaze before she pushed the peacock curtain aside to return to the feast.

He wanted to draw her back, demand she acknowledge the truth of his claim, but now was not the time. She was skittish, and perhaps he understood that better now. But he would woo her and convince her that the past's mistakes could be left there.

He had brought her to Kadar for the reason he'd given her, to help her career, but also because he'd never forgotten her. Not her friendship and not her passionate fire in the bedroom.

He wanted to be warmed by that fire again.

Where that might lead, he did not know, but one certainty existed. He was no longer looking for a perfect princess to share his life.

Iris's reflections on her childhood horrified him. If the two lived among the Sha'b Al'najid, they would have lost not just their daughter, but also their place in the tribe for such unnatural behavior. That parents could be so dismissive of a child was bad enough, but that the child should be his sensitive former lover infuriated him.

One of the first things he had noticed about Iris was the vulnerability she hid behind her shy demeanor. The sensitive child she would have been must have been tormented endlessly by her parents' indifference.

He could not fathom it.

Iris had been right. Asad had not been pleased at his own father's rejection of their heritage and he had determined at a young age never to make a choice that required leaving a child behind, as his parents had him. Yet Asad had never felt ignored by his parents, or that he did not matter to them.

They had made the journey back to the Sha'b Al'najid much more frequently than was convenient for them in order to spend time with their oldest son. And while they had agreed Asad would be raised to be sheikh of his people one day, his father had demanded Asad be allowed to come to Geneva at least one weekend per month throughout his childhood.

Though Asad was not supposed to know it, his mother cried when he left—each and every time.

Still, Asad had fought against more frequent visits, even at the earliest age. He was sure now that his parents had been hurt by that, but then the choice to leave the Sha'b Al'najid—and him, their son—had been theirs.

Regardless, they had been so different from the soulless couple who had given life to his beautiful geologist.

His parents' choice had cost them. Of that he was certain, despite the fact he was equally certain he could never have made that choice himself. The thought of letting Nawar go had been thoroughly untenable from the first time he held her, despite the fact that they shared no actual blood tie.

An inexplicable protectiveness burning in his gut, Asad kept Iris by his side during the rest of the feast, thoroughly enjoying her reaction to his family's way of celebrating.

Badra had always found the ways of the Sha'b Al'najid provincial and never hesitated to say so. The youngest, spoiled daughter of a neighboring country's king, she had rejected Asad's first proposal, saying she would never marry an ignorant goatherd.

Asad, who at eighteen had herded the animals only to learn lessons his grandfather said could not be taught with words, was hugely offended. And equally intrigued by this beautiful, spoiled creature who thought she was too good for him.

Any among the women of his people, or those he had met visiting his parents in Switzerland, would have been more than honored to receive such an offer of marriage. Badra, who was a year his senior, had unaccountably turned him down.

She couldn't have conceived a move more suited to garnering his interest and determination to woo her successfully.

They'd met during a trade negotiation between Asad's grandfather and Badra's father. As was custom, the negotiations had occurred in the home of the king wanting his grandfather's services in moving goods between his country and those nearby.

Asad had found the city-bred and sophisticated young woman fascinating. Besides, she *was* a princess, and as a future sheikh, he should marry a woman of such standing.

Asad allowed himself a small, bitter smile at his own naïveté and arrogance.

Badra had not been impressed with his pedigree, thereby cementing his interest in her. Then and there, he had determined to win her hand. He would attend university and build his tribe into a people others would envy.

And that the Princess Badra would want to belong to.

So he'd gone to university and graduate school, all the while working to build his family's business interests with the help of his father and grandfather. When Asad returned to his desert family permanently, he was determined to do so with Badra at his side.

The only stumbling block to that outcome had been his growing affection for his lover, Iris Carpenter. But a man of considerable will, Asad had forced himself to cut her out of his life and pursue his original goal. It was what was best for his people.

Badra's father would make a powerful political and business ally, the innocent and protected Badra a beautiful and admired lady of his people.

He shook his head. He'd been a fool.

Asad had not been in the least surprised when she accepted his second proposal. He'd assumed her father had convinced her of the advantageousness of the match. It was on Asad's wedding night that he'd discovered the true reason for Badra's capitulation.

Far from the innocent virgin he'd expected to bed, Badra was well versed in the art of sexual encounters.

She was also pregnant. Which he had realized when she woke the next morning nauseated in a way he had witnessed only among the pregnant women of his tribe.

He'd demanded to know the truth and she'd admitted everything amid floods of tears.

She'd had an affair with a married man who had seduced her from her innocence and now carried the man's child. She said she was terrified of what her father's reaction would be if he found out. Claiming to always have a soft spot for Asad, she said she'd learned her lesson and had eagerly accepted his marriage proposal.

She didn't think she was doing him any true harm, as she'd discovered the babe's sex was female. He would not reject a daughter simply because she had come to be as the result of her mother's ignorance and naïveté, would he?

She played to Asad's view of himself as a modern man who knew how to straddle the old world and the new. And he accepted her explanations and perceptions of him because his pride would not allow him to do otherwise, swallowing her words like a camel at an oasis after five days in the desert.

Though he had not forgotten the contempt she'd held for him at eighteen, he believed she had changed her views. He even accepted the role his own pride had played in the current circumstances. He'd been adamant he would marry this woman and no other. She would not reject him, the lion of his people.

He had put himself forward as her unknowing savior and he could hardly withdraw from the field at this point.

Badra claimed she'd broken it off with the married man when she agreed to become the lady of the Sha'b Al'najid, but he'd had his doubts—unspoken and unacknowledged. However, he'd made his vows just as she had. With that truth firmly in the forefront of his mind, Asad had directed his considerable will toward making his marriage with Badra work.

His doubts had come to fruition a month after Nawar's birth when Asad's head of security in the newly created command center had informed him of communications between Badra and her former lover.

But the knowledge of her continued perfidy had come too late. Asad loved his daughter and would not lose her to her mother's selfishness.

He had not realized until much later, in a discussion with his sister during her first pregnancy, that Badra could not possibly have known the babe in her womb was a girl on their wedding night. Not unless she'd had an amniocentesis, which she had not. Badra had been a consummate liar.

And for the sake of *that woman* and his own pride, Asad had let go of his friendship with the one woman whose loyalty and integrity had never once come into question.

Unlike Badra with her deceits and machinations, Iris would always put others first. It was in her nature to do so. Knowing more about her past, he found that trait even more worthy of admiration.

CHAPTER EIGHT

For the second night in a row, Iris found herself walking with Asad toward her room at bedtime. It was much later this night though, the last of Asad's guests having just left.

"There is one chamber you have yet to see in my home," he said as they reached her door.

She'd spent the last hours of the party wrestling with what to do about Asad and had come to a decision.

One thing was certain—he wasn't giving up. She knew how determined he could be and was under no illusions that this time would be any different. He wanted her. He would do his best to get what he wanted.

She could spend the next few weeks doing her level best to avoid him and stifle her own desire for him, but she was not convinced of her own ultimate success.

If she let herself love him again, she was lost. There was another option though, wasn't there?

She'd come to believe that sharing his bed again would help heal her heart. Sometimes the only way to rebirth in life was through the fire. Just like a Phoenix. She would be the one to leave this time and because of that she would not spend the next six years seeing his face every time she looked with interest at another man.

She'd come to the conclusion that the way out of the

isolated existence her life had become was the same way into it. Through Asad. This time she knew he wasn't looking for a future with her and she would not allow herself to look for one either...or fall in love with him again.

That would dictate the difference in the outcome. It had to.

"You're right." Her voice was husky, but not tentative. One thing her feelings about this man had never been was tentative. "I haven't seen your room."

"Would you like to?"

"It will not offend your grandparents?" Iris was not naive enough to believe they would not figure it out, even if she left Asad's bed in the wee hours as she meant to.

This kind of thing always seemed to get out eventually. Physical intimacy had a way of showing itself, even when those involved did their best to hide it. And Asad was too proud and arrogant to even try.

Iris was no good at hiding her emotions, even if she wanted to. She would show the change in her relationship with the sheikh, even if she did her best not to.

He pulled her around to face him, his expression dark and serious. "I am sheikh now. There is no offense in me doing as I see fit in my own home."

She took leave to doubt that culturally it was easy as that, but then this man lived by his own rules, no matter how traditionally Bedouin he could be at times.

"Your arrogance is showing again."

"I am certain of my place."

She nodded, for the moment equally certain of hers. "Show me."

His nostrils flared and his eyes burned her. "It will be my pleasure."

"If I remember right, the pleasure was always very mutual."

"Yes."

He led her into his room and she was surprised to discover that the chamber was the same size as hers, but the bed was much bigger. Covered in pillows and a silk quilt embroidered with a roaring male lion in the center, it was easily twice the width of her bed. Between it and the sparse furniture, there was no extra room as in her chamber.

The sound of rustling clothes had her looking back toward him only to discover he was already disrobing, his *kuffiya* discarded, revealing dark hair that framed his fierce features even better than the head covering had done. He'd also tossed off the ornate robe he'd worn to the feast. Under it he had on the traditional loose trousers and...*an Armani shirt?*

She grinned.

"What?" he asked, arrested in his movements while looking at her.

"You're wearing Armani with your traditional garb."

He shrugged. "I prefer their shirts." He dropped his trousers. "And their shorts."

Her breath caught in her throat at the sight of his muscular legs. Darker than they used to be, and rippling with even more muscle she wanted to touch.

There was a time when she had believed that body belonged to her. She knew now that it did not, but she could still revel in the knowledge that as long as she shared his bed, for all intents and purposes, it might as well be hers.

"Nice," she said, unable to hide the catch in her voice.

His hardness pressed against the black silk of his

Armani boxers, letting her know that his desire for her was real. He unbuttoned the shirt, letting it fall open to reveal the sprinkling of black curls that lightly covered his chest and abdomen.

"You used to shave that," she observed.

He frowned momentarily. "I was trying to be more urbane."

"But why would you want to? You were always so proud of your heritage." It was one of many things about him that had impressed her.

Asad had known who and what he was in a way she had still been trying to achieve for herself. But maybe, he hadn't had it as together as she'd believed. That knowledge cast the past in a different light once again, one that eased old hurts even further.

She'd made the right decision to let him make love to her. This coming together *would* be healing…it already was.

"Another time, we will discuss these things." He moved toward her. "But now is not the time for talking."

She wouldn't argue. It had been six years since she felt the level of excitement coursing through her body now and he hadn't even kissed her yet.

He rectified that with a swift movement, bringing their bodies flush and their mouths together in perfect union. Passion and need exploded inside her with nuclear power.

Everything she'd been suppressing for six years, but especially over the past two days broke through her mental restraints, making her body strain against his even as her lips gave him kiss for kiss, caress for caress.

He broke his mouth from hers, gasping. "It's been so long. Too long."

She had to agree. "Yes."

"For you, as well?" he asked, his brown eyes almost black with the depth of his feeling.

And she could not deny him the truth. "For me, too."

It had definitely been too long since she touched him, as the depth of her excitement showed. They'd had one explosive kiss and she felt like it would take only the slightest touch to her intimate flesh for her to climax.

He'd always known just how to touch her to bring her the ultimate in pleasure, but this was something different. This bliss was coming from deep inside her at the knowledge that, for a little while, they were going to be one again.

But she would not love him. Not this time. Their bodies would join, but not their hearts. She was too smart for that. *Please, God, let her be too smart for that.*

He shrugged his shirt off. "Come with me to my bed. Let us make new memories to supplant the old."

He knew exactly what to say, but that should not surprise her. Other than when he dumped her, Asad had always known exactly what she needed to hear from him.

"New memories," she agreed breathlessly as he gently pulled away the scarf covering her hair.

"I always loved your hair, the red is so rich and unique. It feels like liquid silk." He combed through it with his fingers, his expression intent.

"That's the shampoo and conditioner I use," she said with a smile.

"You think?"

She nodded. She wasn't a vain woman, she didn't think, but Iris had always insisted on using salon quality products on her hair. The way it slipped through Asad's fingers now made her little idiosyncrasy worth it.

"I think it is the magic of the woman, myself."

"You think I'm magic?" she asked softly, tears stinging her eyes that she *would not* let fall.

"I do." He stopped with his hands poised to undress her. "You are sure you want this?"

She was shocked by his question, but maybe she should not have been. No matter how determined Asad was, he was and had always been a man of honor.

She nodded.

"We will erase the ugly memories of the past."

"What memories are you trying to erase?" she couldn't help asking, though she so wanted to move forward with the seduction.

He shrugged, but then surprised her by following it up with words. "You were the last woman I bedded that brought nothing but honesty to our time together."

"You were honest, too." Though for a long time, she'd thought he hadn't been.

"Yes."

"So, this is a reset? For both of us?"

"Yes."

She got that. He'd been hurt badly by Badra's infidelity, Iris was sure. Asad wanted to go back to a time when he could trust the woman in his bed. Iris wanted the same thing. "Then, I'm sure."

He nodded and then removed her galabia with reverent hands, his expression unreadable, but intense and primitive.

Was that possession glowing in his brown gaze? Or desire?

It didn't matter. For a few brief hours, she would let her body be his, just not her heart.

He reached behind her to unclasp her bra. "You still wear such feminine underwear beneath your T-shirts and jeans."

"I wasn't wearing jeans tonight."

"But you brought this with you regardless." He drew the silky champagne lace bra down her arms and dropped it to the carpet under their feet.

She couldn't deny it. She might dress like an asexual scientist most of the time, but underneath, her bras and panties were her one consistent feminine indulgence.

His large hands cupped her breasts, his thumbs brushing over her hardened nipples.

She sucked in a breath.

Approval flared in his dark eyes. "So responsive."

His gaze dipped low and she felt the caress of his eyes on her most sensitive flesh, though it was still hidden behind the stretch lace boy shorts that matched her bra. "This style is new for you. I like it."

"It's been six years since you've seen my underwear."

"I'm keen to see what else you have in store for me."

Which implied this was not a onetime deal. And she'd known that. He'd said as much when admitting he wanted her back in his bed, but this further proof that tonight was not their only and last night together still settled over her in an unexpected delight.

"Take off your panties," he ordered in a guttural tone.

"Why don't you?"

"I can't stop touching you." The admission affected something deep inside her she didn't want reached and she almost pulled away.

But the way he played so intently with her breasts, giving her pleasure and so obviously taking his own from the caresses, made it impossible for her to deny him. Or herself.

Soon, they were both naked and lying together in the big bed, the covers tossed back. His hands mapping her body as if memorizing it, comparing it to memory and marking all the similarities and differences.

She could not remember a time they had made love before when he had been so intent on learning her every dip and crevice. Not even their first time together.

Something about tonight was different for him too, but she wasn't about to speculate what that might be. She'd make the wrong assumptions as she'd done before and her heart couldn't afford such mistakes again.

He leaned up over her, his regard serious. "You are the first woman I have brought to this bed."

But he'd been married. "Badra?"

"Had her own room."

Iris couldn't imagine him having sex with his wife on that tiny bed, so Badra's bed must have gone the way of her other things.

"Do you want me to be flattered?" she asked and then wished she could take back the facetious comment.

It might not be love, but this moment was too profound for sarcasm.

His tender smile said he was not offended. "It is I who am honored to have you here."

So that was what he wanted, for her to feel honored by the distinction. And really? She did. Not that she was going to tell him so. It seemed like too much an admission to make after she'd opened herself to him in a way she'd been determined never to again.

"Kiss me, Asad."

He did, a growl of desire sounding between them, his body moving over hers in that dominating way he'd always had. An aggressive lover, Asad filled her senses with his presence as he caressed her body with the clear intent to seduce and excite. He knew how to draw forth more than she ever intended to give and yet fill her with bliss in the way she responded to him.

She returned his touches, reveling in her ability to once again lay claim to the magnificent man above her.

Their kisses were incendiary, the fire burning inside her in no danger of being extinguished. Tense with need, her body remembered this man's lovemaking and the capacity for pleasure he had taught her that she had.

He brought her to her first climax with his hand, his lips never leaving hers. Once he had swallowed all her cries as his due, he moved down her body, his mouth blazing a trail of heat and want that culminated in a renewed pulsing in the tender flesh between her thighs.

She found completion the second time with his mouth on her, his tongue lashing her clitoris with deft flicks, his hands roving her body and settling on her breasts as he manipulated her nipples to enhance her pleasure until she screamed with it.

She grabbed a pillow to stifle her cries, but he reared up and yanked it from her hand. "I want to hear every sound. I will have all of you."

"But the tent walls…"

"Are far better at muffling sound than you would ever imagine, my sweet little Westerner."

"That was the problem, wasn't it?" she asked, her body still shuddering from the ultimate in pleasure, his resting between her wantonly spread thighs. "I was too Western for your people. Like your mother."

"My grandmother was from the West, as well. She adapted."

"But her son did not."

"No. Why are we talking about my parents right now?" he asked as he thrust his hard and very impressive member against her.

"Because…" She let her voice trail off, unsure what she wanted to say, what she was willing to admit to.

Even though she didn't want to be, she'd been trying to understand how he could let something so good go. What they'd had between them had been incredible, not just something that worked to relieve sexual tension.

"I might have been innocent, but even I knew we were amazing together. The sex was mind-blowing from the very first time." And so had everything else between them been.

The dip of his head acknowledged the truth of her words.

"Why?" she asked, finally able to do so.

"I planned to marry Badra from the time I was eighteen." And he was the type of man that when he had a plan, he stuck to it. Could it really have been that simple?

When she didn't reply, he added, "There was no lack in you. Nothing missing from *us*."

She just hadn't been the Middle Eastern princess he'd wanted. "When you dumped me, I sure felt lacking."

"No." He kissed the join between her neck and shoulder, suckling up a love bite, and sent pleasure zinging through her. "You were the perfect lover."

But not the perfect candidate for wife, even if Badra hadn't been in the wings waiting. That much Iris understood.

Unwilling to dwell on a reality that she had no hope of changing, Iris offered, "You're a pretty amazing lover, yourself, Asad."

He moved over her body, reminding her of the stalking lion he'd been named for. "I would have you beyond amazed."

"What, you want me passed out from pleasure?" she teased.

"It has happened before."

Yes, it had. "Be my guest." She waved languidly with her hand, as if it didn't matter one way or another to her.

But they both knew it did. She'd never been indifferent to him. She never would be, but maybe, just maybe she would learn to move on from him.

"You have a serious expression I do not like," he said with a frown. "You are not thinking of me."

"Of course I'm thinking of you. Who else would I be thinking of while I am in your bed?"

He looked away, telltale color showing on his cut cheekbones. "I used to wonder."

"What? Why?"

"You were not a virgin when you came to my bed the first time." He met her eyes then. "I thought it mattered."

Yes, he had, though she hadn't known it. "If I recall correctly, it was *my* bed we used the first time, and I was as close to a virgin as you can get."

"What do you mean?"

"Did you think I'd had a string of lovers before you?"

"I preferred not to know details."

Arrogant, possessive sheikh. Even though he'd had no intention of staying with her, he didn't like to think of anyone else with her, either. He didn't deserve the truth, but maybe she deserved for him to know it.

Six years before, she'd thought her innocence obvious and had only learned otherwise when they broke up.

"I lost my virginity on a bet."

"That is…a bet…" For the first time ever, she saw Asad bin Hanif al Sha'b Al'najid lost for words.

It made her smile despite the topic under discussion. "For my high school years, my parents placed me in a coed boarding school known for its science programs."

At least they'd cared enough to take the advice of her middle school counselor on that.

"Yes?"

"There were the typical geeks and jocks, though most of the athletically gifted were highly intelligent, as well. It wasn't easy to get placement in the school and required high marks on the standardized tests."

"I imagine you did very well indeed."

She had, but book smart didn't equal people smart as she'd learned unequivocally her sophomore year. "I was the bookish, shy student who didn't make friends easily."

"Because you were afraid to let them in."

"Partly." And partly because she was socially awkward.

He gently tipped her head back toward him. "I would have been your friend."

It was a nice thing to say, but she couldn't stifle her laughter. "No, you wouldn't. You would have been one of the popular people. You couldn't have helped yourself. You wouldn't have even noticed me."

"I noticed you in college and you had not appreciably changed by then I think."

"True." Why was she sharing her past again when

he wasn't going to be in her future? "Are you sure you want to hear this? It's old news anyway."

"Tell me about this bet."

"The year I was a sophomore, the senior boys had a bet going on for who could bag the most virgins."

"Bag?"

"Get in the sack…have sex with."

"I see, and clearly at that age, you were a virgin."

"I was. When the senior boy who decided to make me one of his conquests started flirting with me, I had no clue what was going on. It was only the middle of the school year, but by then, most of the students knew about the bet, so girls were wary of these boys."

"But you are not a gossip and you pay little attention when it goes on around you."

"Right. So I didn't know. It wouldn't have mattered anyway. I thought he just wanted to be my friend. And the funny thing? We ended up enjoying each other's company a lot. He became my best friend."

Asad winced. "Then you had sex."

"Yes. Despite my naïveté, I wasn't an easy mark— simply because the idea he'd want sex with me was so completely outside my thought process."

"And sex would have been an intimate encounter for you, something you'd already learned to avoid."

"You understand me so well." She bit her lip. "So did Darren. We finally had sex the week before graduation. It only happened once. I didn't like it very much."

"He was harsh?"

"No. He tried to make it good for me. He kept asking me if I was okay. He wasn't a cruel boy, not really. But it was my first time and I wasn't doing it because I wanted him. I never desired anyone that way until I met you. I just wanted to be close to him."

"What a little bastard."

"No. Selfish and thoughtless? Yes." She shrugged. "I didn't know about the bet until two days later when one of the other boys in the competition came up to me and complained about how he'd had it in the bag until I won it for Darren."

"The little prick."

"Yes, *he* was. He wanted me to hurt, to know the sex hadn't been about love, but in that, the joke was on him. I never thought Darren loved me." She'd thought he was her friend and she'd felt enough betrayal from that, though they'd worked through it in the end.

"Yet you had sex with him."

"He was leaving."

"So you gave him your virginity?"

"I don't expect you to understand." Darren had, though. He'd known how hurt she was by the bet too, even though she'd pretended indifference. "Darren's guilt was way worse than my embarrassment."

"Don't tell me you forgave him?"

"He's one of my dearest friends." Though they hadn't seen each other more than a handful of times in the intervening years, they stayed in touch with email and telephone.

He'd invited her to his wedding and introduced Iris to his wife as the girl who had made him the man he'd come to be. That bet had had a transforming influence on Darren, changing forever the way he related to others and decimating the power of peer pressure in his life.

He'd told her once that she'd freed him. She'd told him he was an idiot, but knew deep down that in a way he was right. Only it had been his own deep regret at hurting her and the other girls that had truly set him free.

"You cannot be serious."

"I can. Darren learned not to use people." Iris hadn't been so lucky. She hadn't learned not to be used, not then anyway.

"You cannot be this disgusting boy's friend. I forbid it."

She laughed, finding the telling easier than she'd expected it to be. "Too late. And he's no longer a boy. He's an adult man, married with two children and working in the diplomatic corps."

"I will see about that."

"You will do no such thing. Darren hurt me, but he didn't abandon me, not like you did. The boy who told me about the bet? Darren disowned their friendship."

"He was quite the tarnished knight," Asad said with heavy sarcasm.

"He apologized. We moved forward."

"I too apologized."

"And I'm lying here in your bed. What more do you want, Asad?"

CHAPTER NINE

THE question took Asad by surprise. Surely she knew exactly what he needed from her. "Your forgiveness."

She stared up at him in silence for several long seconds, her captivating blue eyes weighing him in a way he rarely encountered and then said, "I forgive you."

Could it truly be that easy? "You don't mean that."

"Would I be here if I didn't?" she asked, again referring to her place in his bed, their naked bodies pressed together, her gorgeous red tresses spread over his sheets.

"You forgive too easily."

"Not really."

"Yes." And why he should chide her about that when he was benefitting, he did not know.

"Are you saying you want me to go back to ignoring you?"

"No." He wanted her to trust him and somehow he knew her forgiveness did not come packaged with that commodity. "I want you to take me into your body."

It wasn't all he wanted, but since he wasn't sure what exactly that did entail, he didn't try to enlighten her.

Her answer was to shift under him, opening herself to him, but there was a part of herself she held back, a shadow in her eyes that had never been there in the past. Probably inevitable considering their history, but Asad did not have to like it.

Her trust was no longer on offer. And only now did he realize it had been a gift he'd taken every bit of as much for granted as that stupid high school boy had done. But Asad had been old enough to know better.

He would make up for it and he would regain that part of their friendship that he had found so comforting, but had been too blind to see the importance of, six years ago.

If she could forgive the little prick who had taken her virginity, call *him* friend and mean it, she could learn to give true forgiveness to Asad.

Asad reached for a condom. It was time to join their bodies in a way she could not hide from, could not pretend did not matter. Not his Iris.

He had brought her to the pinnacle of pleasure twice already because he knew he would not last long. Asad had only known his own hand for sexual release since well before Badra's death. It was not enough, especially now that he had Iris in touching distance again.

The idea of taking another lover, one that might betray him, or even worse, his daughter, had been anathema to him. Nawar's needs had to come first. Leaving her in order to enjoy liaisons to slake his physical hungers had not appealed to Asad.

He guided his head to Iris's soft opening, pressing forward into the heated honey depths he could never forget, no matter how hard he tried. Her body encased him in pure pleasure and he had the undeniable sensation of coming home.

This was where he belonged. For now, anyway.

Iris gasped as his body claimed hers and he kissed the sound right from her lips.

The baffling sense of coming home was so strong, once he was seated fully, he could not move. Despite the need clamoring in his body for release, he remained still, savoring the sensations that came from amazing sex.

"I will not abandon you again," he promised with the full force of his Bedouin honor. "I will be your best and truest friend."

"Possessive."

"I am."

"You always were."

He could not deny it.

Her voice was strained when she asked, "Are you going to move, Asad?"

"You wish for me to do so?" he taunted.

The clenching of her inner body was his only answer, but her eyes demanded he listen.

So he did, making love to her with less finesse than need. And instead of being bothered by his loss of control, he reveled in it. This was what had been missing for so long in his sex life.

Primitive, ungovernable passion.

In this, Asad's Bedouin heritage ruled, not the urbanity Badra had demanded.

His pleasure built like a volcano inside him, his balls burning with the need to erupt. He gritted his teeth, holding off the explosion as he did his best to bring his *aziz* to climax one more time.

Their mouths joined in a primal echo of what their bodies were doing, sweat slickening the skin between them as he thrust into her.

He felt her climax like it was his own and pleasure boiled up out of his cock with all the power of Mt. Vesuvius.

He shouted his triumph even as she continued to convulse around him.

He broke the kiss, still buried deep inside her. "You are mine."

"Your possessive side is showing again," she gasped out, not sounding like it bothered her in the least.

"I am a sheikh. What do you expect?"

She smiled up at him, her eyes filled with sleepy satiation. "Nothing but what you are. I promise, Asad."

He nodded, knowing her further assurances that she understood the parameters of their relationship fully this time around should please him. But a tiny, primitive part of him did not like it and he was not at all certain why. However, the knowledge that she had no hidden agenda and was not trying to get anything out of him with her capitulation into his bed did something in the region of his heart he would have thought impossible.

It moved him when he had been certain his diamond-hard heart could not be moved.

Carefully withdrawing from her body, he rolled to the side and disposed of the condom. Then he pulled her close so she was completely wrapped in him. Despite the niggle of worry at his response to their lovemaking, for the first time in more years than he cared to count, Asad fell asleep feeling replete.

He woke hours later to Iris trying to leave his bed. She'd pushed his arm off her and was trying to scoot away from him without making a sound.

He slipped his hand back over her stomach, tightening his hold on her. "Where are you going?"

"Back to my room."

"No, *az*—" He broke off before saying the word she'd denied him. "Little flower, you belong here."

"I don't, Asad."

"You do." And he set about proving it to her, claiming her with his body and words until she was sobbing her pleasure out in his arms.

Afterward, they slept again, but he woke her in the early hours of the morning.

She blinked up at him with question. "Time for me to go back to my bed?"

No, damn it. If he had his way, she would not sleep another minute in that tiny bed. "Time for a bath."

"But…"

"Come with me."

He led her to the cave his grandfather had never revealed to the rest of the encampment, the place Hanif had only shown to Asad after his marriage to Badra. The private bathing cavern for the lion of the Sha'b Al'najid.

Carrying a high-powered flashlight, Asad led Iris through a complicated series of passages in the caves beyond the chambers for male and female communal bathing. Whenever they came to a fork, he took the one marked with a peacock feather carved in the rock.

He stopped in a rounded cavern. "This is the personal bathing chamber for my family."

"Nawar didn't mention it." Neither had Genevieve.

It didn't surprise her that the sheikh and his family had their own bathing chambers, but there seemed to be an air of secrecy about it.

"Nawar will not be told of this place until she marries and only if she remains with our tribe after the wedding."

Wow, okay. So, definitely a secret. "What about the rest of your family?"

Asad flipped a switch and soft golden light filled the space. "Only my grandparents and parents are aware of its existence. This was my grandfather's true gift to my grandmother upon their wedding, his way of giving her something to make up for all that she left behind."

Iris gasped, unable to believe what her eyes told her she was seeing. "How?"

"In the beginning, Grandfather used real torches to light the space, but I had a solar lighting system installed."

She hadn't meant the lighting, but that was pretty cool, too. It was the rest of the space that had her so amazed.

"How did he have the tiling done?" she asked in awe as she took in the cave that had been made to look like a five-star European spa.

The single hot-tub-size pool in the center had a mosaic tiled surround wide enough to sit on comfortably and dangle one's feet in the steaming water. An ornate wrought iron handrail led into the water, implying steps had been added inside the natural pool.

The cave walls had been smoothed and tiled with another mosaic of Eastern colors and design, a giant peacock centered on the wall opposite the cavern opening. Ornate marble benches graced the area between the wall and two sides of the pool. And on either side of the opening, there were six-feet-high wrought iron shelving units stocked with fluffy Turkish towels, robes and every bathing necessity and luxury Iris could have imagined.

And even some she wouldn't have.

There was even a fully tiled oversize shower stall off to one side. With no door, or curtain, it was clearly intended to be used in luxurious privacy.

"How...the shower...it's not possible."

Asad smiled, pride gleaming in his espresso gaze. "For a Bedouin man with an engineering degree, such things are possible indeed."

"Your grandfather has a degree in engineering?" she asked, feeling more and more like Alice having dropped through the rabbit hole.

Asad nodded. "I told you he'd gone to university in Europe. Many of the modern improvements in our camp are of Grandfather's making."

"He is an amazing man." Just like his grandson.

"He is."

"He acts like he knows only the way of the desert tradition."

"Because at heart, he is that man, but he is more than that, as well."

"Just as you are."

"Yes."

"Thank you for bringing me here." She didn't really understand why Asad had decided to share his family's private oasis with her, but it touched her that he had.

He shrugged, looked pained and then said, "It is what a dear and truest friend would do."

"Ah, so you're still lobbying for that position."

"It would seem I am," he said, sounding a little surprised by that fact himself.

She smiled, not minding in the least. Not when it had such results. She was a woman like any other in this respect...she wasn't about to turn down the opportunity for a bit of pampering.

"It's really wonderful," she said, letting her appreciation of both his grandfather's and Asad's achievements show in her voice.

"It is indeed." He placed his hands on her shoulders,

his expression turning carnal. "Shall we take advantage of the amenities?"

"Yes. Definitely, yes." Dropping her bag with the clean clothes she'd thought she would don after bathing in the communal chamber, she stripped quickly.

She'd never been shy around him, not even in the beginning. Which had always confused her. She'd thought it meant he was the one for her; now she knew he simply brought out the wanton no other man would probably ever meet.

"Beautiful," he said in a husky tone she knew well.

She spun to face him, not in the least surprised to find him watching her. He'd used to watch her all the time, and not just when she was naked. He liked to watch her sleep, to work, to read, to study…doing just about anything.

It used to charm her; she realized it still did. "You like what you see?"

"You know I do."

"Maybe I need you to show me again." She ruthlessly pressed down the guilt at the prospect of getting a late start on her day.

Because with that look in Asad's dark gaze, she knew the last thing she was in for was a quickie.

But Sheikh Hakim had been fine with her taking a full day off simply to get welcomed by the Sha'b Al'najid; a few hours more today wasn't going to make a huge difference in how quickly she got her survey and reports done.

That was her story anyway, and she was sticking to it.

"You need more evidence of how very desirable I find you, my little flower?" he asked, his hands reaching out to tease at her breasts, caress her belly and then dip between her legs.

She moaned, letting her head fall back and just enjoyed his touch for several pleasure-filled moments.

Then she began undressing him, a small tremor of desire in her fingers. "Define need."

All humor drained from his features, leaving a look of such intensity it took her breath away. "What I feel for you."

"Asad…" She tipped her head back again, this time offering her lips.

With a strangled sound he yanked her toward him and took her mouth in a searing kiss. He swept his tongue inside, dueling with hers, tasting her, letting her taste him.

After a night filled with lovemaking, he kissed her as if he had been starved for it.

Needing to feel his naked skin against hers, she scrabbled at his *thobe,* yanking the traditional garment up and over his head, whimpering when that meant breaking their kiss, and going right back to it when the material was out of the way.

She twined her hands behind his neck, pressing her body against his, her already-excited nipples, tender from all his ministrations the night before rubbing against the silky curls on his chest.

She moaned in pleasure at this caress that had always been one of her favorites. Though she liked it even better with his chest hair left to grow naturally. There was just something so wild about her body taking pleasure from his and knowing how much he liked her to do so. Knowing that he was getting every bit as turned on as she was, the need between them growing like an out-of-control tornado.

His hands moved down her body with swift, sure movements to cup her bottom, and then he lifted her so his already-hardened flesh brushed against the apex of her thighs.

Needy sounds filled the steamy air around them, so like six years ago and yet so different. He was stronger now. His reactions were even more primal than they used to be, as if he'd stopped attempting to rein himself in. And she loved that.

She was more aware of what the world of sex had to offer and…not to offer. Innocent embarrassment at her own desires was a thing of the past. She knew how magical this was now, how much she would miss it when it was gone—so she reveled in every second, every breath and touch.

Even the hunger between them was both familiar and altogether different. It was so much stronger now, though she never would have believed that possible. Her craving for him was an ache inside her, but his want was out there for both of them to see and wholly undeniable. He had made love to her short hours before, but the urgency in his touch was as if they had yet to reach their first orgasm.

She felt movement and then her back against the cool tile of the wall. His grip shifted so that he had her thighs over his forearms, her legs spread, her sex open to him.

He pressed against her, but waited as if asking if this was what she wanted. She tilted her hips and pressed down, taking the tip of his engorged sex inside stretched and swollen tissues unused to so much activity.

It didn't hurt; she was experiencing too much pleasure for that, but she felt it. Felt her body stretch to accommodate him, felt the slide of his hard-on against her inner walls, filling her in a way only he could do.

He tilted her just enough so that his head rubbed against her G-spot on both the pull and push of every thrust of his hips.

Ecstasy built inside her one electric jolt at a time until she was writhing against him as he possessed her. She couldn't think, could barely breathe. It was too much and not enough.

He knew. He always knew.

He swiveled his hips, grinding against her sweet spot with his pelvic bone and she shattered. She was barely aware as he shouted out his own release, his hot essence filling her core.

And if a ridiculous wish that she didn't have the uterine insert played through her mind, no one else ever need know.

She'd given up her dreams of babies and her own family when he'd walked out of her life six years ago. So, the dream wasn't quite as dead as she believed. That was a weakness she would forgive herself.

They stayed like that, connected against the wall, for several long moments, the only sound their harsh breathing. Eventually, he made noise that could have been approval or something else, she was too out of it herself to really tell.

But it was followed by him carrying her to the shower and she realized the sound might even have been words. They bathed each other with the delicious-smelling soap Genevieve was so partial to.

They were soaking in the hot spring pool when Asad said with all the seriousness and more chagrin than she'd ever witnessed in him, "I forgot the condom."

Only then did she realize she hadn't told him she was covered for birth control.

"Are you clean?" she asked softly, aware that pregnancy wasn't the only thing a modern woman had to worry about when having sex.

She sincerely doubted he was a reckless lover, but he had forgotten the condom when he didn't realize she could not get pregnant.

He stared at her in confusion for several seconds before understanding dawned in his brown gaze and he growled, "I am not diseased."

"I'm not trying to offend you. It was a legitimate question."

"So you say. I say we have a much more serious worry to consider here."

"No, we don't."

"You are on the pill?" He looked astonished by the idea.

She wasn't about to be offended by that. She didn't date. Her last sex had been with him; she hadn't been willing to trust anyone else with the intimacy since. "No. I have a uterine insert."

"Why?"

"Do we really have to talk about this?"

"Yes. I want to know." He sure didn't sound like it, though.

"You couldn't be like other men and just pretend this part of my life is a great mystery, could you?" she asked hopefully.

"No," he practically snarled.

"Don't get mad." He was such a caveman sometimes. "It's not a big deal. I just had difficult periods and wanted to do something about it. My doctor suggested the insert, and I don't have any bleeding at all now. It's a huge relief, considering how much time I spend in the field and a lot of it in more primitive conditions than this."

She was sure that was more than he ever wanted to know, but she got a perverse pleasure in giving him the gritty details. After all, he was the one who insisted on knowing and got all cranky when she'd hesitated telling him.

"Will it affect your ability to have children?"

"I doubt I'll ever be a mother, but not because I won't be capable of getting pregnant. There's no risk of infertility." She frowned at him, letting him know that this was not her favorite topic of conversation. "Can we be done with this conversation now?"

"Yes." He looked far too complacent.

Maybe that explained what popped out of her mouth next. "Did you bring Badra here?" she asked, realizing almost immediately how much she wanted to bite her own tongue off.

First, because of course he'd brought Badra here; the princess had been his wife. And second, because Iris *really* didn't want to know about it. Not even a little.

Idiot.

"No."

"What?" *No?*

"My grandfather showed me this place on the eve of my wedding, but Badra insisted on being married in her father's palace."

"Wouldn't that be traditional?" And why would it prevent Asad from bringing his wife to the private bathing chamber when they returned to his city of tents?

"Not for a sheikh of my people. Even my parents were married here."

"Oh, but she wanted to get married with the traditions of her family?" That was understandable.

"She wanted to put off joining the encampment for as long as possible, though I did not realize it at the time. She'd convinced me to take her on a tour of Europe for our honeymoon."

"Um, sounds special?" Iris's comment came out more a question than a statement because he sounded so disdainful of their honeymoon plans.

"Our tradition would have dictated I take her into the desert for a time of privacy and bonding. She refused."

"So she wasn't much of a camper."

"She was a poor wife and even worse Bedouin. Badra was not a virgin on our wedding night."

CHAPTER TEN

"THAT must have been a shock to you." A really unpleasant one, too.

Remembering back to their breakup, she knew how important sexual innocence had been to Asad. Probably still was. Iris hadn't realized it when they were dating, but when he told her it was over he'd made a lot of things clear that had been hazy before that. Like the fact that Iris could never be in the running for Asad's future wife because she'd had a sexual partner before him.

Even now, with their friendship firmly intact, she couldn't think of Darren as a former lover. There had been no love in the loss of her virginity. Not even on her part.

Iris had thought Asad's attitude pretty much prehistoric, but her opinion hadn't counted. And he'd walked away to marry the not-so-perfect Badra.

"She was also pregnant."

"What? Nawar isn't yours?" Iris asked in shock.

But there was no doubting the bond between the beautiful little girl and her father.

"She is mine," Asad fiercely contradicted. "Though she carries none of my genetic makeup, Nawar is in all ways that count my beloved daughter."

"But that's…" Unbelievable.

Or kind of funny in a gallows-humor kind of way. Not that his daughter didn't share his gene pool, but because of the way he'd rejected Iris so completely based on her lack of innocence. Only, Iris had been way more virginal in the ways that counted than the already-pregnant Badra. That was for sure.

But mostly, the whole situation with Badra seemed really, really sad. She'd deceived Asad and Nawar had been made a pawn in a marriage paved with bad intention before she'd ever been born.

"I'm sorry." Iris really, really was.

"Do not be. The one good thing I got out of my marriage to Badra was my precious gem, Nawar."

Iris liked hearing that; it gave her confidence that under the more cynical and dour exterior, Asad was still the same man who had once really been her best and truest friend. His willingness to share what had to be his deepest secret with her showed that regardless of the intervening years of silence, he still saw her in that light.

"Nawar said you named her."

"Badra had no interest in parenting from the very beginning. Though at the time, I believed she allowed me to name Nawar to make her more my own. I was wrong about that, just as I had mistaken so much about Badra. At first I believed Badra's lack of interest in my daughter was due to her shame at bearing another man's child. I told her repeatedly how much I loved Nawar. That I did not resent her."

"That's kind of amazing." And so not what Iris would have expected of the arrogant, proud man.

She'd loved Asad, but she hadn't been blind to his faults. Or so she had believed. Perhaps she'd been blinder to more things than even their subsequent break-up had forced her to accept.

"I was not there for the birth, as is the custom of our people, but my grandmother brought the babe to me when she was less than an hour old. I looked down into her beautiful little face and fell in love."

Emotion caught in Iris's throat. "She's very lucky to have you for a father."

"I am far more blessed to have her as a daughter."

Iris thought maybe it was a draw, but forbore saying so.

"I named her flower after the one woman I knew had more honor than my wife ever would."

The import of Asad's words finally registered and Iris gasped in shock. "You named your daughter after me. That's not possible."

"I assure you, it is. Though at the time I was unaware of what my brain had done. I only realized it later, but then so did Badra. When she did, it infuriated her. We fought about it and rather than deny it like I should have because I was totally unaware of having done it, I told Badra I wanted Nawar to share your sense of honor, not her mother's."

"That's…" Iris didn't know what to say. How did you answer a statement like that? "I guess I'm glad to know you think I have strong character."

"I do, very much so. It made you a good friend and trustworthy lover."

There was no denying his words. The trust he was showing in her now matched what she had given him the night before, when she'd shared her past shame with him. It came to Iris then that Asad had not realized what he would lose when he dumped her, or how much he would miss her. Another tiny bit of her shattered heart mended at that knowledge.

"Unless I want a distant cousin to take my place, I will have to marry again."

Well, that came out of the blue and frankly, Iris could have lived without that reminder. Nevertheless, she said, "Yes." And then the import of what he'd said hit her. "Badra intended to stick you with another man's child. What if Nawar had been a boy?"

"He would have been the next sheikh of my people. Nawar's husband may well be my successor."

Iris believed him. And again…wow. This man was everything she'd believed him to be and then convinced herself he wasn't, and so much more.

Asad loved his daughter, and he would have loved a son just as well. That was the kind of man he was. Asad had honor and character to spare. Even if at one time she'd maybe thought he didn't.

"So Badra told you she was pregnant?"

"Only after I figured it out for myself, the day after our wedding."

Their honeymoon must have been a treat, Iris thought rather sarcastically and then felt bad for thinking at all. Poor Asad.

"Whoever I marry must accept Nawar as completely as I do."

"Of course."

He smiled, as if happy with her answer. The man did have a rather well-developed need, or maybe expectation, that the people around him would agree with his opinion. Not that he was great at compromise, or anything. He just liked knowing everyone thought he was right.

Arrogant sheikh. She smiled.

"What is that expression on your face?"

"I'm smiling."

"I am aware."

"That's not exactly a rare occurrence."

"Less common than I remember from six years ago."

"I could say the same."

He shrugged and then pulled her into his arms through the water. "The responsibilities of my position have tempered my humor."

And maybe learning his perfect princess was anything but had robbed Asad of some of his joy in life. Not that Iris expected him to ever admit it.

She let herself relax against him, enjoying this intimacy almost as much as what they'd shared earlier. "You said that Badra died in a plane crash with her lover. Did she leave you?"

"No. She traveled with him several times a year."

"And you put up with it?" Iris asked in shock, turning around to face him, water sloshing over the sides of the pool from her agitated movements.

"I had full control of Nawar's raising. This was the important thing. Badra signed away parental rights to my daughter in exchange for five years of me funding her lifestyle and accepting her choices therein."

"Five years?" Iris asked faintly.

"Yes. I would have divorced Badra a year ago if she were not already dead."

"But that's medieval."

"It was necessary. She could have taken my daughter and I could not allow it."

So he'd bought rights to her daughter. "There were other ways." There had to have been.

"None that guaranteed Nawar, my little jewel, stayed

with me here among the Sha'b Al'najid whom she loved
and who loved her just as fiercely."

"So you gave up five years of your life for her." He
really was the most amazing man ever.

"I was prepared to, yes."

"You're a Superman, you know that?"

"I am glad you think so, but you did not believe this
six years ago."

"Oh, I did. Just not after you dumped me." She took
a deep breath and let it out. "But that's in the past. I
don't want to talk, or even think about it anymore.
Okay?"

"As you wish. The present is enough to keep us both
fully occupied."

She believed he was right about that.

"You slept with him," Russell whispered in cheeky accusation as they completed their first set of measurements at the initial sampling site.

Iris's head snapped around. "Shhh…I don't know
why you'd say that anyway."

She wasn't going to deny it. Iris was a terrible liar,
but admitting she was sleeping with the man who'd
broken her heart once wasn't going to make her look
all that smart to her colleague.

"Give it a rest, cupcake. It's all there in his eyes."

"What's in his eyes?" she couldn't help asking,
though she knew she shouldn't.

The look on Russell's face said he knew he'd gotten
her. "At the palace, and since, he's watched you with
this really intense yearning." He frowned, sadness en-
tering his gaze. "It's an expression I understand too
well not to recognize."

Iris reached out and squeezed his arm in silent comfort. Russell's ex-girlfriend had really done a number on him. And knowing how deeply Asad's defection had affected her, Iris wasn't about to dismiss Russell's love affair gone wrong as a youthful mistake he would get over easily.

"He's not looking at you like that now, though," Russell claimed, his voice cheerful, the look of sadness gone.

She waited several seconds for her nosy colleague to explain, but he just went back to work. Finally, in exasperation, she asked, "How does he look at me, then?"

"Like you're his and anyone thinking to challenge that claim had better protect his balls."

She burst out laughing, but the man who wore T-shirts with humorous sayings only another geologist would really appreciate—today's said Don't Take Me For Granite, Just Because I'm Gneiss—looked as serious as bedrock. "I think you better watch out for your heart, Iris."

That was one warning she didn't need. She already knew how hazardous Asad was to her heart.

"What's so funny?" Nawar asked, skipping up to join them, her father only a few steps behind.

Iris had worried that having them along would make doing her job difficult, but Asad was good with his daughter and this mountainous desert was his homeland. They'd kept busy with an impromptu lesson on geography targeted at the four-year-old's level. Iris had no idea how much the child would remember, but something told her it would be more than she might expect.

"Russell made me laugh," Iris said with a smile for the little girl.

Asad's brows rose, his expression this side of dangerous. "Oh?"

"Told you," Russell mouthed, his head facing Iris and away from Asad.

Iris shook her head.

"He did not make you laugh?" Asad asked.

Iris rolled her eyes. "Does it matter? How are you two doing? Bored?"

"Not in the least, but I believe it is time to take a break for eating and then Nawar will have her nap."

"Where?" Surely the SUV would be too warm for the little girl to sleep in.

Though it was not as hot here as the desert at the base of the mountains, it was still sunny enough to heat the interior to uncomfortable levels.

"There." He indicated the other side of the SUV.

And Iris noticed that while she had been working, he'd erected a small single-room goat-hair tent with an awning that created a second area in front open to any light breezes. It said something about how caught up in her work she got that she hadn't even noticed him putting the tent up. Iris had no doubt the portable Bedouin home would be perfectly comfortable for Nawar's nap.

"You're a good dad."

He shrugged. "I did not want you to feel rushed to return to the encampment."

"Thank you."

"You are welcome." His eyes watched her lips.

She swayed forward, but caught herself before kissing him in front of his daughter and Russell. What was she thinking?

Thankfully Nawar caught their attention then, trying to drag the oversize basket of food prepared for them from the tent by herself.

They chatted while they ate and then Asad put his yawning daughter down for her nap. Afterward, he made himself comfortable under the awning with his laptop, the sheikh of the Sha'b Al'najid working on very modern business in an equally old setting.

Russell caught Iris watching Asad and shook his head.

"What?"

"You've got it bad...you do know that?"

"I *had* it bad, six years ago."

"But not now? Wake up and smell the cordite, Iris. The man is so far under your skin, he's got a direct path to your heart." Russell set the core sampler in the ground.

"No," she said more loudly than she intended. "I'm not going to love him again."

"You're trying to say you ever stopped?"

She glared at Russell, who blithely ignored her while he drew a clean sample of topsoil. "Enough of the personal observations. We've got plenty to do here without you turning into Dr. Phil on me."

"Hey, I resent that." He flicked her a grin over his shoulder. "I've got all my hair."

"You've got a big mouth is what you've got."

He stopped what he was doing and really looked at her, his expression back to the unfamiliar seriousness. "I'm your friend, Iris. I'm not going to lie to you."

"Your truth isn't necessarily my truth."

"Oh, very Zen of you." He was back to being a smart aleck.

"Stop, or I'm going to tell Genevieve you want grasshoppers in your dinner."

"That lady sure does like you. It's almost as if she's looking forward to you joining the family," he said meaningfully.

"Russell," she practically yelled. One thing Iris

could not afford was to allow Russell to plant ideas in her head that would only get her heart shattered a second time around.

"Fine, fine...I'll stop."

Despite their late start, Iris and Russell gathered a good day's worth of samples, measurement and observations. Preliminary indications made her think that mining might very well be in Kadar's future.

But Iris didn't say anything of that nature to Asad or his family over dinner when they asked how her first day on the job had gone. Russell was dining with another family, getting the opportunity to experience more elements of the Bedouin culture.

Iris did not complain about not being afforded the same opportunity. There was nowhere she'd rather be and that was her personal cross to bear. Certainly, she didn't need Russell's observations on the matter.

Iris snuggled against Asad, their early-morning lovemaking having left her feeling drowsy and relaxed. "Are you coming with us again today?"

"But of course. I told you I would be your guide and protector while you are here."

"How can you afford the time?" Challenging enough to be a business mogul, or a sheikh, but to be both?

She doubted many men could handle the pressure.

"I will bring my computer and do work as I did yesterday."

"You spent a good portion of yesterday keeping Nawar occupied."

"She is my joy."

"She is incredibly sweet, but that doesn't answer my question."

"What question is that, *az*—Iris?"

She noticed him stumbling over the old endearment again, but pretended not to. "How you can have the time to babysit Russell and me like this? You can send someone else if you really feel we need looking after. It doesn't have to be you."

"Excuse me, but it does."

"Come on, Asad. You've got what you want. You don't need to keep playing nursemaid."

"And what is it you believe I want?" he asked.

She rolled her eyes, though he wouldn't see it with her head pillowed on his shoulder. Like he thought she wouldn't know. "Me. *Here*."

"I do want that, but there is more I desire, as well."

"What?"

"Your safety, for one."

"Seriously?" She sat up and stared down at Asad. "You don't really think Russell and I are at any risk in the field. Kadar is not exactly a hotbed of crime. And the desert even less so."

"Not all who come to these mountains are as honorable as the Sha'b Al'najid."

"And Russell and I aren't exactly doing our survey in the path of most travelers." They were in foothills of the desert mountains, hours from the nearest village, twice as far from anything resembling a town or city.

"Who do you think knows of the two Western geologists doing their survey here in Kadar?"

"The sheikh and your family. I doubt even the whole camp knows why Russell and I are here." They just weren't that interesting.

Asad got up from the bed and drew on his thobe. "You would be wrong. Every member of my people knows of your purpose and the way you spend your days. Be assured many others do, as well. Gossip travels among the Bedouin like the sand in a storm in the desert."

"So?"

"All who have heard this juicy tidbit of news are not so scrupulous as you would like to believe. The least dangerous are those that might merely covet your equipment for the money it could bring them." He tossed her a hooded robe that swallowed her up when she put it on.

Meant to hit him midcalf, it brushed the carpet on her.

"Who is the most dangerous?" she asked, finding it difficult to keep her amusement at his paranoid worries hidden.

"Slavers."

"Oh, please." Now he was really reaching.

"Modern slavery is a nine-billion-dollar-a-year industry and a worldwide problem."

"But the crime rate in Kadar is almost nonexistent."

"There are always exceptions." He frowned. "You will not be one of them."

"If you're so worried about it, then I'm surprised you're willing to bring Nawar."

He slid traditional leather slippers onto his feet. "You do not imagine that we travel into the mountains alone."

"We did yesterday."

"Did we?"

"Yes?"

"No. My guards are well trained and maintain their distance to give us the illusion of privacy."

"You're not joking."

"Why would I make light of something so important?"

Why indeed, but the idea of having men lurking in

the shadows and watching her was kind of creepy. "So you're saying we've got a troupe of Ninjas hiding in plain sight protecting us?"

"Not Ninja, warriors of the Sha'b Al'najid."

"You still have warriors in your tribe?" she asked with keen interest, her discomfort pushed aside in favor of feeding her curiosity.

"Every man is trained in the ways of stealth, fighting and the scimitar. It is tradition among my people. There is an elite force, my family's bodyguards, that are trained in the ways of modern warfare, as well."

"Your tribe is a lot wealthier than anyone would guess, aren't they?"

"My family is."

"But your family accepts responsibility for the Sha'b Al'najid."

"Yes."

"Amazing."

"It is what it is."

"Badra was such an idiot."

"You think so?" Asad stopped in front of Iris, looking down at her with surprising intensity.

"I do." Iris reached up and traced his lips, smiling when he nipped at her fingertip. "She had you and all of this and still, she wanted something else."

He leaned down and kissed her, not passionately, but not chastely, either. It was intimate and gentle and quick…and it felt really nice. "I am flattered you feel that way."

Iris wished she could share his equanimity about it. She was beginning to have some serious reservations about her current course of action. Yes, her heart was healing bit by bit, but was it just going to shatter again into a million pieces when she left Kadar?

She'd thought she could keep love out of the equation, but a mere two nights in his bed and Iris was already grasping for a lifeline while she felt herself drowning in dormant emotions.

"It would be a lot easier for me if you could simply act like the selfish user I convinced myself you were after you dumped me," she complained with more honesty than she probably should have offered.

But he didn't look like he minded, his dark eyes glowing. "You no longer see me as this person?"

She shrugged, the effect lost under the voluminous folds of his robe on her.

"Iris?" he prompted.

She sighed and admitted, "I'm learning that neither of our perceptions of the past was all that clear."

"You are right. I thought you were far more experienced—"

Her snort of disbelief interrupted him.

"What?"

"How could you not realize how inexperienced I was back then? I was terrified you would get bored with my lack of prowess and go looking for greener pastures."

"The passion between us was always so fiery—there was no room for practiced moves. I assumed you were as overwhelmed by desire as I was."

"I was."

"Yes, but with less experience."

"Bragging now, are you?"

"Never. I have no need to brag. You think I am the most amazing lover ever."

"Conceited."

"Deny it."

"You know I won't."

"Can't," he charged with one raised eyebrow.

She huffed fondly, "Jerk."

"Is that the proper endearment to use for the man who rocks your world?"

"And what of the woman who rocks yours?" she asked facetiously.

"You will not allow me the proper endearment," he accused.

"Poor you."

He shook his head. "You are still determined I should not call you *aziz?*"

"Very." That was one thing she was still absolutely sure about. Though her other beliefs and feelings were in something of a muddle, she knew she didn't want him using the term for beloved when she wasn't.

"One day you will allow it."

"I won't be in Kadar long enough for that to happen." Considering the area Sheikh Hakim had hired her company to survey, Iris would be in Kadar only a month, six weeks at the outside.

It could have been a much more involved study, but Sheikh Hakim had ordered only a first-level survey. Most likely because he would use it to determine which areas to pursue further.

Nevertheless, Asad, did not look like he believed Iris's claim. "Come with me to the baths and I will see what I can do about changing your mind."

CHAPTER ELEVEN

FOR the next two weeks, the days followed the pattern set on that one.

Asad and Nawar accompanied Iris and Russell to their survey sites. Against all expectations, Iris had never enjoyed her job more and found it surprisingly easy to accomplish what she needed to, despite their presence. And that of the unseen guards who joined them every day.

Both she and Russell couldn't help taking time to show the curious little girl how they used their portable geological equipment. And somehow there was always time for play, as well.

Iris found herself falling for the child every bit as heavily as she'd fallen for the father. Her wish that she had been Nawar's mother grew daily, but she kept it hidden. It was dangerous, but Iris allowed herself to wallow in what it would feel like to be a real family.

She thought sometimes that Nawar was doing the same thing, and that both delighted and frightened her. She didn't want Asad's daughter hurt when Iris had to leave.

Iris was currently showing Nawar how to identify a rock, Asad having asked her to watch Nawar while he took a call on his satellite phone. "The first thing we look at is color. What color would you say this is?"

"Brown." Nawar squinted at the rock, as if determining the correctness of her answer.

Iris hid her grin and nodded as solemnly as she could. "Very good. Now feel the rock—is it smooth or rough?"

"It's bumpy."

This time Iris let herself smile. "Right. We can do a test on the rock to see what kind of minerals are in it to get a proper identification."

"What's a min-rall?"

Russell laughed, showing he had been listening.

Iris smiled a little sheepishly. "Minerals are things like iron and zinc."

"Like my vitamins?" Nawar asked, proving she was a very intelligent child.

"Yes, exactly like that. Who told you your vitamins had iron and zinc in them?"

"Papa said I need my iron to grow strong."

Iris remembered Asad saying that Nawar didn't care for meat and ate a practically vegetarian diet. Considering the other foods that comprised the Bedouin diet, she thought she understood why he would want his daughter to take a minimal iron supplement in her children's vitamin.

"He's right, of course."

"Oh. I want zinc in my vitamins."

Iris had no idea if children's vitamins had zinc in them. She would have to do some research before making any promises. "I'll talk to your daddy about it. If you need zinc, I'm sure he'll make sure you get it."

"A mommy would make sure, wouldn't she?"

"I…um…I suppose so."

"Papa said I'm going to have a new mommy soon."

"He did?" Iris asked faintly, a band squeezing tightly around her chest, making it hard to breathe.

Nawar nodded solemnly. "He said it was time."

"That's good." The words cost her, but not nearly as much as the even tone Iris used to say them.

"I'm ever so excited." And Nawar looked it, her eyes so like her father's—even if they didn't share the genes to make it so—glowing brightly with happiness at the thought. "He said I would like her very much."

"I'm glad."

"Me, too. Grandmother says Papa is lonely. My mommy will be his wife."

Oh, gosh, she was going to be sick. "Yes, I do believe that's how it works."

"Do you think she'll be a princess like my other mother?"

"I don't know."

"I don't care. She doesn't have to be a princess." Nawar gave Iris a look she had no hope of understanding.

Not in her current state. It was taking everything she had to remain pleasant and smiling with the little girl so blithely shredding hopes she'd been so sure she hadn't let herself entertain once again.

Badra wasn't the idiot; Iris was.

"I'm sure whoever she is, she'll be a very good mommy," Iris said softly.

"Yes. She'll like me and want to spend time with me." Nawar was back to looking too serious for her years. "Papa promised."

"He loves you very much."

"I love him. He's the bestest."

"He is a wonderful man." Even if he was making

plans to marry someone else while sharing his bed with Iris. Again.

Iris wanted to curse her own stupidity and Asad's plans in equal measure, but she bit back words not appropriate for little ears.

Russell's expression of concern was not helping. She frowned at him and shook her head, her eyes warning him not to say anything.

Asad hadn't made any promises and she'd gone into this thing with him knowing it had a sell-by date of weeks, not even months. So it was no one's fault but her own that hearing of his plans to marry someone else was ripping her apart inside.

It wasn't supposed to be this way this time. Somehow she had to get a handle on her emotions, but Iris couldn't help her quiet over lunch.

She ignored the looks of question Asad kept sliding in her direction. Doing her best to bring her emotions into line, she determinedly focused on eating and not throwing up.

After they'd packed away the lunch things, Asad put Nawar down for a nap and then asked Iris to take a walk with him.

But she shook her head. She wasn't ready to be alone with him, not yet. "I need to work and so do you."

"Nevertheless, we will go for a walk." The set of his jaw said while he'd phrased the initial offer as a request, they would indeed be going, one way or another.

With pictures of herself dangling over his shoulder as he marched along the path, she reluctantly nodded.

Refusing would only delay the inevitable anyway. Iris couldn't hide her upset at Nawar's news and Asad wasn't about to ignore it.

He offered his hand, but she pretended not to see it.

"We're back to that, are we?" he asked as he led her on a narrow path she had noticed earlier doing some measurements.

Iris wanted to deny it, or simply ignore it, or anything but deal with it, but that wasn't going to happen.

"Nawar tells me that you promised her a new mother soon." And the news should not bother her—she knew it shouldn't.

This time around, she had *known* they had no future. But the hurt was there all the same. This man had always been able to get past her defenses and believing this time would be different had been more than short-sighted of her, it had been criminally stupid.

"Yes."

When he didn't say anything else as they followed the trek through some trees and up the side of the mountain, Iris contemplated demanding answers and/ or kicking him in the shin. Neither prospect promised to have an advantageous outcome.

"It's true, then?" she asked regardless.

"It is."

"So this is just like six years ago?"

"No."

She stopped and grabbed his desert robe to halt him, as well. He turned to face her, his inscrutable sheikh face firmly in place.

"How is it different?" she demanded. "You're having sex with me while planning to marry another woman."

For a moment something like pain flared briefly in his espresso gaze. "No."

"No?" Iris asked sarcastically. How could he say that? "You don't have another woman picked out and waiting in the wings to step in as Nawar's mommy?"

As his wife.

"No."

"But…" She did her best to assimilate the meaning of his answers in the face of what Nawar had said.

Asad had promised his daughter a mother. He did not deny it. Yet he hadn't said he knew who that woman was going to be. In fact, if he did, wouldn't Nawar have already met her?

He loved his daughter too much to choose a wife without insuring she was compatible with his daughter.

So the replacement had *not* been chosen. Inexplicably, that knowledge lightened Iris's heart immeasurably. "I see."

"I sincerely doubt it."

"I'm not stupid."

"Just blind."

She let go of the hold she still had on his sleeve and took a step back. "I stopped being blind six years ago."

"Six years ago I was the blind idiot, not you." He turned and started back on the path.

Feeling uncertain, yet oddly hopeful, she followed him. "Yes, well…we both learned our lessons I guess."

"Did we? I'm beginning to wonder."

"So, where does this path lead?"

"To an overlook popular with shepherds and lovers."

"Um…okay."

They'd been walking in an unexpectedly companionable silence for several minutes when he observed, "It bothered you to think I had plans to marry another woman."

Technically he still did, but she didn't want to get into that discussion. "I would never willingly be *the other woman*."

"No, you have too much integrity for that."

"I was, though, six years ago."

It was his turn to stop their progress. He turned to her, his expression grim. "No, you were not."

"You said—"

"That I had plans to marry Badra, not that she'd accepted my proposal. My plans were not hers, nor were they set in stone, no matter that my will insisted it be so. In fact, the first time I asked her, she told me with great contempt that she would never tie herself to an ignorant goatherd."

That explained his oversensitivity on the topic, but Iris couldn't help feeling pleased at the knowledge she had never truly been cast in the role of mistress.

"You were in line to be sheikh, though."

"Of a Bedouin tribe."

"What difference does that make?"

"I live in a *beit al-sha'r,* the house of hair. Not a palace."

"By choice."

"It was not a choice Badra approved of."

"Even if she hadn't been a cheating abandoner of children, you two would have been a really bad match." Iris hoped Asad could see that now.

He really *had* been every bit as blind as she was six years ago.

"You think she abandoned Nawar?" he asked curiously.

There was no doubt in Iris's mind, or her heart. "Didn't she? Badra signed over parental rights in exchange for a cushy lifestyle and the promise of freedom at the end of five years."

It was only as she said the words that she realized that Asad's parents had done much the same to him.

"You mean like my parents," he said, proving that just like in the past, their brains often traveled down the same paths.

"No. I'm not saying I could or even would have made the choices your parents made, but they kept loving, kept wanting to be part of your life. I get the feeling Badra was a little more like my parents, completely uninterested in having her daughter in her life."

"Nawar is my daughter and you are absolutely right."

"You protected Nawar because you understood what it felt like to have your parents put your interests second," Iris said in sudden understanding on a burst of emotion she didn't want to name.

"I did not consider it in the same light. I always had my grandparents and my place here among the Sha'b Al'najid."

But his parents had traded the right to raise their oldest son in their home for the ability to have that home where and at the level of luxury they wanted it. The desire to reach out and comfort him was too strong to deny and she took his hand.

He said nothing, but his grip on her hand was strong.

They continued their walk in silence, Iris's brain too busy to truly appreciate the beauty around her. She could not stop thinking about the fact that if Asad was not actively looking for his next wife, he would be soon.

Not until after Iris had left Kadar, though…from his attitude she was pretty certain of that.

A small voice in her heart asked why that woman could not be Iris? For once, her usually analytical brain could not give an adequate answer. *Why couldn't she be Nawar's mom and Asad's wife?*

Iris would love Nawar as if she'd given her birth;

she was close to doing so already. There was something about the small girl that Iris identified with, a vulnerability she understood all too well. Iris knew what it was to be abandoned emotionally by a parent; she would never let the little girl experience that pain at her own hands.

Beyond that, their relationship six years ago had proven she and Asad were compatible in and out of bed. They had been best and truest friends. That compatibility was very much in evidence again today. As was their friendship, maybe even a deeper one.

They'd shared things they never would have six years ago, being open in ways that they hadn't been then.

And it felt right and good.

So, why not her?

Iris might not be a snooty Middle Eastern princess, but that was a benefit to her way of thinking. Neither Nawar nor Asad had done so well the first time around with one of those. Genevieve hadn't been either and Asad claimed she'd been the most beloved Lady of the Sha'b Al'najid in generations.

His grandfather certainly didn't seem disappointed in his wife's lack of Middle Eastern heritage or pedigree.

Surely Asad had to realize that a woman who loved him and Nawar would be better than any pedigreed pretender.

And Iris did love him, totally and completely. It was inevitable. Staying out of his bed would not have prevented it, because Russell had been right. There had been no danger of Iris falling in love a second time when she'd never stopped in the first place.

No amount of will could prevail against the depth of feeling she had toward Asad.

This time around, she knew she had to fight for what she wanted, that the possibility of having it taken away again lurked around the next bend in the road.

She had to show him that she would make him a better wife than any other woman ever could, just as he would be the ideal husband for her. He might not realize he loved her, but he couldn't make love to her the way he did and feel nothing.

She'd thought at one time he had done, but now she knew it had cost him to leave her. That he'd never forgotten her. He'd even named his daughter after her. And he'd wanted her back in his bed enough to cajole his cousin into making sure she was the geologist sent for this survey.

Any way Iris looked at it, Asad felt more for her than he realized.

Marrying him might mean Iris giving up her current job, but that didn't mean she couldn't start something new. Living among the Sha'b Al'najid and exploring the world they lived in could take a lifetime for even the most devoted geologist.

Six years ago Asad hadn't considered Iris a candidate to become part of his family, but he'd admitted to having been blind and stupid. He implied he wasn't either any longer.

If that was true, then she had a few short weeks to show her new and improved, open-eyed sheikh the light.

It had taken Iris twenty-four years to give up on fighting for her parents' affection. She could be stubborn and determined with the best of them, even if others rarely saw that side of her.

It was time Asad did, at least.

When they reached the overlook, Iris had no trouble understanding why it was popular with lovers. "The view is magnificent," she said with an awe that was becoming familiar.

Asad might not live in a palace, but his home was one of the most beautiful places on earth.

"It is. I come here to think, to ponder my people's needs in the face of the modernization of our world."

She let her gaze travel over the panoramic vista. Off in the distance, she could see a herd and she bet they were animals cared for by the Sha'b Al'najid. "Seeing all this, it helps you keep perspective, doesn't it?"

"You know me well." He turned to face her, his eyes smiling even though his lips were still.

It reminded her of how he used to be at university.

"I want to." She reached up and cupped his face between both of her hands, loving the feel of his closely cropped beard against her fingers. "I want to very much."

He nuzzled into her touch, turning his head so he could kiss each of her palms. "You do?"

"Yes." She wasn't any good at the games women played with men, and she didn't want to be, either.

If Asad decided he wanted Iris in his future, he would have her as she really was, not something she pretended to be to gain his attention.

He gently pulled her to him, his desert robe enveloping them both. "There is one way you know me better than anyone else."

"Really? No other lovers have learned all your body's secrets?"

"No. You do not know them all though, either, not yet."

"Maybe I could learn some more right now."

He jerked as if startled by her suggestion, but then he smiled. "I thought we both had work to do?" he asked, sounding bemused.

"My work can wait a little. Can yours?" She reached up and kissed the underside of his chin.

He shuddered. "Yes, my dove, for you…for this, it can."

"Good."

"It will be." He started to undress.

But she stopped him. "Let me."

Silent, his eyes darkened by lust, he nodded.

She took her time, removing each of his desert layers with intermittent kisses and caresses until he stood naked before her, the timeless Bedouin sheikh.

She took off her own clothes while he stood watching her, his erection so hard it was nearly parallel to his stomach. They had only made love that morning, but clearly something about this was exciting him beyond bearing.

And then she realized it was the first time she'd initiated the lovemaking since they'd renewed their intimacy.

Apparently he missed her feminine aggression.

She let her last garment fall to the ground and stood proudly naked before him. "I want you."

His entire body shuddered at her words, his nostrils flaring, his eyes narrowing, his gut tightening. Her gaze skimmed lower and she noticed a pearl of preejaculate on the end of his penis. More evidence of sexual desire at its peak. She reached out, swiped it with her finger and then brought the bead of viscous fluid to her mouth.

It was sweeter than when he climaxed, which she

preferred not to swallow. He never seemed to mind, but was always complimentary and grateful when she took him in her mouth at all. Even though he gave her oral almost every time they made love.

One thing he had taught her to appreciate six years ago was that if they both enjoyed it, then whatever they did was beautiful.

She loved tasting him and the way he lost himself to her touch when she took him into her mouth. She felt like he truly belonged to her for those frozen minutes in time, no matter what their future held.

She went to drop to her knees in front of him, but he grabbed her under her arms and stopped her.

"Why?" she asked, not understanding.

He loved this.

"You will hurt yourself."

She looked down at the hard ground and shrugged. "I'll survive."

"No. We will fold my robe into a pad for your knees."

She smiled, realizing the man wasn't turning her down, just taking care of her. "All right."

It took only a moment and then she was where she wanted to be. Wrapping her fingers around his engorged member, she said, "Today you are mine."

"You are not usually so possessive." The bemused tone was back.

She looked up and met his dark gaze. "You don't know what goes on in my head when we make love."

"Perhaps I should."

She just shook her head before leaning forward to lick delicately at the tip of his hardness. He groaned, his hips jerking forward. And she did it again. She loved this game, where she licked and mouthed, but didn't quite take him inside.

After a few minutes of that treatment, he cursed. "You are such a tease."

"Am I? I thought a tease did not follow through."

"My knees will give before you are done playing."

"Poor sheikh…his knees are going weak."

He growled and she grinned and then pushed his foreskin back to take him fully into her mouth. She could never take much of him, he was too big, but she didn't need to. Coordinating the movement of her hands and mouth, she soon had him gritting out a warning that he was close to coming. She pulled her head away to finish him with her hand.

She liked being able to see his face as he climaxed, as well. The ecstasy there always excited her and touched something deep in her heart.

He looked down at her as his body went absolutely rigid, their gaze locking in primal connection. He whispered her name reverently and his ejaculate exploded like a geyser between them. He wasn't inside her, but it felt like their very souls connected in that moment.

"Thank you," he said hoarsely, his eyes devouring her naked body kneeling before him.

She kissed the glistening tip and then licked her lips, the flavor more salty and bitter now that he'd come. "I like it."

"You are a very giving lover."

No. She simply loved him. Someday he would understand that, but she swallowed the words back. It wasn't the right time to admit her emotional vulnerability to him, no matter how close she felt to him in that moment.

She let him tug her to her feet and bring her body flush with his, his expression intent and deliciously predatory. "It is a good thing that my powers of recovery are beyond average."

"I would expect nothing less from the lion of the Sha'b Al'najid."

CHAPTER TWELVE

HE STARTED. "How did you know I am called that?"

"Your name means lion. There's a lion on your bedspread. It wasn't much of a leap." She was a scientist after all, making deductions based on observations was one of the things she did best.

"My grandmother told you, didn't she?"

She would dearly love to say no, but Genevieve had mentioned it, confirming Iris's supposition. "She said the mantle of lion had been passed from Hanif to you when you took over the tribe."

"My grandfather is still strong."

"But not the primary protector for the Sha'b Al'najid."

"No. That is now my honor."

She rubbed their bodies together delightfully. "Just as it is my honor to give you pleasure."

"You think so?"

"Yes."

"It will then be my honor to please you, as well."

She wasn't going to argue that. Their lovemaking was always explosive and very, very special. At some point, Asad was going to realize what that meant.

They were meant to be together.

He'd gotten sidetracked six years ago, but this time her eyes were fully open, which meant she could help him get the sand out of his when his vision got a little cloudy concerning them.

He made a bed on the ground with their clothing piled under his robe, and still he insisted on her riding him rather than lying beneath him. It wasn't her favorite position, not because it didn't feel good, but when she got lost in the pleasure, sometimes she forgot to move. He helped her, guiding her with a strong but tender grip on her hips, his own body thrusting upward and sending her into panting delight.

His own lust grew faster than she would have thought possible as his eyes fixed on the way her breasts jiggled with her movement. "You are so lovely in your passion, little dove."

Her feminine pride preened under his heated approval, while the bliss inside her body coiled tighter and tighter.

They kissed to muffle their cries when they climaxed, their bodies shuddering in unison. She collapsed on top of him and lay there quietly for several moments of utter contentment.

"This is right," he said.

"Us?"

"Here in the open, with my land all around us, my people tending their herds in the distance."

He liked making love outside. Before coming to Kadar, that was one thing she would never have guessed. She thought it endearing how he considered the land his, though really, it belonged to the country.

They cleaned up with Asad's *kuffiya,* and then returned to the survey site with him wearing only his shirt and loose trousers. He looked debauched and she found she liked the look on him.

When she told him so, he informed her that she

looked sated and that was a look he found pleasing, as well. She grinned in response and took his hand without hesitation when he reached out to her.

When they got back to the survey site, Russell told them that Nawar was still sleeping. Iris felt the need to check on the little girl regardless. When she backed away from the tent after insuring Nawar was still slumbering, Iris bumped into Asad.

He smiled down at her. "You wanted to make sure she had not woken, despite the fact she has not left the tent?"

"She might have realized we were not here—I mean, *you* weren't here—and been nervous about coming out."

"But she is fine."

"Yes."

He smiled, his white teeth flashing. "When she was a baby, I would go into her room at night and lay my hand on her chest to confirm she was breathing."

"I probably would have done the same thing," Iris admitted with a laugh.

"Yes, I think you would have." He brushed her cheek. "You will make a wonderful mother."

She didn't answer, just kept his gaze for several long seconds filled with profundity she only hoped he felt, as well. Then Russell broke the spell, telling her he needed help with a measurement.

Feeling guilty for neglecting her work, Iris sprang to her feet to do so, but Asad grabbed her wrist.

She looked at him with question.

"I am glad you are here."

"I am, too." And she meant it from the very depth of her soul.

She only hoped she'd feel that way in a few weeks

when it came time to leave. If he did not ask her to stay, she wasn't sure she wouldn't beg him to let her anyway.

What was pride in the face of love and the hope of a family?

Asad's phone rang and he picked it up from his desk. "Hello."

He was enjoying a rare day working in his office; Iris and Russell were testing samples in their portable lab.

"Hey, cousin."

"Hakim."

"How is Project Iris going?"

"What do you mean?"

"Oh, come on. You insisted she be the geologist for this study. You don't think I was blind to your ulterior motives."

"I wanted to help her move forward in her career." And maybe he'd wanted her back in his bed, but now... he wanted more.

The certainty had grown with each passing day. They fit in a way he had never done with Badra, and Iris was so good with Nawar. She would be a fantastic stepmother because she understood what it meant to be rejected. Iris would never visit such a thing on a child, but particularly not a child she had shown so much genuine fondness for already.

"And?"

"Maybe more."

"From the way the air sizzled between you even after six years' separation, I'd say a lot more."

Asad had told Hakim about his former relationship with Iris and expressed his guilt for hurting her when he ended it. The king had been one hundred percent behind Asad's plan for some small restitution. Now he had to wonder if Hakim had not seen something all along that Asad had been blind to.

All he said however was, "Perhaps."

"Have you convinced her yet?"

Into his bed, assuredly, not that he would say so to his cousin. But for the more?

"I do not know." He only wished he did, but his *aziz* seemed to make it her goal in life to confuse him.

Hakim laughed. "Good."

Asad verbally encouraged his cousin to do something with a camel that was not anatomically possible.

The king's laughter sounded over the phone again, this time louder. "You deserve a woman who will keep you on your toes. I am glad you found Iris. I cannot even wish you had not screwed up so badly with her in the past—if you hadn't you would not have Nawar and she is a delight."

Asad could not argue with any of that. At one time, all he'd felt toward the very existence of Nawar was anger and disgust, though he'd been loath to admit it, even to himself. But the first time he'd held her, he'd known. He would love that child forever.

He thought it was possible he was in the same boat with Iris, though he wasn't quite ready to admit it… again, even to himself. "I would stand on my head for this woman, but she seems oblivious to my every effort."

"That's quite an admission. Changed your mind about the whole love thing since the last time we talked?" Hakim asked in a tone that said he knew the answer already.

"What are you? A gossiping old woman? Wanting to know my *feelings*."

Instead of getting offended, Hakim's chuckle said he was mightily amused. "What has you so confused, cousin?"

"She will not allow me to call her *aziz*." He'd made the mistake of letting it slip out the night before and he'd woken up to an empty bed, Iris's pillow cold from her departure.

"Catherine wasn't thrilled with me using endearments she didn't think I meant, either."

"But you meant them?" He had to have. Hakim loved his wife fiercely.

"Yes, though it took me a while to realize it. Have you figured it out yet?"

"I have never heard my grandfather tell my grandmother he loves her, but their marriage is as enduring as the mountains." Personally, Asad could happily live the rest of his life without making himself that vulnerable.

So long as it didn't mean losing Iris.

"You don't know what he says in their private moments," Hakim observed. "But more importantly, he has not given Aunt Genevieve cause to doubt him. My esteemed great-uncle treats his wife like she is the queen of his existence and always has."

"I have done my utmost to treat Iris with great affection and care since she arrived in Kadar. I've given up working in my office, put off meetings with important business associates and politicians."

"Does she know that?"

"Naturally not." He did not wish to make her feel bad for the time he made for her.

"How is she supposed to know she's become the queen of your world if you don't tell her?"

"I did not say she was my queen. She will be my lady."

"She's going to be the *Sha'b Al'najid's lady.* You want her to be *your* wife."

"It is the same."

"Don't believe it."

Asad grumbled, "Catherine ran you a merry chase."

"She did and I have never regretted one moment of it, or joining my life with hers."

"You once told me that Catherine had regretted it," Asad said, carefully.

What if Iris came to regret her time with him? She'd made it pretty clear in the beginning that she'd regretted their time together six years ago. Though he knew that was his fault and no one else's.

"It's true. Catherine almost left me once," Hakim agreed, old horror at the thought tingeing his voice. "Do you want to lose Iris again?"

"No." That was one thing he had no doubts about.

"Then you have to convince her to stay."

"I am doing my best." Asad made no effort to hide his exasperation. "She is more than receptive to my lovemaking. She adores my daughter and my grandparents."

"But you are not sure if she still loves you?" Hakim asked perceptively.

Asad frowned, though his cousin could not see it and then sighed. "Does it matter?"

"You tell me."

"What do I do?"

"Tell her the truth, that you brought her to Kadar to woo her into staying."

But even he hadn't known that was what he was doing at the time. Just as he'd been unaware of naming his daughter after Iris. *Self-aware he was not,* he thought cynically. "She's already figured out that I was instrumental in her arrival here."

"Does she know that most of the land she's surveying is owned by your family?"

"No."

"Maybe you should tell her."

"Badra's only interest was in my possessions." He never wanted to see the light of avarice in Iris's eyes.

Not that he would. Intellectually, he knew that, but there it was.

"Iris isn't like that. Catherine and I only saw her for two days, but we worked that out immediately. The geologist will make you a much better wife than your late princess ever did."

"Badra was never mine, no matter that she spoke vows."

"And you were never hers."

The truth of that would have taken Asad's legs out from under him if he had not been sitting at his desk. *"I love her,"* he said with wonder and no small amount of trepidation. His heart and soul belonged to the introverted scientist irrevocably. "I always did."

"Did you really just figure that out?" Hakim asked with disbelief.

"It's not something I thought about." Not until he'd had no choice but to do so.

"Catherine would say that's something you should be telling Iris, not your cousin."

"That I didn't want to label my feelings for her?"

"That you have those feelings for her. I love you like a brother, I really do, but for all your brains, you can be dense, Asad."

"You're right." It wasn't easy admitting, but he had been beyond blind when it came to his feelings for Iris.

If he'd had an ounce more self-awareness, he would never have left her in the States the first time. And that was something Iris needed to know. She deserved the words. "Your wife, on the other hand, is a brilliant woman."

"She is that. She picked me, didn't she?"

"Iris calls me arrogant. I think it's a family trait."

"Catherine is certain of it and is convinced I've already passed it on to our son."

"Not your daughter?"

"My dear wife is convinced that men are arrogant, but women are merely assertive."

Both men shared a laugh at that.

If Asad's was filled a bit with gallows humor, Hakim did not mention it. Blinded by his pride and stubbornness, Asad had ejected the woman he loved from his life—and paid for that choice every day since.

It was all well and good for Hakim to say Asad should tell Iris of his love, but what if she no longer loved him?

She hadn't said the words since coming to Kadar, not once. No matter how amazing their lovemaking. She had opened up to him in the past weeks, but remained adamant he not call her beloved.

Iris never hesitated to spend time with Nawar, but she changed the topic of conversation every time his daughter, or he, brought up the possibility of him marrying again and giving his daughter a mother.

Iris was close to being finished with her survey. And then she would leave Kadar. She never spoke in a way that indicated she planned anything else.

Her joy in her job was apparent, and from what the man who looked and acted more like a brother than an assistant said, Iris was very good at it. What right did Asad have to ask her to give it up?

If he did not, what kind of mother would she make for Nawar and their future children, gone so many months out of the year? Asad had been looking into other options for her that would give Iris the opportunity to use her education, but would not take her so frequently from his side.

What if none of them appealed to her?

What did he have to offer? His daughter, his family, his tribe…if she did not love them as he did, it would not be enough.

Had his grandfather felt this fear when asking for his grandmother's hand?

To ask a woman not of their people to share their world was no simple matter. After his experience with Badra especially, Asad had realized his grandmother was the exception, not the rule.

But then that should give him hope, because Iris was a special and unique woman in every way, as well.

Iris finished one of the final tests that would confirm the presence of a semi-precious metal in the area near where she and Asad had made love outdoors. The thought of mining happening in the pristine environment made her stomach twist.

That was the least of her findings, though. Preliminary tests, measurements and observations indicated the existence of rhodium, a rare and very precious metal. It also demonstrated the probable existence of aluminum oxide with chromium—or rubies, in lay terms—buried in the mountains of Kadar.

She said as much to Russell and he frowned. "Your boyfriend is not going to be happy to hear that."

"Why? Do you think he was hoping for diamonds?" There were some indicators for the stone, but not as strongly as for corundum.

"I think he was hoping for no strong indicators at all. Haven't you two talked about this?" Russell asked, sounding a lot more concerned than she thought he should be.

"No." They'd talked about his work and her career, but not the work she was doing now. "I've avoided discussing my findings because first reports should be made through proper channels to Sheikh Hakim."

"How very professional of you."

She frowned and tossed her half-finger leather gloves in a wadded ball at him. "Don't make fun. It's harder managing a professional and personal relationship together than I ever imagined."

"But you spend every night with him and his family. None of them have mentioned the way Asad feels about mining to you?" Russell asked, sounding like he found that very suspicious, and not a little upsetting.

"The topic has never come up."

"But you *do* talk about your job?"

"About my career as a geologist, yes. Just not this particular survey." She'd never asked Asad what his stance on mining was. She'd assumed it was favorable, since he'd been the one to convince Hakim to bring her in as geologist.

"Sheikh Asad is one of the Middle East's leading conservationist advocates. He is adamantly opposed to overmining, or mining at all when it's done invasively to the ecosystem."

"What? Are you serious?" Asad was an advocate for conservation? A *leading* advocate?

"Absolutely. He's a spokesperson for preserving the desert habitat and with it the Bedouin way of life."

"But how would mining in the mountains impact that?"

"You really think if a mining company comes in, they're going to be okay with a city of tents as the base of their operations?"

"They'll need workers."

"Not Bedouins who are fiercely opposed to changing the landscape. Besides, do you really think Sheikh Asad wants his tribe working in mines? His whole tourist business is based on the Bedouin lifestyle mystique. He's not going to give up his weavers and shepherds to the mines."

Russell's words made sense, but Asad's behavior didn't. Why hadn't he told her he was so opposed to mining?

And if he was opposed, why agree to be the geologist's liaison?

"You don't think…" Russell let his voice trail off. "No, if he doesn't talk about your reports, it can't be that. It wouldn't make sense."

"What?"

Russell shook his head. "A stray thought and a bad one."

"Tell me."

"I was just thinking that if he was opposed to mining, he might get involved with the geologist responsible for preliminary reports that could influence his cousin to go forward with a more in-depth survey, or leave off the idea of mining altogether." Russell looked very uncomfortable with his own thoughts.

Iris didn't find them particularly palatable herself. Would Asad be that sneaky? Her heart said no, but her brain reminded her that he could be ruthless when pursuing a goal.

They needed to talk.

They were bathing together in Asad's family's private spring later that night, after putting Nawar to bed, when he said, "You will be finished here soon."

"Yes, there is one final site we need to take samples and do our measurements."

"I know. The remote location would make traveling to it daily untenable."

"Mmm-hmm," she agreed, her mind still preoccupied by her earlier conversation with Russell.

"Nawar should probably stay behind in the encampment."

That made Iris's attention snap back to the present and what Asad was saying. "But the fieldwork could take a week, or more."

"She will be content with her grandparents."

"She'll miss you."

"You, as well."

Iris certainly hoped so. She would miss Nawar with a terrible ache in her heart. "Why can't she come? We could bring Fadwa to help keep an eye on her."

"Taking a child into the mountains is no simple task. Despite the way others view us, our encampment has many modern amenities we will not have access to in a primitive camp."

"Don't tell me a Bedouin sheikh is afraid of camping with his daughter, no matter how basic the *amenities?*"

"I simply do not want you overwhelmed with the consequences of having Nawar along. She will not be content to be ignored."

"Of course not." And Iris would never do so to the little girl. "She has a right to expect our attention."

"But your job…"

"Will get done. It may take an extra day, or two, but isn't that better than going without her?"

"For me? Definitely. But *you* have made noises about leaving Kadar, I thought perhaps you tired of us."

"I didn't come here to live, Asad. I came here for a job." And she would stay only if it meant being a permanent part of his life, not a temporary bed partner.

"Perhaps you did come here to live, but did not realize it at the time."

Her eyes narrowed. He was making implications she could not ignore. Iris needed it all spelled out though, not left to hopes and assumptions.

Starting with his role as a spokesman for conservation and his very public antimining stance. "You never mentioned that you spearheaded Our Desert Home."

She'd spent her limited time with access to the internet well that afternoon. ODH was a nonprofit conservation organization started by Asad and his grandfather shortly after Nawar's birth. They weren't militant or extremist by any stretch, but Russell had been absolutely right. Their stance on mining was minimal impact, or no mining at all.

"I did not think it would interest you."

"Really?" She wasn't buying it. "I'd think I made my interest in everything about you pretty apparent lately."

He shrugged, looking as if the topic was of little importance right then. That's not the impression she got from his "Message from the Founder" on the website.

He took a deep breath and then met her gaze, his expression stoic. "There are other things I would discuss with you tonight."

If she didn't know better, she'd think he was nervous.

"First, we talk about this. Did you convince Sheikh Hakim to request me as the geologist on this survey in hopes of influencing what I say in my reports?" she asked baldly.

For a moment Asad simply stared at her in uncomprehending silence, but then the storm came. His eyes flashing, his jaw hewn from granite. "You believe I would attempt to get you to lie?"

"No." She hadn't really, no matter how ruthless he could be, but she'd felt the need to ask.

She wanted to hear his denial from his lips. She needed the words, just like she needed other words to change her life.

"If this is so, when have I ever asked about your findings? Or made a move to discourage you from telling anything but the unvarnished truth in these reports of yours?" he demanded, his voice deep with affront.

"I said *no,* Asad."

"Then why ask the question at all?"

"I needed the words."

Asad shut his mouth and stared for several long seconds, and then nodded. "Hakim said you did."

"Hakim knew I entertained brief doubts about your motivation for bringing me to Kadar?" she asked in confusion.

"Hakim believes I should tell you my true motivation for arranging for your visit to my home."

"We've already discussed this." Hadn't they?

"I wanted to help your career. *You* believe I wanted you in my bed again."

"You did."

"I wanted more, though I did not realize it at first. I *want* so much more." His face was flushed and it wasn't from the heat of the water. "I…six years ago I made the biggest mistake of my life walking away from you. I compounded it by marrying Badra, but you must believe I never stopped loving you."

"You loved me?" she asked faintly, so shocked she could barely breathe.

"Yes, but I was a fool and I did not realize it. I had a plan stuck in my head and I did not know how to let it go."

"You loved me," she said again, this time with a tinge of wonder.

"I did. I do." He surged across the pool in totally uncool urgency and grabbed her shoulders, his eyes intent. "So much. How could I not realize it? But I did not. I know now, though. Surely that counts for something."

"Yes, yes…I think it does."

"I hurt you."

"You nearly destroyed me."

"But you were strong…you are strong, so much stronger than I. I don't think I will survive if you turn me away now."

"What do you want?" she asked quietly, hope burning bright in her heart. "Spell it out for me."

Don't let her be making castles in the air again.

"A mother for my daughter. A lady for my people. A wife for myself."

"Are you asking me to marry you?" she asked in choked astonishment, needing to be absolutely certain they were talking about the same thing.

Without answering, he pulled her out of the pool in silence. Drying them both, he wrapped her in one of the thick Turkish robes, and then, wearing a towel tied round his own hips, he dropped to one knee.

He met her gaze, his own so intent, she could drown

in it. "Will you join your life with mine, until the sands are blown completely from the desert?"

That was a long time, a really, really, really long time. She wanted to answer, but her heart was in her throat...or at least that's what it felt like and she couldn't get even a single word out.

"Why...why...I need to tell you why," he said urgently. Though hadn't he already said? She wouldn't mind hearing it again, just to be sure...to know she hadn't been hallucinating. Right? "Because you are truly my *aziz,* my beloved. I loved you six years ago, but was too foolish to acknowledge it. I love you still. I caused us both great grief with my pride and stupidity, but I have taken no other woman to my bed since the month after Nawar was born."

"You've been celibate for the past four years?" she gasped in total shock, the words exploding from her without thought.

He nodded, no embarrassment at the admission in his features. "I only had sex with my wife a handful of times before that."

"But why?"

"You were my heart." He averted his gaze, but then brought it back to her, determination burning there. "I told myself sex just wasn't working because I didn't trust women after the way Badra deceived me, but I'm the one that messed me up. Not her. Yes, she manipulated me, but only because I made it possible. Because I left you when I should have stayed forever."

"You didn't realize."

"I would not admit it to myself, but it was you I wanted when I got my divorce from Badra—and then after she died, it was you I was waiting to claim when the prescribed time for grieving was over."

And he'd hidden it all from himself because he was really bad at admitting what he needed. Maybe because he'd spent a lifetime hiding from the fact he'd needed his parents but they'd chosen to be elsewhere. She didn't know if he'd ever come to see that, but she would make sure from now on that he didn't go without the love he needed from her.

Not ever again. She wasn't ever going to give up on him again, not like she had six years ago.

It was time she admitted that. "I let you go. I didn't fight for you...for us."

"I didn't give you the chance."

"You walked away. I could have walked after you, but I chose to go home and lick my wounds. I was too used to not getting love from the people I needed it most from. I'm never going to be that tolerant again."

"Good," he said fervently.

She brushed tears from her cheeks. "You really do love me."

"With all that I am. Despite my pride, blindness and outright stupidity, God has seen fit to grant us a second chance. Will you take it?"

"Yes," she gasped out as she fell to her knees with him and kissed him all over his face. "I love you, too. So much. I thought I would die when you left six years ago. I didn't want to go back to the States after my survey. I only wanted to stay here with you and your daughter."

"We will never again be parted."

"My job..."

He stilled. "There are other options for a geologist."

"Yes."

"You would consider them?"

"Of course. I don't want to be away from you and Nawar any more than you want me gone."

"You are too perfect for me."

"We are perfect for each other."

"I will love you until the stars no longer grace the sky."

"Show me."

And he did. Magnificently.

EPILOGUE

Iris learned that Asad owned the mountain his grandfather's bathing caves had been found in, and consequently the land and mineral rights to most of the area she'd surveyed.

He was exploring the possibility of mining with minimal environmental impact, but only if it would benefit the Sha'b Al'najid. As he'd told Iris more than once, he was a man who spanned two worlds, the ancient and modern. He saw the need for the mining, both for the benefit of his people and the rest of Kadar, but only if that benefit outweighed the detriment.

Iris invited her parents to the wedding, but the couple had other plans. For the first time in her life, that caused her no pain because she had a plethora of family attending. Asad had bequeathed all his to her upon the announcement of their formal engagement.

Russell came with another female geology student, who shared his taste in humorous T-shirts. They looked in love and Iris was so happy for them. Darren and his family came as well, surprising Iris. She hadn't invited them.

When she asked Asad about it, he told her that the man was her friend and therefore welcome. Still, Iris had been unsure how Asad would react to Darren, but after a quiet talk with the other man, her sheikh had been nothing but the perfect host.

Darren had looked a little pale after the discussion, but said all was well and Iris believed him.

After all, her sheikh was the lion of his people. He had no need to crush another man to prove his worth.

And he never let her forget hers. He loved her so completely and intensely, she could never doubt it.

* * * * *

The Sheikh's Last Gamble

TRISH MOREY

Trish Morey is an Australian who's also spent time living and working in New Zealand and England. Now she's settled with her husband and four young daughters in a special part of South Australia, surrounded by orchards and bushland, and visited by the occasional koala and kangaroo. With a lifelong love of reading, she penned her first book at the age of eleven, after which life, career and a growing family kept her busy until once again she could indulge her desire to create characters and stories—this time in romance. Having her work published is a dream come true. Visit Trish at her website, www.trishmorey.com.

CHAPTER ONE

BAHIR Al-Qadir hated losing. For a man barred entry to more than half the world's casinos for routinely and systematically breaking the bank, losing did not come often or easily. Now, as he watched yet another pile of his chips being swept from the roulette table, the bitter taste of loss soured his mouth and a black cloud of despair hung low over his head.

For three nights now he had endured this run of black fortune and still there seemed no end to it. And not even the knowledge that roulette was a game designed to give the house the edge was any compensation. Not when he was used to winning. How ironic that Lady Luck had deserted him now, just when he had been counting on a stint at a casino to improve his mood. He might have laughed at the irony, except right now he was in no mood for laughing.

Still, he managed to dredge up a smile as placed his last pile of chips on a black square, and glanced the way of the croupier to let him know he was ready. So what that he had already dropped the equivalent of a small nation's gross national product? He was nothing if not a consummate professional. The back of his neck might be damp with perspiration and his stomach roiling, but he'd be damned if any of the vultures around the table watching him come undone would read how bleak he felt right now on his face or in his body language.

The croupier called for any more bets even when he would have known there would be none. One by one the other players had dropped out, content to watch the unthinkable, to watch Bahir—the famed 'Sheikh of Spin'—lose, until there remained only him and the numbered wheel.

With a well-rehearsed flick of one wrist, the croupier sent the wheel spinning; a flick of the other sending the ball hurtling in the opposite direction.

A feeble and battered thread of hope surged anew. *Surely this time? Surely?*

Bahir's gut clenched as the ball spun. The damp at his collar formed a bead that ran down his back under his shirt. And, despite it all, he forced his smile to grow more nonchalant, his stance more relaxed.

'Rien ne va plus!' the croupier announced unnecessarily, for nobody looked like making another bet. Everybody was watching the ball bounce and skip over the numbered pockets as the wheel slowed beneath it.

Finally the ball lost momentum and caught in one of the pockets, fighting momentum and bouncing once, twice, before settling into another and being whisked suddenly in the other direction. He knew exactly how it felt. He'd felt hope being ripped right out of him in much the same way for three nights running now. Surely this time, on his last bet of the night, his luck would change? Surely this time he might regain some tiny shred of success to take with him, to show him his gift hadn't abandoned him completely?

Then the wheel slowed to a crawl and with sickening realisation he saw: *red*, the colour rendering the number irrelevant.

It was done. He had lost.

Again.

He thanked the croupier, as if he had dropped no more than the price of a cup of coffee, ignoring the shocked murmurings of the onlookers, intending to walk out of here with his head held high, even if he felt like dropping it into his hands. What the hell was wrong with him?

Bahir didn't lose.

Not like this. The last time he had suffered a run like this…

He pulled his thoughts to an abrupt halt. He wasn't going down that path. The last thing he needed to think about on a night such as this was her.

She was the damned reason he was here, after all.

'Monsieur, s'il vous plait,' came a smooth-as-silk voice alongside him, and he turned to see the shark-faced Marcel, the host the casino had assigned to him tonight. The perfect host up until now, keeping both his distance and his expression free of the smugness he was no doubt feeling, Marcel had meantime ensured that he had wanted for nothing during his stint at the table. 'Sheikh Al-Qadir, the evening does not have to end here. If you wish, the casino would be only too happy to extend you credit to prolong your entertainment.'

Bahir read his face. The man's bland expression might tell him nothing, but there was an eagerness in his grey eyes that made his skin crawl. So they did not think he was done with his losing streak yet? A momen-

tary challenge flared in his blood, only to be quashed
by the knowledge that all he'd done here since he'd entered this establishment three days ago was lose. So
maybe they were right. Which gave him all the more
reason to leave now.

Besides, he didn't need their money. He had won
plenty of that over the years not to be worried about
dropping the odd million, or even ten for that matter.
It wasn't the money he cared about. It was losing that
did his head in. It pounded now, the drums in his head
beating out the letters of the word: *loser*. He smiled in
spite of it. 'Thank you, but no.'

He was halfway across the room before Marcel
caught up with him. 'Surely the night is still young?'

Bahir looked around. A person could certainly think
that here. Locked away under the crystal chandeliers,
surrounded by luxurious furnishings and even more
luxurious-looking women, and without a hint of a window to indicate the time of day, it was possible to lose
all concept of time. He glanced at the watch on his wrist,
realising that, even leaving now, daylight would beat
him to bed. 'For some, perhaps.'

Still his host persisted. No doubt he would be amply
rewarded if he hung onto his prize catch a while longer.
'We will see you this evening, then, Sheikh Al-Qadir?'

'Maybe.' *Maybe not.*

'I will arrange a limousine to collect you from your
hotel. Perhaps you will have time for dinner and a show
beforehand? On the house, of course. Shall we say, eight
o'clock?'

Bahir stopped then, fingers pinching the bridge of his
nose, trying to produce enough pain to drown out the

thunder in his head. Not for the first time was he grateful he hadn't accepted the casino's oh-so-generous offer of accommodation in-house. There were advantages in turning down some of the casino's high-roller benefits. The ability to come and go as he pleased, for one.

He was just about to tell Marcel where he could shove his limousine and his show when he saw it—a flash of colour across the room draped over honey-coloured flesh, and a coil of ebony hair held by a diamond clip—and for a moment he was reminded of another time, another casino.

And, damn it all, of another woman; one he had come here expressly to forget. He shook his head, wanting to rid himself of the memories, feeling the blackness inside of him swell to bursting point, feeling the rush of heat from a suddenly pounding heart.

'Shiekh Al-Qadir?'

'Go away, Marcel,' he snarled, and this time the pinstriped shark took the hint and with a hasty goodnight withdrew into the sea of gowns and dinner suits.

It wasn't her, he realised on a second glance, it was nothing like her. This woman's face was all square jaw and heavy brow, her lips like two red slugs framing her mouth, that honey skin more like leather. And, of course, how could it have been her? He'd left her with her sister in Al-Jirad and surely not even someone as irresponsible as she was would abandon her family so soon after the trouble they had all gone to to rescue her from Mustafa?

Then again, knowing Marina…

He cursed under his breath as he headed for the exit.

What the hell was wrong with him tonight? The last thing he needed to think about was *her*.

No, that was wrong. The last thing he needed to think about was her honey skin, and how she'd still drawn him like a magnet, in spite of the passage of time and despite the hate-filled chasm that lay between them. Yet she'd stepped out of that desert tent and he'd still felt the tug in every cell of his body. What was it now—three years? More? Yet still she'd managed to make him hard with just one glance from those siren's eyes, a glance that had turned frosty and cold the instant she'd realized just who one of her rescuers was.

Still she'd moved like liquid silk, mounting the horse like a natural, her limbs as slender as he recalled, her body still willowy slim despite time and the two children he knew she'd borne.

He might be on the losing streak from hell, but he would bet everything he had that her satin skin was just as smooth as he remembered it to be, whether it be under his hands or in the long slide of her legs wrapped around him.

Curse the woman!

He would not think of her or her long limbs and satin skin! There was no point to it. She was trouble, past or present. She was the worst kind of gamble, the wager lost before the wheel was even spun.

A doorman nodded and bade him a good evening as he passed, even though the night sky outside was already softening to grey. He looked to the cool morning air for the balm it should have been to his overheated skin and fractured nerves, searching for the promise of a new day.

Instead he felt only frustration. He rolled his shoulders on an exhale, protesting the unfamiliar stiffness in his back and neck. When before had his muscles ever been bound so tightly? When before had his spirits ever felt so bleak?

But he already knew the answer to that question. He didn't want to go there either.

He curled into a waiting limousine and tugged his bow tie loose as he sagged against the upholstery, suddenly weary of the world, suddenly restless with his life. He'd thought the casino would liven his spirits. Instead, his luck had let him down and ground him further into the mire.

He looked vacantly out of the window, past the palm-lined esplanade, over the white-fringed sea. Monaco was beautiful, there was no doubt, and justifiably a magnet for the rich and famous and those who craved to be. But right now Monaco and the entire south of France seemed stale, empty and utterly pointless.

No, there was nothing for him here.

He needed to get away, but to where? Las Vegas? No, that would be pointless. Casinos in the States offered even better odds for the house. And he was still unwelcome in Macau after his last winning streak.

An image formed unbidden in his mind, a recent memory of desert dunes and a golden sun, heavy, hot and framed between palm trees as it dipped inexorably lower towards the shimmering horizon.

The desert?

He sat up straighter in his seat, his interest piqued, though wondering if he was mad in the next moment. His recent visit to Al-Jirad had reunited him with his three old friends, Zoltan, Kadar and Rashid. It had also brought two brief forays into the desert. But neither of them had afforded more than a taste of the desert as they had raced to retrieve first the Princess Aisha and then her sister, Marina, from the clutches of the snivelling Mustafa.

The first excursion he had found exhilarating, speeding with his three friends in a race against time across the dunes. The second he'd found less so, although the horses had been just as willing, the company just as entertaining and the sunsets and dawns just as magnificent. It was seeing Marina again after all these years that had spoilt that trip for him.

Of all the women in the world, how unfortunate that Zoltan had to marry *her* sister, the one woman he had sworn never to see again in his life. Even more unfortunate that she could still make him hard with just one look.

Maybe a return visit to the desert would cure him. Maybe the desert sun would sear her from his brain, and the crisp desert night air clear all thoughts of her once and for all.

And maybe not just any desert. Maybe it was just time to go home.

Home.

How long since he had thought of the desert as his home?

How long since he'd called any place home?

But why shouldn't he go now? There was nowhere he needed to be. He had no one to please but himself. And this time he could take the time to drink in the colour and the texture of the desert, take the time to linger and to observe and absorb its sheer power, and breathe in air turned pristine under the heat of the desert sun.

But, more than that, out in the desert there would be no flashes of colour across a crowded room; no glimpses of flesh to remind him of another time and another woman he wanted to forget.

He breathed deeply, content for the first time in days, making a mental note to check flights and make enquiries after he had slept. He was glad this run of nights was behind him. Surely now this run of bad luck must be over too? For right now it could not get much worse.

The mobile phone vibrated in his pocket. He hauled it out, curious who would be calling him at this early hour, less surprised when he checked the caller ID. He pressed the phone to his ear. 'Zoltan, what can I do for you?'

He listened while the grey of the dawn sky peeled away to pink and his run of bad luck took a turn for the worse.

CHAPTER TWO

'No.'

'Bahir,' his friend insisted, 'just listen.'

'Whatever it is, I don't need to hear it. The answer is still no.'

'But she can't travel home by herself. I won't allow it.'

'I thought Mustafa was cooling his heels in prison.'

'He is, but I made the mistake of underestimating him once before. I won't do the same again. So long as there's a possibility someone out there is still loyal to him, I'm not taking any chances with Aisha's sister's safety.'

Bahir raked one hand through his hair. 'So get Kadar to do it.'

'Kadar has urgent business in Istanbul.'

He grunted. 'How convenient. Rashid, then.'

'You know Rashid. He's disappeared. Nobody knows where or when he'll show up again.'

He had to be dreaming. Bahir pinched his nose until sparks shot behind his eyelids but there was no waking up. This nightmare was real. 'Look, Zoltan, it doesn't have to be one of us! What's wrong with getting one of the palace guards to babysit her?'

'They're busy.' A pause. 'Besides, Aisha specifically asked that you do it.'

He hesitated. He'd liked what he saw of Zoltan's new bride. Although he'd had his doubts at first, now he could not imagine a better woman as a match for his friend. In any other circumstances, he would not hesitate to do whatever she asked of him. But Aisha had no idea *what* she was asking of him. 'Aisha was wrong.'

'But you know Marina.'

'Which is exactly the reason I'm saying no.'

'Bahir—'

'No. Isn't it enough that I agreed to come with you to rescue her? Don't push me, Zoltan. Why don't you do it yourself, if you're so God damned keen on her having an escort home?'

'Bahir,' came the hesitant voice of his friend at the end of the line. 'Is something wrong?'

'Nothing is wrong!' *Everything is wrong.* 'Listen, Zoltan, we broke up for a reason. Marina hates me and, when it all comes down to it, I'm not that overly fond of her. She might now be your sister-in-law, but you don't know her like I do. She's as irresponsible as they come, the original party girl who's never done a thing for anyone else. She's spoilt and headstrong, and if she isn't given exactly what she wants she goes out and takes it anyway, regardless of the consequences. And, if that's not enough, she's got the morals of an alley cat and the litter to prove it. I tell you now, Zoltan, I am not going back there.'

'God, Bahir, I'm not asking you to marry her! All you have to do is make sure she gets home safely.'

'And I'm telling you to find someone else.'

There was silence at the end of the line. A brooding silence that did nothing to encourage Bahir to think he was swaying his friend's opinion. 'You know, Bahir,' his friend said at last. 'If I didn't know better...'

Bahir felt like growling. 'What?'

'Well, anyone who didn't know you better might actually think you were actually—*worried*—about spending time with Marina.'

'Are you suggesting I'm afraid?'

'Are you?'

'You just don't get it, Zoltan. Even if I agreed to take her, there is no way this side of hell freezing over that she'd agree to come with me. Didn't you hear me say that she hates me? If you'd bothered to ask her you'd already know that.'

There was a telling pause at the end of the line and Bahir felt a glimmer of hope as he saw a way out of this madness.

'In that case, you might try asking her. She'll give you the same answer I have. No. If you're so convinced she needs someone to make sure she's safe, then you find someone else to do your babysitting.'

'And what if she agrees?'

He laughed out loud. 'No way. She'll never agree. Not in a million years.'

'And if she does, will you do it?'

'It's not going to happen.'

'Okay—so, if she says no, I'll find someone else and if she says yes, then you'll do it?'

'Zoltan... There's no way...'

'Is that a bet?'

'She won't say yes.' She wouldn't. If there was one

thing in this world he could be certain of, it was that she would want to be with him even less than he wanted to be with her. Especially after the way they'd parted. 'I know she won't.'

'In which case,' Zoltan said, 'you've got nothing to worry about.'

'No way!'

'Marina!' Aisha called as her sister jumped up from the garden seat where they'd been sitting together. 'Just listen.'

'There's no point,' she said, striding swiftly away. 'Not if you're not going to make sense.'

Aisha chased after her. 'Zoltan and I don't want you going home alone, surely you can understand that? You should have an escort. It's the least we can do.'

'I'll be fine. It's not that far.'

'Like you thought you'd be fine on the way here too, remember?'

Marina shook her head. 'Mustafa's been put away. And this time I won't go overland, okay? Put me on a private jet. Nothing can possibly go wrong.'

'You're going on a private jet, no question, but you're not going alone. Not this time.'

'Fine! So assign me a bodyguard if you must. But I will not go with that man! It was bad enough to find him waiting for me outside Mustafa's tent. If I hadn't known everyone was afraid for me, I would have gone right back inside again.' And it had had nothing to do with the shivers that had skittered across her skin at finding him amongst the party of her rescuers; nothing to do with that flare of heat she had witnessed in his eyes, before they had turned hard, and as cold and unflinching as ice.

Aisha studied her sister. 'You didn't seem that upset when you arrived back at the palace. "A blast from the past", you called him. I got the impression that whatever had happened in the past, it wasn't that serious.'

Not serious. Marina flung her arms out wide, her fingers flicking the flowers of a nearby jasmine creeper in the process and sending its heady scent swirling into the air. She shook her head, reining her arms in and weaving them tightly around her midriff. 'You were all so worried about me, and happy I was safe, how could I make a fuss? Besides, I thought it was over, that I'd never see him again. And clearly he was just as relieved himself that it was over.'

And when she saw the question in her sister's eyes, she added, 'Didn't he take off for Monte Carlo that very same day? No doubt so that there was no chance he could run into me again while I was at the palace.'

'Oh, Marina, I had no idea.' Aisha slid a hand beneath one of her sister's tightly bound arms and coaxed her into a walk through the fragrant garden. 'What happened between you two?'

What hadn't happened? Marina dropped her head, the weight of painful memories dragging her spirits with it. 'Everything and nothing. It all came to nothing.' She frowned. No, not nothing. She still had Chakir. 'I was stupid. Naive. I flew too close to the sun and it's no wonder I came crashing down.'

'Okay. So you had an affair that ended badly, right?'

And this time it was Marina's turn to squeeze her sister's arm. 'I'm sorry, Aisha. I'm not making sense,

I know. But you're right. I met Bahir one night at a party—eyes across a crowded casino, the whole boring cliché, I guess.'

She looked intently at her sister, trying to make her understand. 'But the attraction was so intense, so immediate, and I knew in that instant that we were going to spend the night together. And one night turned into a week and then a month and more, and it was reckless and passionate and didn't look like ending. And I really thought I loved him, you know. I actually thought for one mad moment—maybe more than just one—that he was the one.' She sighed, staring blankly into the distance. 'But I couldn't have been more wrong.'

'Oh, Marina, I'm sorry. I had no idea.'

'How could you? It wasn't as if I was ever home to share my news. And we seemed to have so little in common back then. You seemed content to stay in the family fold while I was continually rebelling against it. Our brothers provided the necessary heir and spare and our father made no bones about it. I figured I was surplus to requirements and so I might as well enjoy myself.'

'A redundant princess,' Aisha said softly to herself, remembering another time, another conversation.

'What did you say?'

She smiled and shook her head as they resumed walking. 'Nothing. It's funny how different we are. But there were times I envied you your freedom and the fact you got to choose your lovers. There were days I wished I could be more like you, headstrong and rebellious, instead of bound by duty. But I guess they both have their down sides.'

'Amen.' Marina sighed and turned her face to the

heavens. 'And now you're married to one of his best friends. Small world, isn't it, when someone who has told you to get out of their life for ever suddenly turns up on your doorstep? Oh, Aisha, I can't go with him. Don't make me go with him!' Tears pricked at the corner of her eyes with the pain of the past. Tears rolled down her cheeks with the complexities of the present and her fears for the future. 'What a mess!'

'He must have hurt you so very much.'

'He hates me.'

'Are you sure? He was there when they rescued you.'

'I doubt that he wanted to be. The others would have expected it, that's all.'

Aisha nodded. 'It's true they are close. Zoltan told me they were the brothers he never had. But hate you? People say things in the heat of the moment—stupid things—but they don't mean them, not really.'

Marina shook her head, her lips pressed tightly together until she could find the words, the burden of her secret suddenly too heavy to bear. 'Oh, he hates me. Even if he had forgotten how much, he will surely hate me when he discovers the truth.'

Aisha stopped walking and turned to her, fear in her eyes. 'Discovers what truth?'

Marina looked at her through eyes scratchy and raw, and her soul bleaker than at any other time in her life. 'The truth about his son.'

Her sister's mouth opened wide. 'Oh no, Marina, surely not? Is Chakir Bahir's child?'

She nodded.

'But you told everyone you didn't know who the father was.'

Marina put a hand to her mouth. 'I know. It was easier that way. And nobody had any trouble believing it.'

'I'm so sorry!'

'Don't be. I had a reputation as a party girl and it came in handy. It made it easier to hide the truth. It was easier to pretend it didn't matter.'

'Even from Bahir.'

'He has no idea.'

Aisha's feet stilled on the path, her gaze fixed on nothing, and when she looked up at her sister Marina was afraid of what she saw in her eyes. 'I think you need to get on that plane. With Bahir.'

Marina pulled back. 'I won't go with him. I can't face him.'

'But you have to tell him.'

'Do I?'

'Of course you do! You have let him know that he is a father; that he has a child.'

She shook her head. 'He doesn't want to know.'

'He has a right to know. It is right that you tell him. And you must tell him. You have no choice.'

'He won't want to hear. He never wanted a child.'

'Then maybe he should have thought about that.' Aisha gave her sister's shoulders a squeeze. 'I'll tell Zoltan it's all set.'

'No! I only told you so you would understand why I can't see him again. I would never have told you otherwise.'

Her sister smiled, a soft and sad smile. 'I think you told me because you already know what you have to do. You just needed to hear it from someone else.'

* * *

Knowing Aisha was right didn't make boarding the Al-Jiradi private jet any easier. No easier at all when she'd seen the plane land and knew he was already waiting inside. How Zoltan had managed to talk Bahir into this was anybody's guess. He would not be happy about it; of that much she was certain.

'You can do this,' Aisha said as she gave her older sister a final squeeze. 'I know you can.'

Marina smiled weakly in return, wishing she believed her, and waved one last time before disappearing into the covered stairs leading to the plane. Right now her legs were so weak and her stomach so tightly wound, it felt like if it snapped she would spin right off the stairs. A fate infinitely preferable, nonetheless, to being enclosed in the cabin of an aircraft with Bahir.

But it had to be done. For more than three years she had wrestled with the question of whether to tell Bahir of Chakir's existence. At first it had been easy to say nothing, the pain of their break-up still raw, the savagery of his declaration never to have children still uppermost in her mind. Why should Bahir be informed of his child's existence, she'd reasoned, when he'd told her he never wanted to see her again? He would not thank her for discovering that, no matter what either of them wanted, they were bound together via the life of a child they had jointly created.

Then, when Hana had come into the world, there had been plenty to think about, and the question of Bahir's rights to know had been easy to ignore. Suddenly mother to two fatherless children, why complicate matters with the father of only one? And Bahir had made it clear he was not a family man; he didn't want her or a child and they certainly didn't need him.

But she'd had reason to wonder lately as she'd watched her young son grow and turn from baby to toddler to young boy, and she'd found herself wondering what Chakir himself would want.

She swallowed back on a lump of apprehension that had lodged in the dry sandy desert that was now her throat. So despite Bahir telling her that he never wanted a child, and even though she was more than happy to accept that as his final word on the topic, maybe for the sake of their son's wishes this would be worth it. For Chakir's sake.

Please God, let it be worth it.

She managed a tremulous smile for the cabin attendant who welcomed her to the plane. Then she was inside the cool interior and he was there, standing with his back to her at a rack filled with magazines, seemingly oblivious to her presence. She wished she could be so oblivious to his, but she could not.

Just the sight of him was enough to make her heartbeat skip and her skin tingle while she sensed a pooling heat building between her thighs. She cursed her body's wayward reaction and wished she could look away. Damn the man! When would she ever be able to look at him and not think of sex? After all the things he had said to her, after the way they had parted, after all the years that separated them, still he conjured pictures of tangled sheets, tangled limbs and long, hot nights filled with sin.

Then again, how was it possible not to think of sex when it was some kind of god that filled your vision?

Was there some kind of formula for masculine perfection; some ratio of leg-length to height or shoulder-width to hip? Some magic number that nature had allocated at conception that marked a man for physical supremacy?

If so, this man was it, and that was just the view of his back.

He turned then, as the attendant ushered her to the seat across the aisle, and the blast of resentment in his eyes made her catch her breath and forget all about magic numbers.

'Bahir,' she uttered in acknowledgement.

'Princess,' he said sharply on a nod before he returned his attention to sorting through the rack. She was amazed he'd managed to pry his jaw apart enough to form the word, it had been so firmly set.

The cabin attendant chatted cheerily while she settled Marina into her wide leather seat, but Marina caught not a word of it, too consumed by Bahir's reaction, too stunned to think about anything else.

So that was what she would get—the silent treatment.

Clearly Bahir was as resentful of being in her company as she was being in his. Equally clearly, he was in no mood for small talk.

Which suited her just fine.

So long as she could eventually find the words to tell him he was a father.

He tried to focus on the business magazine he'd selected from the rack but the words were meaningless scrawl, the article indecipherable, and he tossed it aside. Hopeless. It was no different from the online journal he'd been reading since he'd boarded the jet in Nice, his attention riveted not by the words he was attempting to read but by a simmering resentment that bubbled faster and more furious the closer the plane got to Al-Jirad. Why the hell had he agreed to this again? He still wasn't sure he had agreed. But Zoltan had called and said she'd agreed to go with him and he knew he would have looked weak if he'd refused again.

Much better to look like it didn't matter a bit.

Except that it did.

Because right now, as the attendant stowed Marina's hand luggage and made her comfortable, and as he tried to pretend she wasn't there, his focus was still held captive by the images captured on his retinas—those damned eyes, her pupils large, catlike and seductive. The jut of her collarbones in the vee of the open neck of the fitted ruffled shirt that flirted over her curves, and the jewel-studded belt hugging her swaying hips.

He growled, his nostrils flaring. He picked up his laptop again, determined not to give in, trying to find focus instead of distraction. Because, if it wasn't enough that his mind was filled with images of her, now he could smell her. He remembered that scent, a blend of jasmine, frangipani and warm, wanton woman. He remembered the taste of it on her glistening, sweat-slickened skin. He remembered pressing his face to the curve of her throat and drinking it in as he plunged into her sweet depths.

He shifted in his seat and slammed the computer shut as the plane started to taxi to the runway. How long was the flight to Pisa—three hours? Four? He growled again.

Too long, however long it took.

* * *

How did you find the words to tell someone he was a father? Not easily, especially when that man sat across the aisle from you, rumbling and growling like a dark thundercloud. Any moment she expected to see lightning bolts issuing from his head.

And that was before she had managed to find the words.

What was she supposed to say? *Excuse me, Bahir, but did I ever tell you about our son?* Or, *Congratulations, Bahir. You're a father, to a three-year-old boy. It must have somehow slipped my mind...*

The plane came to a halt at the start of the runway and she glanced across the aisle to where he sat, his posture closed off, his expression grim. Even though she let her gaze linger, even though she was sure he would be aware, still he refused to look her way.

And she wondered how, even if she could find the words, was she supposed to tell him about his child when he wouldn't even look at her?

Did he hate her that much?

How much more would he hate her when he learned the truth?

The engines whined, preparing for take-off, echoing her own nerves, spun tight by his presence, and spun even tighter by the search for the words to tell him.

She closed her eyes and let the jet's acceleration push her deeper into her seat, forcing herself to relax as the whine became a scream and then a roar as the plane launched itself and speared into the sky.

It wasn't as though there was a rush. They had four hours of flight time and then a two-hour drive to her home in the most northern reaches of Tuscany. Why tell him now and spoil the fragile if tense cease-fire that seemed to exist between them? For he would not remain silent once he knew. He would be intolerable. Perhaps with a measure of justification. Still, why make their hours together more difficult than they already were?

No, there was plenty of time to tell him.

Later.

They were an hour into their flight when they were given the news. One hour of interminable and excruciating silence, filled with the static of all the things that were left unsaid, until the air in the cabin fairly crackled with the tension, a silence punctuated only when the smiling flight attendant came to top up their drinks or offer refreshments.

But this time she had the co-pilot with her and neither of them was smiling.

'So fly around it,' Bahir said after they'd delivered their grim message, too impatient for this trip to be over to tolerate delays, whatever the reason.

'That's not possible,' the co-pilot explained. 'The storm cell is tracking right into our path. And the danger is we could ice up if we try to go over. The aviation authorities are ordering everyone out of the area.'

'So what does that mean?' Marina asked. 'We can't get to Pisa at all?'

'Not just yet. We're putting down at the nearest airport that can take us. We'll be beginning our descent soon. Just be prepared as we skirt the edges of this thing that it could get a bit rough. You might want to keep your seatbelts fastened.'

Bahir usually had no trouble sitting. He could sit for

hours at a stretch when his luck was with him and the spinning ball might have been his to command. But right now he couldn't sit still a moment longer.

He was up and out of his seat the moment they'd gone. God, if it wasn't enough that he had to spend six hours in her company, now he would be forced to spend even more time. He raked clawed fingers through his hair. And with her sitting there, her legs tucked up beneath her and those eyes—those damned eyes—looking like an invitation to sin.

'The co-pilot suggested keeping your seatbelt fastened.'

He ignored her as much as it was possible to do. That was the problem with planes, he realised. There was not enough room to pace and to distance yourself from the thing that was bugging you, and right now he sorely needed to pace and find distance from the woman who was bugging him.

Besides, any possible turbulence outside the plane was no match for what was going on inside him. He turned and strode back the other way, covering the length of the cabin in a dozen purposeful but ultimately futile strides, for there was no easing of the tightness in his gut, no respite.

Suddenly he understood how a captive lion felt, boxed and caged and unable to find a way out no matter how many times it turned to retrace its steps, no matter how hard it searched.

'The co-pilot said—'

'I know what he said!' he spat, not needing input from the likes of her.

'Oh, good. Because I thought maybe you'd developed

a hearing problem. I should have realised it was a problem with your powers of comprehension.'

'Oh, I've got a problem all right, and it begins and ends with you.'

She blinked up at him, feigning innocence. 'Did I do something wrong?'

Suddenly the turbulence inside him exploded. He wheeled around and clamped his hands on the arms of the chair either side of her, his face occupying the space hers had been just moments before. He almost grunted his satisfaction, because he liked the way she'd jumped and pressed herself as far back as she could in the chair. He liked knowing he'd taken her by surprise. And, strangely, he liked knowing she wasn't as unaffected by his presence as she made out. 'What do you think you're playing at?'

Inches from his own, those rich caramel eyes opened wide enough until they were big enough to lose yourself in. He watched them, knowing the dangers, watching their swirling depths as she tried to come up with an answer. He'd lost himself in those eyes once before, lost himself in their promises and their persuasion. But that was before, and for all their seductive power he sure as hell wouldn't let that happen again, no matter what pleasures they promised.

'I don't know what you're talking about.'

He shook his head, not believing. 'Then maybe I should spell it out for you. I'm talking about being stuck here—you and me. I expressly told Zoltan I wouldn't do this. I told him there was no way you would agree. And yet here we find ourselves, together. How did that happen, do you suppose? Unless *you* agreed to it. And

I have to ask myself, what possible reason could you have for doing that? What were you thinking?'

She tried to hide her nervous swallow, but he missed nothing of the tiny tilt of her chin and the movement in her throat. He had trained himself to spot the tiniest shift in facial expression or body language of his opponents, a skill that had stood him in good stead through many a poker game. He knew she was hiding something. Did she imagine that there was a chance for them again? Did she think that, because he'd accompanied Zoltan and the others to Mustafa's camp, it meant something? That he was ready to take her back?

She looked up at him, all wide-eyed innocence. 'You think I really want to be here, imprisoned thousands of feet above the earth with you and your black mood?'

Her words were no kind of answer, and he would have told her, only he was suddenly distracted by a stray strand of hair that looped close to the corner of one of those eyes. 'Somebody must have agreed,' he rumbled as he raised one hand. 'And it sure as hell wasn't me.' She flinched as his fingers neared, holding her breath as he gently swept the hair back, surprised when he felt a familiar tremor under her skin, disturbed even more when he felt a corresponding sizzle under his own.

Abruptly he pushed himself away and stood with his back to her, rubbing his hands together to rid himself of the unwelcome sensation. 'Don't you think I've got better things to do than waste my time babysitting a spoilt princess?'

'I absolutely agree,' she said behind him. 'I'm quite sure there's a casino just waiting to be fleeced by the famous Sheikh of Spin. I can't imagine how you managed to drag yourself away.'

His hands stilled. He didn't need any reminders of why he wasn't still at the roulette table. He turned slowly. 'Be careful, princess.'

She jerked up her chin. 'That's the second time you've addressed me by my title. Is it so long that you've forgotten my name? Or can you just not bring yourself to utter it?'

'Is it so long that you've forgotten that I said I never wanted to see you again?'

'Maybe you should have thought of that before you turned up outside my tent that night.'

'Is that what this is about? Why should that change anything? Or were you merely hoping to thank me?'

'Thank you? For what?'

'For rescuing you from Mustafa.'

'Oh, you kid yourself, Bahir. You weren't there for me. You were along for the ride, only there to have fun with your band of merry men. A little boys' own adventure to whet your taste for excitement. So don't expect me to get down on bended knees to thank you.'

A sudden memory of her on bended knee assailed him, temporarily shorting his brain, just as her mouth and wicked tongue had done back then. Not that she'd been thanking him exactly that time. More like tasting him. Laving him with her tongue. *Devouring him.* In fact, if he remembered correctly, he'd been the one to thank her...

He shook his head, wondering if he would ever be rid of those images, knowing he would miss them in the dead of sleepless nights if they were gone. But that minor concession didn't mean he welcomed their presence *now* while he was trying to make a point. 'I wouldn't want your thanks anyway. If I did anything that night, it was out of loyalty to Zoltan and my brothers. It was duty, nothing more.'

'How very noble of you.'

'I don't care what you call it. Just don't go thinking that I've changed my mind about what I said back then. You'd be kidding yourself if you did. What we had is over.'

'You really think you have to tell me that? I have no trouble remembering what you said. Likewise, I have no trouble believing you mean it now, just as you meant it then. And, for the record, it is you who are kidding yourself if you think I am insane enough to want you to change your mind. After what you said to me, after the way you treated me, I wouldn't take you back if you were the last man left on earth!'

He sat back down in his seat. 'So we understand each other, this is merely duty. Of the most unpleasant kind.'

Her eyes glared across at him as he buckled up. 'Finally you say something I can agree with.'

Her agreement offered no satisfaction. His mood only mirrored the darkening sky as the plane descended judderingly through the clouds, icy rain clawing at the windows, the tempestuous winds tearing at the wings—and a sick feeling in his gut that, whatever the weather, things were not about to improve.

CHAPTER THREE

THE plane touched down somewhere on the coast of western Turkey at a small airport not far from where the rocky shoreline met the sea. It was almost dark now, although still only mid-afternoon, and they emerged from the plane into a howling wind that tore at their clothes and sucked the words from their mouths. A waiting car whisked Marina and Bahir through the immigration formalities before surprising Marina by heading away from the airport.

She flicked her windswept hair back from her face and looked longingly back at the airport. 'Shouldn't we stay with the plane?' she asked, concerned. 'So we're ready to take off when the weather clears?'

Was it the lashing from the rain that had eroded her harsh demeanour and left her softer, almost vulnerable? Whatever. With her long black hair in wild disarray around her face, and with her eyelashes still spiked with the air's muggy atmosphere, she looked younger. Softer. Almost like she had when she'd woken sleepily from a night of love-making. All that was missing was the smile and the hungry glint in her eyes as she'd eagerly climbed astride him for more.

'Didn't you hear the pilot's last announcement, princess?' Bahir asked, dragging his thoughts away from misspent days and nights long gone. This was the reason he'd never wanted to see her again. Because he knew she'd make him remember all the things he would never again enjoy. 'Airports all over Europe are closed. We are not going anywhere tonight.'

'But my children… I promised them I would be home tonight.'

Bahir looked away. He wasn't taken in by her sudden maternal concern for her children. It was the first time she had even mentioned them and, if they meant so much to her, why had she left them at home in the first place? Maybe in hindsight it might have been the right thing to do this time, given how she had lumbered into the path of Mustafa, but she could not have known that would happen. And surely they had deserved to be at their own aunt's wedding if not the coronation of Zoltan himself?

'We leave at first light,' he said, already looking forward to it. 'You will be home soon enough.' Though never soon enough for him.

She was silent as they passed through a small town that was seemingly abandoned as everyone had taken cover from the storm, the shutters of windows all closed, awnings flapping and snapping in the wind.

'So where are we going now? Why couldn't we stay with the plane?'

'The crew are staying with the plane. It is, after all, Al-Jiradi property. They will not leave it.'

'So we must?'

'There is a small hotel on the coast. Very exclusive. You will be more comfortable there.'

'And you?'

'This is not about my comfort.'

If there was comfort in this hotel, it was proving elusive to find. There was luxury, it was true: the plushest silk carpets, the finest examples of the weaver's art. The most lavish of fixtures and fittings, from the colourful Byzantine tiles to the gold taps set with emeralds the size of quails' eggs.

But comfort was nowhere to be found. Just as it was impossible to sleep. Even now, when it seemed the worst of the storm had passed, lightning still flashed intermittently through the richly embroidered drapes, filling the room with an electric white light and bleaching the room of colour. But the atmosphere in the room remained heavy with the storm's passing, and the soft bed and starched bed-linen felt stifling. She looked longingly at the doors that led onto the terrace overlooking the sea.

Ever since they'd arrived she'd locked herself away in her suite, wanting desperately to find distance from that man. He'd been impossible on the plane, sullen and resentful at first, openly explosive when the news had come of their flight's delay, as if it had been all her fault.

Maybe it was. She had been the one to agree to him seeing her safely home, but it wasn't for the reason he was thinking—that she somehow imagined that he might change his mind, that he might take her back.

What kind of arrogance led a man to believe a woman would want him back after the things he'd said to her?

Did he think she had no pride?

No, the man was unbearable.

So she'd taken refuge in her room, savouring her privacy and her time alone to call Catriona and explain about the delay. She took her time to talk to each of her children and tell them she would soon be home to hug and kiss them and tickle their tummies until they collapsed with laughter again.

It had seemed such a good idea to lock herself away like this while the storm had raged all around. But like the worst of the storm, hours had passed, and still she could not sleep. Still, she could not make sense of the war going on inside herself.

For she hated him, didn't she? Hated him for the way he had amputated her from his life as quickly and decisively as if he'd been slicing a piece of fruit—as if she had never meant more than that to him. Yet still one sight of him and some primal, some base, bodily response kicked in and she had been wet with wanting him. Even now her body ached with need, as if he had flicked some kind of switch and turned her heartbeat into some kind of pulsing drumbeat of desire.

What kind of woman did that make her?

Was she mad? Or simply wanton? The party princess out for nothing but a good time and not caring who it was who gave it to her.

God, it was hot! The mattress seemed to cocoon her, trapping the heat of her thoughts and slowly roasting her in them. She pushed herself up and a bead of sweat trickled from her hair down her neck.

So much for a refuge. All she'd succeeded in doing was exchanging one kind of prison for another. And, in a few short hours from now, she'd be back on the plane—with him—and the torture would continue.

Another flash of lightning lit up the room, and her gaze went to the doors again. There was a chance they could be opened now, without being blown off their hinges or she being blown away herself. And maybe it would be cooler outside on her terrace. Maybe the wind would tear away some of the heat from her overheated skin, and maybe the air might have a chance to cool her sheets while she was gone.

She slid from the bed and reached for her gown, only remembering then that it was still tucked somewhere deep in her luggage because she had thought the weather too warm to need it. She thought for a moment of the hotel robe waiting neatly on a hanger in the closet, but the thought of towelling against her skin when she was already so hot...

She hesitated only a fraction of a moment. She didn't really need it. It was three in the morning, and she was only stepping onto the darkened terrace. She wouldn't be outside for long, and she so craved the feel of cool air and rain on her skin.

The wind had dropped but still she had to hang onto the door lest it slam open. She snicked it firmly closed behind her, knowing the sound would not carry over the waves crashing on the nearby shore, the wind already whipping her hair around her face and sending swirls of air up the slit in her long nightie, brushing against her legs and fanning against her heated core.

She shivered, not with cold from a sprinkling of rain, but with the wind's delicious caress against her skin, and she turned into the onshore wind, pushing against it until she reached the balustrade overlooking the sea.

This was more like it. The shoreline was thick with dancing foam, bright white against the inky black of sea, the tang of salt heavy in the moisture-laden air. In the distance the storm rumbled and lit up the world for an instant at a time.

Then a wild wave crashed on the rocks below and she was hit with the spray, the wind turning the droplets icy on her skin.

She gasped as it hit, her body electric and alive from her head to her toes, and she flung her arms out wide and laughed into the wind with the sheer thrill of it. It was wild. It was exhilarating. And she felt free, just like she'd always yearned to be.

Like she had been once, before Bahir had stolen her heart.

He watched her from his doorway, where he had been standing for more than an hour watching the storm boil and simmer away. At first he had not heard her, whatever sound she made whipped away by the wind or lost under the crash of the sea, but then he had caught a movement out of the corner of his eye, a vision of a woman in a long white nightgown. But not just any woman. *Marina*. A ghost from his past, moving across the terrace with bare arms and bare feet while her black hair followed, untamed, blowing riotous and free.

He watched and grew hard as the nightdress was plastered against her body by the wild wind and the rain, against her lush breasts and the slight swell of her belly, against the sweet curve of her mound. Plastered hard against all the places he remembered, and plastered so close that she might not have been wearing anything at all.

The wind tore at her gown, peeling the fabric high around her legs, and he grew still harder wondering if she still never wore anything under her nightgown.

He growled. Why would she wear a white nightgown? So very virginal and innocent.

Who was she trying to kid?

She was nowhere near a virgin. She was a sorceress. She was wanton in bed, hungry and insatiable. She was sinuous and lithe, moved and twisted with a dancer's grace, and he knew he should go. He should leave now, while he had the chance, before he was tempted to do something he might regret.

But he could not force his feet to move. He could not turn away. Instead he stayed and watched while she was hit by the spray of a wave crashing below; watched while she flung her arms out wide and laughed as brazenly as the weather, watched while her damp white gown turned transparent—and he knew that he had no choice.

Knew he had to go to her.

Her gown was soaked with spray and clinging to her, her hair blowing wild where it wasn't stuck to her scalp and skin, and she knew that soon she would feel sticky with salt and think herself insane for doing something so utterly reckless when she should have been trying to sleep.

But for now she felt more alive than she had in months. More awake. More liberated.

She spun around, lifting her sodden hair high to cool the back of her neck as another wave sent spray flying, when lightning illuminated the terrace and told her in a chill bolt of realisation that she was not alone.

'Bahir,' she said, dropping her arms and backing away into the spray, the sound wrenched from her mouth before even she could hear it. But her body needed to hear no alarm. Her body was already on high alert, her breasts straining and peaked against the fine wet fabric of her gown, her thighs tingling with urgency and her feet primed to flee.

She might have tried to run, but his expression stilled her feet, his face a tortured mask, as if he'd battled his inner demons and lost. His eyes held her spellbound, dark and fathomless in a shadowed face, while his white shirt clung to him in patches, turning it the colour of the golden skin that lay beneath.

She swallowed, tasting the salt of the sea, or was it of his flesh? For even here she could feel the heat rolling off him as his body called to hers, in all the ways it had done in the past, promising all the pleasures of the past and more.

'Why?' she asked softly in a lull in the wind, wanting to be sure, wary of trusting the chemistry between them.

'You can't sleep either.' He answered with a statement, without really answering at all.

'I was hot.'

His eyes raked over her, slowly, languidly, and the heat she saw there stoked a fire under her skin that even the effect of the night air on her wet gown could not whip away. As she looked at how his white shirt clung to his skin, moulding to one dark nipple, she realised how she must look to him—exposed. As good as naked. She wrapped her arms around her torso in a futile attempt to cover herself.

She had never had reason for modesty with Bahir. There was perhaps no reason for modesty now. He had seen it all before and more. But she was different now. She was a mother, and pregnancy had left its inevitable marks on her body. Would he notice? Would he care? He had no right to care and she had no need to wonder—yet still...

Then his eyes found hers again and he simply said, 'I feel it too. Hot.' And she knew he wasn't talking about the weather.

He took a step closer, and then another, so she had to raise her face to look up at him.

'You should go,' he said.

'I should,' she agreed, because it was right, and because to stay would be reckless. The last thing she needed was to be trapped outside on a storm-tossed terrace with a man she had never stopped lusting after, even when she had tried to hate him so very much. Even when she knew she should.

But her feet didn't move, even when the wind pushed at her back, slapping the wet gown against her legs, urging her to get out while she still had time.

'You should go,' he repeated, his voice gravel-rough against her skin. 'Except...'

She tilted her head up at him, her senses buzzing, every nerve in her body buzzing. 'Except what?'

'Except, I don't want you to.'

She swallowed and closed her eyes, one part of her

wishing she'd already left so she'd never have heard him utter those words. The other part of her, that wanton part of her that belonged to him for ever, rejoicing that he had.

'I want you,' he said, and she started and opened her eyes as she felt his hands lift her jaw and cradle her face.

Suddenly it was much too late to run, even if she could have recalled a fraction of all the good reasons why she should.

When she looked up at him it was to see him gazing down at her with such a look of longing that it charged her soul, for it had been so long since someone had looked at her that way, and that person had been Bahir. Nobody had ever looked at her the way Bahir had.

But that was before…

'This is a mistake,' she said, some remaining shred of logic warning her as his hand drifted towards her face.

'Does this,' he said as his fingers traced across her skin and she forgot how to breathe, 'feel like a mistake?' And she sighed into his touch, for electricity accompanied his fingers, leaving a trail of sparks in its wake, just like his touch had that moment on the plane when he had reached out to her brow and left her sizzling with the contact.

Maybe not right now, she thought, in answer to his question. But tomorrow or next week or even next month she would realise this was all kinds of mistake.

And then his hand curved around her neck, gentling her closer to his waiting mouth. Some mistakes, she rationalised, were meant to be made.

The wind pounded at her back, and she let it push

her closer to him, meeting his lips with her own and sighing into his mouth with that first, precious touch.

It was like coming home, only better, because it was to a home she'd never expected to find again. A home she'd thought lost for ever.

'Bahir,' she whispered on his lips, recognising the taste and scent and texture of him, welcoming him.

For one hitched, exquisite moment the tenuous meeting of their mouths was enough, but only for a moment. Until he groaned and pulled her against him, his mouth opening to hers, sucking her into his kiss.

She went willingly, just as her hands went to the hard wall of his chest, drinking in his hard-packed body with her fingers, pressing her nails into his flesh as if proving he was real, as if proving this was really happening.

He was real, her fingers told her, joyously, deliciously, delectably real.

And so very hot.

His breath, his mouth, his lips on her throat, the flesh under her hands—all of him so hot. Yet when his hand cupped her breast it was she who felt like she would combust with his fingers kneading her flesh, his thumb stroking her hard, straining nipple.

Then his mouth replaced his hand, drawing her breast into his mouth, laving her nipple through the thin gown, and silk had never felt so good against her skin.

A burst of sea spray shattered over them. The clouds parted to a watery moon and she clung to his head in order to stay upright and not collapse under the impact of his sensual onslaught.

But when his hands slid down her back and cupped her behind, his fingers perilously close to the apex of her thighs and the heated, pulsing core of her existence, she knew her knees would not last much longer. 'Bahir!' she cried, but he had already anticipated her need, knowing what she asked and what she needed instinctively, as he always had.

He cupped her face in his hands and kissed her long and hard, until she was dizzy and his own breathing ragged when he pulled himself away enough to speak.

'One night,' he said, his voice thick with want. 'Just this night. That's all I ask.'

She knew what he was telling her—that he hadn't changed his mind, that he didn't want her as a permanent fixture in his life and that he would never want her love—but he was offering her this night. Or, at least, what was left of it.

Would she take it?

If she were stronger—if she was more like her younger sister, Aisha, who had tamed her own potent sheikh—she'd tell him what he could do with his one night. But she wasn't that strong. And the choice was so unfair.

She could have this one night with him, and sacrifice her principles and her pride, or she could have none. But her pride and her principles would never make her heartbeat trip with just one glance or one gentle touch. They could not take her to paradise and back and all the wondrous places in between. And what were pride and principles when compared to paradise?

One excruciatingly short night of paradise. A few short hours before they had to rise and return to the airport and continue their flight.

Was it worth it?

Oh yes.

And tomorrow she would tell him about their son—and it wouldn't matter if he never wanted to see her again, because she would have this one stolen night to remember.

She looked up into his eyes and could see the impatience there, the urgency and the crippling, demanding need that so echoed her own.

'Just one night,' she agreed, and felt herself swept up into his arms as if she were weightless.

He carried her to his suite at the opposite end of the terrace from hers, and laid her reverentially on a bed that looked just as storm-tossed as the one she had left. The covers were piled in disarray on the floor, the pillows thumped to within an inch of their existence. It thrilled her that she might be responsible for at least some of the heat that had kept him from sleep.

He stood at the side of the bed, his eyes never leaving her as he purposefully unbuttoned his shirt and tossed it to the floor, his damp, golden skin glowing in the thin moonlight. She held her breath as his trousers soon joined it, then even the scrap of silk he called underwear was gone, and he was gloriously naked before her, his erection swaying proud and free.

Her mouth went dry as he knelt with one knee alongside her on the bed, every drop and bead of moisture her body contained heading south, where it pooled and pulsed with aching, burning need.

'You're beautiful,' she told him. Not that it was any surprise, she was merely stating a fact. For she had always thought him beautiful, dressed or undressed, but never more so than like this, when his full potent masculinity was proudly on display.

He touched one hand to the hem of her nightgown at her ankle and smiled, his eyes glinting in the pale moonlight. 'And you,' he began, 'are overdressed.'

CHAPTER FOUR

THAT was how it began, with his hands skimming up her calves, peeling the damp silk from her legs as he pressed kisses to her ankles, to the backs of her knees, to the inside of each thigh.

And, just when she was gasping in anticipation and expectation, he lifted himself and eased the bunched fabric over her hips, sliding his hands up either side of her waist and past her sensitive breasts, freeing her of the gown, before raining kisses on her eyes, nose and mouth, her shoulders, breasts and every part of her. With every silken touch of his fingers, every magical glide of his hands on her skin, every hot kiss of his mouth, her fever built, until a tear slipped unbidden from the corner of each eye.

The moment was as poignant as it was bittersweet. For she had dreamed of a night like this so very many times. She had dreamed of him returning to her, of admitting he had made a mistake, of begging her forgiveness, and in a thousand different ways, in a thousand different scenarios, she had welcomed him back.

She had dreamed of a magical night when he would return and say he was sorry, that he had been wrong and that he loved her. And she would take his hand, place it on her ripe belly and tell him that it was his child inside her, created in an act of love.

Until finally she would realise that he was never coming back, that he would never seek her out. That it was finished.

And yet, even though she knew nothing ultimately would change, he was here now—and even if it wasn't what she had longed for, even if it would never be enough, it was *something*.

'You are the beauty,' she heard him say, and she opened liquid eyes to see him kneeling back and staring down at her, his eyes filled with what looked like worship. Yet still she waited, breathless with wondering if he might still notice the changes to her body since they'd last lain together, the changes that motherhood to his child had wrought. 'So beautiful,' he repeated.

She held out a hand to him to pull him down and end this desperate need. 'Please make love to me, Bahir.'

He surprised her by taking her hand, turning it in his and kissing her palm, saying, 'I will. But first...' before he let her hand go to skim his hands up the inside of her legs, parting them, pushing them apart to dip his head lower.

She gasped when she realised his intention, and not only in anticipation of the pleasures to come. But they had so very little time and she had expected him to take his pleasure as many times as he could. She had not expected him to want to spend his time giving it. Besides, as much as she had missed the pleasures his wicked mouth could bring, it was the feel of him inside her that she craved.

'Bahir,' she cried as he wrapped his arms around her thighs and opened her to him. 'Please.'

But her pleas were answered by the heated swipe of his tongue along her cleft, and the arch of her spine in response. 'Oh God,' she cried as his tongue made magic with every flick, sending her senses reeling with no time to recover before his lips closed on that tiny nub of nerves, drawing her into his mouth and teasing her senseless with the skill of an artisan—a man who knew exactly what she needed and when.

'Please!' she called, knowing she was already lost, not knowing what she called for.

But he knew. At the hitched peak of her pleasure she felt his fingers join his mouth, pleasuring her inside and out and sending her over the brink.

And that was how it ended, in a million shattering ways, in a million different colours. Years of ecstasy foregone forged into one shattering rainbow moment as she climaxed all around him.

He had always been the best, she thought as the tremors rolled away. Nothing had changed, it seemed, she registered in the pleasure-filled recesses of her mind.

He pulled her into his kiss as she returned to earth. She tasted herself on him, tasted hot sex, heated desire and his burning need, and that need fed into hers, needing him inside her now more than ever.

'God, you look sexy like that,' she heard him say as he drew back. 'Do you have any idea how much I want you?'

She smiled up at him and thought through flickering eyelids about protection, was just about to say something, but he was already reaching across her to retrieve his wallet from a side table, extracting a packet that he tore open impatiently with his teeth. 'Just as well one of us is responsible.'

She blinked, the fog in her blown-apart world clearing. 'What did you say?' she asked, not sure she'd heard him right, not sure she'd understood what he'd meant if she had.

He rolled the condom down his length, his erection bucking and protesting its latex confines in his hand. 'I said…' he dropped back over her, nuzzling a pebbled nipple with his hot mouth as he moved his legs between hers '…it's lucky one of us can think straight.'

She stilled, the magic his mouth producing negated by the toxic content of his words. 'You think I'm irresponsible.'

'I didn't say that,' he said, before finding her other breast with his teeth, angling his hips for her centre.

'You did,' she said, squirming her hips up the bed and away from his attempts to join her. 'That's what you meant—that you were responsible because you thought about protection. You said I was *lucky* you'd thought of it.'

'It's not important!'

'It is important, if that's what you think.'

'Marina, don't do this. I didn't mean anything.'

'But you did! You think I'm irresponsible, don't you? Just because you mentioned protection before I did. You assume I was never going to ask.'

'Come on, Marina, you're hardly the poster girl for safe sex.'

'And you're the poster boy, I suppose?'

'I'm not the one with two illegitimate children. I

would have thought you'd be happy not to be lumbered with a third.'

Blood rushed to her head at the sheer injustice in his words, pounding in her temples, a call to war. 'How dare you?' she cried, twisting her body underneath him, pushing at him with her hands and pounding him with her fists, desperate to get away. 'How dare you talk about my children and say that *I'm* irresponsible? Get off me!'

'Listen!' he said, grabbing one wrist before it could find its target on his shoulder. 'What the hell is wrong with you?'

She glared up at him, her eyes blazing. 'That's too easy. *You're* what's wrong with me. I told you this was a mistake. I knew it was. I'm just sorry I didn't realise how big a mistake until now.'

'I wouldn't worry on that score,' he said through gritted teeth as he rolled away and let her go so that she could clamber from the bed and swipe up her gown from the floor. 'It won't happen again.'

She tugged the gown over her head, shrugging, uncaring when she realised that the seams were on the outside, already heading for the door. 'You better believe it.'

If the flight thus far had been unbearable, the flight to Pisa was torturous, the atmosphere so strained that this time even the cabin attendants sensed the tension in the cabin and left them alone as much as possible. The lack of distractions was no help at all. Marina put her book down again in frustration, wondering if this flight would ever end. She'd tried to read the same passage at least a dozen times now and still the words didn't stick.

But how could anything stick in a mind already overflowing with self-recrimination and loathing? She hated that she had let herself fall under Bahir's heated spell last night. She hated that he had peeled away every shred of logic, accumulated wisdom and life experience that she possessed, just as easily as he had peeled her nightgown from her body.

She hated herself that she had let him.

And when she remembered the way she had come apart in his bed, she wanted to curl up and die. Oh God, how could she look at herself in the mirror? But one thing she knew. She would not bring herself to look at him.

Oh, she could hear him across the aisle, shifting in his seat, grumbling and muttering from time to time. She could feel the anger rolling off him in waves—even his warm, masculine scent was infused with resentment—but she refused to look his way. She could not face him knowing what she had let him do.

She squeezed her eyes shut. Still her muscles buzzed with the memories, her tender tissues still pulsing, still anticipating the completion that would now never come.

God, she thought, squeezing her thighs together in an effort to quell the endless—the *pointless*—waiting, but she was every kind of fool. Maybe Bahir was right. Maybe she was irresponsible after all. But not in the way he imagined.

Of course, their arrival into Pisa was delayed, the airport busy trying to catch up after the storm disruption of the previous day, the tarmac crowded with charter planes and passenger buses all jockeying for space.

So, by the time they landed, her nerves were strained to breaking point and she no longer cared that he was the father of her child or that she had agreed to tell him so. She just wanted him to be gone.

'I'm good from here,' she said without looking at him, as her luggage was stowed into a waiting car outside the busy airport. 'I have a driver. You might as well go.'

She was dismissing him? His lip curled, and it was nothing to do with the smell of diesel in the air or someone's pizza remains lying discarded and sweltering in the gutter. 'That's not the way it works, princess.'

She glared sharply up at him then, probably the first time she'd looked at him since storming out of his room early this morning, and he knew he'd rubbed her up the wrong way by reverting to her title. *Tough.* The less personal they kept this, the better for both of them. 'The deal was to see you safely home.'

'I won't tell anyone if you don't.'

'It's not up to you,' he said, tossing his own overnight bag into the trunk alongside her bags, before nodding to the driver to close it. 'And it's not up to me. I made an agreement with Zoltan and that agreement stands.'

'There's no need...'

He pulled open the back door for her. 'Get in.'

'But I don't want you...'

He leaned in close to her ear, close enough so that anyone sitting at the outdoor tables nearby might even think he was whispering sweet nothings into her ear. 'You think I want you? You think I want to be here?

But this isn't about what I think of you right now. This isn't personal. This is duty, princess, pure and simple. I said I'd do this and I'll damned well do it.'

He drew back as she stood there in the open door for what seemed like for ever, looking like she might explode, her eyes filled with a white heat, her jaw so rigidly set it could have been wired in place.

'Any time this year would be good, princess. I know how you're in such a hurry to be reunited with your precious children.' *Not to mention how much of a hurry he was in to be done with her for good.*

Her sorceress's eyes narrowed then, and something he'd swear looked almost evil skittered across their dark surface while her lips stretched thin and tight across her face. 'You're right, this is all about duty,' she said. 'I had forgotten that for a moment. Just don't tell me later that I didn't warn you.'

He didn't bother to ask her what she meant. He didn't want to know. He slammed the door behind her, and after a few words, giving the driver a day off, took the keys and the wheel. There was no way he was sharing the back seat with *her*. At least driving along Italy's frenetic *autostradas* would give him something relatively sane to think about.

It sure beat thinking about her.

He headed the car north towards Genoa and the exit that would take them into the northern Tuscan mountain region where she lived, while she sat glowering behind her dark glasses behind him. Such a different woman than the one who had graced his bed last night.

What had that been all about? What was her problem? Had that been some perverse kind of pay-back, a kind of getting even for him cutting her off all those years ago?

Was she still so bitter that she would seek any chance at revenge, including finding any justification that she could to stop him mere moments from plunging into her?

What other reason? Because she could hardly take umbrage at being thought irresponsible. God, the entire world's media had used that word in reference to her at one time or another, and with good reason. It could hardly be considered an insult. One didn't have to look further than not one, but two illegitimate children to prove that.

The traffic was heavy on the *autostrada*, but the powerful car made short work of the kilometres through the wide valley to the turn-off onto the narrower road that led towards the mountain region where she lived. Discovering that had been a surprise. He'd figured she'd still be living somewhere close to a city, somewhere she could party long into the night before collapsing long into the day. But she had children now. Perhaps she left them with their nanny while she partied. Maybe she was responsible enough to do that. That would be something.

The pace slowed considerably after they'd left the *autostrada*, the road wending its way along a fertile river valley flanked by looming peaks and through picturesque villages, where the corners of buildings intruding on the road, and blind corners that left no idea what was coming towards you, became the norm.

He dodged yet another slow-moving farm tractor. This was clearly an inconvenient place to live. But maybe she didn't come home too often.

He glanced in the rear-view mirror to see her leaning back against the leather upholstery, her eyes still hidden under those dark glasses. But nothing could hide the strain made obvious in the tight set of her mouth.

So she was tired. Who wasn't after last night?

He had no sympathy. None at all. At least she'd enjoyed some measure of relief. Unlike him, who had burned unsatiated all the hours till daylight, and then some just thinking about her spread out on his bed, wanton, lush and, oh, so slick.

He had been just moments from the place he had longed to be ever since she had appeared like a sorceress on the terrace, gift-wrapped in a transparent layer of silk...

'Didn't you hear me?' she said from the back. 'You have to turn left here.' He had to haul the car around or he would have missed the turn completely.

'How far?' he said as the road narrowed to little more than a one-lane track up the side of a mountain and a snow sign warned of winter hazards.

'A few kilometres. Not far.' He wanted to snarl at the news, more anxious than ever, the closer they got to her home, for his duty to be done.

On the *autostrada*, with the power and engineering excellence of the car at his disposal, those few kilometres would have taken no time at all. On this narrow goat's track, with its switchback bends and impossibly tight, blind corners, it was impossible to go fast, and the climb seemed to take for ever. Longer than for ever, when all you wanted was for it to be over.

The tyres squealed their protest as he rounded another tight bend, pulling in close against the mountainside as a four-wheel drive coming the other way spun its wheels just enough to the right that the two vehicles slid past with bare millimetres to spare.

He took a ragged breath, relieved at the near miss. What the hell was she doing all the way up here? It would be hard to find somewhere more remote, and there was no way he could reconcile the Marina he knew—the high-living girl who was as wilful as she was wild and wanton—with somewhere so rustic.

Though he could see why anyone not enamoured of the party world would want to live here. For, as they scaled the mountain, the vistas grew more and more impressive, of ridge after ridge, valley after valley framed by even higher peaks to one side of him and a range of grey-green mountains in the distance.

'Just on the next bend,' she said at last. 'The driveway on the left.' And there was the next surprise as he pulled into the gravel driveway—he wasn't sure what he'd been expecting, but it sure hadn't been this.

The stone villa sprawled down the side of a ridge, its windows looking out to what had to be magnificent views in every direction. Climbing bougainvillea up the walls trailed bright vermilion flowers, a brilliant contrast against the painted yellow walls. He stepped out and looked around, feeling the Tuscan sun on his shoulders. Kinder than the desert sun, he registered, even in the early afternoon when it was at its most potent. Or maybe it was always cooler at this height.

She didn't wait for him to finish his appraisal and open her door, or maybe she was just as impatient as him for this ordeal to be over.

'This is where you live?' he asked as he pulled her bags from the trunk.

She reached for them but he held them firm and her lips tightened again. 'It's my home, yes.' She sighed with the resignation of one who knew he was going to see his duty to the bitter end, and led the way down a set of stairs on one side of the house that led to a crazy-paved terrace and covered pergola. From here the views were even better. Across a valley between the ridges, a small village clung in colourful array against the dense green of orchards and forest, and before them the land slipped away, lush and green, fading through to grey with each successive range.

Then from the house he heard footsteps, squeals and cries of 'Mama, Mama!' before a door flew open and two dark-haired children exploded from the house shrieking and laughing.

'Mama!' cried the first, a boy that collided full force against her legs, a tiny girl behind packing no less a punch as she flung herself at her mother.

He felt a growl form at the back of his throat as she knelt down and wrapped her arms around them, felt his gut twist into knots. So these were her children? It was one thing to know about them—it was another to see them.

He looked away, waiting for the reunion to be over. He didn't do families. He certainly didn't want to think about the implication of hers, of the men she had fallen into bed with so quickly after expressing her undying love to him. So much for that.

'You're home at last, thank the heavens,' he heard someone say. And he swung round to see an older woman of forty-something, wiping her hands on a flour-covered apron, standing at the door, not looking at the tableau in front of her, but squarely at him. She raised a quizzical eyebrow at the visitor before turning to Marina. 'Lunch is almost ready. Shall I set another place?'

Marina kissed each of her children and rose, taking their hands in hers. 'Bahir, this is Catriona, my nanny, housekeeper and general lifesaver. And these,' she said, looking down, 'are my children, Chakir and Hana. Bahir was nice enough to make sure I got home safely,' she said to them. 'Say *ciao* to our visitor, children.'

Nice enough to see her home safely? Not really. But this time he had no choice but to look down at them—such a long way down, it seemed. Neither child said anything. The girl clung to her mother's skirts, her eyes wide in a pixie face, her thumb firmly wedged in her mouth and clearly not impressed.

But it was the boy who bothered him the most. He was looking up at him suspiciously, eyes openly defiant, as if protective of his mother and prepared to show it; eyes that looked uncannily familiar...

'I'm not staying,' he said suddenly, feeling a fool when he realised he was still holding her luggage like some stunned-mullet bellboy. He set the cases down by the door and took a step back. She could no doubt manage them from here herself.

'You—should stay,' Marina said, her words sounding strangely forced, as if she was having to force them through her teeth. 'Stay for lunch.'

'No, I…' He looked longingly up the stairs to where he knew the car was parked.

'You should…' she said tightly, trailing off. There was no welcome in her words, but rather an insistence that tugged on some primal survival instinct. Some warning bell deep inside him told him to run and keep right on running.

But he couldn't run.

The nanny-cum-housekeeper was watching him. Marina stood there, looking suddenly brittle and fragile, and as though at any moment she could blow away, except that she was anchored to the ground by the two sullen-looking children at her hands—the wide-eyed girl and the boy who looked up at him with those damned eyes…

And with a sizzle down his spine he realised.

His eyes.

The high, clear mountain air seemed to thicken and churn with poison around him, until it was hard to breathe in the toxic morass. 'No,' he uttered. 'Not that.'

And he was only vaguely aware of Catriona ushering the children inside and closing the door, leaving Marina standing as still as a pillar of salt, her beautiful features gaunt and bleached almost to white.

'It's true,' she whispered. 'Chakir is your son.'

CHAPTER FIVE

'No!' The word exploded from his lips like a missile, intended to be just as deadly, just as decisive, before he wheeled away, his purposeful strides bearing him to the end of the wide terrace, taking him away from that house—but it was nowhere near far away enough from this nightmare. 'No. It cannot be!'

'I'm sorry,' she said behind him. 'I know it must be a shock.'

He spun back. 'A shock? Is that what you call it? To be told that you have a child who is, what, two years old? The first you have heard of his existence, and you call that a *shock*?

'Chakir turned three two months ago.'

He didn't want to hear anything of the sort. His brain scrambled over dates and calendars and what he knew of pregnancy timetables. Three years and two months—plus another nine months or so for the pregnancy, if she was speaking the truth. It was dangerously close to the time since they had last seen each other. But the boy could not be his. It could not be possible.

Except how to explain those eyes…?

He sucked in air as he strode backwards and forwards along the edge of the terrace, fingers clawing through his hair, searching for answers, finding none, only that it was impossible. Just as it was impossible to go back, to unhear what she'd told him and erase those words from his mind, even though it was what he wanted more than anything in the world.

How could it be true? He'd supposedly had a child this past three years and she'd never bothered to inform him of that fact. Why now? Unless...

'So what do you want, Marina?' he said, rounding on her. 'What are you after? Money? Is that it? You need money to fund this house and your lifestyle, and the boy's real father let you down so you saw the opportunity to lumber me with your mistake in an effort to get child support?'

Her hands fisted at her sides. 'Chakir is not a mistake! Don't you ever call *our* child a mistake!'

He pointed towards the house. 'That child is not mine. It is not possible.'

'Why, because the great and infallible Bahir says so?'

'Because I used protection! I always used protection.'

'And unplanned pregnancies only happen to people who are irresponsible, is that right? People like me? Oh, you should hear yourself, Bahir.'

'I never wanted a child!'

'No, I wasn't planning on it either—and yet this baby happened along in spite of everything we did, in spite of every precaution we took, like babies sometimes do. Maybe your gambler's brain might better understand if I put it a different way—we gambled on contraception and we lost. The baby number came up instead.'

He snorted. What did she know of gambling? Of winning and of losing? *Nothing, compared to him.* 'So you have a child. What I don't understand is why you are so desperate to pin it on me? You, who flitted from one man to another the moment I was out of your life.'

She flinched, almost as if he'd physically struck her, stung, no doubt, by the truth in his words. Yet still that defiant chin lifted and she came back fighting.

'I don't understand you, Bahir. How can you begin to doubt that he's yours? You *know* it's true. You saw yourself in his face when you looked at him. I know you did. I saw the moment you recognised it.'

'So there's a resemblance.' He shrugged, his mind scrabbling for an explanation. 'A coincidence. Nothing more. You can't be sure it's mine.'

'I can be sure, Bahir,' she said. 'Because I had just found out I was pregnant that very day I came to you, the day you chose to cut me out of your life for ever.'

'You were pregnant then?'

'I had just found out. I was nervous. Afraid. But excited too. And I thought—I'd dared to hope—that you might be a little excited too.'

'Yet you said nothing about being pregnant.'

'Because there was no point! Not once you'd told me that you weren't interested in my love and to get out of your life for ever. Not once you'd told me you didn't do family and you never wanted children, never wanted a child. Why the hell would I tell you then, when it was already too late?'

He dropped his head onto his fists, his chest heaving with the weight of today's discovery, already buckling under the weight of the memories of the past and of a day so dreadful he had tried to block it from his mind.

'So this is all my fault, is it? You neglect to pass on the fact we have a child, and somehow it's all my fault.'

She took her own sweet time to answer, standing there, looking like some wronged angel when, damn it all, she was not the wronged party here!

Then she sighed. 'No. This is not about finding fault. I'm just trying to explain why I didn't tell you, in words you might understand. You would hardly have thanked me that day if I had told you I was pregnant. You were so vehemently opposed to the idea of children, I could not share that with you. On top of everything else, I could not risk it. I could not risk you telling me what to do…'

He blinked with the realisation of her meaning. She thought he'd have insisted on a termination—was that what she'd been about to say?

He cast his mind back to that day, a day that had always been going to be bleak but a day that had grown progressively worse with the arrival of the mail, a poisoned day that had turned more toxic when she had appeared unexpected and looking like sunshine in a smile. He'd damned well near hated her in that moment. And then she'd asked him if he'd ever wanted a family and the bottom had fallen out of his world.

He'd thought he'd known her. He'd thought they understood each other. Live for the day. Take your pleasure while you could. Party on and then move on.

And it had been good. Better than good.

But then she'd surprised him by turning as needy and grasping as all the others. 'Have you ever thought about having children?' she'd asked. 'I love you,' she'd said. And his mind had turned as fetid and as poisoned as his memories.

She'd known she was pregnant even while she'd been uttering those words.

And if she'd told him that day, if he'd known, would he have insisted on a termination? God. He didn't know. He'd never considered the possibility. It had never been an issue. All he'd known was he'd never wanted a child. But seeing that boy and thinking...

He cursed. Sometimes it was better *not* to think.

'So, why tell me now, if you couldn't tell me then?' he asked, feeling sick with it all, the deceit, the lies, the shock of discovery. 'Why wait until now, nearly four years after the event, to drop this bombshell?'

She shook her head and he tried not to notice the way the ends of the layers in her long hair bobbed around her face when she moved. He hated the way the ends danced and played and caught the sunlight, as if none of this mattered. He hated that he even noticed. 'I didn't want to tell you at all,' she said. 'Not ever. I was happy for you never to know. And you'd told me you never wanted to see me again, so why would I complicate things with news you wouldn't want to hear? That's how I reasoned. But things have happened lately, and—'

'What things?'

'Like you turning up with Zoltan and the others at Mustafa's camp, for a start. I never expected that, not after you'd said you never wanted to see me ever again.'

His jaw tightened. 'I did it for Zoltan and Aisha. I would have done the same for anyone.'

She gave a soft, sad smile. 'Thank you for spelling it out so succinctly, but I'm under no illusions on that score, believe me. What you did was all about duty to your desert brothers. Just as seeing you made me realise that it was my very duty to tell you about your son, no matter how unpleasant that was going to be for both of us. You had a right to know, whether you ever wanted a child or not, whether I wanted you to know or not; it was your right as a father to know that your child existed. Why else would I have agreed to getting on that plane with you?'

'So that's how it happened?'

She paused, that tentative shadow of a smile back on her face. 'Do you really believe I would want you to be the one to escort me home? You were the last person I wanted to be with, and I knew you felt the same about me but I had no choice. How else was I supposed to tell you?'

He sucked in air. 'So Zoltan was in on it too? Did the whole world know before me?'

'No. As far as I know, he knows nothing. Only Aisha knows, and I only told her because she was the one who came up with the crazy idea. She assumed that, because we knew each other before, we'd make the perfect travelling companions. I tried to talk her out of it. In the end, I told her why it wouldn't work.'

'But then you agreed.'

'Aisha helped convince me of what I was already thinking—that you had to be told.' She bowed her head. 'Except, when I got on that plane with you, I still couldn't find the words. You were so angry and I was afraid, and it was easier not to say anything. It was easier to send you away at Pisa and forget about telling you entirely. It was easier...

'But then you insisted on driving.' She shrugged. 'Anyway, it's done now. And, in the end, it wasn't about you. Not entirely.'

'What do you mean?'

'I did it for Chakir. I did it for our son.'

He glanced towards the house. 'You really think the boy cares?'

'Maybe not now, but one day he might. One day he might want to know more about his father, about what kind of man he is. One day he might come looking for you to understand himself and try to work out his place in this world. You need to be prepared for that eventuality.'

'And that's all you want by telling me?'

'Isn't that enough for a man who never wanted a child? A man who already never wanted to see that child's mother again? But now you know. I'll leave it up to you if you want to tell your own family. And I guess…' She crossed her arms, shrugging a little. 'If, say, they wanted to meet him, or a photograph of him or something, you'll let me know?'

'They won't bother you,' he said with grim certainty. 'I know they won't.'

He sighed as he looked around at the wide expanse of view and then back up at the impressive villa. 'Nice place,' he said. *Very nice place for a woman who'd partied on her shoestring allowance for years.* 'Did your father buy it for you? For the children?'

She seemed surprised by the question, blinked and shook her head. 'No. It belongs to a good friend of mine.'

A good friend? The girl-child's father? 'How convenient,' he said.

'I guess you could say that.'

He hesitated, wondering what more there was to say. 'So, that's it, then?'

She looked up him, her arms around her belly, her eyes almost hollow. 'That's it.'

It sounded to him very much like a dismissal, one he was only too happy to accept. 'I have to go. I won't stay for lunch.'

'Yes, of course,' she said, as if she'd expected nothing less. As if she wanted nothing more than for him to be gone. 'Thank you for seeing me home. Excuse me if I don't see you to your car. I should go and see to my children.' And she turned and walked briskly away.

He'd been dismissed. He sat there, the car idling in neutral on the gravel driveway. All he had to do was put the car into first and release the handbrake and he was out of here and away down the mountainside, and he could begin the whole forget-this-ever-happened thing.

That was what he'd intended when she'd calmly walked away. Because if she could calmly walk away from this encounter, then so could he.

Except that he couldn't.

Because this time he wasn't just walking away from her. He was walking away from *him*. The boy. His child? But of course it had to be his child. Just one look in the boy's eyes and it was obvious all the paternity tests in the world would say the same thing.

That the child was his.

He'd seen his own eyes then, just as he'd seen those

of his newborn brother as he'd lain in their mother's arms, all baby wide-eyed innocence. And his father had chipped him on the chin and told him his new brother looked exactly as he had done as a baby. The same dark eyes that looked out at him from every mirror.

The same eyes he saw in the child.

His child.

He thought of his baby brother. Thought of the celebrations that had accompanied his birth, thought of the time with him he'd been cheated of when death had stolen him away with the rest of them. He thought of the amulet he'd found in the lawyer's package, the amulet that had been around his brother's neck when he had died.

And he thought of the child inside the house.

He'd never wanted a child. He'd never wanted family. Never wanted to risk losing what was so very close to him again.

And for so long it had worked. He lost nothing, and when he did, it was only money. He hated losing but it was only ever money.

But now, it seemed, he had a son. A child of his, inside that house, a house she had likely been left by the man she'd moved on to soon after leaving him, if the age of the girl was any guide. Did he want his child raised under such a roof, paid for by just another of his mother's lovers? Surely it should be his money supporting his child. It should be him providing a home to his own.

He might have abandoned all thoughts of having a family, but that did not mean he had abandoned the tenets of the life in which he had grown up.

He was a Bedouin, born and bred.

Family was everything to his people.

So how could he just walk away?

He could not. It was as if Marina had given him a child and then stolen him away in the very next breath. Paying lip service to his parentage. Letting him know like it was some mere formality. That, once she had done her duty in telling him, his role was over.

And that sat badly with him.

Very badly.

He had never wanted a child, it was true.

But now there was this boy. *Chakir*.

And curse luck, chance, happenstance or however it had happened; curse the fact that he was now inexorably tied to a woman he wanted nothing more to do with. He could not simply walk away.

Marina closed the door behind her and leaned against it, taking a deep breath as she wiped the tears from her eyes, hoping to regain some semblance of normalcy before she joined her children for lunch or they would want to know what was wrong and why she was crying.

God, if he'd stayed a moment longer she would have turned into a walking fountain out there. When he'd reminded her of Hana's mother, she'd nearly lost it. All that had kept her together was witnessing the play of expressions on his face. For one who prided himself on his poker face, it had only been too obvious what he had been thinking.

His mind had been working overtime imagining exactly what kind of 'good friend' had lent her this house.

But what of it if she had enjoyed the attentions of some rich sugar daddy? What was it to him if she had

had other lovers who bestowed upon her gifts? She couldn't imagine he had remained celibate all these years. A man of his appetites? Not a chance.

No, all he'd succeeded in doing was giving her all the more reason to be glad he was gone.

And she'd needed that.

Her duty was now done. Bahir knew the truth and it was up to him to deal with it. No doubt, knowing him, he'd disappear back into denial and pretend today's news had never happened.

One could only hope.

She blinked and swiped at her cheeks one final time. It was time to get on with her life.

Time to move on.

Time to put to bed once and for all any forlorn and pathetic hope that Bahir might one day change his mind. How much plainer could he make it that he'd only turned up at Mustafa's desert camp site because Zoltan and his friends had been there? How much plainer could he make his position than by his rapid exit once he'd been confronted with the existence of their son?

Bahir was history. He had no part in her life. Not for the last four years. Not now. Maybe it was time to fully accept that.

From the kitchen came the sound of Catriona serving up lunch to two hungry toddlers, and she smiled softly. It was Bahir's loss that he had turned his back on his child and walked away. Not hers.

She would not let it be hers.

The knock on the door came as they were finishing lunch. A sizzle of premonition down her spine came with it. *Surely not?*

'I'll go,' said Catriona, watching her face, missing nothing.

'No,' she said rising from her seat where she'd been overseeing Hana feed herself. 'I should go.'

'And if it's him?'

Marina gave a smile she didn't come close to feeling. Catriona had asked nothing since she'd returned, though there were questions in her eyes, questions the woman wouldn't ask until the children were asleep and they would have time to talk properly.

'Then he'll want to see me anyway.'

The knock on the door came again, louder and more insistent this time. And something in that knock told Marina that she didn't need to see who it was to know.

'Are you sure?' Catriona asked, collecting plates and keeping her voice light as if nothing was wrong, blessedly keeping the atmosphere in the kitchen on an even keel when Marina's world felt like it was teetering on the edge of a precipice. But the local village woman had a real talent for smoothing the atmosphere, Marina acknowledged, thinking back to when they'd both nursed Sarah those last few months, and how even at the end she'd kept the household together when they could so easily have all fallen apart.

'I'm sure. Don't worry, I'll be right back. It's probably just someone from the village.'

She knew she was kidding herself—anyone from the village would know to come to the kitchen door—even before she pulled open the heavy timber door.

'Bahir,' she acknowledged, stepping out and closing the door behind her as premonition turned to fear. One look in his eyes told her she needed to put as many barriers as she could between this man and her children. For when he'd left, he'd looked like a man defeated, as if he'd had the stuffing knocked out of him. But now he seemed taller and more powerful than ever and, with the cold, hard gleam in his eyes and the resolute set of his jaw, he looked more like a warrior. He looked like the real battle had not yet begun.

Her mouth went dry. He wasn't back because he'd changed his mind about lunch. 'Was there something else?'

'You could say that,' he said, and the chilling note of his delivery made her blood run cold. 'I've come for my son.'

It took a while for the words to register. 'I don't understand,' she said finally, finding no sense in the words; no sense that eased the turmoil inside her. 'What do you mean you've *come* for him?'

'It's quite simple, really. You've had our son to your-self for three years. Now it's my turn.'

CHAPTER SIX

'No,' she managed, her entire body in denial. *'No!'*

'You see,' he continued, as if she hadn't uttered a word, let alone that particular one, 'I've decided it's not enough for me to be some kind of absentee father. If the child is mine, as you are so happy to attest, then I have a responsibility as his father to see that he is raised properly.'

'He is being raised properly! Did he look to you like he is being neglected or is suffering in any way? What are you trying to prove, Bahir? What do you really want?'

'I told you. I want my son!'

She glanced at the house behind her, wondering if Catriona and the children could hear them arguing from inside. 'There's no need to shout,' she warned him, before heading across the crazy-paved terrace, her arms tightly bound beneath her breasts.

'Did you hear me?' he said behind her, his voice lower now but no less menacing. 'I want my son.'

'No. This is madness. You're just angry. You're lashing out, merely wanting some kind of pay-back. Because you can't be serious.'

'I'm perfectly serious. You must have considered the

possibility when you hatched this plan to tell me I was his father that I might actually want a hand in raising my own child?'

She blinked, momentarily struck dumb, because she'd never given a moment's thought to the possibility. It was too fantastical; too unlikely. *Too impossible.* She spun around, hoping he would see the truth of her argument in her eyes. 'But you never wanted children! You were so vehemently opposed to the idea that I was too afraid to tell you I was even pregnant. And now you're telling me that you want a hand in raising him?'

'It's true, I never wanted a child. But what I wanted is irrelevant now, wouldn't you say? Because that child exists. That child is here, and he is mine, just as much as he is yours!'

'But you can't just walk in here and demand your son like he is some kind of package—like a possession to be passed around to whoever it is whose *turn* you perceive it to be.'

'Why not?'

'Because he is not a parcel to be handed from one person to another! He is a child. And because I won't let you take my son.'

He laughed, a short, harsh sound. 'Your son? You seem to have a short memory, princess. Such a short time ago you seemed determined to tell me the boy was mine.'

'He is your son, but you would be no kind of father to him.'

'Has anyone given me the opportunity? How can you be a father to a child you do not know exists?'

'You didn't want to know. You didn't want a child.'

'But the boy is here!'

'His name is not "the boy". His name is Chakir!'

He grunted. 'Something else I was not given a hand in! What other things have you decided for our child, princess? Have you already chosen a school for him? Perhaps he is already enrolled? Have you already procured for him a rich and wealthy bride?'

'Don't be ridiculous.'

'Yes,' he said, his face twisted, his strong features contorted. 'It *is* ridiculous to have to ask when, as the boy's father, I should already know these things. I should have been given a say in such decisions.'

She shook her head, determined not to give ground, no matter how shaky it felt beneath her. 'I didn't think you'd be interested. I didn't think you'd care, given you'd made your position crystal-clear.'

'And so you neglected to tell me he'd even been born!'

She kicked up her chin. 'You didn't want to see me again. I got the impression that meant for any reason.'

'And that…' he paused, the look in his dark eyes damning '…is your pathetic excuse for denying me the knowledge of my own son's existence? That's your excuse for secreting him away for three years?

'And now you think it gives you the right to keep him for ever and only offer me some token parental right, in case one day he might want to look me up?' His chest heaving, he turned and strode away to the balustrade, where the land dipped steeply away below and the valleys and mountains formed his backdrop.

Such a majestic backdrop, she thought, that a mere man should fade into insignificance. No man had a

right to look majestic before such a sight. But this man
did. He was tall and broad like the mountains themselves, and just as impossible to scale, his true self just
as unconquerable and as dangerously unattainable as
the mountains' dizzy heights.

And last night—no, this very morning—he had
taken her to such dizzy heights with the magic of his
mouth and his wicked tongue and she had tasted herself in his kiss…

She shivered. Now this same mouth, lips and tongue
told her he wanted to take Chakir. *Her son.* Why would
he want to do this other than out of spite? Because he
felt slighted? But how could she make him see it, he
who was as stubborn and impossible to move as that
range of mountains behind him? How was she supposed to fight him?

'It doesn't give you that right,' he said, spinning
around, and she blinked and had to rewind the conversation to catch up. 'And now it's time for his father to
exercise some of his rights. I want to take the boy home.'

'Home?' She shook her head. When they had been
together they had lived in a succession of apartments
and hotel rooms always within range of the casino of
choice. 'I didn't know you had a home.'

'I am planning to visit the home of my fathers in
Jaqbar. I want the boy to come with me. I want to show
him the land where his father was raised.'

Jaqbar? Shock punched the air from her lungs. He
couldn't have surprised her more if he'd said he wanted
to take him to Monte Carlo and teach him all he knew
about gambling, for there was nothing in Jaqbar but
endless desert. 'You want to take him somewhere out

in the desert? You must be insane! You can't take him there! He's just a child.'

'He is my child. And the desert is his home.'

'No, *this* is his home. The only home he knows. Besides, you don't know the first thing about children. You wouldn't know how to raise one properly if they came with a manual, let alone out in some desert somewhere. I won't let you take him. I won't let you take him anywhere.'

'Then I won't give you a choice. We will take this to court if that's the way you prefer to play it, princess. Imagine the fun the tabloids could have with that little custody battle: *Party Girl Princess Steals Baby.* Your father would be so proud of his firstborn daughter on reading that.'

She swallowed, the picture he painted too vivid, the consequences too great. For the first time since the onset of her rebellious adolescent years there were the fragile beginnings of a decent father-daughter relationship between the King and her. He still would never understand the circumstances of her becoming mother to not one, but two illegitimate children. That had been her fault too, for never wanting to reveal the truth, but they were at last coming to some kind of decent relationship.

She could not bear it if that fledgling relationship were threatened. And it was so unfair! 'I never stole Chakir!'

'No. You just stole three years of my child's life from me. His first steps; his first words; his first smile. Did you celebrate his birthdays? I hope you enjoyed them.' He glared at her. 'Enjoyed them enough for the both of us.'

His words bit deep, the accusations hitting home. All those milestones she'd enjoyed and celebrated, she had never once realised were in fact crimes against the absent father. 'You didn't want a child,' she said, more like a whimper, in her crumbling defence.

'You didn't give me a choice!'

'I tried,' she said. 'Don't you think I tried? Don't you remember that day?'

'I remember you asking if I wanted a child. I said no. I don't remember you telling me you were already pregnant.'

She wound hands through her hair, twisting it so tightly it pulled on her scalp, welcoming the pain in the hopes it might blot out some of the emotional pain. But it was futile. 'So we can work something out,' she said, scrabbling for solutions. 'Maybe you could visit some weekends or go out for the day? There's a market every Tuesday in Fivizzano, the village at the foot of the mountain, and there's always the beach at La Spezia. It's not far.'

'Or there's a court in Rome where I will be given full custody of my son when I tell them how unsuitable you are to be a mother to my child.'

Was he serious? He'd actually fight her in court for custody? Her jaw dropped open, her mind stunned by the lengths he would resort to. But who was he kidding? Did he really imagine himself the model father? 'You really believe for one moment that they would give custody to you, a man who has spent most of his life in front of a roulette wheel? A man who doesn't even own a home? Not even the famed Sheikh of Spin could find a positive *spin* in your reputation. You'd be laughed out of court.'

He swatted away her protest with one hand like he was swatting at an annoying insect. 'Then maybe we should put it to the test. Which one of us, I wonder, has the most to lose in going public?'

'You bastard!' she snapped. For there was no question in her mind which one of them would come off worst. She could not risk the exposure and the inevitable muckraking that would follow. And she could not risk anyone uncovering the truth about Hana when she had promised Sarah she would not tell.

Oh God, what if they took Hana? What if she lost them both?

Tears pricked at her eyes. How could he do this to her? Was his need for revenge so great? Did he hate her so very much? 'You wouldn't do it,' she whispered, hoping he would realise he was costing her even just in his threats. 'You couldn't.'

'Of course I would, if you continue to try to keep my child from me.'

'Bahir, please,' she said, shaking her head. 'Don't do this. You can't take him. He doesn't know you.'

'Whose fault is that? Not mine. He will come with me to the desert. I will teach him how to ride and how to hunt. I will teach him the ways of his Bedouin forefathers.'

'But he's just a baby. He's barely three years old. He's too young for such a trip.'

'I was born in a tent in the desert! I grew up there. How, then, can he be too young?'

She couldn't take any more in. She was beyond

stunned—already punch-drunk and reeling from the emotional roller-coaster she had been on for the last twenty-four hours—but this latest piece of news sent her mind spinning. She had spent months with this man and never once had he hinted at his origins. But when had they ever spent their time talking? In the dizzy heights of their relationship, nothing had mattered beyond the two of them and their own private sensual world, filled with the taking and giving of pleasure, and it was only now, when their relationship was already ancient history, that she was gleaning any insight into his past.

But that still didn't mean he could take her son away from her.

'Don't do this,' she said. 'You can't expect to just take Chakir away from me and off to some desert somewhere. You don't know the first thing about children and you're a stranger to him. He would be terrified. And it would be irresponsible of me, as a mother, to simply hand him over to you and let you take him.'

He said nothing, his eyes savage, his jaw grinding together, taking his time as if weighing up the truth in her words. Time she couldn't afford to waste.

'You see,' she argued, 'it won't work. He wouldn't go with you. It would be inhuman do that to him.'

'Fine,' he said at last. 'We'll do it your way. I want the two of you packed and ready to leave by ten tomorrow.'

'The two of us?'

'Of course,' he said, looking at his watch as if suddenly bored with the conversation. 'If it will be so problematic—if the child will not come by himself—then clearly you will just have to come too.'

'No, Bahir,' she said, reeling again from this latest twist. 'That's not what I meant.'

'On the contrary, I think it's an excellent solution.'

'You're forgetting Hana.'

'No. Not the girl,' he said with disdain, as if the topic was closed. 'She stays.'

'I'm not going anywhere with Chakir and leaving Hana behind. I will not leave any child of mine behind.'

'Since when? You, the wonderful mother, seemed only too happy to leave your children at home when you gallivanted off alone to their aunt's wedding.'

'You think I should have dragged them out of their sick beds to go to a wedding half a dozen countries away?'

'Chakir was unwell?'

'They both were, with chicken pox. I wasn't going to bother going to the wedding at all except Catriona insisted I should go. They were both over the worst by then and she said she'd cope. Only now...'

'Only now, what?'

Only now she wished she hadn't gone at all. If she'd stayed at home she wouldn't have stumbled into Mustafa's path and needed rescuing. She wouldn't have needed an escort home and this nightmare wouldn't be happening now.

She sucked in air. It *was* happening and somehow she had to deal with it, somehow she had to find a way through, one that didn't involve him calling all the shots.

One that maybe involved calling his bluff.

'Only nothing.' She looked up at him, fired with new resolve. There was a risk, of course, that she could lose everything with this tactic, but she sensed there would always be a risk where this man was concerned. Far better the one that she accepted than the one he imposed on her.

'Nothing at all. But I tell you this, Bahir. We are a family—Chakir, Hana and me—and I will not leave Hana again so soon. I will not do that to my daughter. Either she comes, or none of us do. And if you don't like it, you can abandon any plans of taking Chakir anywhere, and you can take me to court. And don't expect it to be easy, because I will fight you every step of the way.

'And you can feed whatever twisted, sordid little stories you like to the press and let's just see who ends up with custody when they discover that you have nothing; that you're just a gambler with no home and no life outside of the casino. Who in their right mind would award such a man custody of a child? What kind of father could he ever be?

'So take me to court if that's what you must do, and I will wear the consequences, but don't think you can make blanket decisions that concern *my* family and expect me to blindly fall in with them!'

In the end they all went, including Catriona, who had offered to accompany them, an offer Marina had been only too happy to accept. It wasn't just having someone to help keep an eye the children that she was grateful for, it was having someone along who could be both chaperone and the voice of wisdom should Bahir's constant presence turn her thoughts more carnal—or, worse still, made her think that Bahir might somehow manage to fit into their small family on a more permanent basis. Catriona was no fool. They had had a long heart-to-heart last night while she had explained exactly how the land lay. Catriona would soon talk sense into her if she looked like wavering.

Bahir grunted as he loaded the last of the bags and she handed him a hamper of snacks for the children. 'What have you told the boy?' he asked.

'I've told them that we're going on a holiday. What did you expect me to tell them?'

'You didn't tell him—who I am?'

'I think it's a bit premature for that, don't you? Maybe you might try getting to know him a little first.'

She wandered off as Catriona and the children arrived and he watched the women buckle the wriggling children into their car seats, the older woman climbing up alongside them. That addition to their party had taken him by surprise, but now he was quite happy she was coming. She could look after the girl.

'Where are we going?' asked the boy as Bahir climbed into the driver's seat of the big four-wheel drive. 'What's it called again?'

'Jaqbar,' he said, looking at the child in his rear-vision mirror, noticing for the first time the fading marks on his gold-olive skin. The girl had them too, peeking out from under her dark fringe and on her cheeks. If he had noticed them earlier he would probably have assumed they were mosquito bites. So Marina had been telling the truth about their illness? He hadn't known whether to believe her or whether she'd been trying to shore up that 'good mother' myth that she liked to espouse.

'Is it far?' the boy asked.

'We'll be there in time for dinner,' his mother said.

'So long?'

'Don't forget,' she added, 'there's a plane ride first.'

'I like planes,' Chakir said, as the car headed down the mountain. 'I like it when they take off. Whoosh!' And his hand took off into the air.

Beside him the girl giggled hysterically, pulling her thumb out of her mouth to make her own hand plane. 'Whooth!' And she fell into another burst of giggles.

He caught Marina's sideways glance, and sensed she was wondering how long he would cope with all this. He merely smiled as he pulled to the side to let the blue village bus heading the other way squeeze past. The girl he could do without, it was true, but he'd be damned he was going to let Marina think he could be no kind of father for his own child. He might be a gambler, but he was a professional one, who had made millions from his work. Why should that make him a bad father? He would enjoy proving that he could be the father his son needed.

After all, if she could surprise him with her strength last night in arguing her own case, then he could only return the favour. And she had surprised him, he reflected. He hadn't figured on her fighting back. He'd witnessed her arguments crumbling beneath the weight of her guilt—he'd witnessed her almost defeat—and he'd had her in the palm of his hand.

But then he'd told her the girl wasn't invited and she'd transformed into some kind of lioness defending a prized cub, willing to do anything to do so. And why? What was it with the girl? Why was she so special? Because her father had been special to Marina? Was he the one who owned this house?

He growled at the thought of another man making love to Marina while his child lay neglected in his cot nearby.

So much for all her declarations of undying love.

They landed in the heat of Souza, Jaqbar's capital, shortly before six. 'We stay here tonight,' Bahir said as they transferred to a private villa on a palm-studded resort, the air cooled by the spray from a hundred dancing fountains. 'Tomorrow we journey out to the desert, so you might want to take advantage of the pool. There's not a lot of water where we're going.'

'Where are you going?' asked Chakir, with a child's curiosity. He watched the boy's mother warn him with her eyes, but the boy was having none of it. 'Aren't you coming for a swim too?'

'Chakir,' his mother admonished. 'It's not polite to ask so many questions.'

On the contrary, he liked that the boy was bold and not afraid to ask him questions. 'It's fine,' he said, putting a hand to the boy's head—his *son's* head—only to be hit with a sudden jolt of a long buried memory of his father doing the same to him. His long robes had flapped in the desert wind, his face leathery and lined by the sun, his eyes overflowing with love. And for a moment he was rendered speechless. He blinked, clearing his vision of the memories, seeing his dark-eyed son studying him intently.

He smiled. 'I have some things to organise for the morning, to ensure your camping holiday is the very best one it can be. Maybe later I will be back in time for a swim.'

'We're actually camping?'

'That's right. Just like I did, when I was a boy.' Although the tents he had secured were a far cry from the basic squat black tents he remembered as a child. He would not have Marina say he could not provide for his son. He looked over at her now, to where she stood silently watching with something like fear in her eyes. 'We do want this holiday to be perfect, don't we?'

CHAPTER SEVEN

THEY were all in the smaller children's pool when he returned, the children splashing in the shallow water clutching their pool toys, the women close by, ready to reach out a supportive hand if one of the children slipped.

He glanced for a moment at his son, but it was to Marina his eyes were drawn. She was seemingly shrink-wrapped in a red one-piece that showed her long, golden-skinned limbs to full advantage, her black hair restrained in a thick long ponytail that hung, luxuriant, down her back like a heavy cord of silk.

That patch of lycra might have been more than she'd worn two night ago when she'd lain naked and open to him on his bed, but somehow it was also less. For it only accentuated what he knew lay beneath, every glorious curve, every intoxicating dizzy peak, every dip and every dark secret place, so that even now his hands itched to reach out for her, even now his body stirred.

Damn.

She chose that moment to look up and she stilled as their eyes connected, the air between them shimmering, heavy with expectation. Expectation for what? She'd been the one to walk out on him the other night. She'd been the one to walk away. And all ostensibly because he'd implied that she was irresponsible.

Okay, so one of her illegitimate children was his and he might have some responsibility to shoulder for Chakir. But to fall pregnant again so quickly after the birth of his child with another? Hadn't she learned anything?

If not irresponsibility, it smacked of carelessness at the very least.

Was that why she looked at him that way, then, with her eyes like neon signs atop a seedy nightclub promising untold pleasures of the flesh? Because she simply couldn't help herself? Because she looked at every man that way?

He cursed under his breath. She had no right to look at him that way! He balled his towel in his hands and flung it to a nearby lounger before striding to the end of the lap pool. Right now he could do with a cool down, and it had nothing to do with the temperature.

'Bahir!' he heard his son call just before he hit the water. He just kept right on swimming.

Marina sat with her son at the end of the pool waiting for Bahir to finish churning through the water on his seemingly endless laps. But she didn't mind how long he took. First, his preoccupation with his laps had given her the chance to cover herself with her sarong. Something about the way his gaze had raked her body had told her that she needed every bit of protection from his eyes that she could get. Secondly, it had afforded her the time to breathe.

And she had needed the time to remember how to breathe.

For the sight of him dressed in nothing more than a pair of swimming trunks and staring at her like he had done two nights ago just before his head had dipped between her legs had damn near shorted her brain.

It was only luck that he'd dived into the pool when he had or she would still be blindly staring—*wishing...*

The water this end of the pool churned as Bahir's powerful arms sliced a path through and Marina assumed he was about to tumble-turn yet again before powering back the other direction when instead he took another stroke and glided into the wall.

He came up heaving for air, spinning droplets from his hair with a flick of his head as her son—*their son*—jumped up and down at the edge of the pool.

'You swim so fast,' he said in unrestrained awe, and the hero worship in his voice almost broke Marina's heart. He had no heroes in his life, she realised, no male role models close enough to them to make an impact. She bit down on her lip, guilt weighing heavily upon guilt.

Bahir hauled his body from the pool with an ease that belied the work his arms had just done, and she had to force herself to look away and not stare in wonder. 'I bet you can swim faster,' he said to the boy, grabbing his towel and pressing his face into it. 'I'll give you a race right now, if you like.'

Chakir's face crumpled. He shook his head. 'I...' he started, his expression stricken as he struggled with the confession, 'I can't swim.'

'Why not?' His words, intended for the child, were

gentle enough. The black look, on the other hand, was directed squarely at the mother.

She took her son's hand. 'Chakir had a fright when he was two. We thought we'd wait until he was ready before having any more lessons.'

Bahir knelt down and regarded the boy eye-to-eye, a frown marring his patrician brow. 'Is that so?' He looked back at the expanse of inviting pool behind him. 'Tell you what, how about I give you a lesson right now? I bet before you know it, you'll be racing me.'

His eyes opened wide and Marina could see excitement blended with the fear. 'You'd give me a lesson?'

'Of course,' he said, 'but only if you think you're ready.'

Chakir looked uncertainly at his mother. 'Maybe in the shallow pool,' she suggested, trying to encourage.

'But Mama,' he said, puffing out his chest, 'you can't swim there. Not really. Everyone knows that.' She wanted to smile at how brave her boy was being.

'Don't worry,' Bahir said, already leading the boy to the shallow end of the lap pool. 'I'll take good care of him.'

Marina watched on nervously. How would he know how to take good care of a child? He knew nothing of children. But then, as she watched him getting Chakir to kick holding onto the edge of the pool, and showing him how he could relax and float on his back to gain confidence in the water, reluctantly she was forced to acknowledge that he was taking good care of him. When he managed to get him to put his face under the water by himself, she knew it. By the end of the lesson her son even managed to take a few tentative and haphazard freestyle strokes as Bahir supported his body in the water.

As she watched father and son working together, she felt besieged by guilt that she had kept them apart all these years. But there was something more beyond that feeling of guilt, something fragile that bloomed inside her. Something precious that she did not want to put form to, just to feel it was enough.

'Did you see me, Mama?' Chakir said proudly after the lesson was over, running up to his mother, surrounded in plush towel, clutching it at his chin, his teeth chattering in excitement. 'I was swimming!'

'I saw you, Chakir,' she said, embracing him in her arms. 'I'm so proud of you!'

'And I'm having another lesson tomorrow before we leave.'

She shook her head. 'Are you sure he said that? I don't know if there will be time.'

'I'll make time,' Bahir said, catching up with the boy. Once again he was there before her in his swimming trunks and nothing else and this time he was dripping wet. She swallowed, trying not to notice the chest hairs plastered against his skin, forming whorls and patterns. She tried and failed not to notice as they coalesced into a single dark line that trailed southwards to circle his navel before venturing still lower towards those fitted black trunks.

'It's no trouble,' he added. She looked up, her face burning, knowing it was all kinds of trouble trying to think clearly while confronted with such a perfect masculine specimen, especially when your eye was level with his navel.

'Thank you,' she said, standing up as Chakir ran off to tell his sister Catriona was collecting up their things. 'That was good of you.'

He shrugged. 'The boy should know how to swim.'

'But how on earth did you know where to start? You've had nothing to do with children.'

'My father taught me.' And then, before she could pursue that revelation, he asked, 'What happened to him? Why was he so afraid?'

She clutched her arms as she watched her son now showing Hana how to swim, his arms making windmills in the air, and she wondered that Bahir had been able to make such a difference in one short lesson.

'He was just starting to gain some confidence when a boy—the local bully—jumped into the pool while Chakir had his face under the water. I think he only meant to scare him, but Chakir moved and he landed on his back and pushed him right under. He could have drowned.'

She shivered, remembering that day, remembering the panic as his instructor had pulled her lifeless child from the water and she had watched him pump his chest until he had coughed and spluttered and spewed out half the pool.

She sensed him stiffen beside her and turned to see his eyes bleak and cold. 'And then I never would have got to meet my son.'

'No,' she said, realising she'd just racked up one more black mark against her name—but what was one more in her already long list of transgressions? 'I guess not. And now, if you'll excuse me, I must go and help

Catriona with the children. Apparently we have an early start in the morning.'

He watched her go, watching the way her ponytail swayed from side to side with every step, drawing attention to and accentuating the feminine motion of her hips under the sarong she'd wrapped around herself like a suit of armour. It would take more than that for him to not be able to imagine her naked beneath. He watched her go, hating himself for needing to watch.

She must be a sorceress, he wagered, if he could at times hate her with every fibre of his being yet at the same time lust for her so desperately that to throw her to the ground and bury himself deep inside her would not be quick enough.

She had to be.

They did start early, but not too early that Chakir could not have another swimming lesson before their departure. He was full of it as the four-wheel drive headed out of the city and into the wide desert lands, boasting that he would soon be fast enough to beat Bahir.

The motion of the vehicle along the desert highway soon had the two children sleeping in the back seat, Catriona snoozing alongside.

'You handle it well,' Marina said as the car powered through a wide, flat valley, a range of red mountains rising from the rock-strewn desert floor on either side.

'Handle what well?' he asked.

'Chakir and his ambitions to beat you.'

He shrugged a shoulder, his wide brown hands slung seemingly casually over the steering wheel, his eyes alert and constantly scanning the desert ahead for hazards. 'It is good to be ambitious.'

'I'm surprised, that's all. That you take it so good-naturedly.'

'He is a child with a child's sense that nothing is impossible and that everything is attainable, even the stars. I have no doubt I was much the same. Once.'

His words piqued her interest. 'Only once? You don't think that any more?'

'Let's just say I learned the hard way that there are some things the universe will not give you, no matter how much you wish for them.'

'What do you mean?'

He smiled then, if you could call it a smile. 'And you worry that our son asks too many questions.'

'I'm sorry,' she said, falling silent, but not only because of his gentle rebuke. It was the use of the term 'our son' that had stilled her tongue.

Not 'the boy' or 'my son' but 'our son.'

And she surprised herself by liking the sound of it on his tongue, a sound that lit a candle of hope inside her that this did not have to end badly—that they did not have to resort to a heated custody battle, but could forge some kind of truce for the sake of their son.

'He likes you,' she said, musing out loud. 'Especially after the swimming lessons. I think you've made a conquest.'

'Good. I like him too.' He took his eyes from the road again to look at her, and this time they were filled almost with respect. 'You have done a good job with him. He is a fine boy.'

The flickering flame inside her burned a little

brighter. It wouldn't last, she knew enough to know that. Sooner or later she would do or say something that would remind him of the sins she had committed against him and the walls of hostility would rise up between them once again. But right now it was nice not to be at war.

They stopped for a picnic lunch at a tiny oasis, little more than a well and a few hardy palms shading a crumbling mud-brick shelter.

'It's hot,' declared Chakir on climbing from the air-conditioned vehicle into the stifling desert air, then proceeding almost immediately to chase his sister around the well until their picnic was ready, as if totally oblivious to the heat.

'Did someone live here once?' he asked when he had finally collapsed down onto the picnic rug, gasping but ready to eat. He pointed towards the crumbling hut. 'In that building?'

'No,' Bahir answered. 'At least, not all the time. It's a shelter, for shepherds and other travellers passing through. Somewhere protected from the elements when herding sheep and goats on the coldest of nights, and somewhere to take shelter when the dust storms blow in and turn the sky black in the middle of the day.'

Chakir's eyes opened wide. 'Have you ever seen a dust storm?'

'Yes. When I was a boy. The sand blotted out the sun and it was so dark I could not see my hand in front of my face.'

'Were you here for a holiday too?'

'No. I grew up here. Or, not far from here.'

Chakir looked around. 'How could anyone live here, in the desert?'

His father smiled. 'When we get to the camp, I will show you.'

'Will you show me too?' Hana asked, breathless and fascinated and clearly determined not to miss out. 'Please.'

Marina watched the shutters come down in Bahir's eyes. 'I'd like very much to hear too,' she said, adding her support to the chorus. 'We both would, wouldn't we, Hana?'

This time Bahir had no choice but to nod. 'Of course.'

'Why do you do that?' Marina asked later as they loaded the last of the picnic things in the back of the car. 'Why do you answer Chakir's questions in such detail and yet barely grunt when Hana asks something?'

'Do I?'

'You know you do! I know Chakir is the reason we're here, but there is no need to treat Hana as if she doesn't exist.'

'I don't know what you're talking about.'

'I'm talking about the way you try to ignore her.'

'I told you not to bring the girl.'

'And I told you it was all of us or none.'

'Well, you got what you wanted, then. She's here, isn't she?'

'So don't treat her as if she isn't. She's Chakir's sister, whether you like it or not.'

'So maybe I don't.' He climbed into the driver's seat and slammed the door.

She hated him in that moment, hated him with every fibre of her being. Not that he would care. He didn't want anything from her, apart from her son. And now she half-regretted coming. The warm satisfaction of seeing father and son together was waning, for instead of filling a space in her family and providing a father figure for Chakir, the way he was acting could soon drive a wedge between her two children.

It was so unfair, so unjust. Hana had suffered enough in her short life. She deserved happiness too.

And, because she felt like she should make up for his indifference, she caught the girl as she ran puffing up to the car after her brother and swept her up in her arms, spinning her around. Hana squealed and wriggled but she held firm. 'I love you, Hana Banana,' she said, using her pet name for her. 'Never forget that, okay?'

The toddler stopped her wriggling for a moment to hold her jaw in her small hands to kiss her. Her blue-black eyes looked solemnly down at her. 'I love you too, Mummy.' Then she giggled and squirmed to be free.

Very touching, he thought, unable to avoid watching the performance in his side mirror, knowing it was all for his benefit, knowing it was all so false.

For what did she know of love really? She was as fickle and changeable as the desert wind, changing direction and blowing from one man to the next with just as little reason.

No, she knew nothing of love.

The girl proved it.

A herd of ibex scattered as the car topped a rise, the horned goats scampering and leaping at speed in all directions, thrilling Chakir and Hana. Below them lay the camp site, a collection of large tents set around another, more welcoming-looking oasis.

'Wow! Is that where you live?' Chakir asked from the back seat.

'No,' Bahir answered. 'We moved around a lot when I was a boy, but this is not far away from one of the places we camped.' He would not go to that place, now just an empty patch of desert. But a patch of desert that held too many memories and where the mournful wind carried the cries of too many lost souls.

'Are your family there?' Marina asked, a sudden tightness to her voice. When he turned his head he saw she was clutching a pendant at her throat, her eyes filled with fear. Was she worried they would recognise the family resemblance and let the cat out of the bag before she was ready for Chakir to find out the truth about his father? Or was she worried they might try to kidnap Chakir and keep him here for ever?

Whatever, she had no cause for concern. The only people in the camp were those his old friend Ahab had organised to help with their visit, brought in from one of the remaining tribes that still managed to live a simple Bedouin lifestyle despite the call of the modern world.

The simple Bedouin lifestyle, he reminded himself, that he had turned his back on.

'No. They're—not here.' He watched the tension around her expressive eyes ease as she relaxed back against her seat, and he drank in her profile: her dark, lash-framed eyes, her lush sinner's mouth. He wondered why she had to be so beautiful that at times he almost ached to look at her.

He turned away, unable to answer his own question. Not sure he even wanted to try.

The camp grew busier as they neared and their approach was noticed—not 'New York' frenetically busier, or 'Monte Carlo' flourishingly dramatically busier, but *Bedouin* busier, where every movement was purposeful and halfway to poetic. Robed figures swayed rhythmically across the sands, gathering at a point where their vehicle stopped, an impossibly old-looking man at their helm.

Ahab, he realised with surprise as he pulled the vehicle to a halt. He was not arrow-straight as he had always been, but stooped and frail, his face creased with age, his hair bleached whiter than the sands. And it gave him cause to wonder anew about just how long he had been gone. Years he had been away, years that had melded into one long absence, years that knew no numbers.

'Ahab,' he said, alighting from the car to air that brought him up with a jolt, air made of the timeless scent of the desert flavoured with the scent of herbs and roasting meat. Air that made him remember so much that it was a moment before he could embrace his old friend's bony frame. 'It is good to see you.'

'You have come, Bahir,' the old man said, tears squeezing from his eyes. 'You have come home at last.'

Something heavy shifted inside him, like the slide of a weighted box across the deck of a ship in a rolling sea. Uncomfortable. Disarming. He waited, half-anticipating whatever it was to slide back the other direction and right itself, but it stuck fast. When he blinked and told himself to ignore it, Marina and Catriona had the children out of the car and Ahab was smiling down at them through watery eyes.

'Welcome,' he said, after Bahir had introduced the small party, his gaze lingering on Chakir for just a moment longer than it needed to, just a moment that told Bahir that the old man had recognised in an instant what he had so pointlessly tried to deny. 'There is a feast being prepared in honour of your visit, but first I will show you to your tents and then we will sit and have tea.'

Hana and Chakir squealed with delight when shown the interior of the tent they were to occupy. Their low beds were covered with cushions in every bright colour imaginable. The floor was lined with rugs on which sat a toy camp site, complete with tents, camels and tiny people.

Marina was tempted to squeal herself when she saw the room partitioned off for her, lined with silk wall-hangings and the finest, softest carpets with bronze lamps atop carved timber side tables. And the bed? It was every little girl's fantasy but a grown-up version—decorated with sumptuous fabrics in rich jewel colours, bold and beautiful, and surrounded by filmy curtains. A bed fit for a harem. And such a big bed for one.

She thought wistfully about what it would be like to wake up in such a bed in a Bedouin tent in the middle of the desert, in the arms of a Bedouin lover after a night of earth-shattering love-making and with the promise of more to come.

That would make much better use of such a bed.

Her two children burst into the room, wanting to check out her room. Chakir whooped when he saw her bed and launched himself across the room to dive onto it between a gap in the curtains, with Hana in gleeful hot pursuit, her short legs struggling fruitlessly to make the final leap.

She laughed and picked up the squealing girl and jumped onto the bed alongside Chakir, tickling the two of them until tears streamed from their eyes and they begged her to stop. Then she curled her arms around each of her children and they lay there panting, in the big wide curtained bed.

No, she thought as she kissed each of her children on the head, their hair tickling her nose. Such a big bed was not such a waste. Not at all.

They had time to be shown around the camp before the hour designated for their formal welcome, and Hana and Chakir ran gaily from one tent to the next, a clutch of children accompanying them, accepting them in their midst.

But it was the animals that fascinated them the most: the camels and horses the tribe used now for sport rather than transport, and a herd of local goats, black-haired and horned, their new kids bounding in delight. Hana was so entranced with the newborns, it was almost impossible to drag her away.

Soon after, Ahab formally welcomed them at the tea ceremony, the handing over of each cup to their guests an offer of friendship and welcome. Ahab bestowed a special honour on the children, solemnly placing a necklace bearing a pendant of a stylised eye over each child's head.

'What is it?' she whispered to Bahir.

'A token,' he said through a tight throat, unable to

bring himself to believe. 'To ward off the evil eye and keep them safe.' He knew better. Nothing could keep a child safe if the fates chose to take it.

But both children accepted their tokens with the solemnity the ceremony called for, and then the formal part of the ceremony was over and a smattering of children amongst the tribespeople soon drew Chakir and Hana into their games.

As afternoon slipped into evening, they moved to a circle of seats under the darkening sky where a camp fire was already blazing and where three musicians were plucking tunes on their stringed instruments or beating time with their drums. Here they feasted from the endless platters of spiced meats and roasted vegetables, followed by rose-scented sweets washed down with thick, sweet coffee.

It was the perfect evening, Marina thought as she watched her children playing and making new friends, while the air was filled with scented wood-smoke and a haunting song that seemed to expand to fill the landscape.

She watched Bahir talk to Ahab at his side, and she wondered about this place Bahir had brought them to. Wondered again about his family and why they were not here to greet him, when others like Ahab had openly welcomed him home.

Why had he never shared the details of his past?

A bundle of waning energy landed heavily in her lap, short-circuiting her thoughts—Hana, giving up on the game, panting and breathless, her eyelids struggling to remain open.

She cradled the child in her lap, stroking her hair

back from her face. 'Are you tired, Hana Banana? Do you want to go to bed?'

'No,' the toddler said emphatically, rubbing one eye with her fist. 'Not tired.'

'I know,' Marina said, smiling, rocking the child gently in her arms, knowing the exact moment she fell asleep, her head lolling back. She leaned down and pressed her lips to Hana's cheek, thinking of her mother in that moment and wishing that she could be here, a tear sliding unbidden down her cheek.

Mother and child, Bahir thought, listening with one ear to what Ahab had to say, but fully intent on her with the sleeping child in her lap. How could a woman look sexy cradling a child that was not even his? But somehow she managed it. She still had the power to make him burn.

He nodded to Ahab, agreeing on a point as he watched her rise gracefully to her feet, though it could be no easy task to do so with the dead weight of the child in her arms, while Catriona rounded up a weary Chakir.

'You're not leaving already?' Ahab said, rising alongside him.

'It's the children,' she said. 'They've had a long day.'

'I'll stay with them,' Catriona said. 'You come back.'

Bahir rose. She looked so slight and the child so awkward and floppy-limbed. 'Can I help?' he asked, not knowing what that might actually involve.

She responded by clutching the child even closer to her chest, as if she would not trust him with her. 'We'll manage, thank you.'

'We will see you shortly?' Ahab asked.

But it was to Bahir's eyes she directed her gaze, Bahir who felt her uncertainty, her fear and even something like temptation. 'Perhaps.'

'Princess Marina is a fine mother,' Ahab said as the small group padded across the sand towards their tent. 'Her children are a credit to her.'

And, as much as Bahir resented the presence of the girl, and as much as he resented what it meant, he could not disagree.

'Have you gone to visit them yet?' the old man asked a little later as he rose to prod the fire into life, the haunting notes of the stringed *oud* catching on the desert air like a poem on the breeze.

Ahab's question caught him unaware. Bahir didn't have to ask who he meant, but he'd been listening intently for any sound of Marina's return and he had not been thinking of *them*. But he was here in Jaqbar, wasn't he? Wasn't that enough for them? It wasn't as though he could change anything. He shrugged, more carelessly than he felt. 'Is there any point?'

The old man nodded sagely. 'You should go. They have waited a long time for you to come.'

Bahir said nothing, knowing in his bones that the old man was right, that reconnecting with his homeland meant finding his family. But the closer he had come, the more uncomfortable he had felt. After all, what could he tell them? That he might as well have lost his life with theirs for all the good he had done in the world? That he had wasted years of life in the gambling dens of the world?

He could not bring himself to say those things. So

instead, he just answered with the barest inclination of his head and a hand he rested on the old man's bony shoulder, hoping the old man would understand, as Marina returned in a whisper of fabric and a scent that complemented the pristine desert air and made it all the sweeter.

He breathed it in. She was back. And he was relieved, not only because he had been worried she would not return, but because Ahab now had somewhere else to direct his probing questions, affording him breathing space to deal with the demons of his past the way he needed to.

And he *would* deal with them, he thought as Ahab asked Marina about the children and he zoned out, an unswallowable lump in the back of his throat, that sliding weight inside him scraping across his gut at the thought. And, of course, some time he would go.

He owed them that much.

But only when he was ready.

It was late. The musicians had gone and Ahab and the others retired, the fire now a bed of coals. She knew she too should go to bed, but the moon was a heavy golden pearl hanging in the sky, turning the desert into a honeyed nether world, and the air was shimmering with expectation. Expectation of what, she didn't know, except that neither of them seemed willing or able to retire and break this fragile spell that existed between them.

And it occurred to her that, in all the time they had been together, they had never done anything so utterly simple. They had spent time in casinos and ballrooms, and had made love in the bedrooms and bathrooms of some of the most palatial hotels in the world, but they had never enjoyed the simple pleasure of watching a camp fire burn down under a pearlescent desert moon.

He looked beautiful in this light, she thought, stealing a glance when he was staring into the fire. The angles and planes of his face were either lit with a flickering glow or hidden in shadowed mystery.

A face that could still warm her blood with just one glance, so masculinely beautiful that she had to look away. She sighed and lifted her face to the moon, bathing her skin in its brilliance, wanting to drink in the serenity of this moment and hold it close to her for ever, wondering why such a moment should happen upon them now, when it was already too late.

And it was too late. For they had had their time, and it had been amazing, both of them soaring above the world of mere mortals, the sex sublime, the heights of passion reached unimaginable.

Only to be burned up on her savage re-entry into the world.

She closed her eyes, wanting to block out that dark memory. That time was so long ago. And now, for whatever reason, the fates had brought them together again and they had to find a way to move forward.

For now they shared a child.

Dear Chakir, who had turned her life around and made her realise that there was more to life than parties and avoiding responsibilities. For how could you avoid responsibility when you were a mother? You had no choice but to grow up.

The moon felt soft on her face. She would go to bed soon. She had not been going to come back at all, but

Catriona had told her she was far too young to go to bed yet, and there had been something in Bahir's eyes—an invitation? A plea?—and whatever it was had drawn her back, like a moth to the flame, to the fire.

And there had been nothing to fear. Nothing had happened other than they had discovered they could sit in companionable silence around a camp fire and drink in the sounds of the desert night, while tingling with delicious awareness with every breath.

There was something about this woman, Bahir thought as he watched her turn her face to the moon, her eyes closed—something elemental that he had never seen before until that stormy night on the terrace and she had danced when spun in the spray from the crashing waves.

Something that made him wonder if he had every truly known her.

He had always thought her just a good-time girl—and she *had* been then, wild, abandoned and wanton in bed, taking as much as she gave—but there was more to her than that. For she had depths and resources he would never have imagined. And a fiercely protective instinct where her children—one of them his—were concerned.

She was the mother of his child.

His child.

And yet, even though he could see those traits, even though he might otherwise applaud them, the eternal questions still gnawed away at him. Why had she turned to someone else so quickly? How could she have forgotten what they had shared? Out of spite? Or because she had never truly loved him?

It had to be that. What else could it be?

He looked at her upturned face, tracing the noble pro-file, the high forehead, the delicate uptilt of her nose, the long black lashes that swept her cheek, and those lips that had once been his sensual playground and his alone.

He had to ask himself the question—why had he ever let her go? Why had he let her walk into someone else's arms and someone else's bed?

She sighed and turned to him, too fast for him to look away and pretend he hadn't been staring. 'It's beauti-ful,' she said after a moment's hesitation. 'The moon, I mean.'

'Yes,' he simply said, unable to shift his eyes from hers, knowing where the true beauty in this night lay.

Somewhere out in the desert an owl hooted. The fire crackled, spitting sparks into the air, and the moon hung low and fat in the sky, filled with expectation.

He could kiss her now under that moon. The air was ripe for it, the whole desert seemingly poised and wait-ing.

He had no right to make the desert wait.

She watched him draw nearer, shrinking the space between them until she could feel the heat emanat-ing from him, feel the air shift with his approach. His breath was warm around her face, his dark eyes on her mouth, and she knew he was going to kiss her—and knew that there were one hundred good reasons why she shouldn't let him.

But for the life of her, with her senses buzzing and her skin alight, she couldn't remember a single one...

CHAPTER EIGHT

His lips tasted of sweet coffee and promises, of heated desire and the unmistakeable flavour of the man himself.

'It won't work,' she said in spite of the promise in his kiss, some shred of logic filtering through the fog of desire, that shred telling her that they been here before and it had not ended well that time.

He hushed her with his clever mouth and his persuasive lips and she let herself be persuaded for just a moment, giving herself up to his kiss and his touch, his hand at her throat feeling a frantic heartbeat in his touch, not knowing if it was his or hers.

The moment stretched and stretched. But she would stop this, she told herself, remembering another night when she had given herself up to his love-making, another night when she had given in to desire and passion only to be bluntly reminded of what he really thought of her. She remembered the anger she had felt then, trying to summon it up to give her strength when all she could feel was desire, need and the pulsing insistence between her thighs.

The low fire crackled and popped, somewhere close

by a camel softly snorted, and the indulgence of a moment became a minute or longer.

'Come to my tent,' he murmured, his hot mouth at her throat, his big hands molding her to him, his tongue writing its own scorching invitation on her flesh.

'No,' she whispered, turning her face away from his mouth, wishing she had been stronger from the start, wishing she was not so damned weak when it came to him despite all the hurt he had caused her, all the anger and despair. No, she revised—*because* of all the hurt, anger and despair. She should be stronger. 'I can't.'

But he didn't let her go. Instead his hand found one aching breast, brushing his thumb across her straining nipple, and she groaned into his mouth as spears of pleasure let fly to her core. 'Let's finish this, Marina. This time let's finish what we have started.'

With his hand making magic on her breast, and his hot mouth promising every conceivable pleasure, his words sounded so reasonable, so rational, that she almost succumbed.

But she had never wanted reasonable or rational from him. She had only ever wanted his love, in return for hers. And, in the end, that was what had killed their relationship.

She dragged in air, summoning all the strength she could find as she took his face between her hands and eased him away, a tear squeezing from her eye when she saw his eyes looked as tortured as she herself felt. 'Bahir,' she said, shaking her head slowly. 'Our time is past. It is gone. There is no point to this.'

Her words were met with an expression of disbelief, as if he could make no sense of her words. She smiled softly, trying to make him see. 'You know there is no point.' She watched his face as disbelief turned to disagreement and then anger. She waited and hoped that at least a flicker of understanding might follow, when he suddenly spun away from her and stood, clutching his head in his hands like it was set to explode and he needed to keep the two sides together.

'What do you want, Marina?'

She stood and straightened her *abaya*, smoothing out imaginary creases while she searched for an answer to his question. 'I want Chakir to know his father. Maybe even to have a good relationship with him.'

Chakir? He hadn't even been thinking about the boy. He'd been thinking about a woman who could turn him inside out with just one glance, who ran hot and cold in order to torment him.

'And us? What about us?'

She blinked back at him. 'If it is possible, I would like us to be friends.'

Friends!

She could look at him with those damned siren's eyes and that mouth—she could kiss him with that mouth—and yet tell him she wanted to be friends? How could they ever be merely friends? Couldn't she see that?

He looked up at the winking moon and wanted to howl out his anger, his frustration and his rumbling discontent. But instead he just sighed into the desert air. 'It's late,' he said, trying not to snarl, not entirely sure he was succeeding. 'I'll see you to your tent.'

He slept badly, a night of fractured nonsensical dreams filled with an unending and ultimately futile pursuit of something unseen that kept moving and shifting, something always just out of his reach.

Of course he would be frustrated, he rationalised the next morning as he hung over the sink and doused his head with cold water to clear the residual bleariness away. Twice now, she had worked him to fever pitch. Twice now she left him achingly hard with no release.

When had she grown this ability to say no, she who was once so eager for sex that she would not wear underwear in case it slowed them down? She who had never once said no to sex with him in all the time they'd been together, the one who had initiated it just as often as he had?

She thought that after all that, they could go from lovers to just friends? Who was she trying to kid?

Not him. Maybe she was trying to kid herself.

'The vehicles are packed,' Ahab said behind him from the door of the tent. 'Whenever you are ready, Bahir.'

He turned and thanked his old friend, already girding his loins for another day in *her* company. But maybe a day sightseeing in the Melted Gorge and showing his son the wonders of the region would distract him. Maybe a day trying to convince her she was kidding herself would distract him.

He looked at his face in the mirror as he towelled off the last of the water, trying hard not to notice the tiredness around his eyes. He could damned well do with a distraction.

But it wasn't the distraction he was looking for when he saw Marina sitting in the back seat with the children looking subdued and Catriona seated in the passenger seat alongside him. *Interesting,* he thought, climbing behind the wheel, feeling somewhat vindicated. So Marina was determined to stay out of his way? Maybe because she didn't think it was that simple to remain just friends either.

They set out in convoy across the desert floor along a wide flat road edged with random boulders hewn from the mountains around them, half a dozen vehicles filled with half the tribe, a holiday atmosphere prevailing as they set off to spend a day in the mountains.

If Marina was trying to hide from him, so be it. He focused on the excitement of his son, answering his eager questions about where they were going and what they would see. Even managing to answer the girl's one question when it came, without needing *her* prompt from the back seat, smiling to himself when he saw in the rear-vision mirror that she had noticed.

He could play the friends game, if that was what she wanted. He could tolerate a child she had made with someone else—that wasn't his—if it helped get Marina on side and convince her that being merely friends was nowhere near enough.

Onwards the convoy travelled across the stony desert, towards the mountains that loomed blue and imposing before them. They passed by a salt lake where storks rose in a black-and-white cloud that momentarily blotted out the morning sun. They passed by a pointy-eared desert fox standing sentry atop a sand dune, suspiciously monitoring their approach before they got too close and it turned and padded silently away.

He loved that his son got a kick out of these things,

and he got a kick out of seeing his excitement. It was almost like being a boy again himself, except...

No, not that, he thought, knowing he could not bear it if that happened to him. It was too late now to wish he would never have a child, but he would never wish what had happened to him on anyone, let alone a son of his.

She watched his eyes in the mirror, observing him from the back seat, silently applauding him when he explained something to Chakir, cheering him when he finally acknowledged a query from Hana, taking the time to answer. Hana had listened with her fingers in her mouth and with all the concentrated studiousness of a two-year-old. She, on the other hand, had listened with some kind of joy because for the first time she had not had to intercede on her daughter's behalf.

Instead, Bahir had answered her question as if it had been Chakir who had asked him. For that she was grateful and more than a little impressed. For a man who had never wanted children, he showed an interest in his son she would never have thought possible. For a man who had made a point of excluding Hana up until now, he seemed at least to be making an effort not to shunt her aside.

She wondered if Bahir had actually heard her last night, and understood her plea to be friends, and understood what that meant. She should not have stayed so late, getting wooed by the magical desert night, thinking that magic was meant for her. She should never have let him kiss her. But maybe her pleas had broken through some kind of barrier.

Maybe they could be friends after all.

It would not be like what they had shared before—
there could be no return to those heady reckless times—
but it would be something.

The gorge was tucked away like a secret, nothing to
show it was there, the visitors disembarking to follow
a trail that led towards a broad and winding cleft into
the mountains. Excitement among the visitors was high.
The children and adults were eager to enter the gorge—
and not just for the picnic they knew they would enjoy
afterwards—and it wasn't long before Marina could see
why. The track narrowed as they progressed, winding
and twisting its way through the rock, the walls either
side growing higher.

And as they moved deeper into the cleft, the colours
of the rock changed from sun-bleached white to a hundred shades, through honey and caramel and beyond,
like someone had melted the rock and poured it back in
swirling layers, while in other places crystalline colours
of purples and vibrant greens sparkled from the walls.

'Wow,' said Chakir when Bahir had asked them to
look up into a shaft where every colour they had already seen seemed to coalesce and merge in rippled
layered poetry.

Hana just stopped behind her brother and stared upwards, her eyes wide, drinking it in, trying to make
sense of it all. She pulled her fingers from her mouth
to reveal a wide smile. 'Pretty,' she said.

She saw Bahir's eyes on Hana, a small frown hovering at the bridge of his nose, before he turned his gaze
to her and the frown slipped away. He cocked one eyebrow, as if waiting for her reaction, and she had to re-

sist the urge to think he had brought them to the place purely for her benefit and hers alone. She smiled. 'It's amazing.'

But it was the smile he sent right back at her that zapped up her spine and lit all the places that had ached with want last night. And she shivered with the un-wanted pleasure of it, wondering if there would ever come a time when he did not make her sizzle with just one look.

Had she been kidding herself last night with him? Would she ever be satisfied with merely being friends with a man who she knew could blow her world apart with one touch of his clever fingers or one swipe of his wicked tongue?

She swallowed down on a pang of fruitless longing. But they had proved it would not work any other way. She wasn't that reckless good-time girl any more. She could no longer afford to be. And he seemed to be filled with a hatred for something that almost consumed him.

They both had changed in the intervening years. They were both different people, but they were both also Chakir's parents. So for their son's sake, then, it would have to be friendship and they would just have to try to make it work.

The group emerged both awe-struck and panting from the climb out of the gorge to a picnic lunch set in the shadow of the cliff, Chakir and Hana took no more time than it took to grab the first thing they could off a tray before running off to play with their new-found friends.

'They'll be okay?' Marina asked, taking a few steps

after them as her two trailed after the others, itching to follow herself just in case.

She sensed him at her shoulder. 'They'll be fine.'

She took a deep breath and forced her feet to stay where they were, but it was so, so hard to see Hana running so wild and free when she had promised to take good care of her. At home in Tuscany, she knew the local hazards. It was another thing here, in the desert, where everything was so new to them and so unfamiliar. Even when they had visited her father's home in Jemeya, they'd been there for such a short time that there'd hardly been time to venture outside the palace walls, let alone run around in the desert.

'But there are dangers in the desert.'

'As you say, princess,' he said. 'In the desert, there are always dangers lurking.'

His words had her looking at him, looking into his dark eyes, wondering at his meaning and wishing for things that she knew she should not. Knowing he was right. For the dangers of the desert were everywhere.

And right now Bahir was the most dangerous thing of all.

She turned away, shivering, her eyes following the children running and wheeling in circles, their arms outstretched like that flock of cranes they'd seen earlier today. Hana—tiny, precious Hana—lagged behind them all, flapping her arms and making her smile. 'And that's supposed to make me feel more comfortable, is it?'

She heard his sigh beside her. 'Maybe you could cut her some slack.'

'What? Cut who some slack?'

'The girl,' he said, adding, 'Hana,' before she could

correct him. 'You act like she's made of glass or something, always hovering over her. Why don't you let her
just be a child?'

'You don't understand,' she said, shaking her head.
'Hana's special.'

He grunted. 'I can see that.'

She glared at him. 'You just don't like her. Full stop.'

'Why should I? I didn't ask you to bring her. She's
not my child.'

'And that's all that matters is it? The only people who
count are those fathered by your fertile loins?'

'What do you expect me to say? I never wanted a
child. That you present me with one was enough to deal
with, without his sister coming along for the ride.' He
looked over at her and shrugged. 'But she's all right.
Kind of cute, in a way.'

Her head swung around. He'd actually noticed something about Hana besides the fact she wasn't his? Maybe
that question of hers he'd answered in the car hadn't
been an aberration. Maybe his stance was softening towards the tiny girl. 'She's beautiful,' she said, thinking
of Sarah, seeing her mother's pixie face every time she
looked at the daughter. Hana was a miniature Sarah.
Even her laugh reminded her of her friend.

'Not that she looks a lot like you.'

Danger shimmied down her spine, electric and spark-
ing, chasing away any feelings of well-being and putting her senses on red alert. Somehow she managed a
shrug, feigning indifference, while her self-protection
systems registered the need to close this conversation
down and now.

There was one sure way. 'Perhaps,' she said, already

turning back towards the safety of the group, 'that's because she looks more like her father.'

Who was he? he wanted to ask as he watched her go, both dissatisfied with her answer and disgruntled that she could so boldly walk away, her back so stiff and straight, her jaw set high, as if she was claiming some kind of moral high-ground. Who was this wonderful man that his daughter was so special? Where was he now and what was he doing? Was he busy with a wife while he put Marina up in his mountain retreat and let her look after his child?

Whoever he was, one thing was certain: his child would never live in another man's house, no matter who Hana's father was.

He watched her return to the picnic, to a group of women including Catriona where they exchanged words and both glanced over to where the children had been playing before. He followed their gaze to see them all now squatting in a circle, one of the older boys making pictures in the sand with a stick. He would be telling them a story, Bahir knew. He could almost hear drifts of the boy's unbroken voice on the still air.

He remembered sitting in such a circle himself, listening to his cousin telling a story about the first Bedouins and how they had conjured up a camel in their dreams, a soft-footed beast that would carry them safely across the shifting desert sands, and how they had been woken by a terrifying noise only to find the first camels bellowing outside their tents, impatient to be put to work.

He saw his son listen, open-mouthed in wonder. He heard his laughter, and that terrible weight inside him shifted unexpectedly again, jamming up tight against his lungs so he could barely breathe.

The wind lifted and he heard it almost sigh as it swirled past in a rustle of sand and the whispered voices of his brothers, of his mother and his father, of all the people of the tribe calling to him.

He put his hands to his head and spun around, his feet taking him further away, away from the chatter of women and the low murmurings of the men; away from the laughter of children. But the one sound he really wanted to blank out was the sound of the ghosts of the past.

Didn't they understand?

He wasn't ready to face them yet.

Marina watched him go, sensing his pain in every tortured step. 'Will he be all right, do you think?' she asked as Ahab joined them. 'Do you think someone should go with him?'

The old man watched through sun-creased eyes. 'Some things a man can only do by himself.'

She looked at him, wondering at his answer, wondering at the things he was not telling her before she looked back at the retreating form of Bahir in the distance. 'But he's hurting.'

'The hurt he is feeling was inflicted a long time ago. Perhaps he is only now starting to feel the pain.'

'What hurt? What happened to him? Is it something to do with his family?'

'Bahir will tell you,' the old man said, with a nod of his sage head. 'In his own time.'

* * *

He wandered aimlessly, retracing his steps and finding himself back in the gorge, where the coloured walls rose high above him, ancient and full of the wisdom of the world. A wisdom that eluded him, a wisdom he had no clue to understand, until a mournful wind sang through the gorge and drove him away. He then found himself back near the picnic under the cliffs, knowing he was walking in senseless circles and not understanding, but simply driven to walk.

Until it occurred to him that his life was on the same aimless course.

That she was right.

Because, when it all came down to it, what did he actually do? He gambled. What did he produce? Nothing. Not really. Of course, it was easy to think he was producing something when he was winning. He was making money. He had stacks of chips to show for it, he had investments salted away with whatever proceeds exceeded his immediate expenses, and there were plenty of those, because he was good at what he did. But, beyond that, what did he do? What good was he to anyone?

God, he thought, suddenly sick of the soul-searching, sick of it all. He had planned to come to the desert to lift his spirits, not to find fault with himself. So what that he didn't own a home? He didn't need one. So why must he beat himself up about things he could not change and did not need changing?

He was good at what he did. He was the best. When it came to playing the roulette wheel, nobody risked so much or won so much. Wasn't that some kind of achievement in itself?

A cry rang out in the desert air—a child's cry. He'd

half-turned towards the sound, taking in the picture around him, registering a scattering of children across the sands wandering tired and thirsty back to the picnic, when he heard Marina's cry.

'Hana?' she called, half-question in her voice, half-fear, just before the girl's scream came again, shrill and panicked and slicing through the desert air like a sharpened blade. And this time he found the source. The girl was screaming from where she'd fallen on the rocky ground, her tiny limbs rigid. For a split second he assumed she must have hurt herself falling while trying to keep up with the others, and he waited for her to pick herself up off the ground, until he noticed her attention focused on the ugly black shape marching menacingly towards her across the sand.

CHAPTER NINE

'HANA!' he roared, already launching himself towards her. 'Hana, get up. Move!'

But the child was petrified with fear as the arachnid marched purposefully on, its tail curved over its head, poised and ready to inflict its sting.

The air erupted with cries of panic and warning as everyone suddenly realised what was happening. His lungs heaving, Bahir sprinted the distance between them, barely registering others charging for the scene, aware only that there was movement. His eyes were on the girl.

'Mama!' she squealed between sobs, pushing herself backwards across the sand on her hands, her eyes fixed on the approaching terror.

Why didn't she run? She had to run. She was much too small to survive a sting from a scorpion and he would never get there in time. All of these thoughts ran through his head in the seconds it took him to reach her, seconds that stretched and bulged with impossibility as he dived in one desperate lunge and plucked her from the path of danger, rolling away across the desert floor.

For a moment the girl in his arms was too shocked to make a sound, but as he stood she recovered enough to scream again, louder this time if it were possible, howling her protest and twisting her body away, wanting desperately to be free.

And, even though one of the men wielded a stick and flicked the scorpion away, he would not let her go while that thing was anywhere near.

'Hana!' Marina cried, her feet flying across the sand towards them, her robe flapping hard against her legs, and he saw her beautiful face drained of so much colour that she could have been made of the desert sands.

The girl held out her arms to her and, breathless, Marina took the child and clutched her to her chest, pressing her lips to her curls as she sobbed helplessly against her shoulder. 'Oh God, Hana,' she said as her sobs quietened. 'It's okay. You're all right now.'

She looked at Bahir through tear-filled eyes, her voice still shaky. 'I tried not to panic. I thought about what you said and I forced myself not to run to Hana straightaway and pick her up like I usually do. And then I saw it moving on the sand next to her.' She shuddered, rocking the child in her arms. 'If you hadn't got there in time...'

He cursed himself for his ill-timed advice. 'I should never have said anything to you. If I'd thought it was as serious, I would have been there sooner.'

Eyes a man could drown in blinked up at him. 'Thank you.'

He dusted himself off to give his hands something to do other than to pull her trembling form into his arms, child and all, and comfort her. 'You might want to check her for scratches,' he said. 'I tried to keep her off the ground, but she might have got a scrape or two.'

Chakir caught up with them, his eyes bright with excitement. 'Can you teach me how to do that?' he asked, and Bahir almost found it in himself to laugh.

'Maybe later,' he said, thinking that they'd had enough excitement for one day. Besides, there was something he had to do, something he could not put off any longer, the voices in his head became louder and more insistent. But first he had to get this lot home. 'I think right now we should head back to the camp, don't you?'

The journey home was a quiet one, both the children asleep within five minutes of setting off, exhausted after the day's activities, Catriona sleepily staring out of her window and dozing off long before they reached the camp.

This time Marina sat in the front seat alongside him, watching his long-fingered hands on the wheel, looking relaxed and confident, feeling anything but relaxed and confident herself as she tried to make sense of the man alongside her—a man who cared nothing for a child and yet had risked his own life to protect hers. For she was under no misapprehension as to the enormity of his actions. A scorpion sting could threaten the life of a grown man, shutting down his respiratory system, closing his throat and paralysing his lungs. A child Hana's size wouldn't stand a chance, not out here so far from medical assistance.

She glanced behind her, saw that they were all asleep and said softly to him, 'You saved her life today, you know.'

He shrugged, as if it was nothing; as if it was something he did every day. 'I was the closest to her, that's all.'

'Maybe. And I know I thanked you back there,' she said, 'but I'm not sure it was anywhere near enough. Thank you for doing what you did and reaching Hana in time.'

He glanced across at her. 'I would have done the same for any child in danger.'

'I know, it's just that I know you're not that interested in Hana. Whereas Chakir, on the other hand...'

He swung his head around, a scowl tugging at his brows. 'You think I would save my own son and yet leave another's child to suffer a terrible fate?'

'No.' She shook her head, knowing that had come out wrong. 'That wasn't what I meant. I was just surprised that you were the one to act when it wasn't your child in danger, and when you had made such a point in the past about her not being your child.'

He shook his head and looked back at the road. 'So maybe at the time that didn't seem the most pertinent detail.' And she felt his rebuke in his words as he drew a thick black line under the conversation before she'd had a chance to say the things she really wanted to say.

The things she should say.

For in Bahir rescuing Hana, she'd been reminded of her own rescue from the twisted Mustafa, who'd kidnapped her sister, Aisha, to claim the throne of Al-Jirad for his own. And then, when that purpose was foiled, kidnapped her to frustrate his half-brother Zoltan's ascension to the thrown. She'd tried to downplay Bahir's role in her rescue, tried to make out he was only there because his three friends, Zoltan, Kabar and Rashid, expected it—and maybe that had been one element of it—but he had still been one of their party. He had still been there to ensure her safe return to her family.

And now he had rescued her again, for in saving Hana he had saved the promise she had made to the dying Sarah.

She sighed. 'I'm sorry. Now I've gone and offended you. What I was actually trying to lead up to, though so clumsily I'll admit, was to thank you, and properly this time, for your part in my rescue from Mustafa. I don't think I've ever done that. I'm only sorry now that it's so overdue.'

The last thing she expected in return for her thanks was a smile. His features were in profile as his eyes remained on the road, scanning the wide sandy route ahead, but she definitely saw his lips turn up, his cheek creasing along a rarely seen line.

'What? You're actually thanking me, princess, while all the time I was out there I was merely having fun with my friends? What was it you called us—a band of merry men out on some boys' own adventure?'

She slumped back in her seat, mortified. God, had she really said that? It was a miracle he'd bothered trying to save Hana at all, ungrateful as she had been for his part in her rescue. 'You have to forgive me.' She searched for even more words to apologise, searched for the right words, and in the end could only come up with a poor excuse. 'I was angry with you at the time.'

'It's all right,' he said, sounding as though it was anything but, looking over at her then with eyes so devoid of life that she wondered what he was thinking that could have put that look there. 'I know all about anger.'

His words made her shiver, weighted down with

some kind of pain. She didn't ask what he meant as the camp came into view. She wasn't sure she wanted to know. Once before she'd been on the receiving end of his anger and she knew enough not to want to go back there ever again.

She remembered that day now as she watched the desert slide past her window, when he had blown apart her world with the force of his anger and cast her out of his life for ever.

At least, it had been meant to be for ever. Yet here they were, forced together again by circumstances, by the existence of their son Chakir.

Sometimes the anger was still there. It was only too clear, simmering away under the surface, only too willing to bubble up and break free. But at other times it was another emotion, just as heated and potent, that seemed to drive his actions.

And she wondered how she could ever have had a relationship with him for all those months, all those nights, without realising the mystery within the man, those different parts of him, or asking all the questions she had now about who he truly was.

The vehicle neared the camp site, a traditional Bedouin camp complete with opulent tents for their guests, and that raised still more questions in her mind. He'd made the decision to bring Chakir to the desert and, lo, all this had been laid on in honour of their visitors.

'How did you organise all this?'

'You mean the picnic?'

'No. I mean us, here, in the middle of a desert where you haven't lived for years apparently. And one day you decide we will all go to the desert and the next there is an entire encampment set up and waiting for us. How is that even possible?'

He shrugged. 'Cash speaks loudly out here where they have little chance to earn it.'

'But so quickly? One moment you decide to to go to the desert and the next there is this waiting for you?'

'Not really. I was planning to come anyway after taking you home, so I'd already made a few calls and chased up some contacts. Finding Ahab alive made it easy. When I told him there were more coming with me, he knew where to find the tents I needed. He suggested staying with his tribe—one of the last to resist urban-isation and live as traditionally as possible—instead of camping alone as I'd originally intended.'

'I like it,' she said, thinking of the new friends they had already made and the adventures they had enjoyed, despite the traumas of today. 'The tribespeople are so welcoming, to all of us.'

'It's the Bedouin way,' he said with an unexpected note of pride. Unexpected, because he had not thought of himself as Bedouin for years, his lifestyle so removed from that culture. 'Visitors are honoured guests. I had not thought there were any tribes still living in such a simple manner. So much of the world has moved on.'

Hadn't he himself moved on?

'But your people lived this way.'

A pause. And, even though he was sitting behind the wheel of a car driving along a desert road, still it felt like the sand had shifted under his feet like that first step into quicksand when the world tilted and went wrong. 'Mostly.'

'And this is how you grew up—herding goats, sitting around camp fires listening to stories at night, watching the stars and your father teaching you to swim?'

He felt the weight of the years bearing down on him, the oppressive weight of dusty memories. 'A million years ago,' he said, through a throat clogged with the sands of time.

'So where is your tribe now?' she asked as they drove into the camp at the head of the snaking convoy. 'Where is your family? I asked Ahab and he said you would tell me.'

He braked the car to a halt, and sat there while the passengers in the back seat roused and blinked into wakefulness, looking as bewildered as he felt, but knowing the time had come.

All afternoon he'd felt it. All afternoon his duty had called to him. And what better way to explain it to her, if she was so damned curious and when words seemed so thin on the barren ground?

He undid his seatbelt, put one hand to his door handle and looked at her. 'I'm going to visit them after we've unpacked. Maybe you should join me. Maybe then you might understand.'

Should she? There was a power of unspoken meaning in his invitation, along with a measure of challenge in his eyes. But what did it mean? For a while she'd wondered the worst, that he had been hiding some dreadful truth from her about his family. Equally, she had wondered if they had disowned him after he had turned to a life of gambling in the casinos of the world.

But now he talked of visiting them…

Had they now agreed to see him, knowing he was back? Had they heard word via Ahab of their grandson?

'And Chakir?'

'No. Not the boy. It's too soon.'

Relief washed through her. They had not yet told Chakir that Bahir was his father, not even sure he would understand, and for the moment that was how she wanted it to stay. Maybe she was being over-cautious, but she wanted to wait at least until she knew that Bahir wanted to be a permanent part of his son's life. She did not want to have to explain where his father had gone, if he suddenly changed his mind and opted out of Chakir's life.

'Don't worry,' he said, taking her reticence for reluctance. 'It was probably a bad idea.'

'No,' she said. 'I'll come.'

It was a bad idea, he realised as they headed away from the camp and towards a range of craggy blue hills in the distance along little more than a stony track. An exceptionally bad idea to have her along.

But at least she'd stopped asking questions. She was sitting silent alongside him as the vehicle lurched its way forward. Soon enough she would have all the answers she needed and more. Not that it might make any difference, but at least she would be closer to understanding why he had said what he had that day.

And, if she understood, maybe one day she could forgive him. But then he remembered her stricken face and the unshed tears in her eyes—the hurt and desolation—and he would not be surprised if she never forgave him for so completely destroying what they once had.

But she would know the truth of his family.

They scaled one of the ridges rising from the valley and the pounding in his blood grew louder, more urgent, sending heat pulsing around his body until his skin felt almost blistering, sweat broke out on his forehead, marked his armpits and stuck his back to the seat.

One more ridge. It had been years since he had been here and he'd been little more than a child. Just that one time and so long ago, and still he remembered the jagged line of mountain against the sky, still he knew exactly where he was going.

But it was more than memory directing him, for it was almost as if he could feel their hands on the wheel, their collective wisdom guiding the vehicle along the stony track.

Guiding him home.

Home. If that wasn't a strange concept already for a Bedouin, where no fixed address was a way of life and the entire desert was your back yard. So your family and your tribe were your home. How much stranger for him, where his family was gathered in a place of the dead.

And yet still they called to him.

What would he tell them?

What could he possibly say that they would want to hear?

The four-wheel drive ground up the stony incline, the heat in his veins building with it, the weight in his gut lurching with every kick of the steering wheel in his hands.

Just shy of the crest, he stopped and pulled the handbrake on.

'Why are we stopping here?' she asked uncertainly,

looking around, searching for answers. 'What is this place?'

Looking around would tell her nothing, he knew. There was nothing to see but sand, rocky ground and the occasional saltbush, but now they were here he could not find the words to tell her. Soon, he knew she would work it out for herself. But now that they were there, he could not do this with her along. Not yet. First he needed time to make his peace and to collect himself again. 'Wait here,' he instructed, without explaining, leaving the engine on and the air-conditioning running. 'I won't be long.'

Before waiting for her answer, he climbed out into the hot, dry air, pushing the door firmly closed with both hands, his gaze on the track to where it disappeared over the rise, already anticipating the scene that awaited him.

Then with a deep breath he pushed purposefully away from the car and, with a weight in his heart so heavy it was a wonder it didn't fall through his chest, he set off up the track.

He stopped when he reached the crest and looked down into the shallow valley where once a few low black tents had clustered around a tiny oasis, around which a dozen kids had chased each other, laughing and full of life.

Once so full of life.

Where now there was nothing but an eerie wind that coaxed the desert sand into a mournful dance around a few ragged lines of flat white stones set into the rocky earth.

His family.

The wind circled him as he walked closer, imprisoning him, celebrating his capture as it whipped around the stones, presenting him like a prize.

He stood at the base of one of the twenty-six simple stones, now worn ragged with the ravages of the elements, overcome by the enormity of what had happened here.

Overcome with the guilt that there should have been one more flat white stone.

He fell to his knees on the sandy ground and put one hand to the stone, warm under his touch like the living once had been.

'Father,' he said as the first of his tears soaked into the thirsty ground. 'I'm back. I've come home.'

How long was not long in the desert? Bahir had been gone the best part of thirty minutes and still there was no sign of him. A gnawing worry in Marina's gut refused to be ignored any longer.

Why had he not returned? What was taking him so long?

He'd walked up that track and then stood there, looking down at something, and everything about his stance had suggested he was a man defeated.

And then he'd disappeared behind the ridge and she had been left wondering. But from the ridge top she might be able to see.

She leaned over the driver's side and turned off the ignition, slipping from the car into air so dry the moisture was as good as sucked from her lungs. A breeze found her then, playing a haunting tune as it toyed with the ends of her hair, plucking at the hem of her light *abaya* as she headed up the track.

A sad place, she thought, shivering with the premonition, for even though it was as starkly beautiful as any other places she had seen in Jaqbar, there was emptiness mixed with sorrow on the wind, turning the desert desolate.

Then she reached the crest of the hill and saw him a little way away, kneeling on the sand, and for a moment she felt relief that she had found him—until she noticed the flat white stones poking from the earth all around him, and the sad wind moaned its mournful song as her heart squeezed tight. 'Oh no, Bahir,' she whispered, knowing it was as bad as it could possibly be, and still wishing it not to be true. 'Please not that.'

Scant minutes later, she knelt by his side before one of the simple stones, not looking at him, giving him time to register her presence. Only after she was certain he had was she willing to ask, 'Who are they?'

'My family,' he said, his voice sounding strained and choked. 'Let me introduce you to them. He pointed at a stone alongside. 'There is my mother.' He pointed to the next. 'My father.' He listed them as he went. 'My cousins, my uncles, my aunt, her mother. They are all here.'

'And who is this one?'

'This one—this is my baby brother, Jemila. He was three. The same age as Chakir is now.' His voice broke on their child's name. She looked at his face for the first time and saw the tracks of his tears down his cheeks and her heart broke.

'Oh, Bahir.'

'There are twenty-six in all,' he said matter-of-factly

without returning her gaze. 'An entire tribe. All except for one.'

'All except you.'

'I was at school in England,' he said blankly. 'The pride of the family. The chosen one. The one upon whom all the hopes and dreams of the tribe resided.' He shook his head. 'I was twelve years old when I learned a traveller had been found ill in the desert and brought to the camp to be revived. But he died, and one by one, they all fell sick—the old, the young, the strong. The disease made no exception. It wasn't until two weeks after they had been buried that they finally tracked me down to let me know.'

'Bahir,' she uttered softly, not knowing what she could possibly say that might comfort him, instead simply wrapping an arm around his shoulders just to let him know she was there, surprised he felt cold under her hand when the day was so warm. 'I'm so sorry.'

He lifted his face to the heavens then, his features tight and etched with grief. 'I was supposed to be here. It was term break and I had always come home for holidays. Except this time I had an invitation to go home with a classmate. I had never had a Christmas before and I saw the excitement of the other boarders, all looking forward to going home to parties and to presents, and I knew my parents would insist I came home. So I told them that I was held back by the masters, to catch up on my studies. I told her I could not come home.'

He sagged, dropping his head almost to the ground. 'I lied to my father and my mother. I should have been here with them. I should be here now, buried under one of these stones. I should have been here with them.'

Finally she understood the full horror of his past; finally she realised the agony and the pain that had shaped him and made him the man he was, the man racked with survivor guilt. She squeezed his shoulders, trying to lend him her warmth and chase away the chill of the past that possessed him. 'They would have wanted you to survive. They would not blame you. Nobody would blame you.'

'I don't need anyone else to blame me. Don't you think I have blame enough? I lied to my family. I was not here when I should have been, and for my sins I would have to live with that for ever.'

'Bahir, you must not blame yourself.'

'Who else is to blame? Who else is left to blame?' He dragged in air, and she could hear the agony that consumed him and bent him double.

'I swore that day, the day they brought me to this place, that I would sooner never have a child than risk leaving him with nobody and nothing. Nothing but guilt.'

Beside him she ached with the pain that seemed to ooze from his pores. 'You never wanted a child because you never wanted him to suffer as you did. As you still do.'

He shook his head violently from side to side. 'No!' he roared, putting his hands to his forehead before rising, anguished, to his feet, staggering away from the simple graveyard towards a cluster of palms where the sunlight filtered through the leaves and where a tiny spring kept alive a thin border of grass. She followed at a distance, feeling helpless and heartsick, not knowing what to say or do, knowing only that her own heart was breaking as she watched him fall to his knees, dip his hands into the pool and splash water on his face. He rocked back on his heels, his eyes empty, focused on nothing but the past.

'They're the ones who suffered. Not me. I lived through it all. I went home with my friend and laughed and played games and had no idea what was happening out here in the desert.

'And then, in one fell swoop, I had nothing. I had nobody. I should have been with them!' he cried. 'I wish I had been here!'

He squeezed his eyes tightly shut, his face screwed up tight, and she saw the tears squeezing from his eyes as his grief overwhelmed him.

There was not one thing on earth she could say, not one thing she could do, other than to kneel down alongside, hold him, press her mouth to his salty tears and kiss them away.

He sagged against her. He let her hold his head in her hands. He let her kiss his tortured face and stroke her hands through his hair as she nestled his head against her chest. He let her comfort him as the sobs racked his body and his anguished cries rang out across the desert, as the warm breeze wrapped itself around them and held them in its whispering embrace.

Until the wind shifted subtly to a caress and comfort turned to need, and he was kissing her too, his mouth seeking hers. It was done tentatively at first—so hesitant, unsure and so very pained—and then hungrily, like a man starved and falling upon his first meal in days. It was all she could do to keep up with the demands of his urgent mouth and his hot, seeking hands.

She made no move to stop him. She would not stop him. He had lost so very much and all she had to offer him was the comfort of her body in the life-affirming act of sex.

He set her down softly on the grass, his kisses filled with a hungry desperation that wrenched at her soul and made her want to weep for him, to weep for the boy he had been, the boy who felt he had betrayed his family, the boy who had lost everything without the hint of a goodbye. So she put her heart into her kiss, wanting to make up for his sorrow, wanting to take away his pain for ever. Wanting to lend him hope.

He took everything she could give, wanting more. She felt his hand skim down her side, felt the slide of her *abaya* up her legs, and she shifted to enable him to slip it over her hips. She let him tug it over her shoulders, gazing down at her with broken eyes filled with ghosts and a savage, desperate need.

And, while he watched, she slipped off her bra and underwear and lay back on the grassy bank, offering herself to him.

With a groan etched in pain he tore at his shirt and his pants and in a blur of white linen, bunched muscles and golden skin he was back at her mouth, frantic now, his skin against her skin, his hardness pressing into her belly, his legs finding a home between hers.

She arched beneath him, her breath hitched as he found her pulsing core, aching now with her own escalating need, aching for completion. She moaned with the very closeness of it, with the absence and with the promise, forgetting for a moment that this was about pleasuring him.

'Bahir,' she whispered, the sound of his name laced with desperation.

He answered with a growl and a thrust of his hips that drove his hard length into her, filling her so deliciously, so exquisitely that it forced tears from her eyes.

It had always been good with Bahir, she remembered as he remained buried deep inside her. He had always been the best. But surely she would have remembered if holding him deep within her body had been this good?

Then he drew back and all that was good became better in the slide of flesh against flesh and the anticipation of his return. He captured a peaked nipple between his lips, drawing it into his mouth as he drove into her again, and sparks went off behind her eyes. His mouth captured the other breast in time for his next powerful lunge.

All of a sudden there was no time for niceties, no time to cosset. There was only time to cling onto him as she felt her peak building exponentially with every fluid thrust of his hips, every quickening stroke.

Until she could take no more and she shattered around him in a blaze of stars. From another galaxy it seemed she heard his cry, triumph in the desperation, victory in his anguish, and she reached for him as he too reached the stars, holding him close, comforting him as she guided him safely back to earth.

Loving him.

For, even though she knew she could never tell him, she knew in her heart that she loved Bahir. She had never stopped loving him.

They lay there in the dappled shade as day slipped

away and the slanting sun turned the desert into a sea of gold.

'I never cried for them,' he told her, holding her tucked up against him, stroking her hair. 'I couldn't. I was too ashamed. I was too angry.'

'It's okay,' she said, wanting to weep for a boy who hadn't been able to bring himself to cry.

'No.' He sighed, taking his hand from her hair, dropping the back of his wrist on his forehead. 'It's not okay. That day you came, when I got angry...'

'Hush,' she said, with a finger to his lips. 'It doesn't matter. I understand.'

He grabbed her hand, curled it in his long fingers and pressed it to his lips. 'No. There is more. After my family died, the college agreed to extend my scholarship. There was no point, they said, in sending me home. There was nothing for me there. And so a foster family was found for me, an Arab man working in London in corporate finance who claimed to be some distant relative. A cruel man. A man with a simpering excuse for a wife, a man who would beat me with a cane if I didn't top every class, every exam. A man who thought he was grooming me for a career alongside him. I hated him.'

He shook his head. 'I knew I had to get away but I needed money. That's when I started gambling. That's when I realised I had a gift for it. He beat me more when he found out what I was doing and that only made me more determined. By the time I was sixteen, I had made enough that I never had to go back there again.

'That day you came over—that very morning—I had woken to the voices of my family in my head. I had dreamed of them that night, I had dreamed of the day twenty years before when I had stood here and been presented with the truth, that my family and everyone I loved, my whole world, had been taken from me.'

'No wonder you were upset that day.'

'But that wasn't it. It was a package from a lawyer that came that morning—it contained a letter telling me my foster father had died. And it contained my father's ring, a necklace of my mother and the amulet that had been around Jemila's neck when he had died. My family's things. My foster father had kept them all those years. He had never so much as told me they existed.

'And I was so angry—with my foster father, yes, but with my family for leaving me to such a fate. And with myself, for lying and partying with a friend when I should have been with them. On that day, I hated them all and I hated myself, and then you walked in talking family.' He shook his head. 'I savaged you because you stumbled into my nightmare talking about things I never wanted any part of that day more than ever.'

He dragged in a chestful of air and let it go, as if letting the weight of the past go with it. She realised the full horror of her own blundering actions, that she had chosen that day of all days to declare her love and share the excitement of the child they had unwittingly made together. She raised herself up on her elbow and leaned over him. 'I'm so sorry. I didn't know. I had no idea.'

'How could you, when I had never spoken of these things, when I had buried the past under an anger so deep it could never resurface? But that day there was no forgetting any of it.'

She shook her head. She could not imagine.

'To think, I was the chosen one,' he said, bitterness

infusing his words. 'I was the great hope of the tribe, born with a gift for numbers and so sent off to school in England—a rare privilege for my people, one they hoped would bring the tribe great benefits and wealth. They were all so proud of me—my father, my mother...'

He shook his head and turned away. 'And look how I have repaid them—by becoming a gambler. A wastrel. And, even though I finished school and paid for university with my winnings, what point was a degree when I turned straight to the university of spin? What point has been this life that was saved when all others were lost? What good have I ever done for them?'

'What could you possibly do?' she said, stroking the thick hair behind his ear, making circles with her fingertips at his pulsing temple. 'Nothing would bring them back. What could you do?'

'I should have done something! You'd think I would have achieved something other than notoriety in every gambling den in the world.'

'But you had lost everything.'

She splayed her fingers though his thick hair, winding her fingers around its strong waves. 'And maybe that's why you gamble,' she mused, wondering out loud, trying to fit the tortured pieces together. 'Because money is not like people. Money can be won and lost and then won again, and the pain of losing it, if any, is transitory. Maybe because, ultimately, there is no real risk.'

He turned his head back to her, a frown at the bridge of his nose as though he didn't understand, and she wondered if she'd been speaking a foreign language.

'I never wanted a child,' he said. 'I never wanted family.'

'I know. I understand.'

'But I want Chakir. I want my son.'

She nodded, her chest too tight to speak.

Then he pulled her to him. 'And I want his mother too.'

CHAPTER TEN

'Marry me,' he said in the next breath, before she'd had a chance to absorb his previous declaration. Before the beat of her heart had had a chance to settle.

'Bahir, I—'

'It makes sense, don't you see? Chakir needs a father. I never wanted a family, it's true, but I can't turn my back on what's happened. And my father would be so proud to have a grandson and to see that I have done something good with my life.'

'But marriage?'

'I don't want to be a part-time father. I want to be there for him every day. And I swear I will try to be a good father to him. Besides, we're good together, Marina, you know we are. We can make it work for Chakir's sake.'

For Chakir's sake.

How ironic. 'Chakir's sake' was the very reason she'd decided to tell Bahir about their son's existence in the first place, and now he was using it to convince her to marry him.

Was it reason enough?

Maybe it made sense for Chakir, but what about Hana? Wanting to take on Chakir was one thing, but had he even thought about what getting married would entail? That he would have to be a father to Hana too?

And what about love? Was there no place for love in this arrangement? Had he lost the ability to love when he'd lost his entire family?

'I don't know,' she said, conflicted and floundering in uncertainty, only half-aware of the heated stroke of his hand down her body, lingering at her hip, his long fingers splayed over sensitive skin. 'It's too big a decision. I need time to think. And you need time to decide that's what you really want.'

'You're right,' he said, pulling her head down to his to brush his lips against her mouth. 'I could use the time. To persuade you.'

They made love again as the golden desert turned to silver under the rising moon and the desert wind felt like the whisper of silk over their skin. Their love-making was slower this time, Bahir taking his time to taste, explore and revisit; taking his own sweet time to persuade, so that when they joined again, their bodies and senses were at fever pitch and release slammed through her like a thunderbolt in a desert storm. She lay there in the aftermath, her breathing ragged, her body humming, and knew that she was no closer to making a decision.

But there was one thing she knew: that persuasion had never felt so good.

It was only when they were on their way back to the camp, when she felt the warm trickle of his juices in her underwear, that she realised that neither of them had given a moment's thought to protection.

She turned to him, stricken, wondering how either of them could have been so thoughtless—so *irrespon-*

sible—half-wondering if this had been part of Bahir's plan to force her hand. But no, she thought, thinking of the graveyard and Bahir's intense grief, there had been no planned seduction. It had been an oversight, that was all. A foolish one but maybe one without consequences, she thought, rolling over the dates of the calendar in her head. It was late in her cycle. The chances would be slim. Surely fate would not deal her such a hand again…?

Bahir was not slow in backing up his words with action. He proved over the next few days that he would make an excellent father for Chakir. He showed him how to read the footprints on the sand, to tell a camel from a horse, a fox from a wild goat. She watched him teach their son things he would never have learned otherwise.

Even with tiny Hana he showed an interest as she trailed around after him and Chakir, wanting to be included in everything. She wondered and hoped that his resentment of Hana was waning, and that his rescue of her from the scorpion had established some kind of bond between them.

But Bahir saved his most persuasive arguments for their love-making. He was nothing if not resourceful, finding reasons for them to be alone so that he could work his potent brand of persuasion on her. Unlike that reckless evening in the desert, though, when neither had given a thought to protection, he took every care.

Every time they met he asked her if she had made up her mind, if she was closer to deciding.

And every time she shook her head and asked for him to be patient. There was no hurry, she told herself, waiting for him to give her the one thing she craved, to say those tiny words she so longed to hear.

She wasn't brave enough to say them to him—the words he had once flung in shreds back in her face.

In the end, it wasn't the sex that made her decide, or anything he said. It wasn't even watching him with their adoring son, or lifting Hana onto a foal and showing her how to hold onto the reins when her tiny feet dangled way above the stirrups.

It was the new well he paid for and helped build, bare-backed and sweating, slogging it out on the rocky ground alongside the men from the tribe.

It was the books he ordered and had delivered so the children of the camp could learn to read and write at home and not be forced to go to school in Souza, far away from their families.

It was all the changes she witnessed in him that made up her mind.

This was a different man from the one she'd known and partied with all those years ago. This man seemed to have found purpose in his life, even taking to wearing the robes of his people when he was amongst them.

This man had discovered how to laugh and live and maybe, hopefully, how to love.

And she wanted to spend the rest of her life with him.

'He's asked me to marry him,' she confided to Catriona that night as they prepared the children for bed, before she was due to meet him. He'd planned a surprise, he'd told her, 'something special', and her senses were buzzing in anticipation.

The older woman smiled and hugged her. 'I knew

something must be happening because of the stars in your eyes lately. Have you said yes?'

'I'm planning to tonight. Except it means leaving the children with you for a few hours, if that's all right. Bahir has something special planned, apparently.'

Catriona squeezed her hand. 'Of course you can leave them. They'll be just fine! And just think how excited they'll be in the morning when you tell them the news. Children need a father.'

Marina nodded. 'I know.' She'd been the best kind of mother she could be, but already she was seeing Chakir blossom into boyhood under his father's guiding hand. Bahir would be a good father, she knew.

'Does he know about Hana yet?'

She shook her head, setting the large golden hoops in her ear dancing. It was her one last concern—that a man who did not really want a child he had not fathered would turn away that child when he discovered the girl was not even hers. 'Not yet. I didn't want to betray Sarah's confidence until I was sure. But I'll tell him first, so there can be no misunderstanding. Sarah would want me to.'

Catriona smiled and wished her luck, hugging her younger friend again. 'I'm so happy for you, Marina. If anyone deserves happiness, it's you.'

Tonight he was certain she would say yes. Tonight he was taking no chances. The luxurious tent complete with plunge pool he had ordered had been delivered and set up on a ridge overlooking a palm-filled valley, an unexpected treasure in the desert, a relic from dinosaur times and one he'd been saving for a special moment to share. That moment was now.

Bahir took in the scene as he waited for her, smiling at his cleverness, confident that after tonight it would be impossible to say no to him. Inside that plushly decorated and furnished tent, atop the cushioned bed and in the cooling waters of the crystal-clear plunge pool, he would set about making his final assault on her senses, his final step in persuading her to marry him.

Why she was holding out was a mystery when it was so clear that getting married was the right thing to do. The only thing to do.

Yes, he had treated her badly in the past—horrendously, he knew—but she understood the reasons why now. If she hadn't forgiven him, why was she so eager to share her body with him?

Because she wanted to be wooed?

He smiled as he surveyed the desert love-nest he had created, and waited for the car to bring her to him. So he would woo her tonight. Nothing would be left to chance. He had created the perfect place for them to escape to whenever they wanted. He had found a ring, set with an emerald the size of a bird's egg and surrounded by sparkling diamonds. He had found them the perfect house, in the same region of Italy, because she seemed to love it so much, but closer to Pisa to make travelling time between their two homes in Italy and Jaqbar easier. Idly he flicked through the property portfolio, passing time until he heard the sound of an engine in the distance and saw the headlights, and he shoved the brochure under a pile of towels and looked around one more time.

It was perfect.

He had left nothing to chance.

Together with the best sex in the universe, she would not be able to resist.

Tonight he could not fail.

Tonight she would be his.

She was sure it must be a mirage. They had travelled miles from the camp through nothingness, the moon obscured by a lonely cloud, when up ahead there appeared a strange red glow. A tent, she made out as they drew closer, a tent strung with colourful lanterns all around and a tall figure dressed all in white standing waiting outside.

Bahir.

Her pulse quickened. The sight of him in traditional robes, standing so straight and tall like one of the desert sheikhs of old, captured her imagination and stirred her senses. He looked so good in European clothes, in fine fabrics and designer-cut menswear, but in traditional robes he looked magnificent—a true Bedouin leader, standing there like a beacon in the dark.

She swallowed back on a delicious bubble of anticipation, glad she'd taken extra care with her own appearance tonight, her gold silk robe lavishly embroidered with intricate needlework and tiny precious stones that twinkled whenever she moved. She had known tonight would be special on so many levels. The effort Bahir had gone to to make it so proved it was for him too.

She smoothed her hands down the fabric, suddenly nervous. Tonight she would accept his proposal. Tonight she would agree to marry this man.

The car pulled up alongside the tent and Bahir stepped forward to open her door, his dark eyes glinting in the colours of the lanterns' warm glow. She accepted his hand and stepped from the car, and his eyes turned molten, warming her from the inside out. 'Welcome to my tent,' he said, and in the next breath, 'You look exquisite,' before nodding to the driver to leave them.

It was only then, when he had taken his eyes from her, that she noticed the pool behind him. The coloured light from the lamps played on the water and then beyond that the deep valley cut between the cliffs where palm trees sway grew thick and dense down the sides of the valley.

'What is this place?' she asked, taking a step towards the cliff.

'Palm Valley,' he said, wrapping his arms around her from behind, nuzzling at her neck. 'They say it has been here since the days of the dinosaurs. I think it was left here by the universe as a gift to you.'

She sighed as he warmed her skin with his mouth, setting it to tingling, already feeling the drugging effects of his caresses.

'And the tent and the pool?'

'Ah. That, now, is a gift to you from me.'

His hands flattened over her belly, one heading north to her breasts, cupping one in his fingers, his palm exquisite torture against one straining nipple, while the other headed south to cup the feminine mound at the apex of her thighs. She moaned softly as he pressed closer behind her, a reluctant protest, but knowing that there were things that must be said.

'I have refreshments,' he said. 'Sweetmeats with champagne, or sweet, spiced tea if you prefer.'

'No, nothing,' she said, knowing she must tell him about Hana, even as his hands stirred her desires until she felt herself grow slick with need. 'There's something I must do first...'

'I was hoping you'd feel that way,' he growled as he swung her into his arms. 'I can't wait either.'

She meant to stop him and make him put her down, but his mouth was already on hers and she was already too far gone, her senses buzzing, her body happily anticipating the pleasures to come. Besides, would it hurt to wait until after they'd made love to explain? He'd be more patient then, for a start, and most likely more receptive.

And afterwards she would tell him what she had decided—that she would marry him.

Maybe it was better to wait, she thought a few minutes later as his hot mouth blazed a trail up her inner thigh and his tongue flicked her *there*. Why spoil his fun when he was doing his best to persuade her?

Bahir was a master of persuasion, she reflected some indeterminable time later as she lay panting in the pool waiting for him to return with the promised tea. Even if she had come here tonight determined to say no to his proposal, by now she would be utterly convinced of the merits of marriage.

The bed he had laid her upon had just been the *entrée*. What he had dished up then had been a feast of sensual pleasure, a banquet designed to leave her giddy, knowing that it just didn't get any better. She smiled to herself. She would be marrying a man who made making love an art form. How lucky could one woman get?

And to make love to her like that—to worship her body so thoroughly—surely meant he must love her, she reasoned, even just a little. Otherwise she would make him love her. Once they were married.

Marina sighed, lingering in the star-kissed water one blissful moment longer, knowing it was late and that she should move.

Making love in a pool under the desert sky had been heaven but there was no putting off telling him about Hana any more. She would get dressed and tell him over tea and then, when he knew everything, if he still wanted to marry her, she would tell him yes. She groaned, feeling bone-weary after their night of sex, every muscle in her body protesting as she forced herself out of the pool and reached for one of the plush towels piled high on a side table.

The pile slid from the table to the ground, knocking something else off the table too, a mat of some kind. Not a mat, she realised, but a brochure, a real estate brochure. Curious, she wrapped the towel around herself, reached for it and started to read.

'You're out of the pool?'

She turned to see him bearing a tray with an ornate teapot, two tiny cups and a suspicious-looking box.

She looked up at him. 'I was in serious danger of falling asleep. Plus I needed to talk to you. I find I do that better when I'm not naked.' Though the way he looked right now, with a fluffy white towel slung low around his hips accentuating his dark-golden skin and making the most of the taper from his shoulders to his hips...

Maybe him looking naked would be less distracting. At least then she wouldn't have to use her imagination or resort to memories to peel it off...

She shook her head and held up the brochure, wondering if there would ever come a time when the mere sight of him didn't distract her. 'What's this?' she asked, holding it up so he could see. 'It was near the towels.'

'Ah,' he said, looking disappointed, pouring two cups of the sweetly scented brew, 'I was saving that for the finale, after you had agreed to marry me.'

A sizzle zipped down her spine.

So that explained the box on the tray...

Even though she had come here tonight knowing she would say yes to him, something about this latest surprise bothered her. Why was he thinking of buying such a place close to where she already lived in Tuscany, unless he wasn't planning on living with her once they were married? What kind of marriage was he contemplating? 'You are so sure that I would say yes?'

He smiled, looking almost boyish, and she couldn't help but see her son in his face. 'Of course you would say yes.'

She looked back at the brochure so she didn't have to answer beyond the rising tide of colour in her cheeks. Why did nothing suddenly making any sense? 'But I don't understand. What do you want with a house near Pisa?'

He moved to her shoulder and pointed to the pictures of the villa, the sprawling villa spread over several levels on fertile acreage, complete with infinity pool, tennis court and stables, all within fifteen minutes drive of Pisa. 'It's perfect, isn't it?'

Something about the way he said those words alerted her. 'It's lovely,' she said cautiously. Non-committally.

'And it's all down to you.' He put his arm around her shoulders, giving them a squeeze when she frowned up at him, not understanding. 'You were the one who pointed out I didn't even have a home to my name. Do you remember? And, given I have a son who needs a roof over his head, you were absolutely right.'

He pointed to something in the small print, something she could barely make out in the low lighting, not sure she would make sense of it even if the lights were brighter. 'Look where it is. I know you like the area, so I looked for something in the region, only closer to Pisa airport so that the commute between here and there doesn't take so long. I figured we would be spending some time here in Jaqbar as well.'

She held up one hand and shifted away. 'Hang on. What do you mean about Chakir needing a roof over his head? He has a perfectly good roof over his head where he is now.'

He shook his head dismissively. 'No. That is out of the question. I will not have my son living in a house that belongs to that man.'

'What man? Who do you mean?'

'Hana's father. I won't have my son living there.'

Something in her brain fused. She could not believe she had heard what she had just heard. 'What did you just say?'

'I said that my son will not live in a house owned by Hana's father. I am his father. From now on I will put a roof over my son's head. From now on, I will provide for him.'

'Who told you we lived in Hana's father's house?'

'Did you think I wouldn't work it out? A "good friend", you said. Who else could it be but a man only too happy to bury his mistake somewhere deep in the country where no one would ever find her?'

She reeled at his words as if he'd struck her a physical blow. She had suspected he would think the worst when she had told him the house belonged to a friend, but never had she imagined that he might concoct an entire fantasy around a throwaway line and assume it to be true. And she had thought she would never again hear him utter a certain word in the context of her children. 'I thought you knew better than to call either of my children a mistake.'

'I note you don't deny it is his house.'

'Only because it is too ridiculous to be true! Maybe this might convince you.' She slowed her delivery to one deliberate word at a time, hoping it might actually sink in. 'It—is—not—Hana's—father's—house. Satisfied?'

He blinked, then gave a toss of his head as if it didn't matter. 'It is of no consequence, you won't be needing it any more anyway.' He waved the brochure in the air. 'I will arrange to have everything packed and shipped before you leave the desert.'

She put a hand to her forehead, wondering when she had slipped into some parallel universe where Bahir had assumed ownership of her life. Maybe when she had cried out his name in pleasure or when she had dozed in the pool. And, while it would be so easy to set him straight and tell him the truth, this was not the way she had planned to tell him about Hana.

Besides, why should she have to explain at all? His

attitude alone was enough to make her dig her heels in. 'No, you will not do anything of the sort. Chakir has a home already. He is happy there. We all are. I'm sorry you went to all the trouble of buying a house when there is no need, but we have no intention of moving.'

He snorted his disgust and strode, hands on hips, beyond the pool to where the cliff edge fell away into the deep palm-filled valley. 'Why are you being so difficult about this?'

That was rich, coming from him. She was tired, even disappointed, that much was true. 'You think I'm the one being difficult?'

'If the house is so special, there must be a reason. And, if it is not Hana's father's, then whose house is it?' He looked over his shoulder at her, damnation in his eyes. 'Yet another of your lovers?'

Shock punched the air from her lungs. She, who'd been going to tell him tonight about Sarah and the arrangements she had put in place for her daughter, decided that she was glad she had said nothing before now. Because maybe she was getting a glimpse of the real Bahir, the man beneath the persuasive mask he'd been wearing all this week. 'What lovers? What are you talking about?'

'Come on, don't play the innocent. There must have been lovers after me. A woman with your appetites.'

'So what if there were? What about you? Have you had other lovers in the, oh, four years since we parted? Or have you nobly chosen to remain celibate in my honour? How touching! Then again, a man *with your appetites*?' she said, throwing his words right back at him and shaking her head knowingly. 'Somehow I very much doubt it.'

'There have been lovers,' he said, grinding the words out between his teeth. Of course there had been. Or, at least there had been sex. Nowhere near as much as she might think, and nowhere near as satisfying as it should have been, not that she needed to know either of those facts. 'At least I am willing to admit it.'

'What do you want, Bahir? A blow-by-blow description of my life after you threw me out? No! You abrogated all rights to the intimate details of my life when you told me to get out of your life and that you never wanted to see me again.'

Then she seemed to wilt before him, the fire in her eyes extinguished. She put her hands to her face on a sigh. 'And we know why you said that now, don't we? We know why you banished me from your life that day.'

She shook her head, looking up at him plaintively, her dark eyes almost too big for her face. 'Oh God, what's happening here, Bahir? Why are you doing this? Why are we arguing?'

For a moment he didn't know why and he knew even less how to answer. How had they got to this place? And what did he really want? A guarantee that if he gambled on this marriage, that he wouldn't end up the loser? How could anyone give such a guarantee? When had he ever expected one of those?

But he needed to know the odds.

'I just want you to tell me the truth.'

She gave a weak laugh. 'The truth.' She held out her arms by her side and dropped them again. 'Now, there's a concept. Okay, so maybe it's time you heard the truth. Maybe this time you'll be ready to believe it. I love you, Bahir, with all my heart and all my soul. There was never anyone else. There never has been.'

The gears in his brain crunched to a standstill with all he knew and with all he had seen. 'Is that what you told Hana's father?'

She didn't answer. She just looked up at him with those damned eyes that made him almost hurt to look at them, as though she was the one who was wronged. And then she simply said, 'I want to go home.'

She wasn't getting out of it that easily. 'I saw you,' he said. 'A month after we split up I saw you in Monte Carlo. You were wearing that red dress that I'd bought you, the one I loved peeling off. And you were with a man…'

She just closed her eyes and shook her head. 'I want to go home.'

He sighed wearily and looked upwards, seeing the sky and the stars sliding lower on the horizon, recognising that in a few short hours it would be dawn. Recognising that there was no time to fix this now. 'Get dressed,' he said gruffly, looking at the tray with the ring box still sitting there untouched, angry that the night that had started out with such promise had ended so badly. And all because he'd stupidly put the brochure somewhere she could find it. But why did she take offence every time he mentioned Hana's father? Why did she try to pretend the affair had never happened?

'I'll take you back to the camp. We can talk about this later.'

'No,' she said, turning her body away from him, dragging on her clothes as quickly as she could. 'I want to go home. I want to go anywhere that's as far from you as I can possibly get.'

He reached out and touched a hand to her shoulder to turn her. 'Marina, don't do this—'

'Don't touch me!' She shrugged out of his grasp. 'Don't you ever lay a finger on me again.'

'Marina!'

She pulled her robe over her head, lifting out the curtain of her long black hair as she swung around. 'And you know the funny thing in all this? The thing that really cracks me up?'

When it came, his voice was as dry as the desert sands. 'Tell me, if you must.'

She swiped up one sandal from the floor and shoved it on her foot. 'I never even met Hana's father. How's that for a laugh?'

'What are you saying?'

'You work it out, Bahir,' she said, searching for her other sandal. 'You, who thinks he knows so much about who I sleep with and how often.'

'Marina—'

'Oh, and the really funny one? You'll get a good belly laugh out of this one, I promise you: Hana owns the house. Not her father or some other mythical lover from that long list you seem to want to attribute to me, but Hana.' She gave a mock frown. 'But you're not laughing, Bahir. Don't you think it's funny?'

She wasn't making any sense. 'How can Hana own a house?'

'Simple. Her mother left it to her. Now, get me out of this hellhole desert fantasy of yours and then get us to Souza. I'm taking my children home.'

He wasn't laughing. Instead, as he drove back to camp with Marina staring blankly out of the passenger window feigning interest in the inky darkness, he felt like the world as he knew it was coming apart at the seams.

And, battle as he might, he could not get the pieces to fit back together again. Not in any way that fitted with what he knew.

Because she had professed her love to him in one breath and fallen into someone else's arms the next.

Hadn't she?

She had borne his child and gone on to have another's in the blink of an eye.

Hadn't she?

She had been living all this time in the house of her sometime lover.

But then she had said it was Hana's house.

Oh God. These assumptions were the very foundation of his treatment of her all along. These formed the cornerstones of his resentment. How he had resented the way she had moved on so quickly—how that belief had poisoned his mind and turned this night toxic.

And if those assumptions were wrong...

Her words jumbled in his head. *Hana's house. Her mother.* A father Marina had never met. How could any of it make sense? The four-wheel drive tore over the rocky desert track just as realisation sliced through his senses like a scythe.

Unless Hana was someone else's child.

There was no other explanation. Why had he been so blind all this time? Because, apart from her dark hair, she didn't even look like Marina.

Except he knew why he had been blind all this time—because it had been what he had wanted to believe. To prove he hadn't made a mistake all those years ago. To put a lid on his feelings for her and label them with a very different emotion. To protect himself from life's greatest gamble.

Except now he had lost everything.

He had lost her.

There was nothing to see in the inky darkness on the way back to the camp except for the eerie glow from the eyes of a night creature caught in the spotlights before slinking away. There was nothing to say, and if Bahir was curious he didn't let on—which was good, because Marina wasn't inclined to fill him in on the details of how Hana had come to own their villa in Tuscany. He could construct his own explanation. He was a master at that.

Besides, she felt too gutted to speak. There was nothing inside her but a yawning pit into which all her stupid, pointless hopes and dreams had fallen, smashing to dust when they hit rock bottom. Instead she fixed her gaze out of the passenger window and watched the night sky peel away, layer by layer, preparing for the coming dawn, and felt the first stirrings of maternal unease.

What had she been thinking? All those pointless, fruitless hours she had spent with him, thinking this was *the* night, allowing herself to be seduced, imagining it could possibly end in happiness.

What a fool she'd been.

What a damned, stupid fool.

They topped the last rise and a blaze of lights shone

in the distance, bright where surely there should be no more than a lamp or two.

'What's that?' she asked, that curling ribbon of unease snaking and twisting inside her.

'The camp,' he said, putting his foot down on the accelerator, and the feeling of unease in her stomach became a full-blown fear.

She should never have left.

They pulled up in a flurry of dust and stones only to be greeted by the tear-streaked face of Catriona, Chakir clutched tightly in her arms, his dark eyes looking bewildered at the fuss.

'It's Hana,' she said. 'We can't find her.'

CHAPTER ELEVEN

'No!' Ice ran through Marina's veins as she bolted from the car and raced into their tent, needing to see for herself Hana's empty bed. The sheets were cold to the touch when she rested the palm of her hand down on them.

Oh God, she thought, feeling sick. She should never have gone. Why had she gone? Why had she stayed away so long? 'How long has she been missing?' she asked, taking Chakir from the distressed Catriona, needing to hug him, to prove one of her children was still there. 'Where have they looked?'

'I'm so sorry,' Catriona said, distraught. 'She must have slipped out while I was asleep. I don't know how long she's been gone.'

'She can't have gone far,' Marina said, wishing for it to be so.

'They're looking through every tent again. Searchers have started fanning out into the desert in case she wandered off.'

'No!' She collapsed into a chair, clutching Chakir tightly to her chest, her hand cradling his head. He was too big now to be held that way and he squirmed under her hands, but she would not let him go. The thought of Hana wandering off into the dark desert night over shifting desert sands was too dreadful to contemplate.

'I'll find her,' she heard Bahir say, but his voice sounded a long way away.

'I wish I hadn't gone,' she said, rocking her son. 'I should never have gone. I should never have left them.'

He watched her while she rocked, her face bleached white with shock, her arms wound so tightly around their son that he could feel her pain. 'I'll find her,' he repeated as much for his own benefit as for hers.

After the mess he had made of tonight, he had to.

The camp was alive with activity when he emerged from the tent, everyone aware of the seriousness of the situation; of a tiny child, wandering lost and alone in the desert. She couldn't have gone far, he rationalised as he threw the brightly coloured Arabian saddle over his horse, not on her short legs. But, still, which way had she gone? If anything happened to her, she would never forgive herself for leaving the children and he would never forgive himself for taking her away from them.

The sky was lightening now, the promise of a new day also a threat, bringing a scorching sun to the hunt, both a blessing and a curse.

His mount snorted and hoofed the earth, as if sensing the urgency as he leapt onto its back and wheeled it around, preparing to set off. Where would a child go? he wondered, scanning the surrounding dunes now lit with half-light. Where would Hana go?

He had already headed to the top of the nearest dune when he heard the goat bleating, an oddly discordant note to its sound. He turned his mount around and looked more closely at the flock of animals contained in a loose corral. It sounded almost as if something was wrong.

And he wondered.

Animals scattered as he came close, the black Bedouin goats and desert sheep waking in alarm, bleating protests at the stranger in their midst as they skittered out of his way. Then he saw the old mother goat lying at the back, blinking up at him with her sideways eyes, her twin kids nestled together on the ground, a tiny child curled in their midst.

A motionless child.

Hana!

He must have said her name out loud because she woke with a start and burst into tears, confused and disoriented as he lifted her to his chest. And he was so relieved that she was all right, that she had only been asleep, that he just held her and cuddled her close and told her it was all right, even as she wailed against his chest and cried for her mother.

'It's okay, Hana. I'll take you to your mother,' he said, rubbing her back the way he'd seen Marina do, talking to the child in a low voice, hoping to calm her down. 'She was worried about you, and so sorry she wasn't there. That was my fault. I took her away. I should never have done that.'

The child's sobs slowed. She curled closer to him, recognising him, feeling safer. 'And if anything had happened to you,' he said, stroking her hair as her head rested on his shoulder, 'I would never have forgiven myself. You have a special mother, you know, and she deserves better than anything I can give her. Much better. Just as you deserve a father who can keep you safe.'

Hana sniffed against his shoulder and rubbed her eyes and he leaned his head down and kissed her black curls. 'But I will miss you, Hana Banana, when you are gone. And it will be my own stupid fault, for not realising how precious your mother was from the very beginning. For never being able to tell her what I felt because I didn't understand what I felt. For being jealous of shadows. For never realising all this time that I loved her. Only now it's too late.'

'Hana,' she said, looking up at him solemnly as she focused on the important part of his conversation. 'Hana 'nana.'

He smiled in spite of the dampness he felt rising in his eyes, knowing he had missed a chance at life and love. Knowing he was returning to a bleak and point-less future—the future of his own making, the future he *deserved*—and now all the more bleak for knowing what he would be missing. 'You are,' he said, touching a fingertip to the tip of her cute nose, 'the best Hana 'nana ever.'

She giggled and he smiled with her, even as he felt his own world crumbling apart.

The goats! Marina was sitting with Chakir on her lap when she wondered—had anyone checked the goats? She kissed her son and left him with Catriona, who promised a hundred times that she would not take her eyes from him. Marina hugged her and told her to stop blaming herself and ran from the tent.

Hana was in love with those baby goats. Had anyone looked? Was there a chance?

She heard her daughter's screams before she got

there and she almost bolted across the sands towards the sound in relief, until she saw Bahir with his back to her, cradling Hana against his shoulder, his soothing hand at her back; until she heard the words he uttered to her and she paused silent in the cool light of dawn to listen.

'My fault,' she heard him say amongst the snippets of his words she could catch. 'She deserves better.' So true, she thought, knowing she must remain resolute and equally determined not to have her intentions to return home watered down by the picture of him cradling Hana on his shoulder, a picture she had dreamed of happening one day—lots of one days. But why did it have to happen now?

Why now, when everything was lost?

She would have stepped from the shadows then—she almost did—except she heard him say, 'And it will be my own stupid fault, for not realising how precious your mother was from the very beginning.' She paused, and heard him go on to talk of jealousy and shadows, then of love—she held her breath—and of how it was now too late.

Her lungs sucked in air. She must have made a sound, because Hana lifted her head from his shoulder and saw her. 'Mama!' she cried, holding out her arms.

She ran to her child then, scooping her from his arms and hugged her close. 'Oh, Hana, you gave me such a scare. What were you doing here with your goats?'

'Goat,' Hana said, pointing to the babies now drinking at their mother's teats, and she looked up, saw Bahir standing there and smiled. 'Thank you,' she said.

He gave a slight bow of his head. Formally. Distantly.

As if he had already withdrawn from her, knowing she was leaving. 'I will make arrangements for your departure to Souza.'

She knew she should still go home. She had made up her mind to go. But something about his softly spoken words made her hesitate. No, not something—his talk of love made her hesitate. Made her wonder...

'There's no rush,' she said, and he looked back at her, confusion skating across the surface of his dark eyes. 'Hana will need to rest. We all will.'

As if on cue, Hana yawned and dropped her head onto her mother's shoulder. He nodded and turned to go. 'Of course. Whenever you are ready. I will go and call off the search.'

'And Bahir?'

He stopped but this time he didn't turn around. 'Can we talk?' she said. 'Once Hana is asleep? I was going to tell you last night before... Well, I didn't tell you, and I owe you an explanation at least.'

He shook his head, looking down at his feet. 'You owe me nothing. Not after what I have done to you. The things I have said...'

The note of despair in his flat lifeless voice squeezed her heart. 'Come to my tent once you have called off the search and I will tell you about my friend Sarah.' She looked down at the drowsy child in her arms. 'Hana's birth mother.'

Hana was sleeping when he lifted the flap into the children's sleeping quarters a little while later, Marina sitting alongside and watching her as if she was afraid she might disappear again. Though she didn't turn, she must have sensed it was him, because without looking his way she gestured him to enter and sit down on the end of the bed.

'Sarah was a friend of mine,' she started as he sat down softly. 'I'd met her a few times at the casino and we'd say hello, but it was after our split that we grew closer.' She looked over at him then, a sad smile on her face. 'She helped me, you see, in the days and weeks following— Well, you know. She let me move in with her, and when she found out I was pregnant she mothered me a little. She had always wanted a baby, she said. She wanted nothing more in the world. But she had suffered from cancer as a teenager and wasn't sure she even could conceive a child.

'And then Chakir was born and she decided she wanted a baby more than ever, while there still might be a slim chance she might be a mother. She didn't have a partner and so she found a nameless man—I never found out who, I never knew the details—and became pregnant.'

She sniffed, and he could see the glow of moisture in her eyes. 'It was while they were doing the pregnancy tests that they found out the cancer was back, and this time more aggressive than ever. They told her she would have to have an abortion, because the treatment she needed to save her would kill her baby.'

She pressed her lips together. 'She refused treatment. She wanted this baby so much, even though she knew the risk to herself. Even though she knew it might well cost her own life, she knew she would never get another chance. And when Hana was born she said it was the happiest day of her life, even though her body was wasted and she was already dying and there was nothing the doctors could do...'

Her voice trailed away as the tears rolled down her cheeks and he ached to kiss them away, but he knew he had no right to touch her or to soothe her pain when he had caused so much of it himself, pain he now knew was so wrongfully inflicted. He had no right to comfort her.

'She loved Hana so much,' she continued, her hands clenched tightly in her lap. 'And she asked me if I would adopt her, because she wanted Hana and Chakir to grow up together.'

'She had no family of her own?'

'Sarah was estranged from her parents—they were very strict and they cut her off when they learned she was working in a casino. I don't know what they thought she did there, but they said they preferred to think that she'd died of her cancer rather than live with the eternal shame of knowing she worked in such a "den of iniquity". Only her grandmother kept in touch. It hurt Sarah terribly, but it made her stronger too, and more determined to experience everything that she could.

'And then her grandmother died and left her enough money to buy the house in Tuscany. A refuge, she called it, her sanctuary. And when her parents argued the money should be theirs, she told them it was already gone and they assumed she'd gambled it away.'

She sighed and looked down at the hands in her lap.

'She left it to Hana. She wanted her to always have a home, for us all to have a home. And nobody blinked when I emerged from the Tuscan mountainside with another baby to my name. Nobody questioned that the party-girl princess had been irresponsible again.'

Guilt consumed him. He hung his head in shame and horror at the assumptions he had made—at the sheer injustice of them.

'I promised Sarah I would tell nobody our secret. Only Catriona and the lawyers knew and that's how it would stay.' She shook her head. 'She never told me who Hana's father was and I never asked, but Sarah was more afraid of her parents and what they might do if they discovered the truth. So I promised Sarah I would look after Hana as my own. I promised I would keep her safe and never betray her trust.'

He should have seen it coming. He should have guessed. Because hadn't he noticed? Hadn't he re-marked on it himself? Hadn't he infused her answer with yet more damnation? 'You have no idea if she looks like her father, do you?'

This time Marina smiled, her liquid eyes glowing with the memories of her friend. 'She's the image of Sarah. She's beautiful.'

'I was so wrong,' he said, knowing his words to be painfully inadequate. Knowing they were nowhere near enough. Knowing he could never make up for all the wrongs he'd committed against this warm, wonderful woman who had taken another woman's child and nur-tured it as her own. 'I am so sorry, Marina.'

She shrugged and gave a wan smile. 'That day you saw me, in the casino, in your red dress—there were four of us that night. It was Sarah's birthday and she convinced me to go out and wear that dress while I still could, while it still fit.'

The lamp on the tent wall flickered as she sighed. 'I didn't want to go. I didn't want to party, I didn't want any chance of seeing you. But you'd said something about going to Macau, and besides, it was Sarah's birthday and I wanted to be happy for her. She deserved to be happy. But I don't even remember who that man was. I'd never met him before. I never met him again. I went home early that night...'

God. He dropped his head into his hands. 'You must hate me,' he said. 'I don't blame you for hating me. I hate myself for the things I have said to you. For my toxic thoughts and words.'

'I wanted to. I still want to.' She swung her head his way then, a tiny frown between her dark brows. 'Why were you there that night, when you had said you were leaving Europe? Why did you come back?'

He snorted out a laugh. 'I came looking for you. I wanted...' He thought back to that night, to the torture of a month of regret and self-damnation. 'I wanted to tell you I was sorry.' And this time he did manage to laugh, a derisive, self-deprecating laugh. 'The pattern of my life, it seems—apologising to you for treating you so appallingly.'

'You came back to find me?'

'I'd had a month to think about the things I'd said to you in anger. I'd tried to put it out of my mind, but I could not forgive myself. I thought, if I found you and explained, that you might understand and maybe even forgive me yourself.

'Except my anger rose anew when I saw you smiling and laughing, like I had never existed. I told myself I was a fool for thinking you would want me back. I told myself I was a fool for thinking that I wanted your love—that I loved you too.

'God, what a mess.' He rose, raking his fingers through his hair. 'I'm sorry, Marina. I know it's no consolation, but I will never stop being sorry for the way I have treated you.'

'You came back to find me? To tell me you were sorry?' She couldn't get her head around it. The fact he had come back. The fact he had wanted her back. And it was suddenly too much bear—the thought of all these wasted years, all the pointless grief. She dropped her head into her hands as fresh tears flooded her eyes. All that futile, pointless grief.

She felt his strong arms go around her, wrapping her into his embrace. 'I'm so sorry,' he whispered hoarsely, rocking her as she had seen him do with Hana such a short time ago.

'I want to hate you,' she said. 'Because I was prepared to walk away.' She sniffed, sobbing. 'And now you tell me you loved me. Now, when it's too late.'

He drew her to her feet, smoothing the tears from her cheeks with the pads of his thumbs. 'You are better off without me. You are better off going home and forgetting you ever met me. You are better off hating me.'

'But I can't.' She sniffed, grinding the words through her teeth, curling her hands into fists and jamming them in between them, pounding at the solid wall of his chest to stress her words. 'I tried and I tried. But, damn you, I can't!'

'Then try harder. Remember all the things I did and said. Because I am a bad bet, Marina. I will never be good enough for you. You deserve better.' He turned to go, was already out of Hana's room when she caught him, and clamped her hands around his before he could walk out of her life for the second time.

'I don't want better,' she protested. 'I want you, Bahir. I love you. I can't stop loving you. And you told Hana. I heard you. You told her that you loved me.'

He stilled. 'You heard me say that?'

'You told her, I heard you. And now I want you to tell me. Surely I deserve to hear it?'

He looked into her eyes, searching them, almost hopeful, until he blinked and the despair returned to colour their depths. 'What good can it possibly do? There is no point to this, Marina. I have done enough harm. I will not hurt you any more. I will not risk it.'

'I want to hear the words, Bahir. If you are truly sorry, then tell me what I have longed to hear for so long. You owe it to me.'

And this time he hesitated only a moment before he wrapped her in his arms and crushed her to his chest. 'Oh, my love, my sweet, sweet love. I do love you, Marina, and I hate myself for causing you so much pain. I will never forgive myself.'

She sagged against him, relief and hope washing through her. At last the words she'd longed to hear. 'I forgive you. If that helps.'

He took her face in his hands, his eyes looking down at her with a mix of helplessness and hope. 'How can you ever forgive me?'

'Because I love you, Bahir. I have always loved you. Don't you understand? There was never going to be anyone else. There couldn't be.'

'But you are too good for me. You deserve better.'

She pushed away from his chest to look up at him.

'No! Listen, Bahir, why do you think it suited me to take Hana? Do you think I did it purely out of the goodness of my heart? Of course, I would have done anything for Sarah, but it suited me too. For no man would be tempted to get involved with me, the mother of two illegitimate children, for fear that they might end up lumbered with us all. Don't you see? They protected me. I used them to hide behind, just as I used Sarah's house as my own sanctuary. It kept me safely tucked away, where nobody could find me. Where nobody could get close.

'The same with you,' she admitted. 'Because I let you think there was another man or other men. I let you believe what you wanted about who owned the house—out of spite at first, it's true, because you seemed too ready to believe the worst of me. And then it was easier to let you keep believing it. I'm so sorry. But I used Hana as a defence against you. I used her as a reason to hate you. I didn't tell you she wasn't mine only because I'd promised Sarah, but because it suited me to let you think I'd been with someone else, if only as some kind of defence against what I really felt for you. If only like some kind of protection.'

'You shouldn't need protection,' he said, pulling her close, stroking her hair. 'You should have someone to protect you. You should not be alone. You deserve to be loved.'

She breathed in, relishing his warm, masculine scent. 'You're so right, Bahir. I deserve to be loved. Which is why I have to ask you…'

His heart skipped a beat under her ear. 'Ask me what?'

She smiled up at him. 'I'm asking if you will do me the honour of becoming my husband?'

He pushed her away at arm's length. 'You would still marry me? After all that I have said and done?'

'Only if you really wanted to. Only if you would take us all—me, Chakir and Hana—and promise to love us for ever. Promise to make us one family.'

He breathed in, raising his face to the ceiling, before he looked back at her, incredulous. 'Whatever did I do in this world to deserve you? When did luck ever deal a better hand? Because yes, Marina, I will marry you. I will be your husband and I promise that you will never be sorry.'

'I know,' she said, a rush of happiness sweeping through her as she raised her lips for his kiss. 'I'm betting on it.'

EPILOGUE

THEY were married twice. Once in Jaqbar in the desert
in the traditional way—a 'simple' three-day ceremony
filled with much feasting, music and celebration—and
once again in Jemeya, this time a fusion of East and
West, and held in the palace of her father, the King, and
her childhood home.

Chakir solemnly bore the rings on a golden cushion,
his dark eyes concentrating on the pillow and so serious as he walked towards the altar that he looked like
a mini-Bahir.

Hana followed, their tiny flower girl, looking beautiful in a frothy white dress with a circlet of flowers on
her black hair, one gloved hand wrapped around her tiny
posy, the other tucked into the hand of her beautiful
aunt Aisha who whispered words of encouragement as
the wide-eyed child took faltering steps down the aisle.

Marina watched her tiny toddler gait with a bittersweet smile on her face, wishing Sarah could be here
to see how much she'd grown, and how beautiful she
looked with her hair done up and with the coiled ring-
lets framing her face.

As her father told her it was time and they set off
down the aisle behind them, and she looked beyond her

sister and her daughter, she saw Bahir at the front along-side his three friends, Zoltan, Rashid and Kadar, his dark eyes on Hana, his eyes smiling as she approached. He looked up then, and across the distance their eyes snagged and held and she felt the familiar sizzle all the way down to her toes.

Her father patted her hand as he walked her down the aisle. 'He's a fine man you're marrying.'

She only half-turned towards him, nodding to the guests as they passed. 'I know, Papa.'

'And I just wanted to tell you,' he continued, his voice low and gruff, 'that I'm proud of you, Marina. I know we've had our differences in the past, but I just want you to know that.'

This time when she looked across at him she was surprised to see he had tears in his eyes. 'Oh, Papa!' Even as they continued up the aisle, she reached up and pressed her lips to his cheek. 'I love you too.'

Her father beamed with pride and squeezed her hand tighter. 'Two daughters married,' he said as he passed her hand to Bahir's. 'To two fine men. Can it get any better?'

Marina looked up at Bahir as her father passed her hand to his, saw the man she intended spending the rest of her life with form the word 'beautiful' with his lips, and thought with a secret smile, maybe it could, but that would wait just a little while longer.

First of all, she had a man to marry.

Her heart sang as they took their vows. Chakir proffered up the cushion bearing their rings and Bahir slipped the twisted band of tricolour gold onto her fin-ger—white-gold for the endless desert plains, yellow-gold for the sun and rose-gold for sunrise and the promise of a new day.

He slipped the ring onto her finger before lifting it to his mouth and kissing it. 'I love you,' he whispered, a totally unexpected gesture that made her wish they were a million miles away and somewhere private instead of standing in front of a crowded room where every eye was upon them.

Then the ceremony was over and he surprised her again, scooping Hana into his arms before he slipped his arm through hers to walk down the aisle behind Chakir as the guests broke into spontaneous applause. Aboard Bahir's shoulder, Hana clapped her hands and giggled, delighted. She looked up at him, wondering. 'But what…?'

'Chakir and I had it all organised, didn't we, Chakir?' And their son looked over his shoulder and grinned up at her, nodding. 'We're a fambily now.'

'That's right,' said Bahir with a smile at Chakir's mispronuncination. 'We're a family. We should do this together.'

Their formal reception soon became a celebration, and at one stage it seemed everyone was on the dance floor, Bahir with Marina, Zoltan with Aisha and even Chakir dancing with Hana, the two of them spinning until they collapsed in fits of giggles on the dance floor.

Rashid and Kadar watched on from the side, Zoltan and Bahir joining them during a break.

'It looks like Zoltan's set a trend,' Bahir said, sporting the gold band on his finger. 'That's two out of four of us married so far. Who's next?'

Kadar and Rashid took a long look at each other.

'Don't look at me,' they both said together, and Bahir and Zoltan both laughed.

'Don't be so sure of that. You just never know.'

'What's the big joke?' asked Marina as the two women joined the men. Bahir moved to her side, unable to resist slipping his arm proprietorially around his new wife's slender waist in case anyone else thought of asking for the next dance before he could.

'Zoltan and I are laying odds on which one of these two jokers is next for the marriage stakes.'

'Not a chance,' said Rashid, holding up his hands. 'Once a playboy, always a playboy.'

'Besides,' Kadar joined in. 'All the good women are taken.'

'You better believe it,' Bahir said, whisking his bride off for another spin around the dance floor, closely followed by Aisha and Zoltan.

'Did I tell you,' Bahir started as he pulled her close in his embrace, 'just how beautiful you look today?'

Marina smiled. 'Oh, maybe a dozen times, no more than that.'

'I knew I hadn't said it anywhere near enough. You are the most beautiful woman I've ever seen, today more than ever.'

'Because you make me the happiest woman alive, Bahir.'

They kissed in the midst of the dance floor while Zoltan and Aisha spun by with eyes only for each other, the love they felt for each other clearly on display. Bahir smiled when he looked at them. 'To think Chakir and Hana will soon have a new playmate when Zoltan and Aisha's baby arrives. They will like that.'

She smiled up at him. 'Maybe two.'

'They're having twins? Zoltan didn't say.'

'No. Not twins. But there's another baby coming. Another playmate for Chakir and Hana.'

He stopped dancing, his heart skipping a beat, holding her at arm's length to look at her. 'You mean you...? We...? You mean...?'

She laughed. 'I mean we are having a baby, Bahir.'

'But when? How?'

Her smile was softer this time as she stepped back into his warm embrace. 'In the desert where we lay together that day. We have been sent a blessing from your family and from your tribe. We have been sent a blessing in the form of a child.'

He pulled her to him then, wrapping her in his arms, pressing his lips to her head as a joy so profound filled him until it spilled over and coloured the world in rich harmonious light. And when he could breathe again, when he could think, he lifted her chin with his hand and saw the moisture in her eyes, moisture that mirrored his own.

'You have made me the happiest man alive, Marina. You have given back something to me I thought was lost for ever. You have given me back my family. I love you so much.'

'As I love you, Bahir. As I will always love you.'

There were no words he could find to answer her, there were no words that could prove what he said to be true. So he told her with his kiss as they spun together on the dance floor, just as he would prove it every day of their life together.

* * * * *

The Sheikh's Jewel

MELISSA JAMES

Melissa James is a born-and-bred Sydney-sider. Wife and mother of three, a former nurse, she fell into writing when her husband brought home an article about romance writers and suggested she should try it—and she became hooked. Switching from romantic espionage to the family stories of the Mills & Boon® Cherish™ line was the best move she ever made. Melissa loves to hear from readers—you can e-mail her at authormelissajames@yahoo.com.

To my editor, Bryony Green,
with my deepest thanks for all her help
as I tried to make the deadline for this book
during an international move.

CHAPTER ONE

Sar Abbas, capital city of Abbas al-Din
Three years ago

'Is THIS a joke?'

Sitting straight-backed in an overstuffed chair, her body swathed in the black of deep mourning, Amber el-Qurib stared up at her father in disbelief. 'Please, Father, tell me you're trying to make me laugh.' But even as she pleaded she knew it was hopeless.

Her father, Sheikh Aziz of Araba Numara—Land of the Tiger—was also wearing mourning clothes, but his face was composed. He'd wept enough the first day, in the same shock as everyone else; but he hadn't cried since, apart from a few decorous tears at Fadi's funeral. 'Do you think I would make jokes about your future, Amber, or play with a decision that is so important to our nation?' His tone bordered on withering.

Yes, she ought to have known. Though he'd been a kind father, in all her life, she'd never heard her father make a joke about anything relating to the welfare of Araba Numara.

'My fiancé only died six weeks ago.' Amber forced the words out through a throat thick with weeks of tears. He'd been the co-driver for his younger brother Alim, in just one rally. The Double Racing Sheikhs had caused a great deal of mirth and media interest in Abbas al-Din, as had the upcoming wedding.

Even now it seemed surreal. How could Fadi be *dead*—and how could she marry his brother within another month, as her father wanted? How could it even be done while Alim was fighting for his life, with second- and third-degree burns? 'It—it isn't decent,' she said, trying to sound strong but, as ever when with her father, she floundered under the weight of her own opinion. Was she right?

And when her father sighed, giving her the long-suffering look she'd always hated—it made her feel selfish, or like a silly girl—she knew she'd missed something, as usual. 'There are some things more important than how we appear to others. You understand how it is, Amber.'

She did. Both their countries had fallen into uproar after Sheikh Fadi's sudden death in a car wreck. The beloved leader of Abbas al-Din had been lost before he could marry and father a legitimate son, and Amber's people had lost a union that was expected to bring closer ties to a nation far stronger and wealthier than theirs.

It was vital at this point that both nations find stability. The people needed hope: for Araba Numara, that they'd have that permanent connection to Abbas al-Din, and Fadi's people needed to know the el-Kanar family line would continue.

She swiped at her eyes again. Damn Fadi! He'd risked his life a week before their wedding, knowing he didn't want her and she didn't want him—but thousands of marriages had started with less than the respect and liking they'd had for one another. They could have worked it out—but now the whispers were circulating.

She'd endured some impertinent insinuations, from the maids to Ministers of State. That much she could bear, if only she didn't have doubts of her own, deep-held fears that woke her every night.

She'd known he wasn't happy—was deeply unhappy—at the arranged marriage; but *had* Fadi risked death to avoid marrying her?

Certainly neither of them had been in love, but that wasn't uncommon. Fadi had been deeply in love with his mistress, the sweet widow who'd borne his son. But with probably the only impulsive decision he'd ever made, he'd left his country leaderless in a minute. At the moment Alim, his brother and the remaining heir, was still fighting for his life.

'Amber?' her father asked, his tone caught between exasperation and uncertainty. 'The dynasty here must continue, and very quickly. We only gain from the mother of the dynasty being one of our daughters.'

'Then let it continue with someone else! Haven't I done enough?'

'Who do you suggest? Maya is not yet seventeen. Nafisah is but fourteen, and Amal twelve. Your cousins are of similar age to them.' Her father made a savage noise. 'You are the eldest, already here, and bound to the el-Kanar family. They are obligated by their ancient law on brides to care for you, and find you a husband within the family line. Everything—tradition, law, honour and the good of your family—demands that you accept this offer.'

Shamed but still furious, Amber kept her mouth tightly closed. Why must all this fall on her shoulders? She wanted to cry out, *I'm only nineteen!*

Why did some get responsibilities in life, and others all the fun? Alim had shrugged off his responsibilities to the nation for years, chasing fame and wealth on the racing circuit while Fadi and the youngest brother— what was his name again?—had done all the work. Yes, Alim was famous around the world, and had brought so much wealth to the nation with his career in geological surveys and excavation.

And then she realised what—or *who* it was she could be turning down. Even though a sudden marriage repulsed her sense of what felt right in her grief for the man she'd cared for deeply as a friend, the thought of *who* she must be marrying didn't repulse her at all.

Her father laid a hand on her shoulder. It was only with the long years of training that she managed not to shrug off the rare gesture of affection, knowing it was only given to make her stop arguing. For women of her status, any emotion was a luxury one only indulged in among the safety of other women, or not at all if one had the necessary pride. 'You know how it is, Amber. We *need* this marriage. One brother or another, what does it matter to you? You barely knew Fadi before your engagement was agreed upon. You only came to stay here two months before he died, and most of the time he was working or gone.'

Blushing, Amber turned her head, looking at the ground to the left of her feet. *Such a beautiful rug,* she thought inconsequentially; but no matter what she looked at, it didn't block out the memory of where Fadi had gone whenever he had spare time—to his mistress. And always he'd come back with Rafa's smell on his skin, some mumbled apologies and yet another promise he'd never see Rafa again when they were married: a promise given with heartbreak in his eyes.

Amber felt the shadows of the past envelop her. She alone knew where the fault lay with Fadi's death. Sweet,

kind, gentle Fadi had always done the right thing, including agreeing to marry another ruler's daughter for
political gain, when he was deeply in love with an unsuitable commoner, a former housemaid…and Amber,
too, had feelings for another, if only from afar. And
nobody knew it but the three people whose lives were
being torn apart.

She knew Fadi would never wish her harm, but if
it had been Amber who'd died suddenly, it would have
set him free to be with Rafa—at least for a little while,
until the next arranged political marriage.

She truly grieved for the loss of the gentle-hearted
ruler, as she would grieve for any friend lost. Fadi had
understood her feelings and sympathised with her, was
like the moon's sweet light in her darkness. So—was
it awful of her to feel this sudden little thrill that her
wayward heart's feelings were no longer forbidden?

*Fadi, I did care for you. I'm so sorry, but you're the
only one who'd understand…*

'I'm still in deep mourning, and you expect me
to marry his brother while he's still in hospital with
second- and third-degree burns? Won't that look—well,
rather desperate on our part?' she mumbled, wishing
she had something better to say, wishing she didn't feel
quite so excited. Hoping to heaven her father wouldn't
see it on her face. 'Can't you ask Alim if he'd be willing to wait a few months for the wedding—?'

'You will not be marrying Alim,' her father interrupted her bluntly.

Amber's head shot up. *'What?'*

'I'm sorry, my dear,' her father said quietly. 'Alim
disappeared from the hospital last night, unequivocally
refusing both Fadi's position and Fadi's bride. I doubt
he'll return for a long time, if ever.'

Amber almost snarled—almost. Women of her station didn't snarl, not even when the man she—she *liked* had just run out on her; but she managed to hang onto her self-control. 'Where did he go? How did he manage it?'

'Within hours of waking, Alim used his private jet and his medical team from the racing circuit to help him transfer to a private facility—we think he went somewhere in Switzerland. He still needs a lot of graft work on his burns, but he made it obvious that he won't return here when it's done.'

'He must have been desperate to escape from me, leaving hospital when he's at death's door,' she muttered, fighting off a sudden jolt of queasiness in her stomach.

'I doubt it was a personal rejection, my dear. He hardly knew you. I think it was perhaps more of—ah, a matter of principle, or a reaction made in grief.' Her father slanted her a look of semi-apology; so he was capable of embarrassment, at least. 'I find it hard to blame him, after the part he played in Fadi's death… imagine him waking up to find Fadi's skin on his body. He must have felt he'd taken enough from his brother— life, skin…it must be horrifying enough, but wedding and bedding Fadi's bride on top of all that must have felt as if he'd done it all on purpose.'

'Indeed,' she agreed, but with a trace of bitterness. Surely this day couldn't get any worse?

'Since you won't ask, I'll tell you. The youngest brother Harun has taken up the position as Hereditary Sheikh, and has agreed also to become your husband.'

The swirling winds of change had come right from the sun, scorching her to her core. 'Of course he has!' Amber didn't know she spoke aloud, the fury of rejection boiling over. 'So having been rejected by brothers one and two, I'm expected to—to wed and bed brother number three with a smile? There are limits to the amount of humiliation I must accept, surely, Father?'

'You will accept whatever I arrange for you, Amber.' His voice now was pure ice. 'And you should be grateful that I have given such thought to your marriage.'

'Oh, such thought indeed, Father! Why not send me to the princess pound? Because that's what I've become to you, isn't it—a dog, a piece of property returned for you to find a good home and husband elsewhere? Find another owner for Amber because *we* don't want her back.'

'Stop it,' her father said sharply. 'You're a beautiful woman. Many men have wanted to marry you, but I chose the el-Kanar brothers because they are truly good men.'

'Oh, yes, I know that well,' she mocked, knowing Father would punish her for this unprecedented outburst later, but not caring. 'Unfortunately for me, it seems they're good men who'd do anything to avoid me.' She spoke as coldly as she could—anything to hide the tears stinging her eyes and the huge lump in her throat. Alim, the wild and dashing Racing Sheikh, had risked his recovery, his very life to get away from her. As far as insults went, it outranked Fadi's by a million miles. 'Am I so repulsive, Father? What's wrong with me?'

'I see you are in need of relieving your, ah, feelings,' her father said with a strong streak of cold disapproval that she had *feelings* to vent. 'But we are not home, Amber. Royal women do not scream or make emotional outbursts.'

'I can't believe the last remaining brother in the dynasty is willing to risk it,' she pushed in the stinging acid of grief and humiliation without relief. 'Perhaps you should offer him one of my sisters instead, because it seems the el-Kanar men are allergic to me.'

'The Lord Harun has expressed complete willingness to marry you, Amber,' her father said in quiet rebuke.

'Oh, how noble is Brother Number Three, to take the unwanted responsibilities of his older brothers, nation and wife alike, when the other just can't face it!'

'Amber,' her father said sharply. 'That's enough. Your future husband has a name. You will not shame him, or our family, in this manner. He's lost enough!'

She knew what was expected of her. 'I'm sorry, Father. I will behave,' she said dully. She dragged a breath in and out, willing calm, some form of decorum. 'That was uncalled for. I have nothing against the Lord—um, Harun, and I apologise, Father.'

'You should apologise.' Her father's voice was cold with disapproval. 'Harun was only eight when his father died in the plane crash, and his mother died three months later. For the past six weeks he's been grieving for a brother who had been more like a father to him, and he couldn't stop working long enough to stay at the hospital while the only brother he has left, his only close living relative, was fighting for his life. With so many high-ranking families wanting to take over the sudden wealth in Abbas al-Din, Harun had to assume the sheikh's position and run the country in Alim's name, not knowing if Alim would live or die. Now Harun's been left completely alone with the responsibility of running the nation and marrying you, and all this while he's in deepest mourning. He's lost his entire family. Is it so much to ask that you could stop mocking him, be a woman and help him in his time of greatest need?'

Amber felt the flush of shame cover her face.

Whatever she'd lost, Harun had by far the worst suffering of them all. 'No, it isn't. I'm truly sorry, Father. It's just that—well, he's so quiet,' she tried to explain, feeling the inadequacy of her words. 'He never says anything to me apart from good morning or goodnight. He barely even looks at me. He's a stranger, a complete stranger, and now I must marry him in a month's time? Can't we have a little time to know each other first— just a few months?'

'It must be now,' her father said, his voice sad, and she searched his face. He had a way of making her feel guilty without trying, but this time he seemed sincere. 'The sharks are circling Harun—you know how unstable the entire Gulf region has been the past two years. The el-Shabbat family ruled hundreds of years ago, until Muran's madness led to the coup that gave power to Aswan, the greatest of the el-Kanar clan, two hundred and fifty years ago. The el-Shabbat leaders believe the el-Kanar clan are interlopers, and if they ever had a chance to take control of the army and kill the remaining family members, it is now.'

Amber's hand lifted to her mouth. Lost in her own fog of grief, she'd had no idea things were so bad. 'They will kill Lord Harun?'

He nodded. 'And Alim, too, while he's still so weak. It's a good thing nobody knows exactly where he went. All it would take is one corrupt doctor or nurse and a dose of poison into his IV bag, and the el-Shabbats will rule Abbas al-Din once more—a nation with far greater wealth and stability than they ever knew while they were in power.'

'I see,' she said quietly.

'And we need this alliance, my dear daughter. You were but one of twenty well-born girls offered to Fadi—

and to Harun—in the past few years. We are the far poorer, less stable nation, and yet they chose alliance with our family and nation. It's a blessing to our nation I hardly expected; it's given our people hope. And I must say, in my dealings with all three brothers, Harun is the man I'd have chosen for you if I'd had the choice.'

His voice softened on the last sentence, but Amber barely noticed. 'So the contract has been signed,' she said dully. 'I have no choice in this at all.' Her only decision was to go down fighting, or accept her future with grace.

'No, my dear, you don't.' The words were gentle, but inflexible. 'It has been inevitable from the moment the Lord Harun was made aware of his duty towards you.'

She pressed her lips together hard, fighting unseemly tears. Perhaps she should be grateful that the Lord Harun wasn't leaving her to face her public shame— but another man willing to marry her from duty alone left her stomach churning. At least she'd known and liked Fadi. 'But he doesn't even look at me. He never talks to me. I never know what he's thinking or feeling about anything.' *Including me.* 'How am I to face this—this total stranger in the marriage bed, Father? Can you answer me that?'

'It's what many women have done for thousands of years, including your mother and my grandmother Kahlidah, the nation's heroine you've always admired so much. She was only seventeen when she wed my grandfather—another stranger—and within a year, eighteen, pregnant and a new widow, she stopped the invasion of Araba Numara, ruling the nation with strength and wisdom until my father was old enough to take over. Do as she had to, and grow a backbone, child! What is your fear for one night, compared to what Harun faces, and alone?' her father shot back.

Never had her father spoken to her with such contempt and coldness. She drew another breath and released it as she willed strength into her heart. 'I'll do my duty, of course, Father, and do my best to support Lord Harun in all he faces. Perhaps we can find mutual friendship in our loss and our need.'

Father smiled at her, and patted her hand. 'That's more like my strong Amber. Harun is a truly good man, for all his quiet ways. I know——' he clearly hesitated, and Amber writhed inside, waiting for what she'd give anything for him *not* to say '——I know you...admired Lord Alim. What young woman wouldn't admire the Racing Sheikh, with his dashing ways, his wins on the racing circuit worldwide, and the power and wealth he's brought to this region?'

'Please stop,' she murmured in anguish. 'Please, Father, no more.'

But he went on remorselessly. 'Amber, my child, you are so young—too young to understand that the men who change history are not always the Alexanders, or even the Alims,' he added, with a strained smile. 'The real heroes are usually unsung, making their contributions in silence. I believe Lord Harun is one of them. My advice is for you to look at the man I've chosen for you, and ask yourself why I brought this offer to him, not even wanting to wait for Alim's recovery. I think that, if you give Harun a chance, you'll find you and he are very well suited. You can have a good life together, if you will put your heart and soul behind your vows.'

'Yes, Father,' Amber said, feeling dull and spiritless at the thought of being *well suited* and having *a good life,* when she'd had a moment's dream of marrying the man she—well, she thought she could have loved, given time…

At that moment, a movement behind the door caught her eye. *Damn* the officious staffers and inquisitive servants, always listening in, looking for more gossip to spread far and wide! She lifted her chin and sent her most icy stare to the unknown entity at the door. She felt the presence move back a step, and another.

Good. She hoped they'd run far away. If she must deal with these intrusive servants, they'd best know the calibre of the woman who was to be their future mistress—and mistress she'd be.

'If you wouldn't mind, Father, I'd like to—to have a little time alone,' she said quietly.

'You still grieve for Fadi. You're a good girl.' Her father patted her hand, and left the room by the private exit between their rooms.

The moment the connecting door closed, Amber said coldly, 'If I discover any of you are listening in or I hear gossip repeated about this conversation, I will ensure the lot of you are dismissed without a reference. Is that clear?'

It was only when she heard the soft shuffling of feet moving away that Amber at last fell to her bed and cried. Cried again for the loss of a gentle-hearted friend, cried for the end of an unspoken dream—and she cried for the nightmare facing her.

Frozen two steps back from the partially open door to the rooms of state allotted to the Princess Amber, the man who was the subject of his guests' recent discussion had long since dropped the hand he'd held up to knock. Harun el-Kanar's upbringing hadn't included eavesdropping on intimate conversations—and had he not frozen in horror, he wouldn't have heard Amber so desperately trying to get out of marrying him. He wouldn't have seen that repellent look, like a shard of ice piercing his skin.

So now he knew his future wife's opinion of him... and it was little short of pure revulsion. Why did it even surprise him?

Turning sharply away, he strode towards the sanctuary of his rooms. He needed peace, a few minutes to think—

'Lord Harun, there is a call from the Prince al-Hassan of Saudi regarding the deal with Emirates Oil. He is most anxious to speak with you about the Lord Alim's recent find of oil.'

'Of course, I will come now,' he answered quietly, and walked with his personal assistant back to his office.

When the call was done, his minister of state came in. 'My Lord, in the absence of the Lord Alim, we need your immediate presence in the House for a swearing-in ceremony. For the stability of the country, this must be done as soon as possible. I know you will understand the anxiety of your people to have this reassurance that you are committed to the ongoing welfare of Abbas al-Din.'

His assistant raced in with his robes of state, helping Harun into them before he could make a reply.

During the next five hours, as he sat and stood and bowed and made a speech of acceptance of his new role, none of those hereditary leaders sensed how deeply their new sheikh grieved for a brother nine years older. Fadi had been more like a father to him.

Could any of them see how utterly alone he was now, since Alim's disappearance? He hid it behind the face of years of training, calm and regal. They needed the perfect sheikh, and they'd have one for as long as it was needed. Members of the ruling family were trained almost from birth—they must display no need beyond the privilege of serving their people. But during the ceremony, in moments when he didn't have complete control of his mind, Harun had unbidden visions: of eyes as warm as melted honey, and skin to match; a mouth with a smile she'd smother behind her hand when someone was being pompous or ridiculous, hiding her dimples; her flowing dark hair, and her walk, like a hidden dance.

Every time he pushed it—her—away. He had to be in command.

As darkness fell over the city he sat at his desk, eating a sandwich. He'd left the state dinner within minutes of the announcement of the royal engagement, pleading necessary business as a reason not to endure Amber's company. Or, more accurately, for her not to endure his company a moment longer than she needed to. He'd seen the look of surprise and slight confusion on her face, but again, he pushed it away.

His food slowly went stale as the mountain of papers slowly dwindled. He read each one carefully before signing, while dealing with necessary interruptions, the phone calls from various heads of state and security personnel.

In quiet moments, her face returned to his vision, but he always forced it out again.

Okay, so Amber was right; he hadn't looked at her much. What she didn't know was that he hadn't *dared* look at her. For weeks, months, he'd barely looked at her, never spoken beyond politeness, because he'd been too lost in shame that he hungered night and day for his brother's intended wife. Even her name had filled him with yearning: a precious jewel.

But never until yesterday had he dared think that she could ever become *his* jewel.

Lost and alone with his grief, unable to feel anything but pain, he'd been dazed when, out of nowhere, Sheikh Aziz wished him to become Amber's husband. He hadn't been able to say no. So close to breaking, he'd come to her today, touched by something he hadn't known in months, years...*hope.* Hope that even if she didn't feel the same, he wouldn't have to face this nightmare alone. Could it be possible that they might find comfort in one another, to stand together in this living death...?

And the overheard conversation was his reward for being so stupid. Of course Amber wanted Alim, his dashing brother, the nation's hero. As her father had said, what woman wouldn't want Alim?

A dream of twelve hours had now become his nightmare. There was no way out. She was stuck with him, the last option, the sheikh by default who didn't even want to be here.

What a fool. Hadn't he learned long ago that dreams were for other people? For Fadi, there had been his destiny as the next sheikh; for Alim, there was the next racing car, the next glamorous destination, the jets and the women and the adoration of his family and his nation. *Habib Abbas:* Alim was the country's beloved lion, their financial saviour since he'd found oil deep beneath the water of their part of the Gulf, and natural gas in the desert.

His parents would have been so proud of him. They'd always known Alim was destined for greatness, as Fadi had said so many times. *We're all so proud of you, Alim.*

Alim, the golden child. Of course he had Amber's heart—and of course he didn't want it. He'd thrown her away without a thought, just as he'd thrown his brother into his role of sheikh. He'd left them both to their fate without even a farewell or reason.

And yet, he still loved Alim; like everyone else in the country, he'd do anything for his brother. Alim knew that well, which was why he'd just disappeared without a word. 'Harun will do it better than I could, anyway,' had always been his casually tossed words when Fadi had needed him for one duty or another. 'He's good at the duty thing.'

Harun supposed he was good at it—he'd been raised to think his duty was sacred.

I never know what he's thinking or feeling. To her, he was Brother Number Three, nothing but an obliga-tion, a means to enrich her country. She was only will-ing to marry him after being bullied and brought to a sense of pity for his grief by her father.

No, he had no choice but to marry her now—but he had no taste for his brother's unwanted leftovers. He'd dealt with enough broken hearts of the women who'd been rejected by Alim over the years, calling the pal-ace, even offering themselves to him in the faint hope that he had the power to change Alim's mind.

Not this time. Never again. I might have to marry her, but I'll be damned if I touch her.

'It's lust, just lust,' he muttered, hard. Lust he could both deal with, and live without. Anything but the thought of taking her while she stared at the ceiling, wishing he were Alim—

His stomach burning, he found he was no longer hun-gry, and threw the rest of the sandwich into the garbage.

It was long past midnight before Harun at last

reached his rooms. He sent his hovering servants away and sat on his richly canopied bed, ripping the thin mosquito curtain. With an impatient gesture he flung it away; but if he made a noise, the bodyguards watching him from one of the five vantage points designed to protect the sheikh would come running in. So he sat looking out into the night as if nothing were wrong, and grieved in dry-eyed silence.

Fadi, my brother, my father! Allah, I beg you to let Alim live and return to me.

Three days later, the armed rebel forces of the el-Shabbat family invaded Sar Abbas.

CHAPTER TWO

Eight weeks later

'HABIB Numara! Harun, our beloved tiger, our Habib Numara!'

Riding at the head of a makeshift float—two tanks joined by tent material and filled with flowers—Harun smiled and waved to the people lining the streets of Sar Abbas. Each cheering girl or woman in the front three rows of people threw another flower at him as he passed. The flowers landed on the float filling his nostrils until the sweet scent turned his stomach and the noise of the people's shouting left him deafened.

Still he smiled and waved; but what he wouldn't give to be in the quiet of his room reading a book. How had Alim ever endured this adulation, this attention for so many years? Fighting for his country, his men and repelling the el-Shabbat invasion—being wounded twice during battle, and having his shoulder put back in place after the dislocation—had been a positive relief in comparison to this.

You'll never be your brother.

Yet again his parents had been proven right. No, he'd never be like Alim.

As the float and the soldiers and the cheering throng

reached the palace he looked up. His future father-in-law stood beside his bride on the upper balcony, waving to him, looking proud and somehow smug. He supposed he'd find out why when he got some time.

Amber stood like a reed moving in the wind as she watched his triumphal entry. She had a small frown between her brows, a slight tilt to her head, as if trying to puzzle out something. As if she saw his discomfort and sympathised with him.

He almost laughed at the absurdity of the thought. She who loved Alim of racing fame and fortune, the real sheikh? *Right, Harun. She sees nothing in you but the replacement in her life and bed she'd do anything to avoid.*

She half lifted a hand. A smile trembled on her lips. Mindful of the people, he smiled and waved to his bride, giving her the public recognition and honour they expected.

It was all she wanted from him.

At last the wedding night she'd dreaded was upon her.

With a fast-beating heart, Amber stood in the middle of her bridal suite, with unbound hair, perfumed skin and a thin, creamy negligee over her nude body. So scared she could barely breathe, she awaited the arrival of her new husband.

The last of the fussing maids checked her hands and feet to be sure they were soft enough, perfumed to the right scent. Amber forced herself to stand still and not wave them off in irritation—or, worse, give in to her fears and ask someone, anyone what she must do to please a man she'd still barely spoken to. The way she felt right now, even the maid would do—for her mother had told her nothing. As she'd dressed her daughter for the marriage bed, the only words of advice to Amber had been, *Let your husband show you the way, and though it will hurt at first and you will bleed in proof of your virginity, smile and take joy in your woman's duty. For today, you become a woman.* And with a smile Amber didn't understand, she'd left the room.

In the Western world, girls apparently grew up knowing how to please a man, and themselves; but she'd been kept in almost total ignorance. In her world, it was a matter of pride for the husband to teach his wife what took place in the bed. No books were allowed on the subject, no conversation by the servants on the threat of expulsion, and the Internet was strictly patrolled.

She only wished she knew what to do…

More than that, she wished she knew him at all—that he could have taken an hour out of his busy schedule to get to know her.

In the end, she'd had the few months' wait she'd asked for, but it hadn't been for her sake, nor had they had any time to know each other better. The el-Shabbat family hadn't reckoned with Harun's swift action when they'd invaded the city. Handing the day-to-day work to his intended father-in-law, Harun had taken control of the army personally. Leading his men into battle using both the ancient and modern rules of warfare he'd learned since boyhood, Harun had gained the adoration of his people by being constantly in the thick of the fierce fighting, expecting and giving no quarter. The whispers in women's rooms were that he bore new scars on his body: badges of the highest honour. He'd spent no more than a night in the hastily erected Army hospital. Every time he'd been injured, come morning he'd returned to the battle without a word.

Within eight weeks he'd completely quelled the rebellion. By forgiving the followers of the el-Shabbat family and letting them return to their homes with little if any punishment and no public embarrassment, he'd earned their loyalty, his new title—and Amber's deep respect. By assuming control of the el-Shabbat fortune and yet caring for the women and children the dead enemy had left behind, he'd earned the love as well as the respect of his people.

If Alim was their beloved lion, Harun had become *Habib Numara,* their beloved tiger. 'It's a good omen for his marriage, with his bride coming from Araba Numara,' the servants said, smiling at her. 'It will be a fruitful union blessed by God.'

And in the weeks since then, as he'd put down the final shadows of the rebellion and with rare political skill brought together nation and people once more, Harun had had less time for her than Fadi had done. In fact he still barely spoke to her at all; but though he'd never said a word about his heroism on the field, he'd earned Amber's deep, reluctant admiration. If she still harboured regrets over Alim's disappearance, Harun's name now had the power to make her heart beat faster. He'd proved his worthiness without a word of bragging. She was ready to endure what she must tonight, and become the mother of his children.

As the main door opened the maid rushed to leave the room.

Sick to her stomach with nerves, she turned to where he stood—and her breath caught. It was strange, but it was only on the day she'd seen him returning to Sar Abbas as a national hero that she'd truly taken in his deep resemblance to Alim. A quiet, serious version, perhaps, but as, in his army uniform, he smiled and waved to the people cheering him in the streets, she'd seen his face as if for the first time.

Now, she struggled not to stare at him. So handsome and strong in his groom's finery, yet so dark and mysterious with those glittering forest-green eyes. She groped with one hand to the bedpost to gain balance suddenly lacking in her knees. He was the man who'd come home a hero. He was—magnificent. He was hers.

'None of you will listen or stand nearby,' he snapped at the walls, and she was filled with gratitude when she heard the shuffle of many feet moving away.

Lost in awe, she faltered in her traditional greeting, but bowed in the traditional show of deep respect. 'M-my husband, I…' She didn't know how to go on, but surely he'd understand how she felt?

Without a change of expression from the serious, cool appraisal, he closed the door behind him, and offered her a brief smile. 'Sit down, please, Amber.'

Grateful for his understanding, she dropped to the bed, wondering if he'd take it as a sign, or was she being too brazen? She only wished she knew how to go on.

He gave her a slow, thoughtful glance, taking in every inch of her, and she squirmed in embarrassment. Her heart beat like a bird trying to escape its cage as she waited for Harun to come to her, to kiss her or however it was this thing began. 'Well?' she demanded in a haughty tone, covering her rush of nerves with a show of pride, showing him she was worthy of him: a princess to the core. 'Do I pass your inspection, *Habib Numara?*'

For a moment, she thought Harun might actually smile as he hadn't done since the hero's return. There was a telltale glimmer in his eyes she'd noticed when he was in a rare, relaxed moment. Then, just as she was about to smile back, it vanished. 'You have to know you're a beautiful woman, Amber. Exquisite, in fact.'

'Thank you,' she whispered, her voice losing its power. He thought her exquisite? Something inside her melted—

He turned from her, and, drawing out a thin wreath of papers from a fold of his robe, sat at her desk. 'This should cover the necessary time. I forgot my pen, though. Do you happen to have one handy, my dear?'

Her mouth fell open as he began perusing whatever work he'd brought with him. He'd brought work to their wedding night? 'In the second drawer,' she responded, feeling incredibly stupid, but what else could she say?

'Thank you,' he replied, his tone absent. He pulled out one of her collection of pens and began reading, scrolling up and down the pages with his finger, and making notes in the margins.

She blinked, blinked again, unable to believe what she was seeing. 'Harun...' Then she faltered to a stop.

After at least ten seconds, he stopped writing. 'Hmm...? Did you say something, Amber?' His tone was the cold politeness of a man who didn't want to be disturbed.

'Yes, I did,' she retorted, furious. At least five different things leaped to her mouth. *What do you mean by covering the necessary time? What is it with the el-Kanar men? This is our wedding night!*

Don't you want me?

But at the thought of asking it, her confused outrage turned cold inside her, making her ache. *Why should this brother want me when the other two didn't?*

What's wrong with me?

But what came from her mouth, born of the stubborn pride that was her backbone in a world where she'd had

beautiful clothes and surroundings but as much control
over her destiny as a piece of furniture or a child's doll,
she stated coldly, 'If there's no blood on the sheet tomorrow, the servants will talk. It will be around both
our countries in hours. People will blame me, or worse,
assume I wasn't a virgin. Will you shame me that way,
when I've done nothing wrong?'

His back stiffened for a moment.

Amber felt the change in the air, words hovering on
his lips. How she knew that about him, when they'd still
barely spoken, she had no idea, but whatever he'd been
about to say vanished in an instant.

'I see,' he said slowly, with only a very slight weari-
ness in the inflection. 'Of course they will.'

He stood and stripped off his *kafta,* revealing his
nakedness, and Amber's heart took wings again.
Magnificent? Even with the scars across his back and
stomach he was breathtaking, a battle-hardened warrior sheathed in darkest gold, masculinely beautiful and
somehow terrifying. Involuntarily she shrank back on
the bed, wishing she'd found another place to sit. *I'm
not ready for this...please, Harun, be gentle with me...*

She couldn't breathe, watching him come to her.

But he walked around the bed as if she weren't there.
He didn't touch her, didn't even *look* at her. At the other
side of the bed, he put something down, and used both
his hands to sweep all the rose petals from the coverlet.
'I don't like the smell. Cloying.'

'I like it,' she said, halfway between defiance and
stupidity.

He shrugged and stopped brushing them away. 'It's
your bed.' Then he lifted the thing he'd put on the bed: a
ceremonial knife, beautifully scrolled in gold and silver.

'What's that...Harun...?' Her jaw dropped; she

watched in utter disbelief as he made a small cut deep in his armpit, and allowed a few drops of blood to fall into his cupped palm.

'What—what are you…?' Realising she was gaping, she slammed her mouth shut.

'Making a cut where it won't be seen and commented on,' he said in a voice filled with quiet irony. 'Thus I'm salvaging your pride in the eyes of others, my dear wife.'

'I don't understand.' Beyond pride now or remembering any of her instructions for tonight, she gazed at him in open pleading. 'What are you doing?'

He sighed. 'As you said, virgins bleed, Amber. It's my duty to ensure that your reputation isn't ruined. Pull the coverings down, please, and quickly, before the blood drops on the rug. Imagine what the servants would make of that.' His tone was filled with understated irony.

She closed her mouth and swallowed, and then swivelled around in the bed to pull the covers down.

She watched as he dripped blood into his other hand. 'It seems enough, I think,' he said after thirty seconds. Her husband of six hours looked at her. 'Which side of the bed do the servants know you prefer?'

Torn between shock and fury born of humiliation, she pointed.

'Thank you.' As casually as if he'd spilled water, he smeared his blood on the bed. Then he walked into the bathroom; she heard the sound of running water.

When he came out he returned to the desk, picked up his bridegroom's clothing, pulled it back over his head and let it fall to his feet. He sat down again, reading, scrolling and making notes.

Not knowing what else to do, she sat on the bed,

drawing her knees under her chin, her arms wrapped tight around them. And for the next hour, she watched him work in growing but helpless fury.

Why won't you touch me? she wanted to scream. *Why don't you want to touch me? What did I do wrong?*

But she'd made an innocent scene with Fadi when it was obvious he was running from her, and he'd told her about Rafa. *I can't marry her, but I love her, Amber.*

She'd made another scene before her father when Alim fled the country rather than marry her. *He has rejected both Fadi's position, and Fadi's bride.*

She was already the bad-luck bride in the eyes of the servants and the people—but if they found out about this, she'd never recover. Fadi had loved another; Alim fled the country—but neither of them had made the rejection this obvious.

Asking him why would only humiliate her further.

After a while, her husband said without looking at her, 'It would be best if you went to sleep, Amber. It's been a very long day for you.'

She lay back on the sheets, avoiding the smeared blood—but she kept watching him work out of a stubborn refusal to obey anything he asked of her. If he wasn't going to be a real husband, it relieved her of the necessity to be any kind of wife.

Suddenly she wondered how long a day it had been for him. How long had he been working—right up until he'd dressed for the wedding? During the ceremony and after he'd kissed her hand, touched her face with a smile, played the loving bridegroom—for the cameras and the people, no doubt. Now he was working again. Barely two months ago, Harun fought for his life, for the sake of a nation that didn't belong to him.

Did he ever stop, and just be a normal man?

Harun, just look at me, be kind to me for a minute.
I'm your bride, she wanted to say, but nothing emerged from her mouth. She was lying on their marriage bed, his for the taking in this shimmering piece of nothing, and he was doing stupid paperwork.

He didn't even look at her, just as he never had before.

As a soldier, they said, he'd fought with a savagery beyond anything they'd seen before. Like Fadi, had he done it to escape her? What a shame for him that he'd lived, forced into taking a wife he clearly didn't want in the least.

She hated him. She hated this bed…and she couldn't stand this ridiculous situation any more.

Pulling her hair into a messy knot, she got to her feet, stalked into the bathroom, shredded the stupid negligee in her haste to take it off, and scrubbed away all traces of perfume and make-up under the stinging heat of the shower.

Using the pumice stone she scrubbed at her skin until it was raw, and took minimal comfort in the fact that Harun would never know how he'd made her cry.

But as she scrubbed herself to bleeding point she vowed she'd *never* make a fool of herself for an el-Kanar man again. No, she'd show Harun nothing, no emotion at all. She'd be a queen before him at all times, damn it! And one day he'd come to her, on his knees, begging for her…

If only she could make herself believe it.

CHAPTER THREE

Three Years Later

'MY LADY, the Lord Harun has requested entrance!'

Startled, Amber dropped the papers she was reading and stared at her personal maid, Halala. Barely able to believe the words she'd heard, she couldn't catch her breath. All the ladies were in a flutter of excitement... and hope, no doubt.

She could almost hear the whispers from mouth to ear, flying around the palace. *Will he come to her bed at last?*

Her cheeks burned with embarrassment at the common knowledge within the palace of the state of her marriage, the tag of bad-luck bride she couldn't overcome, but she answered calmly enough. 'Please show my husband in, and leave us. I need not remind you of what will happen if you listen in,' she added sternly, holding each of her ladies-in-waiting with her gaze until they nodded.

As the room emptied she smoothed down her dress, her hair, while her pulse beat hard in her throat. What could he want? And she had no time to change out of one of her oldest, most comfortable dresses—

Then Harun entered her rooms, tall and broad-shouldered, with skin like dark honey and a tiny cleft in his chin; she'd long ago become accustomed to the fact that her husband was a quiet, serious version of her dashing first crush. But today his normally withdrawn if handsome face was lit from within; his forest-at-dusk eyes were alive with shimmering emotion, highlighting his resemblance to Alim more than ever. 'Good morning, Amber,' he greeted her not quite formally, his intense eyes not quite looking at her.

He doesn't care what I'm wearing, Amber thought in sullen resentment. How foolish she'd been for wishing to look pretty for him, even for a minute. *I don't even know why I'm surprised. Or why it still hurts after all this time.*

Why had her father wanted her to wed this—this robot? He wasn't a man. He was barely human…at least not where she was concerned. But, oh, she'd heard the rumours that he was man enough for another.

She tamped down the weakness of anger, finding strength in her pride. 'You need something, My Lord?' she asked, keeping her tone meek, submissive, but just as formal and distant as his. 'It must be important for you to actually come inside my rooms. I believe this is the first time you've come here willingly in three years.'

He looked at her then—with a cold flash in his eyes that made her feel like a worm in dirt. 'Since you're taking the gloves off, my wife, we both know it's the first time I've been in here willingly at all, not merely since our wedding night.'

The burning returned in full measure to her cheeks, a stinging wave of embarrassment that came every time she thought of that awful night. Turning from him with insulting slowness, as if she didn't care, she drawled, 'You never did explain yourself.'

Yes, she'd said it well. As if it were a mere matter of curiosity for her, and not the obsession it had been for so long.

She marvelled that, in so long, there'd never been an opportunity to ask before—but Harun was a master at making certain they were never alone. His favourite place in the palace seemed to be his office, or the secret passageway between their bedrooms—going the other way, towards his room. Only once had she swallowed her pride, followed him out and asked him to come to her—

'I'm sure you've noticed that my life is rather busy, my wife. And really, there's no point in coming where you aren't welcome.'

The heat in her cheeks turned painful. 'Of—of course you're welcome,' she stammered. 'You're my husband.'

He shrugged. 'So says the imam who performed the service.'

Knowing what he'd left unsaid, Amber opened her mouth, and closed it. No, they weren't husband and wife, never had been. They hadn't even had one normal conversation, only cold accusation on her part, and stubborn silence on his.

Didn't he know how much it hurt that he only came to her rooms at night when the gossip became unbearable, and that he timed the hour and left, just as he had on their wedding night? Oh, she'd been cold and unwelcoming to him, mocking him with words and formal curtsies, but couldn't he see that it was only because she was unable to stand the constant and very public humiliation of her life? Every time he was forced to be near her she knew that soon, he'd leave without a word, giving her nothing but that cold, distant bow. And everyone in her world knew it, too.

'I didn't come here to start an argument.' He kept his gaze on her, and a faint thrill ran through her body, as delicious as it was unwelcome—yet Harun was finally looking at her, his eyes ablaze with life. 'Alim's shown up at last,' he said abruptly.

Amber gasped. Alim's disappearance from the clinic in Bern three years ago had been so complete that all Harun's efforts to find him had proven useless. 'He's alive?'

Harun nodded. 'He's in Africa, taken by a Sudanese warlord. He's being held hostage for a hundred million US dollars.'

Her hand fluttered to her cheek. 'Oh, no! Is he well? Have they hurt him?'

The silence went on too long, and, seeing the ice chips in his eyes, she realised that, without meaning to, she'd said something terribly wrong—but what?

Floundering for words when she couldn't know which ones were right or wrong, she tried again, wishing she knew something, anything about the man she'd married. 'Harun, what are you going to do about it?'

'Pay the ransom in full, of course. He's the true Sheikh of Abbas al-Din, and without the contracts from the oil he found we'd have very little of our current wealth.' He hesitated for a moment. 'I'm going to Africa. I have to be there when he's released, to find out if he's coming home. And—he's my brother.'

She'd expected him to say that, of course. From doing twelve hours of mind-numbing paperwork to meeting dignitaries and businessmen to taking up sword and gun, Harun always did what was right for the country, for his people, even for her, at least in public—but she hadn't expected the catch in his voice, or the shimmer of tears in those normally emotionless eyes. 'You love him,' she muttered, almost in wonder.

He frowned at her. 'Of course I do. He's my brother, the only family I have left, and he—might come home at last.'

The second catch in her stranger husband's voice made her search his face. She'd never seen him cry once since Fadi's death. He'd never seemed lonely or needy during the years of Alim's disappearance, at least not in her presence. But now his eyes were misty, his jaw working with emotion.

Amber felt a wave of shame. Harun had been missing his brother all this time, and she'd never suspected it. She'd even accused him once of enjoying his role too much as the replacement sheikh to care where Alim was, or if he was alive or dead. He'd bowed and left her without a word, seconds before she could regret her stupid words. She'd wanted to hurt him for always being so cold, so unfeeling with her—but during the past three years she'd been able to call or Skype with her family daily, or ask one sister or another to visit. She'd left him all alone, missing his brother, and she'd never even noticed until now.

The sudden longing to give him comfort when she knew he'd only push her away left her confused, even frightened. 'I'm sorry,' she said in the end—a compromise that was so weak, so wishy-washy she felt like an idiot. 'I hope he does come home, for your sake.'

'Thank you.' But it seemed she'd said the wrong thing again; the smile he gave her held the same shard of ice as his eyes. 'Will it make a difference to you?'

Taken aback, she stammered, 'W-what? How could Alim's return possibly make any difference to me?'

Harun shrugged, but there was something—a hint of fire beneath his customary ice with her. She didn't know why, but it fascinated her, held her gaze as if riveted to his face. 'He surrendered himself to the warlord in order to protect the woman who saved his life, a nurse working with Doctors for Africa. Very courageous of him, but of course one expects no less from the Racing Sheikh. Soon Alim will become the true, hereditary sheikh he should have been these three years, and I'll be back to being—Brother Number Three.'

By this point she wondered if any more blood could possibly pool in her face. Ridiculous that she could feel such envy for a woman she'd never met, but she'd always yearned to have a man care enough about her to make such a sacrifice. To know Alim, the man who'd run from *her,* could risk his life for another woman—

Then, without warning, Harun's deliberate wording slithered back into her mind like a silent snake, striking without warning. Frowning, she tilted her head, mystified. 'What did you mean by that—Brother Number Three?'

'It took you long enough to remember. Thinking of Alim, were you?' He lifted a brow, just a touch, in true understated irony, and, feeling somehow as if he'd caught her out in wrong behaviour, she blushed. Slowly, he nodded. 'I thought you might be.'

Her head was spinning now. 'You just told me he's alive and has been taken by a warlord. Who else should I be thinking about?' He merely shrugged again, and she wanted to hit him. 'So are you going to explain your cryptic comment?'

It took him a few moments to reply, but it wasn't truly an answer. 'You figure it out, Amber. If you think hard, you might remember…or maybe you won't. It probably was never very important to you.'

'I don't understand,' she said before she could stop herself.

His gaze searched hers for a few moments, but whatever he was looking for he obviously didn't find. For some reason she felt a sense of something lost she didn't know she'd had, the bittersweet wishing for what she never realised she could have had.

Before she could ask he shrugged and went on, 'By the way, you'll be needed for a telecast later today, of course, my dear. We're so glad Alim's alive, of course we're paying the ransom, et cetera.'

The momentary wistfulness vanished like a stone in a pond, only its ripples left behind in tiny circles of hurt. 'Of course,' she said mockingly, with a deep curtsy. 'Aren't I always the perfect wife for the cameras? I must be good for something, since you endure my continued barrenness.'

His mouth hardened, but he replied mildly enough, 'Yes, my dear, you're perfect—for the cameras.'

He'd left the room before the poison hidden deep inside the gently-spoken cryptic words hit her.

Brother Number Three.

Oh, no—had it been Harun standing behind the door when she'd discussed her unwanted marriage—no, her unwanted groom—with her father?

She struggled to remember what she'd said. The trouble was, she'd tried to bury it beneath a blanket of forgetfulness ever since she'd accepted her fate.

Brother Number Three…how am I to face this total stranger in the marriage bed?

Her father's words came back to haunt her. *He's been left completely alone…in deepest mourning…*

He'd heard everything, heard her fight with all her might against marrying him—

And he'd heard her father discuss her feelings for Alim.

She closed her eyes. Now, when it was far too late, she understood why her husband had barely spoken to her in all this time, had never tried to find friendship or comfort with her, had rarely if ever shown any emotion in front of her—and remembering how she'd reacted, then and just now…

For three years she'd constantly punished him for his reaction—one born of intense grief and suffering, a reaction she could readily understand…at least she could understand it now. During the most painful time of his life, he'd needed one person to be there for him. He'd needed someone not to abandon or betray him, and that was exactly what she'd done. He'd come to her that day, and she'd treated him with utter contempt, a most unwanted husband, when he'd been the one to salvage her pride and give her the honour she deserved.

No wonder he'd never tried to touch her, had never attempted to make love to her, even on the one occasion she'd gone to his room to ask him to come to her bed!

But had she asked? Even then she'd been so cold, so proud, not hesitating to let him know how he'd failed her over and over. *Give me a child and remove this shame you've forced on me all this time,* she'd said.

With a silent groan, she buried her face in her hands.

The question now was, what could she do to make him forgive her, when it was years too late to undo the damage?

* * *

Harun was climbing into the jet the next day when he heard his name being called in the soft, breathless feminine voice that still turned his guts inside-out.

She might be your wife, but she can't stand you. She wants Alim—even more, now she knows he's alive, and as heroic as ever.

The same old fight, the same stupid need. Nothing ever changed, including his hatred for his everlasting weakness in wanting her.

Lust, it's nothing more than lust. You can ignore that. You've done it for three years. After a few moments, struggling to wipe the hunger from his face, he turned to her. Afraid he'd give himself away somehow, he didn't speak, just lifted a brow.

With that limber, swaying walk, she moved along the carpet laid down for him to reach the jet from the limo, and climbed the stairs to him. Her eyes were enormous, filled with something he'd never seen from her since that wretched night a year ago when he could have had her, and he'd walked away. 'Harun, I want to come with you.'

A shard of ice pierced his heart. Amber hated to fly, yet here she was, ready to do what she hated most. For the sake of seeing Alim? 'No.'

She blinked and took an involuntary step back at his forceful tone. 'But I want to—'

He couldn't stand to hear her reasons. 'I said no.'

Her chin shot up then, and her eyes flashed. Ah, there was the same defiant wife he'd known and ached to have from three feet or three thousand miles of distance for so long. 'Damn you, Harun, it's all I'm asking of you.'

Harun turned his face away. Just looking at her right now hurt. For the first time she was showing him the impulsive, passionate side he'd believed slumbered deep inside her, and it was for Alim.

Of course it was for Alim; why should he expect anything else? In all these years, she'd only shown emotion once: when she'd asked—no, demanded—that he end her public shame, and give her a child. When he'd said no, she'd sworn at him for the first time.

But she'd just sworn at him again.

'You still care for him so much?' he asked, his voice low and throbbing with the white-hot betrayal he barely managed to hide.

She sighed. 'I'm not nineteen any more. I'm your wife. Please, just give me a chance. It's all I'm asking.'

A chance for what? he wanted to ask, but remained silent.

Something to the left of him caught his attention. Her bags were being stowed in the hold. With a sense of fatalism, he swept a hand before him. 'By all means, come and see him. I'm sure he'll appreciate your care.'

No part of her touched him as she pushed past him and into the jet. Her chin was high, her eyes as cold as they'd always been for him…except on that fateful night last year—and a moment ago, because she wanted to see Alim.

Damn her. Damn them both.

Yet something like regret trailed in the wake of the warm Gulf wind behind her. Harun breathed it in, refusing to yet again indulge in the wish that things could be different for them. It was far too late.

She was sitting upright and straight in the plush, wide seat, her belt already buckled. He sat beside her, and saw her hands gripping the armrests. He'd seen this on the times they'd had to go to another country for a state visit. She really hated flying.

His hand moved to hers, then stopped. It wasn't his comfort she wanted.

During the final safety check of the jet the silence stretched out. The awkwardness between them was never more evident than when they sat side by side and could find nothing to talk about: he because all he could think of was touching her and hating himself for it, and she presumably because all she wanted was to get away from him, as fast and as far as possible.

How she must hate this life, trapped in this submissive woman's role, tied to a man she despised.

'You are *not* Brother Number Three.'

Startled, he turned to face her, prompted by a tone of voice he'd never known from his cold, proud wife. The fierce words seemed to burst from her; the passion he'd always felt slumbering in her came to blazing life in a few restrained words. 'I'm sorry I ever said it, and sorrier still that you heard stupid words said in my own shock and grief, and took them so literally. I humiliated you before my father, and I'm sorry, Harun.'

Surprise and regret, remembered humiliation, yearning and a dozen other emotions flew around in him, their edges hitting him like the wings of a wild bird caged. He could only think of one thing to say, and he couldn't possibly say it to his stranger wife. *What am I to you now?* As ever, he resorted to his fall-back, the cool diplomacy that told her nothing about what he was thinking or feeling. 'It's all right.'

'No, it isn't. It's not all right between us. It never has been, and I never knew why. But we've been married for three years. In all this time, why didn't you try, even once, to talk to me?' Touching his cheek, she turned him to face her before he could school his stunned surprise that her hands were on his skin. 'I always wanted to know why you hated me. You were outside the door that day.'

Taken aback, he could only answer with truth. 'I don't hate you.'

An encyclopaedia could be written on the doubt in her eyes. 'Really? You don't?'

Reluctant understanding touched a heart shrouded in ice too long. 'No,' was all he said.

She sighed. 'But you don't trust me. You won't treat me even as a friend, let alone your wife.' She shook her head. 'I thought you were a servant when I heard your footsteps behind the door. I would never have done that to you—don't you know that?'

Her face was vivid with the force of her anger and her regret. She thought she wanted to know about his emotions—but she didn't have a clue. If he let out one iota of his feelings, it might break a dam of everything he'd repressed since he was eight years old.

I need you to be strong for me again, little akh, Fadi had said at his mother's funeral, only three months after their father died, and Alim had stormed off within minutes of the service beginning. *We have to stand together, and show the world what we're made of.*

I need you to stay home and help me, little akh, he'd said when Alim was seventeen, and his first race on the circuit gave him the nickname the Racing Sheikh. *What Alim's doing could change the nation for us, economically and socially. You can study by correspondence, right? It won't make a difference to you.*

I need you to come home, little akh. I feel like I'm drowning under the weight of all this, Fadi had said when Harun was nineteen, and had to go on a dig to pass his archaeology course. *I'll fix it with the univer-*

sity, don't worry. You'll pass, which is all you want, right?

'I suppose I should have known,' he answered Amber now. From the vague memories he had of his mother, he knew that it was dangerous not to answer an angry woman, but it was worse to answer with a truth she didn't want to hear.

'And—and you heard what my father said about—' her cheeks blazed, but her chin lifted again, and she said it '—about the—the feelings I had for Alim back then.'

As a passion-killer, hearing his wife say she had *feelings* for the brother who'd abandoned him to this half-life had to rank up there as number one. 'Yes,' he said, quiet. Dead inside.

'Harun, don't.' She gripped his chin in her hand, her eyes fairly blazing with emotion. 'Do you hate me for it?'

He closed his eyes against the passion always beneath the surface with her, but never for him. 'No.' So many times, he'd wished he could hate her, or just take her for the higher duty of making an heir, but he could do neither. Yes, he still desired her; he could live with that. But he'd shut off his heart years ago. There was no way he'd open it up, only to have her walk all over it again with her careless rejections and stinging rebukes.

'Stop it, Harun,' she burst out, startling him into opening his eyes again. 'Hate me if you want, but stop showing me this uncaring wall of ice! I don't know how to talk to you or what to do when you're so cold with me, always pushing me away!'

Cold? He felt as if he were bleeding agony whenever he looked at her, and she thought his feelings for her were cold? Harun stared at her, the wife he barely knew, and wondered if she was blind, or if it was because he really had covered his need too well. But wasn't that what he'd always done? How could he stop doing what had always been expected of him?

So he frowned again. 'I don't know what you want me to say.'

'Talk to me for once. Tell me how it hurt you.' Though she spoke softly, almost beneath her breath, it felt like a dam bursting, the release of a long-held pressure valve. 'I was *nineteen,* Harun, one of a legion of girls that dreamed of capturing the heart of the world-famous Racing Sheikh. I didn't know him any more than I could touch or talk to a literal star.'

She hadn't said so many words to him at one time since he'd rejected her one attempt at connection last year—and the bitter self-mockery in her voice and her eyes lashed even harder at him than herself.

So she thought of Alim as a star. Well, why not? Even now, years later, it was how the world saw him. The headlines were filled with adoring references to the missing sheikh, reinforcing his own aching emptiness. *He's my brother. Not one of you misses him like I do.*

When he didn't answer, she snapped, 'Do you feel nothing about it, Harun? Do you not care that I married you believing I was in love with your brother?'

The pain of it gripped him everywhere, like a vice inside him, squeezing the blood from his heart. Not care that she—

Believing she was in love with Alim? What did she mean?

Did he want to know? Could he stand to ask what she felt for his brother now?

This was too much. She'd changed so suddenly from the cold, imperious woman she'd always been with him; it left him wondering what the hell to say to her that wouldn't make her explode. After three years of icy disdain and silence, without warning she was demanding thoughts and feelings from him that threatened to take the only thing he had left; his pride.

'Of course I cared,' he said coolly. 'Quite humiliating, isn't it, to be the last brother in line in the eyes of your prospective bride—good old Brother Number Three. I didn't enjoy knowing that my wedding only took place because one brother died and the other brother ran away. Worse still to know she'd have done anything to have my runaway brother there instead of me.' He was quite proud of himself. Total truth in a few raw sentences, years of grief, loss and anguish— but told as if it were someone else's life, as if it didn't twist in his guts like a knife he couldn't pull out of him.

The fire in her eyes dimmed. 'I suppose it is,' she said dully. 'Thank you for your honesty, at least.'

And, too late, Harun knew he'd blown this last chance she'd given him to connect with her. She might have said and done it all wrong, but at least she was trying.

I never know what he's thinking or feeling.

For years the words had haunted him, leaving him locked deep inside what had always been his greatest strength—but with Amber, it felt like his deepest inadequacy. He'd grown up always aware that, hereditary sheikh though he was, he was the last in line, the spare tyre, the reliable son or brother. His parents had been busy running a nation, too busy to spend time with their children. The only memories he had of his mother was that she'd resented that the last child she could have wasn't the girl she'd longed for. His father, who wanted sons, contemptuously called him a sissy for his love of history and hiding in his room reading books instead of playing sports and inventing marvellous things as Alim could, or charming the people, as Fadi did. *He'll grow up to be a real man whether he likes it or not,* their father said with utter disdain when Harun was six. From that day, he'd been enrolled in all the action-man activities and ancient and modern knowledge of war-craft that made the family so popular with the people.

He'd learned to fight, all right…he'd had no choice, since his father had arranged constant martial-arts battles for him. But he'd also read books late at night, beneath the blanket with a tiny hand-torch, so the servants wouldn't see it and report to his father.

After their parents' deaths, Fadi had become the father he'd never known, raising both his brothers with greater love and acceptance than Harun had ever known from his parents, and yet he'd had to learn how to run the small, independent emirate. Harun adored Fadi, and Fadi had always loved him dearly, giving him the affection he'd craved for so long; but Fadi always comforted himself in the knowledge that, while Alim would travel the world, and put Abbas al-Din on the world and economic map, Harun would stay home and help.

Alim had always counted on it, too. *You've got Harun,* Alim would always say when Fadi asked him to come home for this duty or that. *He'll do it better than I can.*

So Harun supported Fadi's heavy load as Sheikh, kept learning war-craft and how to lead all the armed forces, continuing the studies that were his secret passion by reading books late at night. Since he'd been recalled home at nineteen from his one trip outside the palace, he'd never dreamed of asking to leave Sar Abbas, except on matters of military or state. His interests were unimportant beside the demands of nation, honour, family, and their people. Good old Harun, doing the right, the decent and honourable thing, always his brothers' support and mainstay.

The thing was, nobody ever asked him how he felt about it, or believed he had feelings at all. And so, as long as he could remember, he'd kept his thoughts to himself.

So how did he suddenly begin talking now, after all these years?

Amber sighed aloud, reiterating his failure with her. 'Say something, *anything,* Harun!'

What was he supposed to say? 'I'm sorry, Amber.' At this moment, he wished he'd realised how very young she'd been when they wed—as she'd said, only nineteen. He sat beside this wife who despised him, feeling the old chains of silence holding him in place, with a rusted padlock he could never seem to open.

'If it ruined everything we could have had, I wish I'd never thought of Alim,' she burst out, yet said it very quietly. She dropped his hand, and turned away. 'I never even knew him, but I was all alone here. Fadi loved Rafa, and you never looked at me or talked to me. And—and he smiled and was nice to me when he came. It was just a lonely girl's stupid crush on a superstar,' she mumbled, her cheeks aflame.

The finality in her words dropped him into a well of unexpected darkness. *Don't you understand, Amber? If he'd been anyone else, I could have ignored it.* 'What could we have had, Amber?' he asked, as quietly as she'd spoken.

Her left shoulder lifted in a delicate shrug. 'We married because you were a sheikh and I was a sheikh's daughter, for the sake of our nations. Harun, you've been so amazing the past three years. You've been a strong and loving leader for your people in their need, giving them everything they asked of you. But the only good part of our marriage was for the cameras and in front of the people. Now, if Alim comes back—well, what's left for us?'

Us. She'd said *us.* As if there were an *us*—or could have been. She'd admired him for the things he'd done? He couldn't get his head around it.

'I don't want a sham for the cameras any more. I don't want to live the rest of my life alone, tied to a man who never touches me, who doesn't want me.'

Harun had never cursed his habit of silence more than now. Strong, brave, lovely Amber had burst out with everything they'd kept locked in silence all these years, and his mind was totally blank. He'd been too busy keeping his nation intact and his heart from bearing any more scars to say a word to her about his wants and needs, and he'd presumed she didn't care what he wanted anyway, because she still loved Alim.

But if that wasn't the truth, why had she walled off from him so completely? He'd thought it was because she found him repulsive—but now?

But last year, she'd come to him. She'd asked him to make love to her…

'I never knew you wanted me to desire you,' he said, fighting the husky note of long-hated yearning with all he had. His pride had taken enough battering from this woman, and he'd been celibate far too long. *Say it, Amber, tell me if you want me—*

But with a jerky movement Amber unlocked her seat belt and got to her feet. Her eyes blazed down at him, thwarted passion burning bright. 'Can't you just talk to me like you're a normal man, and show me some human feeling? Can't you stop—stop fencing with words, asking questions instead of answering me honestly? Can't you stop being so cold all the time? I'm not your enemy, I'm your *wife!*'

Stop reading books, Harun! Stop saying yes and do it, be a real man like your brothers!

He rubbed at his forehead in frustration. 'Amber, stop talking in circles and tell me what you want,' he grated, knowing he sounded harsh but no longer caring. He felt as if he had enough to deal with right now without her baffling dramatics. Couldn't she see that she was expecting too much, too fast? 'Can we do this thing later? In a few hours I'll be facing my brother for the first time in years. Alim's my only family, all I have left.'

'It only needed that.' With a slow nod, those beautiful, liquid-honey eyes iced over, frozen in time like her namesake. 'We don't have to do this *thing* at all. Thank you, Harun. You've made my decision easy.' And she walked—that beautiful swaying dance she put into every effortless step—into the cockpit and asked in a voice as curt as her walk had been shimmering, 'I don't want to go now. Open the exit door, please.'

When it was open, she moved to the exit, her head high. At the opening, she turned—only her head—and glanced at him. She spoke with regal dignity, the deposed queen she was about to become. 'I hope your reunion with Alim is all you wish it to be. I hope he comes home to be your family.'

He opened his mouth, but she rushed on, as if unable to bear hearing his formal thank-you. 'When Alim becomes the sheikh again, I hope you find what you want out of your life. I hope you find a way to be happy,

Harun, because I'm going to find my own life from now on, without you or anyone else telling me what to do.'

Then, like a dream of beauty abruptly awakened, she was gone.

CHAPTER FOUR

Fifteen Days Later
The Sheikh's Palace, Sar Abbas

HARUN had asked Amber to be here at this private handover of the nation to the real Sheikh of Abbas al-Din, and so she'd come, from curiosity if nothing else—but it seemed as if nobody else would begin speaking, so she'd have to.

Maybe that was what Harun wanted from her, to break the ice?

Right now she felt as if she'd give anything to be able to do just that—to break the ice of Harun's withdrawn politeness. In the last fifteen days she'd come to regret her outburst. When would she learn to control her tongue and temper? Neither had got her anywhere with the el-Kanar brothers, least of all Harun.

'Welcome home, Alim,' she said, trying to smile, to repress the emotion boiling like a pot beneath the surface. 'It's good to have you back.'

Her long-lost brother-in-law looked older than the handsome, daring racing driver she remembered. The scars on his face and neck, the mementoes of the race that took Fadi's life, weren't as bad as she'd feared. He was still the kind of man who'd draw admiring looks from women wherever he went, though, from the wariness in his stance when any woman was nearby, she suspected he didn't know it.

Alim flicked a glance at Harun, but he stood impassive, neither moving nor speaking. After a few moments Alim bowed to her, a smile on his mouth as stressed as the look in his eyes. 'Thank you, Amber.'

It seemed the charming daredevil who'd grabbed her youthful fancy was gone—like her long-disappeared crush. But this man was her brother-in-law, a stranger to her—and this was not her reunion. So she waited, casting small glances about the room. The awkward tension between the brothers was too hard to keep watching.

This beautiful, airy but neutral room was almost as hard to look at. This had been Fadi's reception room to meet foreign dignitaries, and it was where she'd met all three el-Kanar brothers for the first time. The dear friend who'd loved another woman, the glamorous racing hero who'd disappeared rather than wed her, and the man of ice who'd done his duty by her in public, but would do anything rather than talk to her or touch her.

Harun must have noticed that she and Alim were both awaiting their cue from him. He spoke with an odd note in his voice. 'I've moved out of your room, Alim. It's ready for you, as is your office, as soon as you want to resume your duties.'

Alim took a step towards his brother. 'Let's not pretend. Don't talk as if I've been sick for a few weeks. I was gone for three years. I left all the grief and duty to you. Harun, I wanted to say that…'

Harun shrugged, with all his eloquent understatement, and she realised he did it with Alim, not just with her. It seemed he was skilled at cutting off more people than her alone. He shut off anyone's attempts at emotional connection, freezing them out with that hint of blue-blooded frost. *Come no further.* 'There's no need to say anything, Alim. It wasn't as if I had anywhere better to be at the time.'

But Alim wasn't having it. With a determined tone, he went on, 'I wanted to say, the choice is yours now. You've done a magnificent job of running the country, of picking up the pieces after Fadi's death and my disappearance. You're the nation's hero now, not me. If you want to remain the sheikh—'

'No.'

The snarl burst from her mouth, shaking her to the core, but it had a masculine note as well. Harun had echoed it even more forcefully than she had; he sounded almost savage.

Amber felt Alim staring at her, waiting. Maybe it was easier for him to hear her out first than to know what he'd done to Harun by his disappearance.

She flushed, and glanced at Harun—but as usual, he stood locked inside those walls of silence she couldn't knock down, even with catapults and cannons.

She fiddled with her hands, shuffled a foot. Did she want to hear Harun's reasons for wanting out before she'd spoken? Suddenly she couldn't bear to know, to hear all the reasons why she'd failed him, and heard words tumbling from her lips.

'I won't play sheikh's happy wife for anyone's sake any more. I'm tired of the pretence that everything's all right. I don't care what my father says. I want a divorce.'

She turned and walked out of the room, trying to contain the trembling in every part of her body. She reached her suite of rooms and closed the door behind her. It almost felt like a miracle to make it this far without being stopped, but she'd managed it by staring down anyone that approached her. She encountered more than twenty people, staffers or servants, all asking if they could serve her—all burning to know the answer to one question. Who was the sheikh now, Alim or Harun?

Sitting on the straight-backed chair at her desk, she counted in silence. If he didn't come this time—

In less than three minutes, the door swung wide open without announcement. 'Guard every possible listening place, but stay well away from it,' Harun snapped to someone outside, and several masculine voices lifted in assent. From behind the walls of her suite, she heard the soft shuffling of feminine feet moving away in haste, and smiled to herself.

'He comes to my rooms twice in a month of his own free will,' she murmured, as if to herself. 'Will the walls fall flat in shock?'

Harun's gaze narrowed. 'Is that really how you want to conduct this conversation, Amber, in sarcasm and anger?'

She lifted her chin. 'If it actually makes you feel something, I'll risk it.'

'You needn't worry about that,' he said grimly. 'I'm feeling quite a lot of things right about now.'

'Then I'm glad,' she said with sweet mockery. It seemed the only way to break through that invisible, impenetrable wall of concrete around him.

And it worked. With a few steps he was right in front of her, his chest rising and falling in abrupt motion, his normally forest-green eyes black with intensity. The emotion she'd hungered to see for so long had risen from his self-dug grave and the satisfaction hit her like a punch to the stomach. 'How dare you make an announcement like that with my brother there?'

'I had to,' she said with false calm, heart hammering.

'Without him there it would have done no good, because it seems to me that you don't care what I say or what I think. You've never once asked or cared what I want. What's right for Abbas al-Din is all that matters to you.'

Ah, why did there have to be that little catch in her voice, giving her away?

But it seemed he didn't even notice it. 'He wants to marry the nurse that rescued him. He loves her, just so you know,' he replied in a measured, even tone—but the fire in his eyes showed the struggle he was having in commanding his emotions.

Incensed, she jerked to her feet. 'Is that all you can say? I tell you I want a divorce, and you only want to remind me of a stupid crush I had when I was nineteen? How long will you keep punishing me for words I said and feelings I had when I was barely out of childhood? I was grieving too, you know. I cared for Fadi. He was like a big brother to me.' Afraid she'd burst into unseemly tears in front of him, she wheeled away, staring hard out of that beautifully carved window, blinking the stinging from her eyes. She'd rather *die* than cry in front of him. 'I've always known I meant nothing to you beyond the political gain to your country, but I hoped you respected me a little more than that.'

The silence stretched out so long, she wondered if he'd left. He had the knack of moving without sound. Then he spoke. 'You're right. I apologise, Amber.' As she whirled around he gave her a small smile. 'I had my own stupid crush at nineteen—but I didn't marry you while I was in love with your sister. Do you understand?'

They were the first words he'd ever spoken that felt real to her, and she put a hand on the chair to feel something solid; the truth had hit her that hard. She'd thought of it as a silly crush on a superstar all this time—but Alim was his brother. Though he'd said it simply, it sickened her. She'd married him with a crush on his *brother*—the brother that had publicly humiliated her. As far as deeply personal insults went, it probably couldn't get much worse.

'I understand,' she said, her voice croaky.

He nodded. 'We both know you can't divorce me, Amber. It would bring dishonour on the family and threaten the stability of the country, so I don't believe that was what you want most.'

Hating that he'd called her on her little power-game, she said wearily, 'I don't have to live here, Harun.' She rubbed her eyes, heedless of make-up. What did it matter what she looked like? He didn't want her, had never wanted her.

His jaw hardened. 'You'd make our problems public by leaving me?'

'I was never *with* you to leave you, My Lord. The little scar in your armpit is evidence enough of that.' But instead of feeling triumph at the taunt, she just wanted to cry. Why did she always have to attack? And why did it take attacking him to make him *talk?*

'So you're saying you'll drag us both through the mud by proving I didn't consummate the marriage?'

She lifted her face, staring at him in disbelief. 'Is that all you care about—if I embarrass you in public? When you've been humiliating me publicly for years!' she flung at him. 'Everyone in the palace knows you don't come to my bedroom! I'm known as the bad-luck bride, who's ruined the lives of all three el-Kanar brothers. Even my parents bemoan my inability to entice you—not to mention the lack of grandchildren—every time they visit or call me!' She was quite proud of herself, laying her deepest, bleeding wound before him with such flaming sarcasm instead of crying or wailing like a weak woman. 'And of course everyone's very well aware your lack of interest must be my fault, since our wedding night was apparently consummated, and you never came back.' She paused, and looked at him reproachfully, before delivering the final blow. 'Oh, and nobody in the palace has hesitated to tell me about your lover and daughter. Do you know how it feels to know that while you continue to leave me alone, you gave another woman the only thing I've ever asked of you—and even the servants know about it?'

Harun closed his eyes and rubbed his forehead, shoulders bent. He looked unutterably weary, and part of her ached to take the words back, to make this conversation any time but now. 'I would have thought you'd know by now that servants only ever get things half-right. The child's name is Naima. Her mother is Buhjah, and she's a good woman.' His words were tight, locking her out again.

Amber stared in disbelief. She'd just bared her greatest shame to him, the very public and family humiliation she had to endure daily, and he could only speak of his daughter and lover—the family he'd allowed her to learn about from the servants?

Did he love Buhjah? Was that why he'd never cared how she felt or what she needed? Just like Fadi, all over again. Oh, these el-Kanar brothers were so faithful to the women they loved. And so good at doing their public duty by her and then leaving her in no-man's-land, stuck in a life she could no longer bear.

'Get out,' she said, her voice wobbling. She wheeled away, her breast heaving with her choppy breathing. 'Just go. Oh, and you'd better lock me in, because it's the only way your precious name won't be dragged through the mud you're so afraid of.'

'No, I won't leave it like this,' he said, hard and unbending. Oh, no, he wouldn't plead, not with her. Probably the mother of his child roused his gentleness and touch and had the man on his knees for her. For Amber, there was only an unending wall of ice. But then, why should she expect more? She was only the wife.

She buried her face in her hands. 'Oh, by all means, master, stay, and force me to keep humiliating myself before you. You're in control by law and religion. I can't stop you.' The words scraped across a throat as raw as the desert, but she no longer cared. It wasn't as if he gave a fig if she did weep or how she felt about anything—but the embarrassment at her less than regal behaviour might just get rid of him for a little while.

'Amber, I don't want to keep going like this. I can see you're hurting, but I don't know how to help you.'

Seconds later she heard the door close softly behind him, and heaved a sigh—whether in relief or from the greatest misery she'd ever known, she wasn't sure. Had she got her point across to him at last, or had she driven him away?

There would be no divorce. Her father would see her dead before he'd allow it, and she couldn't just disappear. Even if she weren't hemmed in by servants, she'd put her family through public shame, the scandal would leave her younger sisters unmarriageable and, worst of all, she'd have to leave her family behind for ever.

Unthinkable. Impossible. They were all she had, and, despite her ongoing conflicts with her father, she loved them all dearly.

So she was stuck here, for ever bound to this man—

'So why do I keep driving him away?' she muttered through her fingers. If she wanted any kind of amity in her life—and, most importantly, a child to fill the hole in her heart and end her public shame—she had to let Harun know the truth. That, far from hating him, she punished him for his neglect of her because she admired and desired him, and had since before their wedding day. Even now she pushed him in some desperate attempt to get him to really speak to her, to feel something, anything—

No. She'd die before she told him. He had to give her some sign first! But how to—?

The rag crossed her mouth with shocking suddenness. Panic clawed at her and she struggled, but within moments it was tied at the back of her head. Another bound her hands together behind her. She kept fighting, but then a sickly sweet stench filled her nostrils, and made her head spin before everything turned black.

Three steps from her door, Harun stopped and wheeled around. What was he doing?

Amber was crying, and he'd left her. He'd never believed he'd ever have the power to make her cry, but he had…talking of Naima and Buhjah—

'Idiot!' he muttered when at last a light went on in his brain and his heart after years of darkness. Was it possible? Could Amber be jealous? He struggled to think. Did she yearn for the child she'd demanded of him last year, the child he'd never given her—his children that were her right as his wife…or—dear God in heaven…he'd let her keep thinking Buhjah was Rafa's real name—that she was his lover, not Fadi's—

Amber was his wife. He owed her his first loyalty, not Buhjah and Naima, much as he cared for both of them. He owed Amber a lot more than the public presence he gave her. And—what if all her roundabout talking, her probing and proud demands for more than the child she'd asked him for a year ago were supposed to help him to work out that she wanted more? That she wanted him?

He stalked back through the door before he could change his mind. 'Amber, I'm not going anywhere—'

Then he jerked to a standstill, staring at the sliding door of the secret passage that joined the back of their bedrooms—the one that was never watched, at his strict order. It led to freedom through a tunnel below the palace, created during the seventeenth century, when many brides were taken by abduction. Amber's feet were all he saw as the door began to slide closed again, but they were sliding backwards.

Someone had her! If it was the el-Shabbats...or worse, the more virulent of the el-Kanar supportive factions who'd kept sending him messages to rid himself of her, that she was bad luck—dear God, the return of Alim might have spurred them to action. The faction of reactionary, old-fashioned autocrats hated Alim for his western ways, and wanted to keep Harun as Sheikh. If they'd taken Amber, they'd use her as leverage to make Alim disappear for good—and then they'd kill her to leave Harun free to wed a more fertile bride.

No!

'Amber!' he yelled, bolting for the door. He reached it before it slid shut, yanked it open and shouldered his way through.

Turning left, he ran down the passage—then a cloying scent filled his senses and mind; the world spun too fast, and he knew no more.

CHAPTER FIVE

THE screaming headache and general feeling of grogginess were the first indications that life wasn't normal when Harun opened his eyes…because when he tried to open them they were filled with sticky sand, and he had to blink and push his lids wide before they opened.

The second indication was when he saw the room he was in. Lying on a bed that—well, it *sagged,* he could feel his hip aching from the divot his body had made— he knew this was a room he'd never been in before. It wasn't quite filthy, but for a man who'd spent every day of his life in apartments in flawless condition, he could smell the dust, breathe it in.

The furnishings were strange. After a few moments of blinking and staring hard, he thought he hadn't been in a room so sparse since his tent during the war. The one cupboard looked as though it had been sanded with steel wool, the gouges were so messy, and it was old. Not antique, but worn out, like something sold at a bazaar in the poor quarter of the city. The one carpet on the wide-boarded wooden floor looked like an original eighteenth-century weave, but with moth-holes and ragged ends. The dining table and chairs had been hand-carved in a beautiful dark wood, but looked as if they hadn't been polished in years. The chairs by the windows were covered in tapestry that had long lost its plushness.

Thin, almost transparent curtains hung over the wide, ornately carved windows and around the bed, giving an illusion of privacy; but in a life filled with servants and politicians, foreign dignitaries and visiting relatives, he barely understood what the word meant.

He moved to rub his eyes, but both hands came together. His hands were tied with a double-stranded silken string. Could he break it if he struggled hard enough—?

The silk was stronger than it appeared. The bonds didn't budge, no matter how he struggled, and he swore.

A little murmur of protest behind him made him freeze halfway through pulling his wrists apart. A soft sigh followed, and then the soft breathing of a woman in deep sleep.

He flipped his body around to the other direction, his head screaming in protest at the movement, and looked at his companion. Pale-faced, deeply asleep, Amber was in bed with him for the first time, wearing only a peignoir of almost the same shimmering honey-gold as her skin.

For that matter, he wore only a pair of boxers in silk as thin as Amber's peignoir.

A memory as blurry as a photo of his grandparents' youth came to him—a vision of Amber's feet being dragged backwards down the secret passage. But, try as he might, nothing more came to him.

They'd obviously been kidnapped, but why? For money, or political clout? Why would anyone want to take them now, when it was too late? It made no sense, with Alim back and able to take his rightful place as Sheikh—

Unless…could this be part of an elaborate el-Shabbat plot to reduce the el-Kanar power base in Abbas al-Din? He'd just paid one hundred million US dollars for Alim's safe release. If Alim paid the same for his and Amber's safe return, it wouldn't bankrupt the nation, but it would be enough to create a negative media backlash against the family. *Why do these people keep getting kidnapped?* Once was forgivable, but twice would be seen as a family weakness. If they'd taken Alim as well, it might destroy the—

An icy chill ran down his back. If it was the el-Shabbats, it would mean their deaths, all of them. Alim had just been taken hostage, beaten badly, and released only by ransom. How could he stand it again so soon? If Alim was taken or, God forbid, dead—his only brother, the only one he had left in the world—

He had to get out of here! When a guard came in, he'd be ready. He jerked to a sitting position, looking around the room for something, anything that could be used as a weapon.

Amber's tiny murmur of protest let him know he'd disturbed her. He dragged in a slow breath, taking a few moments to reorient himself. If anything had happened to Alim, right now he couldn't do a thing about it. Getting Amber out safely had to be his first priority—but even if they managed to escape, how could they reach home, almost completely undressed?

He'd wondered what kind of kidnapper would put him on a bed dressed in almost nothing, lying beside his scantily clad wife, but now he saw the point all too well. Without clothes, with no dignity, what could he do?

Find some clothes—and I will find a way out of here.

Slowly, gently, he got to his feet, making a face at the swishing slide of the shorts against his skin. He wore silk clothes only for ceremonial occasions, preferring cotton. Jeans and T-shirts had been his favoured fashion in his private time, until it had been made clear to him that, as replacement sheikh, he had to be seen to be the perfect Arabic man at all times.

With only two rooms, searching their cage didn't take long. Besides the bed, the dining set, the chairs by the windows, and the cupboard, there was only a prayer mat. He realised that was what had woken him, the call to prayer being made somewhere behind the building.

But even with his hands tied, he could look around.

The massive double door was locked. The only other doors, to the bathroom and the balcony, showed no chance of escape. The room they were in was five storeys up, without convenient roofs nearby to leap onto. Even if there were, he couldn't ask Amber to leap from one roof to another, and he couldn't leave her alone to face the consequences of his escape.

On the bedside tables were water glasses, and paper tissues. In the drawer on Amber's side there were about twenty hairpins.

They even knew how she preferred to do her hair, he thought grimly.

He crawled awkwardly under the bed, finding only dust. Using both hands together, he opened the cupboard—nothing at all but the hanging rail.

That had possibilities, if only he could get it out. But pulling and tugging at the rail made his head spin.

He checked through the bathroom, including the two small cupboards there. Even the most basic of bathroom goods could be used together to create something to help them escape.

'No floss, not even toilet paper in here,' he muttered moments later, resisting the urge to slam a cupboard, or throw one of the little bottles of oil at the wall. 'What kind of crazy kidnappers give their captives scented oils for their bath?'

Then his mind began racing. With the right oils, combined with the toothpaste and some water—he assumed they'd be fed and given water, at least—he might be able to make something...perhaps one of Alim's infamous stink-bombs from childhood, or some kind of fluid to throw in their kidnappers' eyes.

How he wished he'd paid more attention to Alim's scientific pranks when they were kids!

The bathroom held no more secrets. The bath was old and large, scrubbed clean. The toilet had a hose beside it. The towels were close to threadbare, useless for anything but basic drying. Their abductors weren't taking any chances.

He'd run out of options for now. With a clenched jaw, Harun let the pounding of his head and eyes dictate to him. He fell back on the bed, closed his eyes and breathed in the scent she wore. Intoxicating as an unfurled desert bud, soft and tender as a mid-spring night—was it perfume or the essence of Amber herself? He wished he knew. Drinking it in with each breath, savouring an intimacy so new and yet somehow familiar because of so many dreams, he returned to sleep.

Amber couldn't remember waking so peacefully since she was a child. In fact, had she ever woken feeling this warm and snuggly, secure and happy?

There was a sound beside her, a slow, rhythmic cadence she couldn't recognise. There was a scent she couldn't define, filling every breath she took. Where was she?

Opening her eyes, she saw the light sprinkling of

dark hair scattered across an unclad male chest lying right before her eyes. She took in a slow, deep breath, and it came again, the scent of belonging, as if she'd come home at last.

She barely dared lift her gaze—but she knew the scent, the feeling it gave her. She'd known it for so long from so far away. It was him. The perfectly sculpted statue of ice had become all warm, solid male. Her untouchable husband was within her reach at last.

They had so many problems to overcome. Their hopes and fears and most of their lives were unknown to each other—but at this moment, she didn't care. He was here. She was gripped by a long-familiar urge.

Could she do it?

It had started on their wedding night when he'd come to her, dressed as a groom ready to love his bride. It had persisted even after she'd emerged from the bathroom that night, clad only in a towel. With a glance, he'd gathered his blasted paperwork and bowed to her, the movement fairly dripping with irony, and, with a twist to his lips, he'd left the room without a word. She hadn't slept in weeks after that—and she'd endured three hundred and forty-four restless, hungry, angry nights after he'd refused her bed last year. Sometimes she thought she'd give anything to have this farce come to an end, and she could find a man who would actually desire her. But he didn't, and he wouldn't let her go, either.

The *thunk* came again, a sickening hit in the stomach at the remembered rejection. So why did the aching need to taste him with her lips and tongue still fill every pore of her? Why did she want him so badly when he was so cold and uncaring? She could never seem to break this stupid desire for the husband who despised her. The need to touch him was like the heat of a gold-refiner's furnace. There was no point in ignoring facts when just by her looking at him now, by her lying so close to him, her pulse was pounding so hard she wondered if it would wake him. Wondered and hungered, as she danced on a fine blade-point of need and pride and the soul-destroying fear of another rejection.

Do it. Just kiss him once, a little voice in her head whispered, soft and insistent. *Maybe it will cure you of all this wondering. Maybe it won't be as good as you think.*

Was she leaning into him, or was she dreaming again? His lips, parted in dreams were so close, closer than they'd ever been—

His eyes opened, looking right into hers.

Her breath caught, and she danced that razor-fine point again, aching and fearful as she scrambled to find her pride, the coldness that had been her salvation in all her dealings with him. Was the returning hunger she saw in his eyes merely a product of her overwrought imagination? If only she knew him well enough to find the courage, to ask.

If only every chance she'd ever taken hadn't left her alone with her humiliation.

Harun's gaze drifted lower. Torn between slight indignation and the spark heating her blood at the slow flame in his eyes, familiar pride rushed back to save her, won over the need for the unknown. She lifted a hand to tug at the neckline of her negligée, but the other hand jerked up with it. Looking down, she saw she was tied in silken bonds, as soft as the silken negligee that barely covered her nudity beneath.

As if she had never seen him before, Amber turned back to Harun. She let her gaze take him all in. He was almost naked...and he was fully aroused.

Blushing so hard it felt like fire on her cheeks, she saw his knowing, gentle smile. He knew she wanted him, and still he didn't say a word, didn't touch her. Wouldn't give her the one thing she craved, a child of her own. Someone all her own to love.

A beautiful, almost poetic revenge for my stupid words—isn't it, Harun?—always leaving me alone? When will you stop torturing me for the past?

Taking refuge in imperiousness, she demanded, 'Who dressed me this way? Who *undressed* me? Where are we?'

His gaze lifted to hers. For a moment she saw a flash of reluctance and regret; then it vanished, leaving that unreadable look she'd come to hate. 'I'm afraid I can't answer any of those questions. I can only tell you that I didn't undress you.' He lifted his hands, tied together in front of him, with silky white bonds that would only hurt if he struggled to free himself.

Her hands were tied with the same material—and she hated that some small part of her had been hoping that he'd been the one to undress her, see her naked, touch her skin. Foolish, pathetic woman, would she never stop these ridiculous hopes and dreams? She'd always be alone. The lesson had been hammered into her skull years ago, and still she kept aiming her darts at the moon.

Feeling her blush grow hotter, she retorted, 'Well, I think I can take it for granted that you wouldn't undress me after all these years.'

His gaze roamed her body, so slow she almost felt him touch her—tender, invisible fingers exploring her skin as she'd hoped only moments before, and she had to hold in the soft sound of imagined delight. It felt so *real*.

In a deep growling voice that heated her blood,

he murmured, 'I don't think you should take that for granted at all.' After another slow perusal, her body felt gripped by fever. 'We don't have the luxury of taking anything for granted in our situation.'

Even spoken with a gentle huskiness, the final words doused the edge of her anger and her desire, leaving her soul flooding with questions. 'What's going on here, Harun? Why would anyone—anyone…just leave us here, dressed like this?'

Say it, you coward. You've been abducted! But just thinking the word left her sick and shaking with impotent terror. *So much for being like Great-grandmother…*

'I don't pretend to know.' His gaze met hers, direct. 'We just paid one hundred million dollars for Alim's safe return. How much do you think Alim and your father between them can afford to pay for our ransom now?'

'I don't know about Abbas al-Din's treasury, but the recent troubles in the Gulf have drained Father's resources, paying the security forces.' Amber bit her lip. 'Do you think the el-Shabbats are behind this?'

'I certainly wouldn't rule them out, but this could be any of a dozen high-ranking families, not just the el-Shabbats. There are many families eager to take over rulership of our countries if they only had the funds,' he said quietly. 'Your father and Alim would have to take that into consideration before making any decision.'

'Do you even think either of them knows we're gone?' she asked, hating the piteous note in her voice, pleading for reassurance.

Harun sighed. 'I don't know. Alim's got so much on his mind at the moment. We walked out saying we weren't staying. I think he'll assume we left, possibly to talk out our troubles, patch up our marriage.'

I wish we had. Why didn't you want that? she almost blurted, but there were far greater necessities to talk about right now. She looked down again, frowning. 'Why are our hands tied, but not our feet? Why aren't we gagged?'

He moved his hands, and she felt a finger caress the back of hers. 'Maybe someone wants us to talk?' he suggested, his eyes glimmering.

Her mouth opened and closed. The surprise of his making a joke was too complete for her to quite believe in it. 'Oh, I wish,' she retorted at last, rolling her eyes. 'Perhaps they could make you talk to me if they repeatedly used an electric prod—you know, those things that shock animals?'

He grinned at her, and it relaxed his austere handsomeness, making her catch her breath. 'Do you think it's worth a try?'

Choking back a giggle, she fixed a stern expression in her eyes. 'Can you please be serious? How can we get out of here?' She bit her lip.

His eyes sobered. 'I don't think they need to gag us, Amber. We're at least five storeys up. The walls are thick, and the nearest buildings are a hundred metres or more away. There are guards posted outside the doors and at every building through the windows, and they'll be very hard of hearing. I doubt that any amount of screaming will bring help.'

Absurd to feel such warmth from the motion of one of his fingers when they'd been abducted and could be dead by nightfall, but right now she'd take whatever comfort she could get. 'You've already looked?'

He nodded, his face tight. 'There's no way out of here until they let us out. This abduction's been perfectly planned.'

'Do you think anyone's looking for us yet?' she asked almost piteously, hating to hear the word. *Abduction.* It made her feel so powerless.

He gave that tiny shrug she'd always hated, but this time she sensed it was less a brush-off than an attempt to reassure her. 'That depends on how clever our abductors have been, and what they heard us saying beforehand.'

She frowned. 'What could they have heard us say?'

He just looked at her, waiting for her to remember—and after a few moments, it struck her. In her need to push Harun into action of some kind, she'd stated her intention to divorce him, where a dozen servants or any palace or government servant could have heard. She'd shown her contempt for the existing laws and traditions. Any traditional man would have been shocked.

She closed her eyes. By coming to her room to discuss their problems instead of punishing her in front of Alim, Harun had treated her with the utmost respect. But she'd given him none. She'd ploughed ahead with her shocking announcement, thinking only of humiliating Harun in a public place to spur him into some kind of action. She'd thought only of herself, her needs—and now they both had to endure the consequences.

'I'm sorry, Harun,' she whispered. 'This is all my fault.'

'Let's not waste time pushing blame at each other or on ourselves, when we don't know what's going on.' Softly, almost hypnotically, his fingers caressed hers. 'Playing that kind of game won't help either of us now. We need to keep our minds clear, and work together.'

Her head was on his shoulder before she knew she'd moved. Or maybe he had, too. Either way she rested her head halfway between his shoulder and chest, hearing him breathe, drinking it in. 'Thank you.'

'For what?'

She smiled up at him. 'A more insecure man would have wasted an hour lecturing me on my unfeminine behaviour, on my presumption in challenging you in the first place, where others could hear. A less intelligent man would blame our situation totally on me. A man who felt his masculinity challenged might have beaten me into submission.'

He smiled—no, he grinned back. 'I never even thought of it. Whatever made you think I wanted a wishy-washy kind of wife?'

In all this time, I've never seen him smile like that.

Had she seen him smile at all, apart from the practised one for the cameras?

Maybe he knew she needed distraction from this intense situation, as weird as it was terrifying; but Harun was providing distraction and reassurance in a way she never would have expected—at least from him.

Was this why his men had followed him into battle with such blind ferocity? Had he made them feel they could survive anything, too?

Whether it was real or a trick, she had no desire to argue with him. Right now, he was all she had, just as she was all he had—and the thought of losing this smiling man, teasing and caressing her hand, was unbearable. 'Well, maybe if you'd talked to me about what kind of wife you did want, I could answer that,' she replied, but in a light, fun tone, 'but right now I'm rather clueless.'

At that, he chuckled. 'Yes, you're not the only one who's told me that I keep a little too much to myself.'

Fascinated, she stared at his mouth. 'In all this time, I've never heard you laugh.'

She half expected him to make a cool retort—but instead one end of his mouth quirked higher. 'You think it took being abducted for me to show my true colours? Maybe, if you like it, you can arrange for it to happen on a regular basis.'

She was in the middle of laughter before she realised it. The look, the self-deprecating humour, set off a strange feeling low in her belly, a cross between muted terror and an inexplicable, badly timed hunger. 'How can you be so serious all the time when everything is safe and normal, and be this…this *charming* man now, when we might—?' To her horror, she couldn't go on, as a lump burned its way up her throat and tears prickled behind her eyes.

'Well, you see, I'm trying to distract myself from a horrendous itch on my back that I can't scratch.' He lifted up his bound hands.

Even though it was delivered deadpan, it made her laugh again. If he'd spent all those years before being too serious, now it seemed she couldn't make him become so. And she knew he'd done it to distract her. His thoughtfulness in this terrifying situation touched her. 'I could do it for you,' she offered, gulping away the painful lump in her throat. 'Roll over.'

He did, and her breath caught in her throat as she realised anew that he was naked from the waist up. She looked at the wealth of revealed man, unseen in three years. He didn't have time for extensive workouts, but he was toned and a natural deep brown, with broad shoulders and a muscular chest and back.

'Where?' she asked, fighting to keep the huskiness

out of her voice. It was the first time she'd touch his body, and it was for a stupid itch.

'Beneath my left shoulder blade.' He sounded odd, as if his throat was constricted, but when she scratched the area for him, using both hands at once since they were both there, he moved so her fingers covered a wider amount of skin. 'I don't remember anything ever feeling so good,' he groaned. 'You have magic hands, Amber. How about you? Is there anywhere you can't reach that needs scratching?'

Yes, my curiosity as to why you never talked to me before now, why you never wanted anything but to hurt and humiliate me until now—when we could die at any moment. 'You scratch my back and I'll scratch yours?' she murmured, aiming for the light tone of moments before, but she was too busy fighting her fingers, aching to turn the scratch into a caress, to feel his body.

'Sounds good to me,' he said, and now he was the one that sounded husky. 'I'll scratch any itch you need me to. You only need to ask, Amber.'

Her breath snagged in her chest. Her rebel eyes lifted to his face as he rolled back to her, and his awkward, tied movements brought him far closer to her than he'd ever been. His thighs were against hers, and his eyes were nearly black as his gaze slowly roamed her silk-clad form, and lifted to her mouth. She'd never seen a man's desire before, and it felt like sunlight touching her after a long, black Arctic winter. 'Harun,' she whispered, but no sound emerged from her. Her body moved towards him, and her face lifted as his lowered…

Then Harun rolled away from her, hard and fast, and she felt sick with anger and disappointment.

CHAPTER SIX

AT LEAST Amber felt sick until she realised Harun was shielding her with his body. 'Who's there?' he demanded in a hard tone. 'I heard the door open. Show yourself!' He'd blocked her effectively from seeing the door, and whoever stood there couldn't see her, either.

She tugged fast at the peignoir, but realised that trying to cover herself with this thin bit of nothing was a useless exercise.

A man walked around the curtain, his bare feet swishing on the old woven rug. He was dressed in anonymous Arabic clothing the colour of sand, most of his face swathed in a scarf. Without a word he bowed to them both, an incongruous gesture, and ridiculous in their current setting. Then, covering Amber's scantily clad body with the sheet first, his eyes trained away, he used a thin knife to untie her, and then Harun. When Harun was free the man waved to the small dining table by the window, which had two trays filled with food and drink, and bowed again.

Harun leaped to his feet the second he was untied, but the man lifted a strong hand, in clear warning against trying anything. He clapped, and two guards came around the curtains, armed with machine guns. Both guards had the weapons aiming directly at Harun.

Amber balled her hands into fists at her sides, instead of holding them to her mouth. If they knew she wanted to be sick at the sight of the weapons trained on Harun, they'd know their power over her.

If Harun felt any fear he wasn't showing it. 'What is this?' he demanded, and his voice was hard with command. 'Where are we, and what do you want with us?'

The man only kept his hand up. His eyes were blank.

'So you're a minion, paid to look anonymous,' Harun taunted. 'You can stay silent so I don't know your dialect, but the money you're hoping for will never be of use to you or your families.'

In answer, the man moved around the room. He pointed to one possible escape route after another, opening doors, lifting curtains to show them what lay beyond.

Armed guards stood at the door, and at each flat building roof facing a window, holding assault weapons trained on them.

Amber scrambled to her feet and, clutching the sheet, shrank behind Harun, who suddenly seemed far bigger than before, far more solid and welcoming. 'Those men are snipers, Harun,' she whispered. Allah help them, they were surrounded by snipers.

'Don't think about it. They're probably not even loaded,' Harun whispered in her ear. He kept his gaze on the guard, hard and unforgiving as he said aloud, 'I promise you, Amber, we'll get out of this safely.' He flicked the man a glance. 'These men know who we are. They won't take any risks with us, because we mean money. The cowards hiding behind them are obviously too scared to risk dealing with us themselves.'

The guard's eyes seemed to smile, but they held something akin to real respect. He bowed one final time, and left the room. A deep, hollow *boom* sound followed moments later.

The door wasn't simply locked. They'd put a bar across it.

Amber shivered. 'That was—unnerving.' Hardly knowing it, she reached out to him with a hand that shook slightly. Right now she was too terrified to remember it was weak to need anyone else's reassurance.

His hand found hers, and the warm clasp was filled with strength. 'It was meant to paralyse us into instant obedience,' he said, in equal quiet, but anger vibrating through each syllable. 'Remember, we're their bankroll. This is all a game to them. They won't hurt us, Amber. They need us alive.'

'So why surround us with snipers?' She shivered, drawing closer. 'Why put us in the middle of nowhere like this? How can we be such a threat?'

After a short hesitation, he took her in his arms. 'The Shabbat war,' he said quietly.

He said no more, made no reference to his heroic acts three years ago—he never had spoken about it, or referred to his title, *the beloved tiger*. But his acts were the stuff of legend now, and the stories had grown to Alexander-like proportions during the past few years. The people of Abbas al-Din felt safe with Harun as their sheikh. 'You mean they're afraid of what you'll do?'

'Thus far it seems there's nothing *to* do.' He made a sound of disgust. 'They want us to believe they're prepared for every contingency, but even the guard's silence tells me something. They don't want us to know where we are. They know if he'd spoken, I might have known his nationality and sub-tribe through the local dialect.'

She frowned, looking up at him, glad of the distraction. 'Why would you know his nationality or tribe or dialect?'

His voice darkened still further. 'Whoever took us knows that I have a background in linguistics, and that I know almost every Arabic sub-dialect.'

'Oh.' Another cold slither ran down her back, even as she wondered what he'd studied at university, and why she'd never thought to ask. 'I think I'd like to eat now.'

'Amber, wait.' He held her back by trapping her in his arms.

More unnerved by the events of the last hour than she wanted to admit, she glared at him. 'Why should I? I'm hungry.'

He said softly, 'You've been unconscious for hours, and you haven't eaten in a day. You came around the bed in fear, but your legs might not support you any further.'

So have you, she wanted to say but didn't. *I can stand alone,* her pride wanted her to state, but, again, she couldn't make herself say it, because more unexpected depths of the man she'd married were being revealed with every passing moment. And, to her chagrin, she found her legs weren't as steady as she'd believed; she swayed, and he lifted her in his arms.

'Thank you,' she whispered. It was another first for them, and the poignant irony of why he held her this way slammed into her with full force.

'Come, you should eat, and probably drink.' He seated her on one of the chairs. 'But let me go first.' This time she merely frowned at the impolite assertion. With a weary smile, he again spoke very softly. 'I don't think your body can take any more drugging, Amber. You slept hours longer than I did, and you're still shaking. Let me see if the food is all right.'

Touched again by this new display of caring for her,

Amber tried to smile at him, but no words came. Right now, she didn't know if the non-stop quivering of her body was because of the drugging, or because he was being so considerate…and so close to her, smiling at her at last. Or because—because—

'I've been abducted,' she said. She meant it to come out hard, but it was a shaky whisper. But at least she'd said it. The reality had been slammed into her with the guards' entrance. There was no point in any form of denial.

'Don't think about it.' His voice was gentle but strong. 'You need time to adjust.'

Grateful for his understanding, she nodded.

After making a small wince she didn't understand, he tried the water, swilling it around in his mouth. 'No odd taste, no reaction in my gums or stinging in the bite-cut I just made in my inner cheek. I think it's safe to drink.' He poured her a glass. 'Sip it slowly, Amber, in case it makes you nauseous.'

She stared at him, touched anew. He'd cut himself to protect her. He'd shielded her from the guard. He'd carried her to the table. The Habib Numara she'd heard so much of but had never seen was here with her, for her.

'How do you know about the effects of being drugged?' she asked after a sip, and her stomach churned. She put down the glass with a trembling hand. 'Were you a kidnapper before you were a sheikh?'

Her would-be teasing tone fell flat, but he didn't seem to care. He kept smiling and replied, 'Well, I know about dehydration, and you've been a long time without fluids. When I did a stint in the desert, it affected me far more than it should for a boy of nineteen. The next time, during the Shabbat war, I knew better.'

Curiosity overcame the nausea. She tilted her head.

'What were you doing in the desert at nineteen? Was it for the Armed Forces?'

'No.' He lifted the darker fluid out of the ice bucket and poured it in his glass. When he'd sipped at it, swilling it as he had the water before swallowing, he poured her a glass. 'I was in Yemen, at a dig for a month. There was a fantastic *tell* there that seemed as if it might hold another palace that might have dated back to the time of the Queen of Sheba. Sip the water again now, Amber. Taking a sip every thirty seconds or so will accustom your stomach to the fluid and raise your blood pressure slowly, and hopefully stop the feeling of disorientation. I'll give you some iced tea as soon as I know you can tolerate it.'

'Why were you at a dig?' she asked before she sipped at the water, just to show her determination and strength to him. She didn't want him to think she was weak because she needed his help now.

He looked surprised. 'You didn't know? I assumed your father would have told you. I studied Middle Eastern history with an emphasis on archaeology. That's why I minored in linguistics, especially ancient dialects—I wanted to be able to translate any cuneiform tablets I found, scrolls with intimate family details, or even the daily accounts.'

She blinked, taken aback. Her lips fell open as eager questions burst from her mouth. 'You can read cuneiform tablets? In what languages? Have you read any of the Gilgamesh epic in its original form, or any of the accounts of the Trojan wars?'

'Yes, I can.' His brows lifted. 'What do you know about the Gilgamesh epic?'

She lifted one shoulder in a little shrug. 'I learned a little from my tutors during my school years, and I read about it whenever it comes up in the *Gods and Graves* journal.'

It was his turn to do a double take. 'Where do you get the journals? Have you been in my room?'

She shrugged, feeling oddly shy about it. 'I'm a subscriber. I have been for years.' She hesitated before she added, 'I can't wait for it to arrive every month.'

'You know you can get it online now?' He looked oddly boyish as he asked it, his eyes alight with eagerness.

'Oh, yes, but I like to *feel* it in my hands, see the things again and again by flipping the pages—you know? And the magazine is shinier than printing it up myself. The pages last longer, through more re-reads.'

'Yes, that's why I still subscribe, too.'

They smiled at each other, like a boy and girl meeting at a party for the first time. Feeling their way on unfamiliar yet exciting ground.

'When do you find time to read them, with all you have to do?'

'Late at night, before I sleep,' he said, with the air of confession. 'I have a small night light beside the bed.'

'Me too—I don't want the servants coming in, asking if they can serve me. I just want to read in peace.'

'Exactly.' He looked years younger now, and just looking into that eager blaze of joy in his eyes sent a thrill through her. 'It's my time to be myself.'

'Me too,' she said again, amazed and so happy to find this thing in common. 'What's your favourite period of study?'

He chuckled. 'I'd love to know who the Amalekites were, where they lived, and why they disappeared.'

Mystified, she demanded, 'Who? I've never heard of them.'

'Few people have. They were a nomadic people, sav-age and yet leaving no records except through those they attacked. *Gods and Graves* did a series on them years ago—probably before you subscribed—and I used to try to find references to them in my years of univer-sity. I have notes in my room at home, and the series, if you'd like to read about them.'

'You'd really share your notes with me? I'd *love* to,' she added quickly, in case he changed his mind. 'Did you always want to be an archaeologist?'

He shrugged and nodded. 'I always loved learning about history, in any part of the world. Fadi planned for me to use it to help Abbas al-Din. He thought Alim and I could use our knowledge in different ways. Alim, the scientist and driver, would be the way of the future, bringing needed funds to the nation, and exploring en-vironmentally friendly ways to use our resources rather than blindly handing contracts to oil companies. I would delve into our past and uncover its secrets. Abbas al-Din has had very little done in the way of archaeology be-cause my great-great grandfather banned it after some-thing was found that seemed to shame our ancestors.' He grinned then. 'When I told Fadi what I wanted to do, he gave me carte blanche on our country's past. He thought it would be good for one of the royal fam-ily to be the one to make the discoveries, and not hide any, shall we say, inconvenient finds. After the dig at Yemen, I organised one in the Mumadi Desert to the west of Sar Abbas, since Fadi didn't want me to leave the country again—but it turned out that I couldn't go.'

As he bowed his head in brief thanks for the food, and picked up a knife and fork to try the salad, she watched him with unwilling fascination. She didn't want to ruin the mood by asking why he hadn't gone that time, or why he hadn't taken it up as a career. She knew the answer: Alim's public life had chained Harun to home, helping Fadi for years. Then Fadi's death and Alim's desertion had foisted upon him more than just an unwanted wife.

He nodded at the salad, and served her a small helping. 'I think everything is okay to eat. The most likely source for drugging is in the fluids.'

After she'd given her own thanks, she couldn't help asking, 'So you keep up with it?'

'Apart from subscribing to all the magazines, I have a collection of books in my room, which I read whenever I have time. I keep up with the latest finds posted on the Net. I fund what digs I can from my private account.'

'It must be hard to love something so much, to fund all those digs you fund, and not be able to be there,' she said softly.

His face closed off for long moments, and she thought he might give her that shrug she hated. Then, slowly, he did—but it didn't feel like a brush-off. 'There's no point in wanting what you can't have, is there?'

But he did. The look of self-denial in those amazing eyes was more poignant than any complaint. She ached for him, this stranger husband who'd had to live for others for so many years. Would he ever be able to find his own life, to have time to just *be*?

As if sensing her pain and pity for him, he asked abruptly, 'So, do you have any thoughts on who might have taken us, and why?'

Wishing he hadn't diverted her yet, she bit her lip and shook her head. 'I've been thinking and thinking. This feels like the wrong time. If the el-Shabbats were going to do it, it should have been a year or more ago— and they would have paid for the African warlord to kill

Alim while they were at it. What's the point of taking us now? Alim's back, he'll probably marry the nurse… the dynasty continues.'

'I know.' He frowned hard. 'There doesn't seem to be a point—except…'

Amber found herself shivering in some weird prescience. 'Except?'

He looked up, into her eyes. 'We didn't continue the dynasty, Amber. Too many people know we've never shared a bedroom. The most traditional followers of the el-Kanar clan think you've brought me bad luck, and hate Alim's Western ways. They probably think we've already poisoned any future union, given who and what the woman is who Alim intends to marry.'

She frowned deeper. 'What do you mean, who and what she is? How could we affect his chances with this woman?'

He shrugged. 'You might as well know now. Hana, the woman Alim loves, is a nurse, and, yes, she saved his life—but though she was born in Abbas al-Din, she was raised in Western Australia, and isn't quite a traditional woman. Not only that, but Hana's not the required highborn virgin—she's a commoner, an engineer and miner's daughter. And that's not the worst.'

'There's more?' she asked, as fascinated as she was taken aback. This was sounding more and more like one of the many 'perils of Lutfiyah' films she'd enjoyed as a child.

'Believe it…or not,' he joked, in an imitation of the 'Ripley's' show she'd seen once or twice, and she laughed. 'Though Alim's arranged for her illegal proxy marriage to a drug runner to be annulled, the man's still in prison. You know how the press will use that—"our sheikh marries a drug runner's ex-wife". What's left of the Shabbat dynasty will make excellent mileage of it, perhaps start another insurrection.'

Amber gasped. 'How can Alim possibly think he'll get away with it? The hereditary sheikhs will never allow such a marriage!'

He gave another, too-careless shrug. 'Alim has brought our country much of its current wealth. And Hana's become a national heroine by saving his life at the risk of her own—without her, he'd be dead now, or he might never have come home. That belief is likely to start a backlash against the worst of the scandalmongers. And, given our lack of an heir in three years, the sheikhs that profit most from the el-Kanar family, and are desperate for the dynasty to continue, will vote for the marriage. By now Alim's probably made his planned public announcement that he either marries Hana or I remain his heir for life. To Alim, it's her or no one. He's determined to have her. He loves her.'

The bleakness of his eyes warned her not to touch the subject, but a cold finger of jealousy ran up her spine and refused to be silenced. 'She's a lucky woman. Is that how you feel about—about—what was her name?'

'Buhjah, you mean,' he supplied, with an ironic look that told her he knew she'd deliberately forgotten the woman's name. 'You really don't know me at all, Amber.'

She felt her chin lift and jut as she faced him, willing her cheeks not to blush at being caught out. 'And if I don't, whose fault is that?'

'Too many people's faults to mention, really.' He turned his face, staring out into the afternoon sky. 'And yes, the blame is mine, too—but blaming each other for anything gets us nowhere in our current position.'

'All right,' she said quietly, shamed by his honesty.

'So I'm thinking perhaps this abduction could be a reactionary thing—those who love Alim most are taking us out of the equation, or some relations of Hana's are doing this to force the media and hereditary sheikhs to accept the marriage, which means we'd be safely returned once the marriage is accepted and the wedding arrangements begun.'

She frowned at him. 'That's a very pretty story, and very reassuring, but what is it you're not saying? Who do you really think it is?'

His shoulders, which had been held tense, slumped just a little. 'Amber...'

'I'm not a child,' she said sharply. 'This is my life, Harun. I need to know what I'm facing if I'm going to be of any help to you.'

After a few moments, he came around the table and stood right over her. A quick, hard little thrill filled her at the closeness she'd so rarely known from him. 'Those who hate Alim's Western ways might have taken him, too,' he said so quietly she had to strain her ears to hear him, 'and they've put us here, in these clothes, this enforced intimacy, to create the outcome they want.'

'Which is?' she asked in a similar whisper, unwillingly fascinated. He was speaking so low she had to stand and crowd against him to hear.

'The obvious,' he murmured, moving against her as if they were playing a love-game. 'They want a legal el-Kanar heir from a suitable woman—and who could be more suitable than you?'

She felt her cheeks burning at the unprecedented intimacy. 'Oh.' She couldn't think of anything to say. But the stark look in his eyes told her something else lay deeper. 'There's something wrong with that happening, isn't there?' she mouthed against his ear. Again he didn't answer straight away, and she said, soft but fast, before she lost her courage, 'Whatever it is you fear most, just say it. It's my life, too. I deserve to know.'

The silence stretched out too long, and she wondered if she'd have to prompt him again, or make him angry enough to blurt it out, when he whispered right in her ear, 'But if we make love and you get pregnant, Amber, they'll have no reason to keep my brother alive.'

CHAPTER SEVEN

Who was constantly conspiring against them? Even half naked and moving against each other as if they'd fall to the bed at any moment, it wasn't going to happen.

Would they ever enjoy a normal marriage, or was it Amber's pipe dream?

Then she looked into Harun's eyes, and saw the depth of his fear. *Alim is all I have left.*

An icy finger ran down her spine as she understood the nightmare he was locked in. How could she find it in her to blame him for putting his brother's life first?

Slowly, she nodded, trying to force a calm into her voice she was far from feeling—for his sake. 'Then we won't make love,' she said softly.

The intensity of his gratitude shone in the look he flashed at her. 'Thank you, Amber. I know how much you want a child. This is a sacrifice for you.'

'If it was one of my family in danger, I'd be saying the exact same thing to you.' Her voice was a touch shaky despite her best efforts. 'So tell me what's next?'

With a brief glance she didn't quite understand, he moved back to his side of the table. 'I checked the room pretty thoroughly while you slept. There's no window that isn't watched, no door or way out that isn't fully guarded, including the roof. And as you saw, there are snipers everywhere.'

'So that's it?' she asked in disbelief. 'We're stuck in this golden cage until someone pays our ransom?'

Slowly he nodded. 'Yes,' was all he said, and her stomach gave a sick lurch. Then he gave her a knowing look. It clicked into place—of course, the guards were listening in. They had to be careful what they said aloud. 'We're stuck here—and if you don't like it, remember you agreed to marry me.'

Not knowing what he wanted from her, she made herself give a delicate shrug, as if being abducted were something she was used to. 'Well, at least they're treating us better than Alim was treated in Africa.'

'And that's just as well, since Alim was always the action man in the family.'

The look in his eyes said he'd almost rather be treated badly. She frowned.

'You feel shamed by this abduction?'

He didn't look at her as he said, 'I can't get you out of this danger we're in, Amber. I searched out every possible way, but there's none that gets us both out, and in safety. I don't know what they want, but we have no choice but to comply.'

'And that makes you feel incompetent? Harun, you were drugged and brought here against your will—'

'But that didn't happen to Alim, did it? He sacrificed himself. He was even a hero in being abducted.' His jaw tightened. 'What sort of man am I if I can't even fight, or find a way for us to escape? If Alim couldn't rescue himself, what hope does someone like me have of getting us both out of here?'

The unspoken words shimmered in the air. *Even when he was taken, Alim had sacrificed himself, risked his life to save the woman he loved. I am less than a man in comparison to my brother.*

His voice rang with conviction—the kind that came from intimate knowledge of truth of feeling. And she wondered how many times he'd felt that way before he'd become a hero in his own right. How hard had it been to be the younger, quieter brother of the nation's hero, to live in the shadow of a world superstar?

'Someone like you?' As she repeated the words an unexpected surge of hot anger filled her, at what she wasn't yet sure, but its very ferocity demanded she find out. 'How did they take you?' she shot at him.

He shrugged again. It was another cool, careless thing, a barrier in itself, and, three years too late, she realised that this was what he did, how he pushed people away before he'd say something he might regret. 'Tell me, Harun!'

'Fine,' he growled. 'I came into the room, and saw you being dragged away. I had no time, I just ran after you, and they took me, too. Because I didn't stop to think it through, I failed you. And yes, before you say it, I know Alim would have done better!'

'*How* would he have done that?' she snapped, even angrier now.

He shook his head. 'If I'd stopped to think—if I'd called the guard—'

'Then they might have got away, and I'd be here alone, terrified out of my mind.' She slammed her hand down on the table. 'I don't *care* what Alim would have done. He isn't here. *You're* here, because you tried to save me. You didn't have to do that!'

'And what a wonderful job I did of it, getting drugged myself, and ending up with us both in this prison,' he retorted, self-mockingly.

As if incensed, she grabbed his shoulders. 'You're here with me, Harun. You think you're nothing like Alim? You're just like him! You're more of a hero to me than he can ever be. Do you think he'd have sacrificed his freedom for me the way you have? Don't you know what you did—how much it means to me?'

He looked up at her, a look she couldn't decipher in his eyes. 'You've never willingly touched me before,' he said slowly.

Lost in an odd wonder, she looked down, to where his fingers curled around her arms. 'Nor you me, before today,' she whispered. Suddenly she found it hard to breathe.

Too quickly, they both released the other, and she felt as bereft as he looked, for a bare moment in time, both breathing hard, as if from running an unseen race. It felt so real. Was it real? She only wished she knew.

'I—I'm so glad you're here with me, Harun,' she said, very quietly. 'No matter how it happened. Without you, I…' She shook her head, not sure what it was she was going to say. 'I'm glad it's *you*,' she whispered, so soft he probably couldn't hear it.

'Amber.'

So quietly spoken, that word, her name, and yet… She was torn between so many remembered humiliations and unfamiliar, almost frightening hope, her lips parted. She looked into his eyes, and saw—

The door rattled and opened.

Just as she'd looked up into his eyes like that—with a softened, almost hopeful expression, the real woman, not the part she was playing, he knew, could *feel* it— the noise of the rattling handle broke the moment. At the entry of the man swathed in his sand-hued outfit and headscarf, Amber had started, flushed scarlet and looked back down at her plate as if nothing else existed.

Harun couldn't stand up until he had control of his body—and that was a task of near-impossible proportions, given what she was almost wearing. Thus he'd desperately thought of this farce of play-acting for those watching them. If they'd known he was hurtling down the invisible highway of a man condemned to fulfilling the prophecy they'd put in place for him, they'd leave him totally alone with Amber—*your wife, she's your wife*—and she looked like the gates to paradise…

Stop it! Just don't look at her.

She wasn't looking at him like that now. In fact she wasn't looking at him at all. She waited until their guard had cleared away their food trays and left the room, before murmuring, 'Are you sure there's no way out of here? I think we should check the rooms together. There might be something…'

Pride reared its useless head for a moment, but with a struggle he subdued it. Even if he could easily take offence, he chose not to start another fight. Besides that, they both needed something to distract them right now—at least he did, and desperately.

'Good idea,' was all he could manage to say. 'I was drugged still when I looked. I might have missed something.' He knew he hadn't, but he had to get away from her.

She must have seen him stiffen. She peered at him, anxiety clear to read in her eyes. 'I just want to be sure—and, really, what else is there for us to do right now?'

He could think of something else incredible, amazing, and dangerous to do—but he nodded, trying not to look at the sweet delight before him. 'You need to know for yourself. I would have, too.'

Her voice was filled with warmth and relief. 'Thank you.'

Why wasn't it a cold evening? Then he could cover her with the bed sheet—a towel—anything. Not that it would help; the image of her unfettered loveliness had been burned in his brain since their wedding night. 'You try out here, while I do the bathroom.'

After shoving her chair back, she froze. 'I—I don't... I think I'd prefer if we stayed together. That is, if you don't mind,' she said in a very small voice. She still wasn't looking at him, but, from the fiery blush before, she was far too pale.

Harun cursed himself in silence for thinking only of himself, his needs. Amber was frightened, and he was all she had. Who else could she turn to for strength and reassurance? 'Of course I'll stay with you,' he said gently. 'Where would you prefer to begin?'

Without warning she scraped the chair back and bolted to him. 'I c-can't think. I don't know what to do.' She pushed at his shoulders in obvious intent.

Forcing compassion and tenderness to overcome every other need right now, he pushed his chair back, and pulled her onto his lap. He held her close, caressing those shining waves of dark-honey hair. 'I'm here, Amber. Whatever happens, I won't leave you.'

'Thank you,' she whispered in a shaky voice, burrowing her face into his neck. 'I'll be better in a minute. It's just that man—his silence terrifies me. And those guns...I can't stop seeing them in my mind.'

'It would scare anyone senseless,' he agreed, resting his chin on her hair. *Don't think of anything else. She needs you.*

'Were you scared? In the war, I mean?' she whispered into his neck. Her warm breath caressed his skin, and sent hot shivers of need through him. Every moment the struggle grew harder to not touch her. Just by being so close against him, she made his whole body ache with even hotter desire.

Could she feel what she was doing to him? He'd been permanently aroused since waking up the first time; his dreams had been filled with fevered visions of them that he couldn't dismiss, no matter how he tried.

For Amber's sake, control yourself. She doesn't want you, she needs reassurance.

'Of course I was scared,' he said quietly, forcing the safe rhythm, palm smoothing her hair. 'Everyone was, no matter what they say.'

'They said you showed no sign of fear.' She looked up, her eyes as bright as they'd been before, when they'd made a connection over their shared love of archaeology. It seemed his bride wanted to know about him at last. 'Everyone says you fought like a man possessed.'

Everyone says... Did that mean she'd been asking about him, or drinking in every story? What had she been thinking and hoping in those years he'd ignored her?

'I had to lead my men.' He wondered what she'd think if he told her the truth: he'd fought his own demons on that battlefield, and every man had Alim's face. Where his brother was concerned, the love and the resentment had always been so closely entwined he didn't know how to separate them—and never more so than when he discovered his bride wanted Alim. And he was paying for that ambivalence now, in spades. If Alim had been taken, or God forbid, was dead...

'Everyone said you took the lead wherever you were.' She sounded sweet, breathless.

But though something deep inside felt more than gratified that she wanted to know about him, had been thinking of him, he sobered. 'Even killing a man you perceive as your enemy has its cost for every soldier, Amber. The el-Shabbats had reason for what they did. I knew that—and Alim had left the country leaderless; he clearly wasn't interested in coming home. I wondered what I was doing when I took the mantle.'

'So why did you fight?' she murmured, her head on his shoulder now.

He wanted to shrug off the question, to freeze her out—but his personal need for space and silence had to come second now. Amber's and Alim's lives were on the line because he'd put his *feelings* before the needs of the nation. 'When the el-Shabbats chose Mahmud el-Shabbat for their leader, a man with no conscience, who was neither stable nor interested in what was best for anyone but his own family, they forced the war on me.'

'You became a hero,' she murmured, and he heard the frown in her voice. Wondering why he wasn't happy about it.

Harun felt the air in his lungs stick there. He wanted to breathe, but he had to say it first. 'I can still see the faces of the men whose lives I took, Amber,' he said jerkily. 'War isn't glorious when you live it. That's a pretty story for old men to tell to young boys. War's an undignified, angry, bloody mess.'

'I saw you coming in on the float,' she said quietly. 'I thought you looked as if you wanted to be anywhere but there.'

He almost started at her perception. 'All the glory I received on coming back felt wrong. I'd taken fathers from children, sons from parents, made widows and orphans, all to retain power that was never mine to keep.'

At that she looked up. 'That's why you gave it back to Alim without a qualm?'

Slowly, he nodded. 'That, and the fact that the power wasn't mine to give. I was only the custodian until his return.'

'You related to the people you fought against.' It wasn't a question; her eyes shimmered with understanding. Her arms were still tightly locked around his neck, and he ached to lean down an inch, to kiss her. His yearning was erotic, yes, but beneath that some small, stupid part of him still ached to know he wasn't alone. Where Amber was concerned, he was still fighting inevitability after all these years.

'To their families,' he replied, struggling against giving the uncaring shrug that always seemed to annoy her. 'I became an orphan at eight years old. I lost both my brothers almost at once.' He held back the final words, unwilling to break this tentative trust budding between them.

'And you lost your wife even before the wedding day.' She filled in the words, her voice dark with shame even as she kept her head on his shoulder. 'You were forced to fight for your family, your country while you were still grieving. You gave everything to your country and your family—then you were abandoned by Fadi, by Alim, and, last, by me. I'm sorry, Harun. You were alone. I could have, should have tried to help you more.'

How could she say those things? It was as if she stared through him to see what even he didn't. She seemed to think he was something far more special than he was. 'No, Amber. I never told you. I shut you out.' Tipping her face up to his, he tried to smile at her, to keep the connection going. 'All of it was my fault.'

'No, it wasn't, and we both know that—but blame won't help us in our current situation,' she retorted, quoting his words back to him with a cheeky light in her eyes, and her dimples quivering.

He grinned. 'Someone's feeling feisty.'

She winked. 'I told you I'd feel better in a minute. Or maybe five,' she amended, laughing.

'Then let's begin the search,' he suggested, not sure if he was relieved or resentful for the intervention. Her lips glistened like ripe pomegranates in the rose-hued rays of the falling sun through the window, and he was dying to taste them. And when she wriggled off his lap, he couldn't move for a few moments—so blinded by white-hot need for her, all he could see was the vision of them together in bed as they could have been for years now.

What sort of fool had he been? Within a day of giving her some attention her eyes were alight with desire when she looked at him, or when he was close. If he took her to bed right now, he doubted she'd even want to argue.

'Wrong time, wrong place—and Alim could die,' he muttered fiercely beneath his breath, feeling the frozen nails of fear put the coffin lid on his selfish wants.

Keeping Alim's face in his mind, Harun fell to his knees, looking for loose boards in the floor with ferocious determination. He wouldn't look at her again until his blood began to cool; but whenever he heard her husky voice announcing she still hadn't found anything, he looked up, and with every sight of her wiggling along the floor in that shimmering satin the fight began over. Hot and cold, fire and ice—Amber and Alim...

The suite of rooms was small. Amber unconsciously followed the path he'd taken while she slept, knocking softly on walls, checking bricks for secret passages. But then she hung so far out of the window he grabbed her by the waist to anchor her, and had to twist his body so she wouldn't know how much she affected him. Fighting also against the burning fury that those men with assault rifles would be looking at her luscious body, he pulled her back inside with a mumbled half-lie about her safety.

She sighed as she came back into the room. 'We're so far up, even if we tied the sheets and bedcover together, we'd have a two-storey drop or more.' She glanced at him. 'You could probably make it to the ground, but I'd probably break my legs, and then they'd just take us again.' Biting her lip, she mumbled, 'I wish I'd had the same kind of war training as you—dropping out of planes, martial arts and the like. I wish I could say I was a heroine like my great-grandmother, but the thought of breaking my legs makes me sick with fear.' She looked him in the eyes as she said, 'You should go without me. You have to save Alim.'

Hearing the self-sacrifice in her voice, remembering how she'd been so furious when he'd run himself down earlier, even if it was an act, he felt something warm spread across him. After all these years where he'd ignored her, did she really think so much of him?

Or so little, that she could even suggest he'd go without me, put his brother first, and abandon her to her captors?

Quietly, he said, 'I dropped out of planes with a parachute and spare. And even if I could use a sheet as a makeshift parachute, and jump in the darkest part of the night, I'd still have to outrun the guards, and find a place of safety or a phone, and all without water or food—and wearing only these stupid things.' And there was no way he'd leave Amber alone to face the consequences of his escape.

He was taken aback by the success of his diversion when Amber giggled. 'Oh, the visions I'm having now—the oh-so-serious Sheikh Harun el-Kanar escaping abduction, but found only in his boxer shorts!'

Though he laughed with her—because it was a funny thought—right now he wasn't in the mood to laugh. 'I would never leave you, Amber. That probably seems hard to believe—'

Her eyes, glowing with life and joy, a smile filled with gratitude, stopped him. She did believe him, though he'd done nothing to earn her trust. That smile pierced him in places he didn't want to remember existed. The places he'd thought had died years ago…trust, faith, and that blasted, unconquerable hope.

Trust had died even before his parents, and, though he still prayed, a lot of his faith had eroded through the years. And hope—the last shards of it had smashed to bits when he'd heard her agree to marry him, despite loving his brother.

Or so he'd thought, until today.

'Let's check the bathroom again,' she suggested. 'Sometimes there's a loose tile on the floor that is the way out—or even in the bath itself. My great-grandmother had one egress made through the base of the tap in the bath, after the war ended. We should check it out thoroughly.'

Grateful for the reprieve from his dark thoughts, he followed her in and got down on hands and knees beside her, but turned to search in the opposite direction.

Anything rather than endure the torture of memory—
or of watching her lovely body wiggling with every
movement.

This time he forced his eyes to stay away. If she held
a shadow of desire for him now, it was just through enforced proximity and her need for human closeness.
She'd never shown a single sign of wanting him, or
even wanting to know him better, until now. He'd never
seen anything from her but cold duty and contemptuous
anger until the day she'd heard Alim was back.

That was the way his life would be. How many times
did he have to convince himself over and over that
duty and supporting family was his only destiny? How
many times had his parents told him that he'd be useless for anything else? How many times in the twenty-
two years since they'd died had Fadi enforced his belief
that duty was first, last and everything for him, that
he was born to be the supportive brother? Yet here
he was, no wiser. At thirty years old, he still hadn't
learned the lesson.

Was it the after-effects of the drugs that had weak-
ened his resolve, or was it just a case of too many years
of denial? But the desire in her eyes, the curve of her
smile, the music of her laughter—and everything that
was almost clear to see beneath that peignoir—were
killing him to resist. Even the sight of her bare feet was
a temptation beyond him right now.

This was the exact reason he'd avoided her so long
before. But now he couldn't make himself avoid her,
even if he could parachute out of here with that stupid
sheet. He couldn't leave her alone…and so here they
were, only the two of them and that delicious bed…
and with every moment that passed, it became more

impossible to resist her. How long could he last before he made a fool of himself?

But that was exactly what the kidnappers wanted, and damned if he'd give it to them.

CHAPTER EIGHT

BY NIGHTFALL, they had covered almost every inch of both rooms, and found no way out. All her hopes dashed, she sat on the ground, slumping against the cool bath tiles in despair. 'We're not getting out of here, are we?'

'Not until they let us out.' There was a strange inflection in his voice.

Arrested, she turned to look at him. 'What is it?'

Harun didn't reply.

'I'm not a child, Harun, or an idiot. I'm in this with you, like it or not, and there's nowhere for you to conveniently disappear to here, no excuse or official or quiet room for you to get away from me. So you might as well share what you're thinking with me.'

After a moment that seemed to last a full minute, he said, 'I think your father may be our abductor.'

'What?' They were the last words she'd expected. Gasping, she choked on her breath and got lost in a coughing fit to be able to breathe again. Harun began using the heel of his hand in rhythmic upward motions, and the choking feeling subsided. Then she pushed him away, glaring at him. 'Why would he do that? What would be the benefit to him, and to Araba Numara?

How could you even think that? How dare you accuse my father of this?'

Harun was on his haunches in front of her, his face had that cold, withdrawn look she hated.

'For a daughter who doesn't share my suspicions, a daughter who believes implicitly in her father's innocence, I notice you put the two most natural questions last. Instead, you asked the most important questions first—why, and what benefit to him in abducting his own child. You believe it's possible at the very least, Amber. Everything makes sense with that one answer. Why there have been no demands or threats as yet, why we were left in this kind of room dressed this way, and why we're alone most of the time. Your father has probably endured some ridicule and speculation over our not producing an heir, and he wants it to end.' He gave her a hard look. 'He has no son, and you're the eldest daughter. He hasn't named his brother, or his nephews or male cousins as his heir. Any son we have will be qualified to become the hereditary sheikh for Araba Numara, so long as he takes his grandfather's name…and I assume that keeping the line going is important to him.'

Every suspicion he'd voiced could be exactly right. And it all fitted her father too well. Though he came from a very small state in the Emirates—or maybe because of that—he enjoyed manipulating people until they bent to his will. And yes, he'd want a grandson to take his name and the rule of Araba Numara.

'If you're right, and I'm not saying you are, I will never, never forgive him for this.' Then she shot to her feet, and cried, 'Hasn't he done enough to me? Three years of being his pawn, left in a foreign country and shuffled from one man to another, none of whom wanted me! Can't he just leave me be?'

The echoes of her voice in the tiled bathroom were her only answer. The silence was complete, just as it had always been when she'd tried to defy her father's will, and she slid back down the tiles. 'I hate this, I hate it. Why can't he let me have my life?'

Harun's eyes gleamed with sadness. 'I don't know, Amber. I'm no expert on family life. I barely remember my father, or mother.' As he slid down beside her, the feeling of abandonment fled along with her outrage—and, as natural as if she'd done it for years, she laid her head on his shoulder. 'It's probably best not to think about it,' he said quietly, wrapping his arm over her shoulder, drawing her closer. 'And remember I could be wrong.'

'We both know you're not. It makes too much sense.'

'There is the other solution I told you before,' he said very quietly.

She nodded.

'If they won't let us out until you're pregnant, we may have little choice but to comply.'

A tiny frisson of shock ran through her. 'B-but what if we are wrong—wouldn't that risk Alim's life?' she stammered.

'Only if he has been taken. We just don't know.' His eyes hardened. 'I can't keep living my life for honour alone, Amber. Alim's the one who left his family and his nation too many times to count—and why did he finally return? For the sake of a woman he can't even marry. I've done everything for him for ten years, and it's time I did something I want to do.'

Softly, she murmured, 'And now you want me?'

'Yes,' he replied, just as soft.

His mouth curved; his eyes softened. And he brushed his mouth against hers.

With the first touch, it was as if he'd pulled a string inside her, releasing warmth and joy and need and—and yes, a power she hadn't known existed, the power of being a woman with her man, *the* man for her. She made a smothered sound and moved into him as her lips moved of their own will, craving more. She turned into him, her hands seeking his skin, pulling him against her. Eager fingers wound into his hair, splayed across his back, explored his shoulders and arms, and the kiss grew deeper and deeper. They slowly fell back until they lay entangled on the floor. Amber barely noticed its cold hard surface. Harun was touching her at last, he was fully aroused, and she moaned in joy.

'As far as first kisses go, that was fairly sensational,' he said in a shaky voice. 'But we're only a few hours out of the drugs. Today hasn't been the easiest for either of us. Maybe we should rest. If we feel the same tomorrow…'

Bewildered by the constant changes in his conversation, she sighed. 'Yes, I think I need to sleep again. But I really should have a bath.'

After a short silence, Harun said quietly, 'No, sleep first. Come, I'll help you to bed.' He swept her up again, as though she weighed nothing, and carried her back out to the main room. He could have taken her to bed and made love to her all night and she'd have loved it.

Reaching the bed, he laid her down. 'Rest now, Amber. I swear I won't leave you,' he whispered, his voice tender, so protective. Had the *habib numara* become her very own tiger—at least for now?

She ought to know better than to think this way. They barely knew each other, and he'd never shown any interest in touching her until today.

She ought to feel grateful to their abductors. For

the first time Harun was looking at her as a person. For a captive, she felt happier than she had in a very long time.

Too tired to work through the confusion, she allowed her heavy eyes and hurting heart to dictate to her. She needed temporary oblivion from the events of the past day, to blank it all out. But even as she slid towards sleep, she felt Harun's presence in the chair he'd drawn up beside the bed. Touched that he was standing guard over her, keeping her safe without presuming to share the bed, she wanted to take his hand in hers and cradle it against her face, to thank him for all he'd done today. But he'd done so much for her; she couldn't demand more than he'd already given. She sighed again, and drifted into dreams.

And shaken far beyond anything she knew, too aroused to sleep, Harun sat beside her the whole night. He didn't get on the bed—he didn't dare—but he remained on guard, ready to protect her if there should be a need.

She's a stubborn, rebellious daughter, with no regard for law or tradition. I wouldn't pay a single dinar for her return. Let Sheikh el-Kanar pay it, if he's worried about her at all, but I doubt it. He ran from her in the first place, didn't he?

Shivering in the night suddenly turned cold, the echoes of her father's uncaring tone still ringing in her ears, Amber jerked to a sitting position in the bed. Praise Allah, it had only been a nightmare—

But this bed, sagging slightly, definitely wasn't hers, and choppy breathing came from a few feet away. Adjusting to the darkness and unfamiliar room, she gradually took in the form of her husband sleeping in a chair beside the bed.

Although the sight of him made her ache somehow—he looked like a bronze statue of male perfection in the pale moonlight, even half crumpled in the chair—reality returned to her in seconds, the reasons why they were here. And what they'd done to convince their abductors that they were cooperating…

A hot shiver ran down her spine.

She looked again at her sleeping husband, realising anew the masculine beauty of him. His face was gentle in repose, seeming so much younger.

She reached out, touching him very softly. His skin was cool to the touch. He was shivering as she'd been; there were goosebumps on his arms. His sheet must have slipped to the floor long ago, and he was still half naked, only clad in those silky boxers. Obviously he'd left her the blanket, but she'd kicked it off some time in the night.

During the search earlier, neither of them had found a second covering of any kind, so she could do nothing but share the blanket they had. The modesty he'd given her in sleeping on the chair was touching, but it was ridiculous when they were married. If either of them took sick, they had no way to care for the other.

'Harun,' she whispered, but he didn't move. Taking him by the shoulder, she shook it, feeling the flex and ripple of muscles beneath her fingers. 'Harun, come—' she stopped herself from saying *come to bed* only just in time '—under the blanket. You're cold.'

An indistinct mumble was his only response.

Impatient, getting sleepy again, she grabbed his shoulders with both hands, pulling him towards her.

'Come on, Harun. You'll be in agony in the morning, sleeping like that. I can't afford for you to get sick.'

Something must have penetrated, for he fell onto the bed, landing almost right on top of her, his leg and arm falling over her body, trapping her. 'Mmm, Amber, lovely Amber,' he mumbled, moving his aroused body against hers, his lips nuzzling her throat. 'Taste so good…knew you would. Like sandalwood honey.' And before she could gather her wits or move, he kept right on going, lower, until he was kissing her shoulder, and she had no idea if he was awake or seducing her in his dreams.

She couldn't think enough to care…her neck and shoulder arched with a volition of their own as he nibbled the juncture between both, and the bliss was *exquisite*. And when his hand covered her breast, caressing her taut nipple, the joy was sharp as a blade, a beautiful piercing of her entire being. 'Harun, oh,' she cried aloud, craving more—

His eyes opened, and even in the moonlit night she saw the lust and sleepy confusion. Gazing down, he saw his hand covering her breast. 'I'm sorry…I was dreaming. I didn't mean to take advantage of you.' He shook his head. 'How did I get on the bed?'

A dull ache smothered the lovely desire like a fire-retardant blanket. 'I woke up—you were shivering, and I pulled you over. The sheet wasn't warm enough for you,' she replied drearily. Who had he been dreaming of when he'd said her name? 'It's all right. Take the blanket and go back to sleep.'

'Amber…'

'Don't,' she said sharply. *Don't be kind to me, or I*

might just break down. She rolled away from him so he wouldn't see her humiliation. 'Goodnight.'

The next afternoon

Any moment now, he'd pick her up and throw her on the bed, and make love to her until they both died of exhaustion.

He'd been going crazy since last night. Pretending to sleep for her sake, he'd lain still on the bed until his entire body had throbbed and hurt; he knew she was doing the same. Then, just as his burning body talked him into rolling over and making love to her, her soft, even breathing told him she slept.

That he'd made Amber cry simply by not continuing to make love to her was a revelation to him. In three long, dreary years, all he'd known was her contempt and anger, even the night she'd asked him to come to her bed. But within the space of a day, he'd seen her show him regret, budding friendship, trust, need and—for that blazing second when he'd awoken with his hand on her breast—pure desire for him. He'd come so close to giving in, giving them what they both wanted—only a tiny sound from outside the room, a shuffle of feet, a little cough, had reminded him of their watchers, had held him back.

And how could he risk his brother's life?

It kept going back to that choice: their personal happiness, or Alim's life. If there was a way to know Alim was safe, if they could escape and have some privacy, he'd give their abductors what they wanted, over and over. Now he knew Amber wanted him…

But without meaning to, he'd hurt and humiliated

her. His apology had wounded her pride in a way she was going to find extremely hard to forgive.

After hours of silence between them and no touching, he spoke with gentle deliberation. 'I'm sorry about last night.'

Her lips parted as her head turned. 'You already apologised. Anyway why should you apologise? You were dreaming, right?' Oh, so cold, so imperious, her tone—but his deepest male instincts told him it was the exact opposite of what she felt inside.

He looked into her eyes. 'I heard a cough outside the room. The first time I make love to you will not be by accident, with an audience of strangers through holes in the wall.'

A surprised blink covered a moment's softness in her eyes. 'That's a fairly big assumption to make.'

Despite the cold fury in her voice, he wanted to smile. 'That we'll make love? Or that you can forgive me for neglecting you all these years, and welcome me in your bed?'

'Either. Both,' she said quietly, 'especially considering the neglect was of epic proportions, and publicly humiliating.'

At that, he offered her a wry smile. 'I had no wish for a martyr bride, Amber. I'm fairly sure you didn't want a dutiful, reluctant husband, either. I believed you had no desire for me; you believed that I never desired you. All this time we both wanted the same thing, if only we'd tried to talk.'

She looked right into his face, her chin lifted. 'Did you really just say that—if *we'd* tried to talk?'

He had to concede that point if he wanted to get anywhere with her. 'You're right, I'm the one that didn't try—but ask yourself how hard you'd have tried, if you'd thought I was in love with your sister.'

Another slow blink as she thought about it. 'Maybe—'

But just as the frost covering her hidden passion finally began to soften he heard the door open, and he cursed the constant interferences between them—but then, with a smothered gasp, Amber bolted off the window seat and cannoned into him. 'He's pointing that rifle at me,' she whispered, shaking, as his arms came around her. 'And…and he's looking at me, and I'm only wearing this thing.'

Like a whip he flung around to face the guard, putting Amber behind him. 'What is this?' he demanded four times over, in different dialects. 'Answer me, why do you terrify my wife this way?' Again he said it in another few dialects—all of Amber's home region.

The man never so much as glanced their way; he answered only by moving the rifle inward, towards the dining table.

Amber's chest heaved against his back as she tried to control her fear.

Three men followed him into the room, bearing a more substantial meal than they'd eaten yesterday, or at breakfast, three full choices of meal plus teas, juice or water. The men set the table with exquisite care, as if he and Amber were honoured guests at a six-star hotel. Then they held out the seats, playing the perfect waiters—only the maître d' was holding an assault rifle on them.

Harun stood his ground, shielding Amber with his body. 'Move away from the chairs. Don't come near my wife. Stop looking at her or I will find who you are after this and kill you with my bare hands.'

After a moment, with a look of deep respect the head

guard bowed, and waved the others back. When they were out, he took several steps back himself before he stopped, staring at the furthest wall from their captives.

Harun led Amber to her chair and seated her himself, blocking her from their view so they could see no part of her semi-exposed body. 'Now get out,' he barked.

He bowed again, and left the room.

'Thank you,' she whispered, hanging onto his hand when he would have moved.

'There's nothing to thank me for.' Some emotion he couldn't define was coursing through him, as if he were flying with his own wings. He didn't trust it.

'I can't take much more of this—this terrifying silence,' she muttered, her free hand clenching and unclenching. 'Why did he point the rifle at me? What did I do?'

Harun had his own ideas, but he doubted saying, *Their objective is achieved, Amber, you ran straight to me,* would help now, or bring her any comfort. She might even begin to suspect him.

Instead of sitting, he released her hand, and wrapped his arms around her from behind. 'I know I may not seem like much help to you in this situation, Amber, but I swear I'll protect you with my life if need be.'

She twisted around so her face tilted up to his. 'You know that's not true. Last night, I told you how glad I am you're here…and you saw, you must have seen that…' Her lips pushed hard together.

It was time; he knew it, could feel it; but still he would give her a gift first. 'Yes, I saw that you desire me, how you loved my touch.' With a gentle smile, he touched her burning face. 'And you had to see how much I desire you, Amber. If it hadn't been for the guards, we'd have made love last night.'

She said nothing, but her eyes spoke encyclopaedic volumes of doubt. 'You said my name. I wasn't sure if you meant it.'

In the half-question, and the deep shadows in her eyes, he saw the depth of the damage he'd done to her by his neglect. She had no idea at all; she'd never once seen his desire until last night, and she even doubted it had been for her.

It seemed he'd hidden his feelings too well—and at this point he doubted just showing her would be enough. He had to open up, starting now.

'I did mean it, Amber. My dreams were of you. My dreams have been of you for a long time.' Taking her hand again, he lifted it to his mouth and pressed a lingering kiss to her palm. When she didn't snatch her hand away, but drew in a quick, slightly trembling breath, he let his lips roam to her wrist. 'Sandalwood honey,' he murmured against her skin. 'The most exquisite taste I've known.'

She didn't answer him, except in the tips of her fingers that caressed his face, then retreated. So tentative still, she was afraid to give anything away. Unsure if, even now, he'd walk away again and leave her humiliated. He'd damaged her that much through the years, which meant he had the *power* to hurt her—and that meant more than any clumsy words of reassurance she could give.

It was time to give back, to be the one to reach out and risk rejection.

So hard to start, but he'd already done that; and now, to his surprise, the words flowed more easily. 'You need to know now. I haven't been with any woman since we married. I kept my vows, as difficult as that's been at times.'

Her look of doubt grew, but she said nothing.

He smiled at her. 'It's true, Amber. I didn't want a replacement. I wanted you.'

The little frown between her brows deepened. 'Then why…?'

Walking around to face her, he took both hands in his and lifted her to her feet. 'I refused to continue last night because our audience made it clear they were there watching us. I'm not a man who likes applause and cheering on, and I didn't think you'd want your first time to be here, where any of them could see us.'

'No, I wouldn't. Thank you for thinking of it,' she murmured, her gaze dropping to his mouth, and his whole body heated with a burst of flame at the look in her eyes. 'But I don't understand why you didn't come to me before—oh.' She nodded slowly. 'Because of what I said to my father.'

'I'm not Alim. I'll never be like Alim.' She had to know that now. He'd rather burn like this the rest of his life than be his brother's replacement in her eyes, or in her bed.

'I know who you are.' And still she stared at his mouth with open yearning that made him define the alien, flying feeling—he was so *glad* to be alive, to be the man she desired.

Then her head tilted, and he mentally prepared himself: she did that when she wanted to know something he wouldn't want to answer. 'Why do you think you can never compare to Alim? I barely knew him. You must have known that; he left for the racing circuit days after I met him, and then ran from the country as soon as he could leave the hopspital. He never wanted me, and you say you did. So why didn't you try for me?'

As far as hard questions went, that was number one.

He felt himself tensing, ready to give the shrug that was his defence mechanism, to walk away—

Trouble was, there was nowhere to go, no place of escape. And he knew what she was going to say before she said, very softly, 'You promised to talk to me.'

At that moment he almost loathed her. He'd never broken a promise in his life, never walked away in dishonour; but trying to put his disjointed thoughts together was like trying to catch grains of sand in a desert storm. What did she want him to say?

'Just tell me the truth,' she said, just as quietly as before, smiling at him. As if she'd seen his inner turbulence and wanted to calm it.

Nothing would do that. There was no way out this time. So he said it, hard and fast. 'I don't compare to him. I never have. What was the point in trying for you when you wanted a man that wasn't me? I was never anything but a replacement for him, with Fadi and with you. I always knew that.'

CHAPTER NINE

IF THERE was anything she'd expected Harun to say, it wasn't that. She'd hoped to hear a complaint about his family, or about how he'd lived in the shadow of a famous, heroic brother—but never that calmly spoken announcement, like a fact long accepted. *I don't compare to him. I never have.*

A sense of foreboding touched Amber's heart, a premonition of the hardships facing her if she chose to spend her life with this man. *How would I have ended up, had Alim been my brother, if I'd lived in the shadow of a famous sibling and ended up taking on all the responsibilities he didn't want?*

The thought came from deep inside her, from the girl who'd never really felt like a princess, but a commodity for sale to the highest bidder. And she spoke before she knew what she wanted to say. 'That's another big assumption to make, considering my total acquaintance with Alim has been five days, and I've known you three years.'

He flicked her another resentful glance, but she wouldn't back down. He had nowhere to go, and his honour meant more than anything. He'd answer her, if she waited long enough.

Lucky she wasn't holding her breath; she'd be dead

by the time he finally said, 'I know what I am in your eyes, Amber. And I know what Alim is.'

She frowned. 'One sentence made in grief and not even knowing you, and that's it? You just write me off your things to do list? *Marry her and ignore her because she insulted me once when she didn't know I was listening? I don't care if she apologised.*'

Another look, fuming and filled with frustration; how he hated to talk. But finally he said, 'I'm not Alim.'

By now she felt almost as angry as him, but some instinct told her he was deliberately pushing her there to make her stop talking to him. So she'd keep control if it killed her. 'That sounds like a statement someone else told you that you're repeating. And don't tell me Fadi ever said it to you. He adored you.' After a long stretch of silence, she said it for him. 'How old were you the first time your parents told you that Alim was better than you?'

The one-shoulder shrug came, but she didn't let herself care. So he said it, again with that quiet acceptance. 'I don't remember a time when they didn't say it.'

He wasn't angry, fighting or drowning in self-pity. He believed it, and that was all.

Bam. Like that she felt the whack of a hammer, snatching her breath, thickening her throat and making her eyes sting. His own parents had done that to him? No wonder he couldn't believe in her; he didn't know how to believe in himself. And the truth that she'd pushed away for years whispered to her inside her mind, why she'd fought to push him out of his isolation and to notice her. *I love him.*

Every messed-up, silent, heroic, inch of him. He'd crept into her soul from the time he'd marched away with his men, and returned a hero, hating the adulation.

She'd been amazed when he'd handed everything back to Alim without wanting a thing. She'd thought him so humble. Now she knew the truth: he didn't think he deserved the adoration of the nation; that was Alim's portion. He'd been in the shadows so long he found the limelight terrifying.

Don't you see, Amber, I'm doing everything I can do?

The words he'd given her in rejection of creating a child with her finally made horrible sense…and she knew if she pushed him to tell her everything, he'd never forgive her.

'Before our wedding, my father told me that the lion draws obvious admiration, but you need to look deeper to see the tiger's quiet strength. I've known that was true for a long time now,' she said softly, and touched his face. Warm and soft, not the unyielding granite she'd found repellent and fascinating at once; he was a man, just a damaged, honourable, limping, beloved hero, and she loved him.

He stared at her, looked hard and dazed at once. He shook his head, and her hand fell—but she refused to leave it like that. She touched him again. *'Habib numara,'* she whispered. 'I've wanted you for so long.'

He kept staring at her as if she were a spirit come to torture him—yes, she could see that was exactly what he was thinking. He needed time to believe even in this small miracle. So she smiled at him, letting her desire show without shame or regret.

After a long time, he took her by the hands. *'Mee johara,'* he said huskily. *My jewel.*

Her heart almost burst with the words, pounding with a joy she'd never known.

Don't hesitate, or he'll think the worst. So she wound her arms around his neck. 'I've been alone so long, waiting for you,' she whispered so softly only he would hear it. 'Kiss me and call me your jewel again.'

But instead, the hard bewilderment filled his eyes again. 'You've waited for me?'

'So long,' she murmured against his ear, and let her lips move against his skin. She felt him shudder, and rejoiced in it. 'You fascinate me with the way you can make me hate you and want you and love you—'

He stilled. Completely. And though she waited, he didn't ask her if she meant it. She felt his pain radiating from him, the complete denial of what she'd said because he didn't dare believe, not yet. Lost in a life of expectation and self-denial, in a world where his own parents didn't seem to love him, at least in comparison to Alim, how could he believe?

In a life where both of them had hidden their true selves from self-protection, one of them had to step into the light...and at least she'd known her family loved her. For once, she was the strong one; she had to lead the way.

'I love you, Harun. I have for a long time.' She pulled back, her hands framing his face as she smiled with all the love she felt. 'It began when I saw you march away to war, and I kept wondering if I'd see you again. I heard all the stories of your courage, leadership and self-sacrifice, and was so proud to be your woman. And when you came back and refused to talk about it, but just kept working to help your people, I began to believe I'd found my mate for life.'

His frown grew deeper with every word she said. 'Before we married.' The question was hidden inside the incredulous statement. He didn't believe her.

With difficulty, Amber reined in her temper and said, 'I never looked at you before we were engaged—

but once we were, I couldn't stop looking at you. But on our wedding night, I thought you didn't want me at all. I thought you hated me. I was only nineteen, I was told nothing but to follow your lead...I didn't know what to do.'

At last his features softened a little. 'So you followed my lead, all these years.'

She murmured, 'Pretending to despise you when all I wanted was to be in your life, in your bed. I cried myself to sleep that night.' Inwardly her pride was rebelling more with every word she spoke, but the relief at finally getting the words out was greater. Besides, pride wouldn't help either of them in this situation. Neither would useless worry over who heard their conversation—given the people they were, that would happen no matter their location. 'If I'd known why you avoided me...'

He moved an inch closer, his features taut with expectation, and she exulted in the evidence that he wanted her. 'What would you have done?'

'This,' she whispered, and kissed him.

It was a clumsy attempt, a bare fastening of her lips on his, and she made a frustrated sound. She felt his lips curve in a little smile as he put his hands to her hips and drew her closer, and took over, deepening the kiss, arousing her with lips and hands until she forgot everything but him.

Let your husband show you the way. For years she'd felt nothing but contempt for her mother's advice—it had only led her to utter loneliness and self-hate. But now Harun showed her the way, and the joy spread through her like quicksilver. He had one hand in her hair, another caressing her waist while he kissed her, and she found her body taking over her will. She moaned and kissed him even deeper, moving against him and the fire grew. Oh, she loved his touch, the feel of his body sliding on hers—

Were they in bed? She didn't remember moving her feet, or landing on the mattress; his hand was on her breast again and it was that knife-blade touch of exquisite perfection…

Then there was only the soft swish of air on her skin, and she made a mewing sound of protest before she could stop it. 'Harun?' she faltered, seeing him standing beside the bed. 'Did I do something wrong…?'

'No…something very right.' He finished pulling the curtains around the bed, and turned to smile at her. 'It will only be wrong if you tell me you want to stop.'

The black blankness was gone from his eyes; the ugly memory had been chased away, and by her. She felt her mouth curving; her eyes must be alight with the happiness and desire consuming her. 'After waiting three years for you, do you think I could?' No matter who was there, or why they'd come to this place, or what happened in the past, they were here now. He was all hers at last. 'Now, Harun. Please.'

And she held out her arms to him.

CHAPTER TEN

The next morning

So THIS was what she'd waited so long to know…

Through the cracks in the curtains he'd pulled around the bed last night, the rising sun touched Harun's sleeping face; his breathing was soft and even. Slowly Amber stretched, feeling a slight soreness inside her, but what they'd shared had been worth every discomfort.

He'd been right. With each touch, each kiss and intimate caress, the feeling went from wonderful to exquisite to an almost unbearable white light of beauty, until the ache inside her, the waiting and the wanting was intolerable, and she thrashed against him in wordless demand. And still he kept going, teasing her in kiss and touch until she'd pleaded with him to stop the sweet torture, and take her.

She was so ready for him that the pain was brief, a cry and a moment's stiffening, and it was done; soon the ache was to know the joy again. She kissed him and moved her body so he moved inside her. He smiled and called her his jewel again, and the familiar endearment, one her parents had given her years ago, was so much more beautiful from his lips, with his body on hers, inside her.

They made love slowly, Harun giving her infinite tenderness and patience. The beauty built higher as she became ready for the next step, and he took her there. The joy became bliss, and then something like being scorched by the sun, and yet she couldn't care, couldn't fear it or want to stop. And just before she cried out with joyful completion, he whispered, 'I can't wait any more—Amber, Amber...'

He shuddered in climax almost at the same time she did. As he held her afterwards, he caressed her hair and whispered, *'Mee habiba `arusa.' My beloved bride.*

She smiled and refused to give in to the temptation to ask if he meant it. The whispers in the women's rooms the past few years told her that men could become tender, poetic even at these times, but could forget it in minutes.

They made love twice more in the night, once at her instigation. If she was awake, she couldn't stop herself from touching him or kissing him.

Looking at him laying beside her now, his face almost boyish in sleep, his brown skin aglow in the light of sunrise, she felt her body begin the slow, heady tingling of arousal. Leaning into him, she kissed his chest, loving the taste of his skin. Unbearable to think of stopping now—she kissed him over and over, in warm, moist trails across his body.

His eyes were open now, and he was smiling at her. Her insides did that little flip at the relaxed, happy man who was finally her lover, and she was lost in wanting him. 'Come here,' he growled, and pulled her on top of him.

Laughing breathlessly, she whispered, 'I'm sorry I woke you.'

Now the smile was a grin. 'No, you're not.'

She bit her lip over a smile. Was she a fool to feel so happy? Did she care? 'No, I suppose I'm not sorry at all.'

'So this is how it's going to be, is it? I'll be worn out by your constant demands?' His twinkling eyes told her how much he hated the thought.

'I'm sure you knew I was a little on the demanding side when you married me,' she retorted, mock-haughty, but she moaned as his lips found better uses than teasing.

This time he taught her new things that pleased him, and she let him know what she loved, and it was beyond beauty, more than physical bliss. It was joy and peace. It was deep connection, communication without words. It was happiness so complete she couldn't think of anything to match it.

She'd heard about the endless pleasure of making love, but never had she dreamed this act of creation could be so life-changing. It was far from just her body's gratification; it was giving a part of herself, her trust, her inner self to Harun, and he gave himself to her.

She wondered if he felt the same, or whether it was this way every time he—

No, she wouldn't think of his former lovers now. She couldn't bear to think of him in this intimate position with another woman. She was his lover now, and he was hers. And she'd make sure it stayed that way.

'Are you in pain at all?' he asked as he held her afterwards.

'A little,' she admitted.

'Stay there a minute.' He got out of bed, and walked into the bathroom, wonderfully naked, and she couldn't help staring at his body. Unable to believe that, because of an abduction of all things, she finally had him all to herself. And within two days, they'd become lovers.

Had the passion been there all along, simmering beneath the surface? What might have happened long ago had he not overheard her silly girl's romantic dream of marrying a superstar? If she hadn't overreacted to his coldness on their wedding night—a decision she knew now he'd made in a mixture of intense grief and betrayal—would they always have had this joy together?

The sound of running water was soon followed by a lovely scent, and she smiled when he came back into the room. Then the mere sight of him, unclad and open to her in a way he'd never been, made her insides go all mushy with longing. 'Come.' He lifted her into his arms with ease. How had she been so blind, never realising until now just how big and strong he was?

He placed her in the bath, which was hotter than she normally liked it, and she squealed, and squirmed.

'The heat will help with the discomfort,' he said, his voice filled with tenderness. 'The bath oils can be good for that, too, I've heard. Just wait a few minutes.'

Deciding to trust him in this, she settled into the water with a luxurious wriggle, and soon she discovered he was right; the soreness lessened. 'Thank you, this is really helping,' she said as he came back into the room with the bed sheet. 'What are you—?' She stopped as he began washing it at the sink. 'Oh…thank you.' She blushed that he'd do something so intimate for her, and not think it beneath his masculine dignity.

He turned his face and smiled at her. 'What happened is nobody's business but ours. It's a hot day, so it should be dry by tonight. Besides, you need time to recover.'

She'd wondered what their kidnappers would make of the bloodstain on the sheets—or even the sheet hanging out of the window to dry; but his thoughtfulness touched her anew, even as his unashamed nakedness, and just his smile, made her insides melt. 'Are you sure about that?' she murmured huskily.

He made a sound halfway between laughter and a groan. 'You're going to kill me, woman. I need time to recover.'

'Oh. I didn't know men had to recover,' she said, rather forlornly. 'I just thought you might like to share my bath…there's plenty of room, and it's so lovely and warm…'

The sheet was abandoned before she finished the thought, and he was in the enormous, two-person bath with her, hauling her onto his lap. 'Recovery be damned. You're definitely going to kill me, Amber el-Kanar my wife,' he muttered between kisses growing hotter by the moment, 'but at this moment, I can't think of a better way to go.'

As she dissolved under his touch neither could she.

The next day

It was only as they finished breakfast that the conversation of the first night began working its way up Harun's consciousness from the dazed mist of contentment and arousal he'd been happily wandering in. The guards no longer intruded on them, but knocked on the door and left food there. They waited in silence at either end of the corridor, not moving or speaking. The assault rifles were no longer trained on them from the windows.

'How much longer do you think they'll keep us here?' Amber asked, as lazily content as he.

He didn't want to break their bubble by saying *when they know you're pregnant*. And then Alim was in real danger. 'So you're tired of my company already?' he teased.

Predictably, she blushed but smiled, too. 'Not quite yet.' As if to negate the words, the underlying fear they'd both been ignoring—that if their abduction wasn't the work of her father, the danger was still real and terrifying—she came around the table and snuggled into his lap, winding her arms around his neck. After a long, drugging kiss, she whispered, 'No, not quite yet—but this has got to be the strangest honeymoon two people ever had.'

He smiled up into her face, so vivid with life, flushed with passion. 'That's a bad assertion to make to a historian, my bride.'

'I love stories about history,' she murmured, nibbling his lips.

Between kisses, he mumbled, 'In the Middle Ages, a honeymoon was a very different thing from what it is now. A man who wanted a woman—or if he needed her wealth, dowry or the political connections she brought, but couldn't have her by conventional means—drugged her, kidnapped her and constantly seduced her. He did so by keeping her half drunk on mead—that's a honey-based wine—for a month, until the next full moon, so her father would know she'd been very properly deflowered. Then he'd bring her back to her family, with the woman hopefully pregnant, and present the father with the fait accompli. If the father didn't kill him, but accepted the marriage, he'd then ask for the dowry, or the hereditary title and lands, or whatever it was he'd wanted.'

'So what's different from this situation?' she demanded, smiling, with more nibbling kisses. 'Okay, we didn't have the wine, but we had the political marriage, the drugs, the abduction, and the deflowering.'

'True,' he conceded the point, deepening the kiss before saying, 'but I assure you I didn't organise this, I didn't drug you, and I have no further demands for your father. I'm perfectly happy with what I have right now.' *Apart from not knowing whether my brother is alive or dead...*

Her eyes seemed to be always alight now, either with teasing or with passion. 'I'm enough for you, then?'

More than enough—you're everything I've ever wanted, he thought but didn't say. They were lovers now, but he had no idea where they'd go from here. She wanted him, she'd even said she loved him; but he couldn't begin to believe she wanted more from him than this time. Proximity, passion, fear, curiosity—to end her three-year shame, or to have the baby she'd demanded from him a year ago. Whatever the reason she'd given herself to him, he didn't know. Since they'd made love, neither of them had spoken beyond the here and now.

The only thing he knew for certain was that they must get out of here, and soon. Their private time here was running out, and the only emotion he could bring up was regret. Could they keep up their amity, their passion, when the world intruded on them once again?

'I should have thought of this plan myself, years ago,' he said, grinning and kissed her to distract himself from his dark thoughts. 'We could have been doing this for years.'

'Who says it would have worked on me then?' she demanded, mock-haughty but with twinkling eyes, and he laughed and showed her how easily it would have worked with a touch that made her moan in pleasure.

'Tell me more historical titbits,' she muttered between kisses growing more frantic by the moment. 'I love the way you teach me about history.'

He didn't know if she meant it or not, but he began telling her of ancient marriage rituals in their region, while she kept murmuring, 'Mmm, that's so fascinating, tell me more,' between explorations of his body with her hands, fingers and lips.

They soon returned to bed, whispering historical facts to each other in a way they'd never been intended.

'I want to please you, *mee numara*,' she whispered as she caressed his body with eager innocence. 'Show me how your—how to make you happy.'

How your other women touched you. He heard what she'd left unspoken, but again he barely believed she could be jealous. 'You please me constantly already.' Surely she could see that in the way he couldn't stop touching her?

A fierce look was his answer. 'So you won't return to her.' It wasn't a question or a plea, but a demand. She wanted him all to herself—she did care—and some deep core of ice he'd never known existed inside him began to melt.

Caring for him made this her business now; it was time to tell her the truth.

'You have nothing to fear, Amber. You never did,' he said in a jerking voice because telling anyone someone else's secret wasn't in his nature. 'You know Buhjah means joy. It was Fadi's nickname for Rafa, the woman he loved, and she loved to hear it again when Fadi was gone, from the other person closest to him. Naima is Fadi's daughter, my niece. I've never touched Buhjah; I see her as my sister-in-law. In fact I arranged a very advantageous marriage for her a few months ago, and, though part of her still loves Fadi, she's very happy.'

Amber's mouth fell open, and her eyes came alight. 'Do you mean that? There is no other woman?'

The ice inside him was melting so quickly it unnerved him, but she'd been open with him, and deserved the whole truth. 'There never has been. I've never knowingly broken a promise in my life. I wasn't going to start with our marriage vows.' He saw the look in her eyes; he had to stop her, because she was about the say the words he couldn't yet believe in, and he wasn't sure he wanted to hear them. So he grinned and said, 'So long as you're in my bed, I'm content. Even if there were fifty other women in the room right now, you leave me too exhausted to think of looking at them.' Exhausted, sated and so incredibly joyous: how could she be worried? She was a demanding and giving lover beyond any he'd known.

Her face, her whole body glowed with a furious kind of intent he'd never seen until he touched her, his warrior woman. 'No other woman but me.' Again, it wasn't a question; she was demanding her rights with him. No other woman had ever demanded so much of him, but her fierce, unashamed possessiveness made him come as vividly alive as she. In making love, Amber had none of that cold, queenly pride, but a ferocious need for him, an attitude of *'you're mine'* that translated in every touch, throbbed in every word, and made him feel so glad to be her lover. 'While you're in my bed, I don't want to look at another woman,' he vowed solemnly.

With an inarticulate little cry she leaped at him, and with a kiss he took them both beyond thought.

They spent the afternoon in bed. Not that there was much else to do, but he thought now it wouldn't matter if there was a choice; their need for each other was almost blinding. Once in a while he wondered who was listening or watching, but then she'd touch or kiss him, and they were gone again.

Later that night, contented once more, Amber wrapped herself in the sheet to use the bathroom, and trod on the bed curtain, pulling it down. Scrambling behind the ones still hanging in place, and making sure she was covered by the sheet, she whispered, 'Fix it, Harun, quickly!'

Loving that she could be so demanding and uninhibited with him and yet was so modest otherwise, he rolled off the bed. Then he felt himself being jerked back down to the bed with a thump. Half indignant, half laughing, he was about to kiss her when she shook her head, and her mouth moved to his ear. 'Harun, I think I know how we can escape.' She laid her hand across his lips. 'Put the curtains back in place, but leave the end with me.'

The imperative command spoken beneath her breath put his brain back in order. He hung the cheesecloth back in its place. He'd just turned to her when she put a finger to her lips. He nodded, and crawled across the bed to reach her. 'Make sounds as if we're making love,' she mouthed.

Puzzled but willing to indulge her, he made a soft groaning sound, and another, and bounced, making the old bed squeak, and he heard the soft swishing of feet moving from the holes in the wall. The guards had obviously been ordered to give them privacy.

She nodded and waved her hand. *Do it again.*

As he continued she folded the end of the curtain over, and looked closely. She probed it with her fingers. Pulling something from the bedside table, he couldn't make out what in the darkness, she moved it into the material. Then she whispered in his ear, 'This is one of the hairpins they gave me. If we twist them a bit, we can use them like clothing pins. We can use a curtain each, doubled over, and weave the pins through to hold the edges together.'

'You're going to make us wear togas?' he whispered back, trying hard not to laugh, but intrigued nevertheless. He made another necessary noise.

She nodded, her face adorably naughty in response to his groan. 'We girls played dress-ups enough as children. I destroyed sheets and curtains regularly until the servants complained, and Father made materials available to me. I made my sisters be my emperors or slaves. I was always Agrippina or Claudia, of course.' And then her grin faded. 'And the rest of the curtains we can tie together with the sheets.'

The simple brilliance of the plan caught him by surprise, as did her knowledge of Roman empresses' names. *She really does love history.* 'In the middle of the night, I take it?'

She nodded again. 'You go first, since you have the greatest chance of making it safely down, while I make, ah, appropriate sounds.' She nudged him, and he groaned again, while she sighed and moaned his name. 'Then I follow.'

He shook his head. 'No, you'll go first.' The slowest person had to go first. Then if anyone saw them, or the light came early or a check, he could jump down and—

'No,' she whispered urgently. 'You weigh more than me, and these curtains might not last long. I'm not athletic, and I might panic if the curtains begin to give. If you're already down…'

'I could catch you,' he whispered back, seeing the sense in that.

'You can get away,' she finished at the same time. 'You're the important one—you have to live. I couldn't bear it if you were hurt, or caught because I let you down.' Then she moaned again. 'Oh, my love, yes…'

Words she'd said while making love, but he'd taken them with a grain of salt in his experience, women became very affectionate during the act when he pleased them, and he'd never had a more compatible lover than Amber.

But she'd said it now: *My love*…and it disturbed him somehow, left him with that restless, needing to get out of here feeling. Yet she was willing to sacrifice herself—she saw him as the important one—and it caught him like a jab to the solar plexus. He'd always been the replacement, with the disposable life. Until now. Until Amber.

Did she really mean it? The doubts were insidious, but part of him now, a part so intrinsic he wouldn't know how to get them out of his system.

'Amber,' he groaned, and then whispered, 'I'll go first, but only because I can catch you—and because you're more vocal than me, during, ah…'

With a grin, she jabbed him in the side with her elbow, and he chuckled low. *Objective achieved,* he thought with a wry twist to his lips. She was distracted—and more, she was laughing. It was stupid, but he wanted her to stay happy for what would probably be their last day together. He could see her plan working. Already he was adding to her plan, with his commander's training—and planning what to do when he had Amber safe somewhere. If his brother had been taken, or, Allah forbid, killed, he knew what he had to do. If Alim was safe, the plan barely changed.

Though he had no choice but to go ahead with finding their abductors, he could no longer conjure up anger, humiliation or regret. In this abduction, he'd been given a gift beyond price. He could barely believe Amber had been in front of him for years and he'd been too angry, too betrayed or just too plain stupid to look for the passion beneath her ice when she looked at him, and her courage under this extreme test.

But for now, he had to go forward. If she was still willing when he'd found their traitors... 'So we do this tonight. We can go home.'

A few seconds too long passed before she answered. 'Yes. Um, wonderful.'

He looked at her, frowning, and saw the uncertainty he heard in her voice mirrored in her forlorn expression. 'This is your plan, Amber. Why are you hesitating?'

Still wrapped only in the sheet, she wiggled her toes, and shook her head. 'It's silly.'

'I can't agree or disagree with that statement until I know what "it" is,' he said, concerned. Though it was hard to see her expression clearly in the waxing moonlight to the east, he thought she looked lost. After a while, she gave a little half-shrug—and with a small start, he realised it was an unconscious emulation of his own act when he wanted to hide his emotions. 'Tell me, Amber.'

'You'll think I'm stupid,' she muttered. 'You'll laugh at me.'

So Amber really cared what he thought about her. Touched, he took her hands in his. 'No, I won't, no matter what. I promise. Now tell me.'

She couldn't look at him; her hands pulled out of

his as she looked anywhere but at him. Frowning, he watched her, and waited.

After a few moments she spoke, her voice low, but clearly fumbling for words. 'Out there—' her arm shot out, her finger pointing towards the window '—everything will change; we won't be able to control what happens. You'll have duty—your responsibilities, or your work, or maybe at last you can do whatever you want to do with your life. I don't know what I'll have.' She lifted her face, and she was so beautiful and so sad he wanted to haul her close, kiss her and tell her it would be all right; the world, their families and life wouldn't come between them. But he couldn't guarantee anything at this point, and she knew it.

'I ruined your plans, didn't I? I never thought beyond here and now, or what you wanted.' He tipped her face up to his. 'Did you want your freedom so badly?'

An almost violent shake of her head answered him. 'I regret nothing. You—you've made me so happy, if only for a few days.' Her hair fell over her face. She seemed very small and fragile. 'I don't know what to do now. I don't know what's in my future. It's different for you, the whole world's there for you, anything you want, but what do I do, Harun? Where do I go from here?'

An ache filled him, not for his sake but hers. Raised only to be a sheikh's wife, to be a political helpmate and child-bearer, Amber had now lost her chance to be another man's wife, to bear children. From what Aziz had told him, the only career she'd been trained for was that of a powerful man's virgin bride, his consort and mother of his children. If she'd been taught to believe it was her only use, no wonder she was lost now. 'I can't answer those questions. Only you can do that.'

Her head shook almost violently. 'I can't. I'm not—I'm not ready.'

'You're not ready for what?'

'To leave, to give up, to go back to—to the life I had before. I don't want to go back to that…that emptiness. I've been so happy here.' She looked up again, and in the time between sunset and moonrise he still saw a look of sadness so profound, the ache grew and spread through his body.

The irony didn't escape him. It had only taken being abducted to show him how little palace life meant to Amber. He felt awful, having left her alone in it so long; but how could he have dreamed the imperious princess who'd cried at the thought of marrying him could be so happy here, in a place with few creature comforts, and being alone with him? With just a small amount of his attention she'd become the most giving, ferocious, amazing lover he'd ever known.

He was happy now with what they had, so happy, but she was lost. He wanted to help her, but at this moment he didn't know what she needed most—his reassurance or her freedom. 'What can I do to help?'

She leaned forward and whispered harshly, 'We could die tonight.'

'Yes,' he agreed quietly, wondering where she was going.

She shuffled her feet on the bed, twisting her hands around each other for a few more moments, and finally whispered, 'I'm not ready to let you go, Harun. I need you one more time before the world comes between us.'

He almost let out a shout of laughter, an exclamation of amazement and the pure joy of it, but, remembering his promise, he held it in. 'That's all you want?'

She gave a tiny headshake. 'It's all I'm asking for

now…no decisions to make, no family to please, no duty to perform, no anger or pride or servants' gossip. Just give me tonight.' Dropping the sheet, she burrowed her body against his, burying her face in his neck. 'Just give me you, one more time.'

Shaking, his arms held her tight against him. How had he ever been so stupid as to believe he'd married a cold wife? By heaven, this woman was a warm-hearted, generous miracle, a gift from God who'd given him chance after chance every time he'd screwed it up or hurt her again. But this time he wasn't going to leave her crying, alone with her pain, leaving her to hide behind her only solace, her pride.

He laid her tenderly back on the bed, and closed all the window shutters and the bed curtains before returning to her. 'Just you and me.'

Her lips fell apart, and her eyes glowed. 'Thank you,' she breathed, as if he'd offered her a treasure beyond price.

'You're welcome.' Was his voice as unsteady as it sounded to him? After three long, lonely years, he realised what he could have had with Amber all along: a willing wife and lover as generous as he could have dreamed, a woman who didn't care in the least about his family name or position; all she wanted was him.

Give me a chance. It's all I'm asking.

It was all she'd ever asked of him: to give her a chance to show him the woman she really was inside. But he'd just kept pushing her away until he'd been given no choice in the matter. The chance she'd asked for had been forced on him, and he'd only given her grudging trust. Their alliance had been years too late, forged from desperation. And still, when he thought of what Amber had given him in return…

Praise God for their abductors, and this ruthless method of bringing them together.

How could he let her go after this? Was this the last night he'd ever have with her?

'You can have whatever you want. Just ask and it's yours, I swear it,' he said, even now only half believing she'd take him up on it.

Her eyes shimmered at his words. 'Do you think, when we go back, we could maybe go on a honeymoon? Just us, you and me?'

Something inside him felt as if it burst open, something tightly locked away too long. 'Of course we can. I'll have a few things to do first, but as soon as they're done...'

She nodded, and kissed him. 'Of course. I can wait.'

She'll wait for me. He smiled, and wondered if he'd ever stop smiling again. 'We know we don't need to take the honey-wine with us.'

'No, and you don't need to drug me.' Her returned smile was a thing of pure beauty. 'You'll ravish me day and night, and I'll let you.'

'I'll do my poor best.' He bowed as he laughed. 'Let me? I doubt you'd let me stop, my jewel. And you'll ravish me.'

'Of course I will,' she replied earnestly, as if he'd asked her for reassurance.

In all his life, he'd never remembered feeling like this—as if he could fly. The hope he'd believed dead was back, the terrible, treacherous thing he hardly dared to believe in was whispering to him that, this time, he wouldn't be hurt or left alone; he'd finally found the one who would want to stay with him. 'I have a yacht off Kusadasi on the Adriatic Sea. I haven't used her in years. We could cruise through the Greek Islands, or we can head to the east if you prefer. It'll be just you and me, for however long you want.'

'Oh, Harun…' She wound her arms around his neck, and buried her face in his shoulder. He heard her mumble some words, but, though he couldn't make them out, he felt the warmth of her tears against his skin, and then her lips roaming him in eager need.

Squelching that traitor's voice inside him, knowing he had to leave her first, he lifted her face and kissed her.

CHAPTER ELEVEN

How long do I want with you? I want for ever.

Had he heard her say it? She didn't know. All she knew was that in the last few days, she'd truly become a woman—and the frustrated desire she'd known for so long, the admiration and longing for her husband had become total and utter love without her even noticing. Harun had ignored her, but he'd never intentionally hurt her; he'd left her alone, but he'd fought for peace in Abbas al-Din, and worked himself half to death to hand his brother a country in good economic and political shape when Alim returned.

Had Alim ever really been a champion in her eyes? Perhaps in a public way, but it was nothing in comparison with the way she saw Harun.

During the past three years, Harun had shown her the real meaning of the word *hero*. Being a hero didn't have to come in flashy shows or trophies or spilling champagne in front of cameras; it wasn't in finding wealth, writing songs or poetry or giving flowers; it was in wordless self-sacrifice, doing the right thing even when it hurt, giving protection and—and just giving, expecting nothing in return.

She loved the man he was, and she no longer needed or even wanted fancy words or riotous acclaim. She just needed him, her quiet, beloved tiger, her lover and her man, and now she had him to herself, she never wanted to let him go again.

But she knew there was little choice in that. She'd lose him again; but for now, she'd take what she could with him.

'What do you want most to get from your job?' she asked while they waited for the deepest part of the night.

He didn't ask her to explain; he knew what she wanted: to connect with him, to know him. 'It's the really ancient history that fascinates me—our early ancestors. The Moabites during the Ishmaelite period, and Canaan, with the Philistines to the west. I want to know who they were beyond the child sacrifices and the multiplicity of gods.'

She held in the shudder. 'They sacrificed children?'

'Yes, they sacrificed their firstborn to the god Malcam, believing it brought his blessing to their crops. Archaeologists have found the sites of newborn cemeteries all over modern-day Israel and Lebanon, Jordan and Syria.'

This time she couldn't hold it in. 'That's disgusting.'

'Our ancestors weren't the most civilised people.' He grinned. 'But what I want most of all is to discover traces of the real people called the Amalekites. It's still hotly contested by historians as to who they were, because they just seemed to disappear from the human record about three thousand years ago.'

'How can that be?' she asked, wide-eyed. 'How can a whole nation of people just vanish without trace?'

'They didn't—there are records, but none belonging to them. It seems they were a warrior-nation that didn't keep their own records. Other contemporary nations speak of them as the most terrifying warriors of their time…oh, sorry, I must be boring you to sleep,' he teased as she tried valiantly to hold in her third yawn.

'No, no, I want to know,' she mumbled, snuggling deeper against his chest. 'I'm listening, I promise—just sleepy.'

Harun smiled down at her, and stroked her hair as she fell into a deep sleep. He could give her an hour; it was just past midnight.

It was heading for two a.m. when he woke her.

Instinctively Amber reacted to the gentle shaking by rolling into him, seeking his mouth. It was amazing how quickly she'd become accustomed to needing him there. 'I'm sorry, I let you sleep as long as I could,' he whispered, after they'd shared a brief, sweet kiss. 'We have to start on the plan.'

With difficulty, she reoriented herself. 'Of course, I have the pins ready. We'll need to be as silent as possible.'

'If we make any noise, I'll make some lover-noises to cover it, and you do that laughing thing you do.'

She felt her cheeks heating, but smiled. 'I can do that. Now help me pull the curtains down. We'll just take one down at a time—and while I'm making one toga, check the windows to see how many guards are stationed.'

The curtains proved no hardship in pulling off the rail, except in the slight swish and slide of falling off the rail, once it was loosened. She pulled him to her and deftly wound the doubled fabric over his shoulder and around his waist. 'What I wouldn't give to be able to rip the towels into strips,' she murmured as she had to push the pin-head through the fabric every time. 'Then we could have a waist-sash.'

He groaned her name softly, and pushed the bed

down with his hand. If they got quiet for any length of time, the guards would return. 'Here, let me.' He twisted the ends of the pushed-through pin so each end bent back on itself. 'No chance of its undoing now. Put one at my waist and it should be fine.'

'Two is better.' She worked two pins into the waist, at the rib and hip level. 'Now if one goes the other will hold.'

They both made appropriate noises while he got down another curtain and she made her toga; he helped her twist the pins, and the cheesecloth felt surprisingly strong under his hands. Amber felt breakable in comparison, or maybe it was the fear in her eyes.

They continued making sounds of love as he twisted the remaining curtains and sheets together in sailing knots.

It was time. It was nearly three a.m. and they couldn't keep up the noises much longer, or the guards would become suspicious. Seeing the fear growing in her eyes, he held her hands, smiled and whispered, 'You know what to do. I'll pull the rope three times when I reach the bottom. Be strong, my Kahlidah, my Agrippina.'

She gulped at the reference to her great-grandmother. 'I'm trying, but right now I don't think I take after her.'

She was falling apart at the worst possible time, and he had only seconds to pull her back together. 'I'm relying on you, *mee numara,* my courageous tigress. This is your plan. You can fulfil it. You *will* do this.' And he kissed her, quick and fierce.

'I think I'll leave any roaring until later,' she whispered with a wavering smile.

Harun winked at her. 'I'll be waiting for you.'

With one swift, serious look he kissed her a final time; with a little frown and eyes enormous with fear and strangely uncertain determination, she waved him off.

He crept to the window, and checked as best he could. If guards were posted around he couldn't see them—but then, he thought the numbers of guards had thinned out in the past day. They'd achieved their first objective, he supposed, and would let them enjoy their faux honeymoon.

At first, he had thought that with every piece of furniture but the chairs being nailed to the floor, he could use a bigger piece as a ballast. The closest to a window least likely to attract attention was the dining table— but now it looked too old, fragile; it might break under his weight. After scanning the room again, he saw the only real choice was the bed, since the wardrobe was too wide, taking rope length they couldn't afford.

The bed was the furthest from any window. This was going to be tight.

He looked at her again, and pulled at each corner of the bed, testing its strength, while Amber covered the noises as best she could with cries of passion, but her eyes were wide and caught between taut fear and held-in laughter.

The sturdiest part of the bed was the corner furthest from the window, but he estimated that would leave their rope at least eight feet short. Having jumped from walls in his army training, he knew they couldn't afford the noise he'd make in landing, or in catching her. If she'd come that far, seeing the gap.

This was Hobson's choice. A swift prayer thrown to heaven, and he made his decision, tying the rope with a triple winding around the nearest bed leg and through the corner where the mattress rested.

Then, slowly and with the utmost care, he let the

makeshift rope out of the window closest to the bed, and in the middle of the room, an inch at a time. It was frustrating, wasting time they didn't have, but throwing the rope could lead to its hitting something and causing attention.

At last the rope could go no further. He leaned out, and saw the rope was only short by about three feet, and he breathed a quiet sigh of relief, giving Amber a thumbs-up.

Her smile in the moonlight was radiant with the same relief he felt. With a short, jaunty wave and another wink he hoped she could see, he climbed over the sill, gripped the cheesecloth in both hands and began the drop.

The hardest part was not being able to bounce off the building, but just use his hands to slide down. By the time he'd reached the smoother sheet part of the rope, his hands were raw and starting to bleed. He and Amber had discussed this even as they'd loved each other the final time; she knew what to expect.

He only hoped her courage saw her through. But she was only twenty-two—what had he done with life by then? Yes, he'd passed all his training exercises with the armed forces, but that was at the insistence first of his parents and then Fadi. He'd replaced Alim and Fadi at necessary functions, but again, he'd been trained for it all his life. He'd told Amber how to rappel down the rope, but if she panicked—

In his worry over her, he'd rappelled automatically down the final fifty feet. His toga was askew, but his pins held. Running even by night in their bare feet would be hard, harder on Amber; would they make it?

Stop thinking. He looked around and again saw no guards. Vaguely uneasy, he checked out their surroundings, and tugged on the rope slowly three times. Within moments he saw her looking out of the window. Beckoning to her lest she back out, he hoped he'd done enough.

It was long moments before she moved—time they didn't have; the eastern sky was beginning to lighten. Then she slipped over the edge and, using only her hands, began dropping towards him. His heart torn between melting at her bravery and pounding with fear that she'd fall, he braced himself to catch her.

She stopped at the point where the sheets took over from the curtains, and he almost felt the raw pain her hands were in. He did feel it; his hands took fire again, as if in sympathy.

Come on, Amber. I'm waiting for you...

A few moments later, she began sliding down—literally sliding—and his heart jack-knifed straight into his mouth.

Allah help me!

A slight thump, and a madly grinning Amber was beside him, looking intensely proud of herself. 'You thought I was falling, didn't you?'

He wanted to growl so badly the need clawed around his belly, but instead he found himself kissing her, ferocious and in terrified relief. 'Let's go.'

'Which way?'

He pointed. 'I can't believe I didn't recognise where we were before, but from above the perspective changes, I suppose. This was one of the first battle areas during the el-Shabbat war. We're only about fourteen miles from Sar Abbas.'

Her face changed, losing some confidence. 'Fourteen miles. I can do that,' she whispered, frowning like a child facing a wall. 'Let's run.'

His uneasiness growing—why wasn't anyone trying to stop them?—he took her hand and ran southwest. Towards the dimly lit road only a mile away where he hadn't been able to see it before, behind the part of the building without windows. The brighter lights of Sar Abbas glinted in the distance like a welcoming beacon.

CHAPTER TWELVE

The Sheikh's Palace, Sar Abbas, a few hours later

In the opulent office that had been Harun's but was now his, Alim stared at Harun when he walked in the door unannounced, and then ran headlong for him. 'Praise Allah, you're back, you're alive! *Akh, mee habib akh!*'

Brother, my beloved brother. Harun had the strangest sense of déjà vu with Alim's outburst, the echo of words he himself had spoken only a few weeks ago in Africa. But Alim sounded so overwhelmingly relieved, and Alim's arms were gripping his shoulders hard enough to hurt. He didn't know what to make of it. 'So you were given demands?'

'No.' His brother's face was dark with stress and exhaustion as they all sat down on respective chairs around his—*Alim's* desk. 'This never went public, but two guards were found drugged in the palace the night you disappeared, and another almost died saving me from an abduction attempt. I came to check on you and you were gone—and Amber too. We sent all our usual guards away, and filled the palace with elite marine guards. Under the guise of army exercises I've had the best in the country looking for you, and hunting down your abductors. How did you get away? What happened?'

'I wish I knew.' Harun frowned. 'It was like they wanted us to get away. The guards disappeared, and we rappelled down a rope of sheets and curtains. We ran to the highway into the city and I called in a favour from an army captain who drove us the rest of the way.' He grinned. 'We only stopped to change, since our attire wasn't quite up to palace standards.' He flicked the grin over to Amber, who was watching him with a look of mingled pride and exasperation—at his cut-down version of events, he supposed.

'Maybe their plan was contingent on us all being taken,' Alim said quietly. 'Any thoughts on that, *akh?* You're the tactician in the family.'

'He's more than that,' Amber interjected sharply, the first words she'd spoken.

'Alim didn't mean anything by it, Amber.' He reached over, touched her hand to quiet the protest he felt wasn't yet done.

'I meant it as a compliment, actually, Amber.' Alim was frowning. 'Harun's the one that saved the country while I was lying in a bed in Switzerland, and he ran the country while I drove a truck.' He met Harun's eyes with an odd mix of admiration and resentment. 'I've only been here a few days and I've got no idea how you did it all so well.'

Harun felt Amber gearing up for another comment born of exhaustion and—it made him want to smile— the urge to protect him, and he pressed her hand this time. 'We think it might have been some el-Kanar supporters who wanted an heir.'

'You mean they wanted an heir from you and Amber?' At his nod, he earned a sharp look from Alim.

'And who don't support my, shall we say, less than tra-ditional ways, and my choice of bride.' When Harun didn't answer, he was forced to go on. 'Then I can as-sume the rumours about the state of your marriage were correct?'

Neither moved nor spoke in answer.

After a flicked glance at them both, Alim avoided the obvious question. Amber's face was rosy, her eyes downcast. It was obvious she was no longer the ice maiden she'd seemed to be the week before…and Harun could almost swear Alim's left eye drooped in a wink. He certainly seemed a little brighter than before.

'So I'd guess you think the plan was to kill me and install you as permanent ruler.'

It wasn't a question, but still Harun nodded and shrugged. 'That's what they planned, but they left one thing out of the equation.' He met his brother's enquir-ing look with a hard expression. 'I never wanted the position in the first place. I still don't want it. Stepping into Fadi's dead shoes was the last thing I wanted three years ago. Less still do I want to be in your shoes now.'

Alim stilled, staring at him. 'You don't want to be here at all, do you.'

Again, it was a statement of fact.

'He never did.' Amber spoke with the quiet venom of stored anger. 'Tell him, Harun. Tell him the truth about what you've sacrificed the last thirteen years so he could do whatever he wanted.'

Alim only said, almost pleading, *'Akh?'*

'Amber, please,' Harun said quietly, turning only his head. 'I appreciate what you're trying to do, but this is not the time.'

'If not now, when…?' Then Amber's eyes swivelled to meet his, and she paled beyond her state of exhaustion. 'You're going to sacrifice yourself again—you'll sacrifice us, even—to fulfil your sacred duty. And for *him*.' She jerked her head in Alim's direction. 'Is he *still* all you've got?'

'Harun?' Alim's voice sounded uncertain.

Harun couldn't answer either of them. He was lost in the humbling knowledge that she could read him so easily now—that he had no time to formulate an explanation; she knew it all. And she wasn't going to support him.

When he didn't speak Amber made a choking sound, and turned on Alim. There was no trace of her old crush as she snarled at his brother, 'You'll let him do it for you again, won't you? Just as you let him do everything *you* were supposed to do, all these years. He gave up *everything* for you, while you were off playing the superstar, or feeling sorry for yourself in Africa, playing the hero again. Did you ever *care* about what he wanted? Did you think to ask him, even once?'

In the aftermath of Amber's outburst, all that was audible in this soundproof room was her harsh breathing. She stared at Alim in cold accusation; Alim's gaze was on Harun, tortured by guilt. Then Amber turned to him, her eyes challenging. She wasn't backing down, wasn't going to let him smooth this over with pretty half-truths.

The trouble was, his mind had gone totally blank. It had been so long since anyone asked him for unvarnished truth or stripped his feelings bare as she'd just done, she'd left him with nothing to say.

At length she turned back on Alim. 'Harun never told me any of it, just so you know. Fadi did. I hope you've appreciated your life, because Harun gave it to you! And he's going to do it again. For once, Alim, be a real man instead of a shiny image!'

Then, pulling her hand from Harun's, she turned and ran from the room.

Harun watched her go, completely beyond words. Devastated and betrayed, she was still loyal to him to the end. Why was it only now that he realised how loyal she'd always been to him?

Loyalty, courage and duty…Amber epitomised all of them, and he'd never deserved it.

'Have you hated me all these years?' asked Alim.

The low question made him turn back. Alim's eyes were black, tortured with guilt. 'Don't,' he said wearily when Harun was about to deny it. 'Don't be polite, don't be the perfect sheikh or the perfect brother, just this once. Answer me honestly. Have you hated me for having the life I wanted at your expense?'

For years he'd waited for Alim to see what he'd done, to ask. For years he'd borne the chains that should have been his brother's—and yet, now the question was finally asked, he couldn't feel the weight any more. 'I hated that you never asked me what I wanted.' Then he frowned. 'What do you mean, the perfect brother?'

Alim pulled a face of obvious pain, and rubbed at the scars on his neck and cheek. 'I need some of Hana's balsam,' he muttered. 'Don't pretend you don't know what I mean. It was always you with Fadi—Harun this and that, you did such a wonderful job of something I should have done or been there to do. Even if I'd come home, I'd have done a second-rate job. I was always well aware you were the one Fadi wanted, and I was second-best.'

It was funny how the old adage about walking in another's shoes always seemed so fresh and new when you were the ones in the shoes. 'I never knew he did that.'

Alim shrugged, retreating into silence, and it looked

like a mirror of his own actions. So it meant that much to Alim. It had hurt him that much.

He'd just never realised they were so alike.

'It must have hurt,' he said eventually, when it was obvious Alim wasn't going to speak. This was new to him, being forced to reach out.

Another shrug as his brother's face hardened and he rubbed at the scarring. Though it wasn't quite the same, it was a defence mechanism he recognised. He thought Amber would, too…and she'd have tried again from a different position. Poking and prodding at the wound until he was forced to lance it.

Suddenly Harun wanted to smile. All the things he'd been blind to for so long… Amber knew him so well. How, he didn't know. She must have studied him at a distance—or maybe it was just destiny. Or love.

That the word even came to him with such clarity shocked him. What did it mean?

'Do you know what it's like to be inadequate beside your little brother at your mother's funeral?' Alim suddenly burst out. 'Fadi never let me forget it. No matter what I achieved or did, I never measured up to you.'

Harun stared at him. '*Fadi* said that?'

'All the time,' Alim snarled.

It was hard to get his head around it: the brother he'd always adored and looked up to had played favourites, just as their mother and father had. The insight turned all his lifelong beliefs on their heads—and the indestructible Racing Sheikh became a man like any other, his big brother who was lost and hurting.

The trouble was he didn't have a clue what to do with the knowledge that the brother he'd resented so long was the only one who could understand how it felt to be him. 'Did you hate me for that?' he faltered.

A weary half-shake, half-nod was his only answer, yet he understood. 'I'm sorry, Alim,' he said awkwardly in the end, but he wasn't sure what he was apologising for.

Alim gave another careless shrug, but he saw straight through it. Some scars bled only when pulled open. Others just kept bleeding.

'So, what did you want to do with your life that you didn't get to do, while I was off being rich and famous?' Alim tried to snap, but it came out with a humorous bent somehow.

Willing them both to get past what had only hurt them all these years, Harun grinned. 'Come on, *akh*. I don't change. Think. Remember.'

Alim frowned, looking at him with quizzical eyes... and slowly they lit. 'The books, the history you always had your nose stuck in as a kid? Do you want to be a professor?'

'Close.' The grin grew. 'Archaeologist.'

'Really?' Alim laughed. 'You want to spend your life digging up old bones and bits of pottery?'

'Hey, big kid, you played with cars for years,' he retorted, laughing.

Alim chuckled. 'Well, if you put it that way...okay, I'm growing up and you're getting to go make mud pies.'

The laughter relaxed them both. 'So you have no objections?'

'I have no right to object to anything you want to do, even if I have the power.' Alim came around the desk, and gave Harun a cocky grin. 'I promise to get the job right, and not bother you or force you home for at least the next thirteen years.'

Harun looked up, his expression hardening. 'Thanks, but I'm not applying for digs just yet. I have something I need to do first.'

Alim tilted his head.

'You just said you wouldn't object to anything I wanted.' Harun shook off Alim's hands as they landed on his shoulders, and stood. 'First, I have to renounce my position formally, publicly state I don't want the job.' He met his brother's eyes. 'I have to disappear until everyone in the nation accepts you in the position, or our friends will try again…and this time they might get it right.'

'I guess I'd better let you do it…but you're all I have left, Harun.' Alim's face seemed to take on a few more lines, or maybe the scars were more pronounced. 'Take care with your life, little *akh*. Don't leave me alone to grieve at your funeral.'

The words were raw, but still Alim squared up to him, looking him in the eye. And Harun realised he was the taller brother—something he'd never noticed before. 'I'm doing this *for* you. I'm the soldier in the family. I have to hunt them down.' He spoke through a throat hurting with unspoken emotion. 'Until the group's disabled, you'll never be safe—and neither will the woman you love.'

'And if I don't want you to do this? If I say that without you, I have nothing?'

Too late, he heard the choked emotion, and understood what Alim wasn't saying. 'What about Hana?'

His brother's jaw hardened still more. 'That's no more open to discussion than your private life with Amber. But let me say this now, while I can, because I know you're going to disappear, no matter what I say. Are you leaving because you hate me for Fadi's death—or can I hope one day you'll forgive me?'

The words sliced Harun when he'd least expected it.

He wheeled away, just trying to breathe for a minute, but his chest felt constricted.

'I have to know, Harun.' The hand that landed on his shoulder was shaking. 'Despite the fact that you were his favourite, I loved him. He was more father than brother to us both from the time we were little.'

All he could do was nod once.

After a stretch of quiet, Alim asked, 'Do you blame me for his death?'

'Stop,' he croaked, feeling as if Alim had torn him in half.

'I need to know, Harun.'

There were so many replies he could make to that assertion, but he'd been where Alim was now. He knew better than Alim did that staffers and servants and all the personal and national wealth that oil and gas could bring, even the adoration of a nation, the whole world, didn't halt the simple loneliness of not having the woman you wanted love you for who you really were inside.

It seemed this was a week of unburdening, whether he wanted to or not.

'Fadi made his own decision,' he said eventually, staring out of the window. 'I always knew that. He was so unhappy at the political marriage he had to make— not just with Amber, but any suitable woman. He loved Rafa with all his heart. I don't think he wanted to die, just to escape from inevitability for a few days.'

After a long time, Alim answered, sounding constricted. 'Thank you.'

He shrugged again. 'You saw how unhappy he was, didn't you? I saw it too, but I didn't know what to do; I had nothing to offer him. You gave him escape for a little while, because you loved him. His death was a terrible accident, one that scars you more than me. I never blamed you for it.' *Only for running off when I needed someone the most,* he thought but didn't say. Alim had more burdens on his shoulders than he'd ever dreamed. He found himself hoping Hana would come back to him, and make him happy.

'Thanks, *akh.*'

Two words straight from the heart, the word *brother* filled with choked emotion, bringing them both a measure of healing—and yet Harun wondered when it was that he'd last heard someone speak to him that way. Fadi had never been one for pretty words, just a clasp on the shoulder in thanks for a job well done.

Do you think...we could maybe go on a honeymoon? Just us, you and me?

Amber had spoken to him from the heart, probably as much as she'd dared when he'd never once told her what he wanted with her—and he realised what he'd done by making his decision without involving her.

He turned back to Alim. 'I need to find Amber.'

Alim nodded. 'That you do, brother. I think it's time—or way past time, actually—that you told her how you feel about her.' Startled, Harun stared at him, and Alim gave a small smile. 'I saw it on your face the day you first saw her, and even in the way you looked at her today. I knew then, but I understand it now. It's how I felt when I first saw Hana. It's how I still feel even though she's gone.'

'You...knew how I felt about Amber?' he asked slowly, taken aback by his brother's insight. Alim saw more about him than he'd ever realised.

Alim shrugged. 'Why do you think I left so quickly after meeting her? I saw the way she looked at me—but the crush was on the Racing Sheikh.'

'So you knew that, too,' he jerked out.

Alim nodded. 'Of course I knew. Do you really think I'd have left you with all this responsibility three years ago if I didn't think you were going to be rewarded with your heart's desire? Leaving without a word to either of you would make her turn to you, because you were as hurt as she was by my disappearance.' By now they were both staring hard out the window, looking at the city view as if it held the answers to life's mysteries.

'Why?' Harun asked eventually. 'Didn't you know I'd rather have had you?'

'Not then, I didn't. I do now.' From the corner of his eye, he saw Alim shrug. 'I was the wrong man for her. I knew you'd step up, take the marriage and position I couldn't bear to. It was selfish, yes, and I wanted to run; but I couldn't stand the thought of taking someone so precious from you—again.'

Fadi. Oh, the guilt Alim carried on his shoulders...

Beyond an answer, Harun shook his head. Unable to stand any more emotion, he joked mildly, 'You always did have the gift of the gab. The only one of us who did.'

'It hasn't got me very far with Hana,' Alim muttered.

Harun resisted the urge to touch his brother's shoulder, and asked again, brother to brother. 'She won't marry you?'

This time Alim shook his head. 'She's running from all the stories. She thinks she isn't worthy to be my wife. I hoped when I met the family that they'd know her worth, but they agreed with her. Her father all but told me to forget her. I can't do that, I'll never do that! As if bloodlines matter when we're all descendants of the one man!'

Harun shrugged. 'There's a world of practical difference between the theory of being a fellow descendant of Abraham, and the reality of being royalty or a miner's daughter.'

'Not to me,' Alim growled. 'Would your ice princess have risked her life to save you—not once, but a half-dozen times?'

'I was only saying what she might be thinking,' Harun replied mildly. He knew when a man spoke from love and pain, and the foolishness of words regretted later, but unable to take back. 'I agree with you. Hana's a heroine, and she has a courage far more suited to the role you want her to take than any pampered princess— but it's what she thinks that counts.'

Mollified, Alim nodded. 'Sorry I jumped on you.'

'Forgiven—but I'd appreciate it if you'd never call Amber an ice princess again,' he added, gently frigid. 'She might not have saved any lives, but she's put up with quite a lot from the el-Kanar brothers, mostly without complaint, and with the kind of loyalty not one of us have earned from her. She forgave you not half an hour ago without even telling you about the very public embarrassment she suffered when you disappeared rather than marry her.'

Alim sobered once more. 'You're right. I apologise— and I think it's time you did, too. Go,' he said, half forceful, half laughing as Harun turned on his heel to stalk down his quarry.

It took him over an hour to find her—and in a night of surprises, she was sitting at a desk in the extensive library, her nose buried in a book on the archaeology of the Near East local area. She glanced up at his approach, but, with a flash of defiance in her eyes, she lowered her gaze to her book, and kept reading.

Fervently wishing for Alim's gift of the gab about

now, his ability to turn a phrase into something emotional and beautiful, Harun could only find his own words. 'I'm sorry. I know you were only trying to help.'

With careful precision, she turned a page, as if she was absorbed by the book. 'What is your plan?'

He didn't hesitate. 'I'm leaving tonight. I have a few leads—I have to find out who abducted us and why. Alim and the entire royal household cannot be safe until they have been brought to justice.'

Her gaze drifted a little further down the page. 'Goodbye, then. Enjoy your escape.'

'Amber, please understand. I have to do this.'

'And of course I'm far safer here, left alone in the place where I was kidnapped last time,' she remarked idly, turning another page. 'But then, I don't suppose my fears and wishes come into this. You're going, and leaving me here, no matter how I feel about it.'

The observation jolted him. 'I thought you of all people would understand. You said there wasn't anything you wouldn't do to save your family.'

'Hmm? What was that?' She ran her finger down a page before she looked up with a cloudy-eyed expression.

'Don't be childish,' he rebuked in an undertone.

Her brows lifted in a look of mild surprise. 'Sorry, I can hardly believe you're still here talking to me. You should be off saving your brother, your nation or anything else. After all, isn't he all you have? Isn't your duty to your brother and country above everything, especially me?'

That hit hard. 'I have to do this, Amber. If I don't disappear and hunt them down, they'll just take us again— or kill Alim to make me step up, now they know we're lovers.'

'We were lovers,' she replied, still in that indolent, I-don't-care voice. 'Rather hard to be anything when you're going undercover commando on me.'

Right now he wished she'd just say what she wanted, but she'd gone Ice Queen on him again, and it was taking all he had left after this long, very hard day not to respond in kind, or just walk away. 'When I'm done with this, I'm coming back for you.' He tried to smile. 'I want that honeymoon we agreed on.'

At that, she closed the book with a tiny snapping sound. 'Again, it's rather hard to believe that there will be a future at all when you're going to be outnumbered and if they find you, they'll probably kill you—' With a choking sound, she jumped up, wheeled around and ran from the room.

But not before he'd heard her gasp for breath on a sob, and seen her dash the tears from her eyes—and when he tried to find her, to make things right somehow, she'd retired to the section of the palace reserved only for women, where even Alim could not enter.

CHAPTER THIRTEEN

Four months later

'I UNEQUIVOCALLY refuse any position that belongs right-fully to my brother. I was never more than his care-taker while he healed. I have now handed over the full power to my brother Alim. I am leaving Abbas al-Din tonight, and will not be returning for a long time. I wish my beloved brother happiness in the life ordained for him by God, and fully approve of his choice of bride. Hana al-Sud is a fine, strong woman of faith, worthy of the highest position. Thank you and good evening.'

For the five hundredth time Amber felt the potent cocktail of hunger and fury as she watched the re-run of the security closed circuit TV. Harun stepped down from the podium at the ruling congress, refusing to an-swer any questions after reading his statement. A five-minute presentation before the people he suspected of abducting them, and then he'd disappeared. No one had heard from him since.

At least, she hadn't. She assumed Alim would tell her something if he knew, but he was very busy, taking the reins of power, planning his wedding—and since com-ing to the palace to accept Alim's proposal, Hana had a

terrible habit of dragging him into secret corners to kiss
and touch him whenever he had a minute to himself.

*Why didn't I think of doing that with Harun years
ago?*

*Because Hana's secure; she knows Alim loves her.
She's a blessed woman.*

With an angry snap she switched off the TV, resolv-
ing for the five hundredth time to never watch again,
but she knew she would. Again before bed tonight, leaving her to pace the floor until exhaustion drove her to
bed; again tomorrow when she'd finished the studies
she loved, but he did too—and before dinner, driving
her to eat next to nothing as she uttered polite inanities
with the family to prove to them that she was coping
with her isolated life, studying an archaeology course
in half the time, and living in the old women's quarters
with only one maid and guard for company.

Hana and Alim's wedding was to take place in two
days. She didn't even assume Harun would return for
that event. She'd made that mistake for their engagement party, dressing in her finest, making sure she
looked her best…and it was all for nothing.

Alim had no best man. He said if Harun didn't come
he didn't want anyone.

She knew exactly how Alim felt. Why, why couldn't
she just leave him behind, as he'd done with her? Why
didn't she just get on with her life?

'Because I have nowhere to go,' she muttered, leaping to her feet and crossing the room rather than give in
to the temptation to throw something at the TV. Despite
her station, she had no personal fortune, or even a bank
account. Not one of the staff in the palace, even a foreign worker, would help her, at the risk of deporta-
tion; her face was too well known. Her father refused

to allow her to stay with them, or even send the jet for a week's visit.

Come when your husband returns to claim you, he'd said inflexibly.

And unless it was to family, the law of the land forbade her from leaving her husband unless she could prove ongoing physical abuse. She had no friends outside her family circle, nobody close that would offer her shelter, or believe her if she tried to claim abuse; they'd all loved Harun from the start.

No, she was a royal wife in a traditional land: just another possession left unwanted in the treasure room until her owner remembered her.

Instead of pacing the floor for the five hundredth time, she stared fiercely out of the window. What she wouldn't give to grow wings right now! She'd escaped once, but this time she was surrounded less by snipers than a thousand servants catering to her every need, and watching her every move. They were her protectors until her husband came back to take over the job. So until Harun chose to return from his wanderings and release her, she was caged as effectively as she'd been for her abductors.

Two days later

'So, *akh,* I hear you're one best man short.'

With an hour until the wedding Alim, standing alone in the sheikh's magnificent bedchamber and dressed in his groom's finery, whirled around to see Harun in the doorway, with a cheeky grin. Tired to the point of falling down, he was still ready to give his brother support during his day of days.

He threw Alim a mock salute. 'Your Highness.'

And found himself smothered in a hard embrace. '*Akh*, little *akh*, praise God you're alive.' Alim was trembling. 'I thought…feared…'

'I can hardly breathe here,' he complained with a laugh. 'I'm okay, *akh*, really—and when you come back from your honeymoon, I have good news to report.'

Alim pulled back, but hugged him again. 'I'll be grateful for that later. Right now, my little brother's back from the dead… It was so damn *hard* going through my transition and engagement alone. I wanted you with me, to share my happiness and hardships.'

Harun willed away the sense of irony in everything Alim had just said. Telling Alim he'd felt the same for years would only damage their fragile relationship; he understood, and that was enough. 'If it helps, I worked day and night the past few months to get here today.'

Alim peered at his face, and frowned. 'You do look like you're ready to fall down. Come, take some coffee. I can't have you falling asleep on me during the ceremony.' Alim led him inside, and poured him a cup of thick, syrupy black coffee. 'There's more. I've been drinking it all day.'

Harun chuckled and shook his head. 'No wonder you seem like one of those wind-up toys. Why are you so nervous? You know Hana loves you.'

Alim sobered. 'You know her first marriage was a sham. It's her first time tonight, as well as our first time. If I don't—'

Harun silenced him with a lifted hand, smiling. 'I was there a few months ago, *akh*. Take it from one who knows now. I've seen the way she looks at you in news reports, and heard how she drags you into cupboards.' Alim chuckled at that, as Harun intended. 'She loves you, Alim; she's ready. It will be everything she's dreamed of, because in her eyes, that's what you are.'

'That was—the perfect thing to say.' He was taken aback by Alim's hand cupping his cheek. 'I can't believe you came back for me.'

So much left unsaid, but it no longer needed to be said. 'Ah, you know me. I'm always hanging around just waiting to be useful.'

Alim grabbed the coffee cup from him and drew him into the stranglehold hug again, thumping him on the back. 'I don't deserve you, but I thank Allah every day for the gifts you've given me.'

'You found life's best gift all by yourself. You came home all by yourself, too. I had my bride and my life handed to me—by you, I should add.'

'You know what I mean. I can't believe we could have been friends all these years, but—'

Neither wanted to say it. Separated by those they'd loved and needed most, they could always have been allies. 'Nothing's stopping us now,' Harun said huskily.

'And nothing will again.' Another massive hug.

'You're choking me,' Harun mock complained, 'and crushing my best man's outfit.'

'Who was it that abducted you?' Alim asked abruptly, releasing him.

In answer, he handed Alim the file he'd dropped during the first hug. 'The entire group has been put out of action.'

'Hmm.' Alim scanned the first sheet rapidly. 'I wouldn't have thought it of the Jamal and Hamor clans, but yes, they are very conservative. With financial and armed backing from our more conservative neighbours, I guess they thought they could try. I think it's time we did something about our neighbours, too.'

'I did all that's needed, My Lord.' Harun bowed, laughing again. 'I told you I worked night and day. I found out who it was by word of mouth months ago—but proof had to be absolute. When it was, the perpetrators were easy to rout, especially after my public announcement. Now go, enjoy your wedding. It's time to go see your bride.'

And he pushed Alim out of the door. One relationship on track...but he had the feeling this lifelong breach would be the easier of the two to heal.

The wedding banquet was beautiful, filled with the daintiest dishes of the region. Sheikhs, presidents and first ladies sat at the tables, mingled and laughed, probably proposed or made new deals over a relaxing extended meal, while Alim and Hana ignored the world, feeding each other, giving small touches, their eyes locked on the other. So absorbed were they that when someone approached them, they jerked out of their own little world with obvious surprise that anyone else existed.

To think he could have had a similar wedding, if only he'd known Amber wanted him the way he'd wanted her...

But right now, even his memories of their two days of joy seemed false. Dressed in full, traditional clothing, covered from head to foot apart from her face, Amber sat at the royal table between two first ladies, speaking only with them. She was thinner, paler, wearing none of her soft make-up that made her face glow with life; her eyes were too calm, holding no emotion at all; her hands remained at the table instead of waving around as she talked.

She'd lost herself somewhere in the past few

months—or hours. She'd whitened when she'd seen him standing beside Alim, and looked away before he could move or even smile at her, and she'd avoided him ever since. He'd been trying to get her attention discreetly, but she wasn't responding. Any moment now, she'd excuse herself and retire to the women's quarters.

So he stalked over to her. 'I wish to speak to you, my wife.'

Amber's head snapped around to him, her lips parted in shock that he'd come right into the open; but trapped by law and convention, she could either cause a scene, or acquiesce.

The cheeks that had been pale were now rosy; her eyes were fiery with indignation. 'As you can no doubt see, I am fully occupied at present, my husband.' With the slightest sarcastic inflection on the title *husband,* she waved a hand at the important women sitting either side of her, who both immediately demurred, insisting that if her husband wished to speak with her, they'd be fine together.

Obviously fuming, she rose to her feet; but Harun, inwardly grinning—at least she was alive again—held out his hand, which again she had to take in seeming grace. He led her around the table, and out through the state banqueting rooms onto the back balcony of the palace, semi-private and with no public or press access.

Once there, she jerked her hand away, and folded her arms, waiting.

Instinct told him a joke wouldn't get him far this time. Neither would she reach out to him. This time, he had to be the one to give. Anything that would get her to talk to him, tell him what she was thinking and feeling, even if she hated him.

So he started there. 'Do you hate me for being away so long?'

She sighed, looking out into the night. 'Why don't you tell me what you want from me this time, so we can get on with our lives once you're gone again?'

The question confused him, but he felt it wasn't a topic to pursue, not yet. 'You look so thin,' he said softly. 'Are you feeling well?'

'I'm fine, thank you.' Cold words, with no compromise. She wasn't giving anything away, wasn't going to play his game. She wanted her question answered.

'You're my wife. I've come back for you, as I promised I would.'

'Like a dropped-off package, or a toy forgotten about until you want to play again?'

'No, like a wife I hoped would understand that what I was doing had to come first.'

Another sigh, harsh and rather bored, and she kept looking out into the night. 'Just tell me what you want.'

He shook his head. 'I don't understand. You're my wife. I've come back for you.'

'Your wife.' The words were flat, as was the laughter that followed. 'So says the imam that performed the service. Isn't that what you said?' Still she wouldn't look at him. 'What is a wife to you?'

She'd obviously had far too much time alone to think; every question she asked left him feeling more bewildered. 'I think you have ideas on what I think a wife is.' Soft, provocatively spoken, designed to break the wall of ice around her and get to the pain of abandonment hiding beneath.

She lifted her brows in open incredulity, but remained silent.

Feeling hunted and harried into a position he didn't

want to take, wishing fervently for the wife who'd pushed and prodded her way into his bed and heart, he snapped, 'Okay, Amber, I don't know what I think a wife is, but I know what I want. I want those two days we had. I want them again. I want a honeymoon with you, to find the life we both want—'

Loud, almost manic laughter sliced his words off. Amber was doubled over herself, laughing with a hard, cynical edge that told him he'd better not join her. 'A life we both want?' She gasped, and laughed over again. 'What do *I* want, Harun? Do you even know that much about me? Do you know anything about me?'

Daylight began cracking apart the icy darkness she'd wrapped herself in. 'I know you're brave and beautiful and loyal to me even when I don't deserve it,' he said softly. 'I know you gave me chance after chance, and forgave me time and again. I know you're the wife I want, the woman I want to spend my life with. But you're right, I don't know what you want. That's what I'm here to find out. Doesn't that count for something?'

'Not right now, no.' Hands on hips, she seemed challenging, except she still refused to look at him, or make a connection of any kind. If she'd heard how he felt about her written between the lines he'd spoken she wouldn't acknowledge it.

'All right, Amber, I understand.'

A little snort was her only answer.

'Oh, I do understand.' With swift, military precision, he whipped the burqa from her head, ignoring her outraged gasp. 'You're hiding from me the way I hid from you all those years. You're not going to make it easy for me, and I don't deserve you to.' Grabbing her and hauling her against him, he held her hard with one hand, while he slowly played with a thick tress of hair, unbound beneath the veil she'd worn. 'Have I missed anything?' he asked huskily, inhaling the rosemary scent in her hair.

'Ask yourself,' she retorted in a voice that shook just a little.

'Ah, thank you, *mee johara*. That means I did.' He grinned at her as her eyes smoked with fury. 'Ah, of course…you still want to know what I think a wife is?'

Her chin lifted.

'You,' he answered, trying to douse the flames in her heart. 'That's all. When I think of "a wife", I think of you. Just as you are.'

'Don't,' she snarled without warning. 'Don't worm your way in with pretty words and compliments. I thought you were dead—that—that they'd killed you. Or that you were never coming back. Why else would you not contact me once? What did I do to—to…?' She pulled at his hands until he released her. She'd startled him right out of his cocky assurance, and his belief that he'd win. She faced him, panting, her eyes shimmering with pain. 'I *loved* you. I loved you with all of me, I gave you everything I had, and you just left. You left me for the sake of the brother who'd abandoned and betrayed you. Do you have any idea what that did to me?'

Bewildered, he spoke from depths he hadn't known were in him. 'But he's my family, Amber. I had no choice. It was my duty.'

'What about me?' she cried. 'Was it your *duty* to seduce and then abandon me, to hurt me the way Alim hurt you? Do I have to run off like he did to make you see I'm alive and that I *hurt?*' She held up a hand when he would have spoken. 'I—I can't do this any more. I tried, Harun, I tried to make things work with you for three years. I tried to show you that love isn't manipulation and emotional blackmail, but you won't see it. I'm tired of hitting my head against a wall. Believe Fadi and not me, and spend your life alone!'

She ran for the balcony doors.

Love isn't manipulation and emotional blackmail... believe Fadi...

That was what Fadi had done to him since childhood, and he'd never known it until now. But she had. She'd seen that he'd gained Fadi's love and approval by doing anything asked of him, no matter what it cost him personally. Fadi hadn't known any better, but followed the example set by their parents. Alim had found a way to escape from it, and somehow, somewhere in his worldwide travels, had learned how to love. But he, Harun, had stayed like a whipped dog, always saying yes, because he accepted the manipulation—because he didn't know any better.

In three long years, Amber had asked only one thing of him—and he hadn't even given her that, because she didn't manipulate or blackmail him into it.

*If someone loves you, they ask the impossible over and over...*and he'd believed it was normal, even right; his duty.

Amber hadn't asked him to change, or to slay dragons for her. So he'd never believed she loved him. Not until now, when she'd stripped his lifelong beliefs in a moment, left him bare and bleeding, and she was leaving him.

He couldn't stand it, couldn't take losing her. This time would be for ever—

'I love you.' Three raw, desperate words. *God, let them be enough, let her stay. Come back to me, Amber...*

Her hand on the door handle, she turned, and hope soared—

She made a small, choking sound, the one she made when she was about to cry. 'I can't believe you'd be so cruel, after what they did to you. Don't ever use those words against me again.'

Then she was gone. Harun stood by the balcony rail, exposed to the bone, the world's greatest fool.

CHAPTER FOURTEEN

It was 3 a.m. and Harun was pounding the road, gasping with each breath and pushing himself still harder. At least ten miles from the palace, his guards were running behind him and finding it hard to keep up. It had been hours since he'd seen Alim and Hana to their bridal chamber. He'd shepherded all of the guests downstairs, made sure the food and drink still overflowed for anyone who wanted it. He'd chatted amiably with heads of state he'd known for years, had quietly warned their friendlier neighbours against trusting certain people among the nations surrounding them, and in general played the perfect host.

The perfect host, the perfect brother, he thought now, with an inner wryness that never made it to his expression. *Why can't I be the perfect husband?*

He wished he knew how to be everything Amber wanted…

What does she want? an imp in his mind prodded. *All she ever wanted was you. But you pushed her away and abandoned her until it was too late. What does she want now—the freedom from you she'd asked for months ago?*

Her words replayed over and over in his brain. *I*

thought you were dead. Or that you were never coming back. Love isn't manipulation and emotional blackmail.

He was missing something. It wasn't in Amber's nature to hurt him without a reason; he knew that now. Everything she'd said taught him what love wasn't.

So what the hell *was* it, then? It seemed she had the secret, but he'd been deaf and blind the whole time she was trying to tell or show him.

He thought she'd *wanted* to hear he loved her. So what had gone so wrong?

At four a.m., he came to the inescapable conclusion: there was only one way to find out. He wheeled around and ran back for the palace, much to the relief of his stitching, gasping guards.

Five a.m.

'My Lord, it's written in the law! You cannot come into this place!'

'Unless you are the ruling sheikh—or the woman in question is your wife. I know the law. Is there any woman in here but my wife?'

'There is the maid, My Lord!'

'Then I suggest you send her out immediately. I will give you three minutes, then I am coming in no matter what—and I suggest you don't argue with me. I doubt you possess the skills to stop me.'

'Your wife is sleeping. Would you wake her?'

'No, she's not. She's behind the door, listening, as she has been since about a minute after I began yelling for her. I knew she'd be awake, or I wouldn't have come.'

The tone was more grim than amused. Even with her throat and eyes on fire, Amber smiled a bit. The door had no glass; he'd just known she'd be waiting for him.

'Let him in, Tahir,' she called, opening the door. 'I'll send Sabetha out.'

The maid, wakened by Harun's first roar for Amber, scuttled past her. Harun shouldered past the guard, snarling, 'No listening. If there's any gossip about this, you both lose your positions.'

'We love the lady Amber, My Lord,' little, delicate Sabetha said, with gentle dignity.

His face softened at that. 'I'm grateful for your loyalty to the lady Amber. I beg your pardon for insulting you.'

Sabetha smiled up at him, not with infatuation but instant affection. Tahir smiled also, but with a manly kind of understanding; he'd forgiven his lord.

Harun seemed to have the knack of making people care. She just wished he knew how to care in return.

In softer mode now, he walked into the room and closed the door. But instead of talking, he just looked at her until she wanted to squirm. 'Well?' she demanded, or tried to. It sounded breathless, hopeful.

Would she ever stop being a fool over this man?

'You are the most beautiful thing I've ever seen or will ever see,' he said, with a quiet sincerity that made her breath take up unmoving lodgings in her throat. 'I thought that the first time I saw you, and I still think it now.'

She lifted her chin, letting him see her devastated face clearly, her tangled hair and the salt tracks lining her cheeks. 'I've spent the past six hours crying and hating you, so it might be best if you use less practised lines. You have five minutes to give me a compelling reason to let you stay here any longer.'

'That you've cried over me only makes you more beautiful in my eyes.'

'That's nice.' Tapping her foot, she looked at her watch. 'Four minutes forty-five seconds.'

He closed his eyes. 'I don't know how to love any other way but through doing what I perceived as my duty. I thought it was all I had to give.' Taking her by the shoulders, he opened his eyes, looked at her as if she was his path to salvation and rushed the words out, as if he didn't say everything now, he never would. 'Those two days we were together, I felt like I was flying. Now it's gone, and the past few months I felt like I was starving to death. I'm suffocating under duty, lost and wandering and alone, and nothing works. I need you, Amber, by God I need you. Please, can you teach me how to make you happy—because without you, I never will be. I can't sleep, I can't eat, can't think about anything but touching you, being with you again.' He dragged her against him, and she didn't have the heart or will to pull away. 'Don't deny me, Amber, because I won't go, not tonight, not any night. Teach me the words you want to hear. I'll say whatever you need, do whatever it takes, because right now I need you more than my next breath. I can't let you keep shutting me out, not when you're everything to me.'

Ouch—it hurt to try to gulp with her mouth still open. How did he turn up just when she'd given up hope, and say the words she needed to hear more than life?

With a tiny noise, she buried her face in his neck. 'Me too, oh, me too, I need you so much,' she whispered as she cannoned into him, her fingers winding in his hair to pull him down to her. 'You just said everything I needed to know.'

'Except one thing,' he muttered hoarsely between kisses. 'I love you, Amber. I have from the day we met.

I just never knew how to say it, or how to believe you could ever love me in return.'

'Do you believe it now?' she whispered, pulling back a little. This was something she had to know now.

He smiled down at her. 'I knew it the day you yelled at Alim, my jewel. It's why I came back today so full of confidence. I'd hoped missing me would have softened you. But you taught me a valuable lesson tonight—that I have to trust in our love, and talk to you.' He nuzzled her lips. 'I'll never put you last again. From now on, you're my family, my first duty. My desire, my passion. My precious jewel.'

'I'm so happy,' she cried, kissing him. 'But though your words are wonderful, I want you to show me the desire and passion. I've missed you so much!'

He didn't need to be told twice. Devouring each other in desperate kisses, mumbling more words of desire and need, they staggered together back to the bed.

Later that morning

The sun was well up when Harun began to stir.

Amber was curled against him like a contented cat, her head on his chest, her body wound around his, one leg and arm holding him to her. He smiled, and kissed the top of her head. Her hair was splayed across his body; her breaths warmed his skin.

Unable to make the mat to give his morning prayer, he gave his thanks in silence, deep and heartfelt. *Thank you for helping me find the way back to her again.*

They'd made love twice, first in a frenzy and then slow and ecstatic. They'd said words of need and pleasure and love during the past four hours.

Now it was time for the next step.

'Amber.' He bent his head to kiss the top of her head. 'Love, we need to talk. No, I said *talk,* my jewel.' He laughed as she kissed his chest, slow and sensuous. 'I've made some arrangements for us I hope you'll like.'

'Mmm-hmm,' she mumbled through kisses. 'Tell me.'

'Are you listening?' He laughed again. She was peppering his torso with kisses and caresses, and he was getting distracted.

'Uh-huh, I always listen to you. Mmm…' More kisses. 'Hurry, *habibi,* it's been at least two hours since we made love. I need you.'

'I've secured us two part-time, unpaid places on a dig only half an hour's drive from the University of Araba Numara…and while I do my doctorate, you'll be finishing your course face to face.'

That stopped her. Completely. She gaped up at him. 'You know about my course?'

'Why do you think I applied for positions near that university? I've known everything you've been doing the past four months—and it made me so proud of you.'

'You—you don't mind?' she asked, half shyly. 'About being a woman and getting all high distinctions, I mean?'

'No, of course not—I've heard you've got lots of distinctions—I'm so proud of you. I've never felt threatened by your intelligence, Amber,' he said quietly. 'And I trust you completely. As I said, your success has made me so proud of you, *mee johara.* I married a woman of great intellect as well as good taste—in loving history and her husband.' He winked at her. 'Do my arrangements meet with your approval?'

'Approval? Oh, you have no idea! I love you, I love you!'

'We'll be living in the same tents as everyone else,

I warn you,' he put in with mock-sternness, but was turning to fire again at her touch. 'And it will mean no babies until you're done with your course.'

Again she looked up at him, almost in wonder. 'You don't mind waiting for children?'

'I've waited all this time for you,' he murmured, with the utmost tenderness. 'I can wait a little more for our family to start.'

'I love you,' she whispered again, with all the vivid intensity of her nature, and pulled him down on top of her.

Strange how falling down actually felt like flying…

EPILOGUE

Eight years later

'IT's a girl!'

In the sorting tent, deep in diagnosis of the siftings he'd just dug up, Harun frowned vaguely at his wife's excited voice coming from behind him. 'Hmm? What was that?'

'Harun, we have a new niece. Hana had a girl about an hour ago.'

'That's great. Look at this piece I found, *mee johara*. Is this beer jug belly Sumerian, do you think?'

'Harun, look at me.' Gently he was turned around. He knew, having finished her archaeology degree last year, as excited by the past as he could ever hope for, Amber wouldn't risk disturbing his findings. But, as she always said, *without families there wouldn't be history to discover.* 'Hana had a girl an hour ago. They named her Johara.'

The look in Amber's eyes warned him to return to the present. He blinked, focusing on what he'd only half-heard, and slowly grinned. 'That's wonderful! We have a niece at last. Kalila will be thrilled.'

Their five-year-old daughter always felt left out of her boy cousins' rowdy play. She was a girly-girl, and even though she was as enthusiastic as her parents on the digs, she somehow managed to stay clean. The only time she had someone as fastidious as her on the digs was when Naima stayed for the school breaks. Kalila adored her cousin, and followed her around like a puppy.

At not yet four, their son Tarif fitted in splendidly with his male cousins, rolling around as happily on the palace floors, indulging in masculine play with his father and uncle. But when on the dig, he confined his rougher antics to the hours Harun kept sacred for play with his son. He knew better than to disturb any promising-looking holes in the ground, though Harun swore their son was a genius from the day he'd inadvertently found the site of an ancient temple's foundations when he was trying to poke in a snake hole. 'Abi, Abi, pretty rocks over there,' he'd said, growing distressed until Harun followed his little son to the other side of the *tell,* where they hadn't yet sectioned off the ground to look.

Amber grinned. 'I've booked the jet for Monday. I can't fly after that, as you know—' the slight stress on *know* told him if he didn't remember she was twenty-seven weeks pregnant, he'd better catch up with real life and fast '—and I want to see my…well, my sort-of namesake.'

'Oh, of course she is.' Harun grinned again. 'I'm sure they named her for you, my jewel,' he assured her with mock-gravity.

Laughing, she swatted him with her fingers. 'You could at least pretend to believe it. You know I'm in a very delicate state right now.'

Both brows lifted with that one. 'Um, yes, very delicate,' he agreed. 'Remind me again how your delicate condition meant you had to crawl ahead of me five days ago into an unstable subterranean chamber?' Not to mention that, at night, she was the one to instigate loving as often as he did. They'd have at least six children by now, if they hadn't planned their family carefully around Amber's studies.

Finding no answer for his teasing, Amber put her nose in the air; then she looked at the small piece he'd found. 'Oh, I do concur, it is part of a beer jug, and it definitely looks the right period. It's a shame it isn't Amalekite. We're still not there,' she teased, backing off as he mock waved his fist at her. 'It's a very good piece. But you might want to call the family and congratulate them before you get lost in the Sumerian period again,' she suggested, turning his face back to her as her opinion distracted him. 'One more,' she murmured, kissing him again, deepening it to keep him in the here and now.

'One more kiss like that and I'll forget the Sumerian artefact as well as our new niece,' he mock threatened as his body awoke.

'Not you, my love,' she retorted, laughing. 'And anyway, there's always tonight.'

As if on cue, the baby kicked its father, squirming around as if to say, *Not again, you two!* It was a chant almost everyone on any dig said to them, sooner or later. Whether it was over their almost scary connection over their love of ancient history or their knowledge of ancient finds, or their touching and kissing so often when they were together, the protest was as loud as it was meant in fun. *I wish I could find what you two have,* was the lament of so many people on the digs, when another relationship failed with someone who could never understand the archaeologist's absorbing passion for the past.

'Okay, little one, okay,' he said softly, caressing Amber's

belly, leaning down to kiss his child. 'I think you're being told to rest, my jewel.'

'I think I am.' She smothered a yawn. 'Tarif will wake in about an hour, so I'd better get there.' She gave him one final kiss. 'But I want to hear all about the jug later—and don't think the other part of tonight's forgotten, either.'

'Never,' he assured her with a wink. 'Both have been duly noted.'

'And call Alim,' she reminded him a final time, at the tent flap. 'Don't forget to call Naima too. Tell her the car will pick her up the day we arrive, if Buhjah doesn't have anything else planned for her.'

Grinning, he waved in acceptance. Amber returned to their family tent where Tarif still slept in a partitioned-off section, and at the other end Kalila endured her long-suffering tutor's lessons on mathematics.

Harun, smiling as he always did when Amber had been with him or when he thought of his family, pulled out his phone to call his niece. Naima was thrilled she had a new girl cousin, and, after consulting with Buhjah, told him she could join in the family celebrations. He chatted with her for a few minutes longer, hearing all about her studies and her other family, the antics of her younger half-brothers at home, before hanging up with a smile.

Then he called the palace to congratulate Alim and Hana, and to hear about his new niece. The bubbling joy in his brother's voice when he spoke of their new 'little jewel' made Harun's cup run over.

He was a blessed man.

* * * * *

MILLS & BOON®

Why shop at millsandboon.co.uk?

Each year, thousands of romance readers find their perfect read at millsandboon.co.uk. That's because we're passionate about bringing you the very best romantic fiction. Here are some of the advantages of shopping at www.millsandboon.co.uk:

* **Get new books first**—you'll be able to buy your favourite books one month before they hit the shops

* **Get exclusive discounts**—you'll also be able to buy our specially created monthly collections, with up to 50% off the RRP

* **Find your favourite authors**—latest news, interviews and new releases for all your favourite authors and series on our website, plus ideas for what to try next

* **Join in**—once you've bought your favourite books, don't forget to register with us to rate, review and join in the discussions

Visit **www.millsandboon.co.uk**
for all this and more today!

The World of Mills & Boon

There's a Mills & Boon® series that's perfect for you. There are ten different series to choose from and new titles every month, so whether you're looking for glamorous seduction, Regency rakes, homespun heroes or sizzling erotica, we'll give you plenty of inspiration for your next read.

By Request
Relive the romance with the best of the best
12 stories every month

***Cherish*™**
Experience the ultimate rush of falling in love.
12 new stories every month

INTRIGUE...
A seductive combination of danger and desire...
7 new stories every month

***Desire*™**
Passionate and dramatic love stories
6 new stories every month

n o c t u r n e™
An exhilarating underworld of dark desires
3 new stories every month

For exclusive member offers go to
millsandboon.co.uk/subscribe

Which series will you try next?

*Awaken the romance
of the past...*
6 new stories every month

*The ultimate in romantic
medical drama*
6 new stories every month

MODERN™

*Power, passion and
irresistible temptation*
8 new stories every month

MODERN
tempted™

True love and temptation!
4 new stories every month

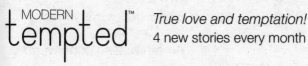